THE RIDER FALL

The Lost Riders

Book 7

JASPER ALDEN

D.K. HOLMBERG

ASH
PUBLISHING

Chapter One

IF THERE WERE THREE THINGS THAT ANIJA HAD LEARNED TO hate the most about the Glacians since the war started last month, it was their war balloons, their ice bombs, and their smug attitudes.

Their war balloons—'zeppelins,' they called them, though Anija refused to use their correct name to avoid giving them more respect than they deserved—were deadly. Despite their ungainly size, they regularly sneaked up on the northern border that Malarsan shared with the Glacian province of Hosar, dropped their ice bombs, and then left before anyone could mount a defense.

Then there were the ice bombs. Huge spheres of ice that, when detonated, created massive, thick ice spikes that would instantly kill or maim whoever was unlucky enough to get caught in the middle of them. That was usually the ground soldiers on loan from the Malarsan Army, whose armor was certainly not strong enough to protect them from the icy death that the war balloons rained down on them. Plus, the spikes from the ice bombs would linger on the battlefield for hours even in the hot sun, making it more difficult for the rest of the ground troops to maneuver and provide backup to their fellow troops.

But Anija truly thought that the worst thing about the Glacians was their sheer arrogance. More than once over the past month, Anija had come face to face with Glacian soldiers who seemed to believe they were actually helping free Malarsan from the council's 'tyrannical' rule. Not only that, but they also regularly taunted her by claiming that the glory of the Glaci Empire eclipsed that of Malarsan and that it was only a matter of time before Kryo Kardia crushed them under his frozen fist.

That was usually about the time Anija had her dragon, Rialo, rip them to shreds or set them on fire.

Unfortunately, that wasn't always possible. As Anija had noted before, the Glaci Empire's offense primarily consisted of sending their war balloons to bomb the Malarsan and Hosarian border, while occasionally sending in small groups of ground troops just to make things more difficult for the Malarsan forces. Anija supposed she should be happy that Kryo Kardia had not yet sent in his Dragon Riders, who would undoubtedly be much more difficult to fight than the war balloons.

But it was hard to be grateful while fighting six war balloons, which had already taken out half of her fellow Riders and were in the process of gunning down the rest, at once.

Soaring through the sky, the cold winds biting at the exposed portions of her skin, Anija gazed down at the half dozen or so war balloons below. Flashes of ice moulash erupted from the cannons on their sides, aiming mostly for Anija's fellow Dragon Riders and the few ground troops they had decided to bring with them to this battle. Even though dragons had superior mobility to war balloons, the aim of the war balloon fighters was unmatched.

Even as Anija watched, a war balloon ice cannon struck one of her fellow Riders, forcing them to make a crash landing on the rocky ground below. Yet even as the Rider and Steed landed, the same war balloon that had shot them out of the sky dropped an ice bomb directly overhead.

And unfortunately, Anija and Rialo were too far away to save the Rider and Steed. Anija had to look away, having already seen her fair share of young, innocent Riders and Steeds getting slaughtered during this war.

We need to get on the offense. Rialo's voice echoed in Anija's mind, the dragon flapping its wings powerfully underneath her. *We cannot remain reactive forever.*

Anija felt Rialo's emotions through her bond. Frustration. Anger. Hate, even.

We've been on the defense for this whole freaking war, Anija replied, trying not to sound too annoyed with her Steed. *And besides, you know we have a plan to deal with the war balloons now. We just need to be patient.*

Rialo laughed. *You, patient? I cannot think of a more impatient human than you, other than perhaps Surrels.*

Can it, Rialo, Anija said. *You're one to talk. You're just as impatient as me, if not more so. Maybe that's why we make such a great team.*

Probably, Rialo agreed. She sighed. *I just wish we could go in and attack them now. I feel like we are losing.*

Anija did not repeat Rialo's words, but she also could not deny that she felt similarly.

Even so, they *did* have a plan. And it was a good one, as far as Anija was concerned.

Another flap of wings nearby drew Anija's attention to her right. Lieutenant Ragnol and his Steed, Dinne, flew up out of the clouds toward her and Rialo.

"Report on the battle?" Anija said.

Dinne came to a stop, hovering in the air with each flap of his wings, while Ragnol cleared his throat. "Not good, Vice-Captain, but not as bad as it could have been. We've lost half of our Riders and Steeds, though mostly injuries and few deaths so far. We did lose one pair, however, to an ice bomb, but that is our only casualty at the moment."

Anija shuddered. "Yes, I saw that. But are the war balloons in range of the mages yet?"

"Almost," Ragnol said. "Archmage Fralia told me that the air and fire mages are at the ready. They await only your command, Chief."

Anija nodded. "Good. Tell them to start attacking the war balloons once they get close enough. We will handle them from there."

Ragnol nodded and then he and Dinne flew away, disappearing into the clouds as they returned to the battle-field below.

Ragnol seemed oddly patient, Rialo observed. *He's usually the first to want to rush into battle and prove himself.*

He likes putting plans into action, so he knows he'll get his chance to shine soon enough, Anija said. *As long as we stick to the plan, that is.*

Anija briefly reviewed the plan in her mind as they hovered there.

The plan was simple, which was how Anija liked her plans: They were going to attack the war balloons from two directions at once.

Over the past month, Anija had studied the movements

of the war balloons carefully. She noted that they were excellent at attacking anything below or level with them, such as ground troops or flying dragons, but they seemed to have no real defense against attacks from above. As well, they were heavily dependent on the weather being good, because if the weather was stormy or less than ideal in some way, it would have a considerable impact on their speed and maneuverability.

Therefore, Anija, working with Fralia, Surrels, and some of their lieutenants, had put together a plan that involved using both Dragon Riders and mages to double-team the Glacian war balloons. Fire and air mages from below would use their magic to attack the airships directly and create powerful winds that would push the war balloons around while the Dragon Riders would attack from above. The idea was to make it impossible for the war balloons to focus on any one given target and make it difficult for them to move easily, which should, in theory, make it easier to down them.

Of course, the plan was already off the rails somewhat. Anija had been betting on Kryo Kardia to send one, maybe two, war balloons. That Kryo Kardia had instead sent six— about as much as he had sent to support them during the rebellion against Queen Marial—complicated things somewhat.

But not enough to ruin the plan entirely, Rialo reminded her. *It just gives us more targets to destroy.*

Anija grinned. *Yeah.*

Without warning, Anija felt a powerful gust of wind pass by her, followed by a glimmer of green light through the clouds below. The war balloons shuddered in the wind, only for fire bolts to launch up at them from the ground, forcing the war balloons to point their cannons toward the ground to deal with that threat.

The air mages and fire mages. The war balloons must have finally gotten within range of their magic, meaning they were beginning the assault already.

"Riders and Steeds!" Anija yelled. "Attack!"

From out of the clouds around her, a dozen Dragon Riders and their Steeds burst forth. They flew straight down toward the war balloons below, shouting, whooping, and roaring as they neared the enemy airships.

Anija and Rialo were in the lead, the wind whipping through Anija's long red hair as she drew a sword from the sheath at her side. A wild grin crossed her lips as they drew closer and closer to the war balloons, the Glacians below seemingly unaware of the death coming at them from above.

"Fire!" Anija roared, her voice barely audible over the shrieking wind and flapping of dragon wings.

Nonetheless, everyone seemed to have heard her, because the Steeds fired dragonfire balls from their mouth toward the war balloons. Not all of them hit, but the drag-onfire balls that did hit set their respective war balloons ablaze.

Already, Anija could see some of the war balloons moving their cannons around to try to aim at them, but Anija wasn't going to let them react. She and Rialo, along with the other Riders and Steeds, circled the war balloon farthest from the others, bathing it with dragonfire from above.

The war balloon did not stand a chance. With a shudder and a *bang*, the hulking ship began careening through the air. It clipped the war balloon closest to it, causing the second war balloon to also careen, before crashing into the trees below with a loud *boom*. Tall flames shot up out of the trees as the explosion ripped through the air.

From above, Anija could see the surviving crew members of the airship spilling out from the burning remains of their war balloon. She also spotted Malarsan ground troops making their way through the forest to the site of the war balloon, no doubt going to make sure that there were no survivors.

Good, Anija thought, smiling. *The plan is going well.*

As for the other war balloons, they were as confused as Anija hoped they would be. Some of them were still shooting ice cannons at the mages while others were trying to shoot Anija's Dragon Riders out of the sky, and a handful were even futilely attempting to make an escape.

Our surprise attack ruined their formations, Rialo said triumphantly. *You were correct. It was a good plan, after all.*

Anija chuckled. *What can I say? I can be pretty clever sometimes, you know. Anyway, we need to finish off the war balloons quickly before they can reorient themselves.*

Before Anija could send that order out to the rest of the Dragon Riders, however, she heard the flapping of wings above her, and a huge shadow passed over her.

At first, Anija thought that it was one of her fellow Dragon Riders flying nearby. She almost ignored it until she heard a growl above her that definitely *wasn't* one of their own.

Looking up, Anija caught a glimpse of dragon wings in the cloud overhead, but they moved too fast for her to identify them. "Rialo, did you see that?"

"I did," Rialo said, turning her head this way and that.

She sniffed the air. "I smelled it, too. And it didn't smell at all like one of our dragons. It smelled like—"

A piercing roar filled the air, interrupting Rialo and forcing all of the assembled Dragon Riders to pause and hover in the air, looking for the source of the roar.

That turned out to be a mistake, however, because a dragon flew out of the clouds overhead and tackled a Dragon Rider and Steed approximately a hundred yards from Anija and Rialo. The Rider and Steed, along with their assailant, disappeared into the clouds around them with screams and the sounds of dragons biting and clawing at each other.

"The hell was that?" Ragnol yelled as Dinne beat his wings hard to keep them afloat.

Anija gulped and looked around at her fellow Riders. "We're under attack! Everyone, get into formation before —"

Anija did not get a chance to finish her sentence before another roar pierced the air and then a dozen Dragon Riders, clad in the armor of the Glacian Army, flew out of the clouds overhead. Their dragons, though slightly smaller than the dragons of the Malarsan Riders, nonetheless immediately engaged in battle with Anija's allies.

Soon, the whole sky around her was a midair battlefield between the Malarsan Dragon Riders and the Glacian Dragon riders. Fireballs flew freely, claws and teeth ripped and tore at scale and skin, wings flapped powerfully, and humans yelled commands as both sides tore into each other as viciously as wild animals, all thoughts of organization and military formations lost in the frenzied insanity of war.

Anija and Rialo, however, managed to separate themselves from the chaos before it could envelop them. Anija watched with horror and confusion as the two sets of Dragon Riders brutally fought each other.

"Damn it," Rialo said, a deep growl emitting from her throat. "The frozen bastard finally sent his Dragon Riders. I was wondering when he would get the balls to do that."

Anija, despite the horror she felt, could not help but agree with Rialo. The truth was that, ever since the start of the war, everyone had been wondering when the Glaci Empire would send their Dragon Riders to the front lines. The Glacian Riders' absence until now had been puzzling, especially considering how powerful they were, but Anija had appreciated the respite.

Evidently, however, Kryo Kardia was growing tired of the war already and probably thought that this would be the quickest way to end it. The Glacian Riders were the Glaci Empire's shiny new most powerful weapons, after all.

Anija shook her head. She couldn't afford to freeze up here, not when her fellow Dragon Riders were fighting for their lives. As the current Co-chief of the Clawfoot Clan and Vice-Captain of the Dragon Rider Order, Anija needed to be fighting alongside her fellow Riders.

Let's go help them, Anija told Rialo, *before they get overwhelmed by the Glacians.*

A fireball suddenly flew out of nowhere, forcing Rialo to duck to the side to avoid getting struck. Tightly clinging to Rialo's saddle, Anija looked around, trying to spot the source of the fireball. "Who did that?"

"Darn," said a familiar female voice in the clouds around them. "Your dragon has such quick reflexes for being such a big beast. I was hoping you wouldn't be able to dodge that attack."

From out of the clouds overhead emerged another

Glacian Dragon Rider. She was a bald woman, a spear in her hand, sitting atop a purple-and-green dragon that Anija had only seen once before, though she had no trouble recognizing either of them.

"Nege," Anija said, scowling. "Long time, no see."

"That's *Princess* Nege Kardia, third daughter of Kryo Kardia, to you, Malarsan scum," Nege said with a huff. "Remember that, because it is the last name you will ever hear."

"I'm not planning to die, if that's what you mean," Anija said with a shake of her head. "Although I can't say the same for you and your dragon. What was his name again? Snout?"

"My *name* is Prika, woman," said the dragon in a rough, raspy voice. "Show some respect."

Rialo's eyes widened. "I thought I recognized you, Prika. I remember when my father and your mother would meet to discuss military strategies during the Dragon War."

"His mother—?" Anija blinked. "You mean Prika is Frozas's son?"

"Indeed I am," Prika said. "The firstborn of Chief Frozas, chief of the Fang Clan."

Anija shook her head. The Fang Clan had been the second biggest dragon clan in Malarsan until the end of the Dragon War, after which the Fang Clan immigrated all the way to the Northern Circle under the belief that they would be safer from humans there than in Malarsan. The Glacian Riders primarily rode Fang Clan dragons, which seemed a bit ironic to Anija given how anti-human the Fang dragons were, but she supposed that it wasn't any of her business.

"Speaking of Kryo Kardia and Frozas, where are

they?" Anija said, glancing around the sky. She gave Nege a mocking look. "Did Daddy decide he didn't want to dirty his precious hands and so sent his favorite daughter to die in his stead?"

Nege scowled. "Father is doing very important work back in the Northern Circle. He has no time to waste invading a tiny, almost irrelevant kingdom like Malarsan. Frankly, I don't even see why he wants it, but I suppose it's not my place to question Father's commands."

"Your dad wants Malarsan because he's a power-hungry jerk who wants to take over the world," Anija said. "Seems pretty simple to me."

Nege chuckled. "Poor, naive Anija. Is that what you really think this conflict is about? Merely taking over the world? Adding another spit of land to our already glorious Empire? Father has much higher goals than mere world domination. He has set his sights on a power greater than anything in this mortal realm."

Anija narrowed her eyes. "And what, pray tell, is that?"

"None of your business," Nege said. She raised her spear. "We did not come here to chitchat. We came here to fight, to conquer, to put the kingdom of Malarsan under the glorious heel of my Fa—"

Nege never got to finish her sentence because a beam of pure light shot down from the sky above. Prika just barely managed to duck to the side at the last minute, the beam passing by in a flash.

But the beam did hit a target. It struck one of the war balloons below, making the entire thing explode. Burning in the air, the war balloon careened toward the ground below with a *bang*, sending more smoke and flame into the wind.

Clutching tightly onto Prika's back, Nege looked up into

the sky, a shocked and angry expression on her face. "The hell was that? Another one of your Malarsan tricks?"

Anija shook her head. "Don't look at us. We are just as surprised by the light beam as you are, maybe even more so. It's not one of ours."

Nege scowled. "Then who is——?"

Multiple beams of light shot out of the clouds, mostly aiming for the war balloons. The beams struck the war balloons head-on, making each one explode in midair, raining flaming debris down on the trees and soldiers below.

"Our zeppelins!" Nege said in shock. "How were they taken down so easily?"

Rialo, did you see that? Anija said mentally to her dragon.

How could I not? Rialo said. *But where did those beams come from? Whoever wields that kind of power must be incredibly, well, powerful.*

And they seem to be on our side, too, Anija said. *That's good for us.*

Without warning, a brilliant golden light shone in the clouds overhead, forcing Anija to cover her eyes with her hand to avoid getting blinded. Out of the corner of her eye, Anija also spotted Nege covering her eyes.

"Light?" Nege said. "What is this?"

Nege's question was soon answered when the light finally faded, revealing two familiar yet different figures hovering in the air above them.

It was another Dragon Rider pair, but not one of the Glacian pairs. It was a young man, clad in gold and white armor, sitting atop a dragon with scales as white as snow and eyes as pure as the purest silver. Power unlike anything

Anija had felt radiated off of the pair in waves, like the rays of the sun beating down on them.

But it was an energizing feeling, sapping the weakness and tiredness from Anija's bones and making her feel more alert and alive than ever. Based on Rialo's movements, she could tell that her Steed also felt renewed by the presence of this pair. In fact, a quick glance around the battlefield showed Anija that the other Dragon Riders and Steeds seemed to have gotten their second wind as a result of the arrival of this mysterious pair.

Even so, Anija's jaw dropped when she saw them, because she knew exactly who the 'mysterious' newcomers were.

"Hal?" Anija said. "Keershan? Is that you?"

Hal turned his gaze toward Anija and said, "It's us. And today, the Glaci Empire will know why they should fear the Dragon Riders of Malarsan."

Chapter Two

ANIJA HEARD SOMETHING DIFFERENT IN HAL'S VOICE WHEN he spoke. It was deeper, more reverential, and possibly divine? She couldn't think of a better word to describe Hal's appearance and demeanor. For that matter, Keershan seemed similar, looking less like the goofy scholar she'd always known him to be and more like Rialo or some other powerful dragon.

It was different from how Hal and Keershan looked when they used the Final Relic. Somehow, she sensed that they were now on a level above mere relics, that they had ascended to something beyond what she and the other Dragon Riders were capable of.

And she wasn't yet certain if that was a good thing or a bad thing.

Nege, apparently, had already gotten over her shock at seeing Hal and Keershan again, because she said, "So there you two are. I had heard you had perished in the Abode of the Gods, but it seems like I was given incorrect information."

"Your father lied to you," Hal said. "Although that's not surprising. I'm sure your father has lied to you about many things. You are probably used to it by now."

Nege scowled. "How dare you besmirch the name of Father in front of me. Do you want to die, or are you just stupid?"

Hal cocked his head to the side. "Given how we just downed the rest of your war balloons by ourselves, I think the better question is if *you* want to die or not."

Nege laughed. "Are you threatening *me*? Don't make me laugh. I still remember quite clearly how Father defeated you and your runt of a dragon the first time you fought. You only survived through sheer luck. I will make sure to finish what Father started."

Hal shrugged. "I suppose the gods did smile upon us that day. Although I suspect they are currently frowning upon you and your father."

"Who needs the approval of the gods?" Nege said. She raised her sword. "Talking solves nothing. I will bring your head back to my father and—"

Nege never got to finish her sentence before Hal drew his sword, pointed it at her, and tilted it slightly to the side.

A cage made of light suddenly warped into existence around Nege and Prika. The princess and her dragon looked around in alarm at the cage, which began rotating around them in a pattern that threatened to make even Anija feel dizzy if she stared at it for too long.

"What kind of magic is this?" Nege said. "Prika?"

"I-I don't know, Nege," Prika said, "but whatever it is, I doubt it will be a match for my dragonfire."

Prika opened his mouth and unleashed a stream of

white-hot dragonfire onto the cage. Anija and Rialo flew backward to avoid getting caught in his dragonfire breath.

As it turned out, however, they didn't need to, because the dragonfire dissipated when it touched the bars of the cage. It didn't even smoke. It was as if the dragonfire simply ceased to exist once it came into contact with the bars of the mysterious cage.

Cutting off his own stream of dragonfire, Prika stared at the bars of the cage in disbelief. "Why did my dragonfire not melt the bars?"

"Because they aren't made of metal, genius," Keershan said in an unusually harsh voice. "That's divine light, which even the hottest dragonfire is no match for."

Anija raised an eyebrow. *When did Keershan get snarky?*

I don't know, Rialo said, *but there seems to be something different about those two. And I'm not just talking about their appearances, either.*

Anija agreed. *Yeah. They look and talk almost like gods.*

Nege snarled and hit the back of Prika's head with the hilt of her sword. "Stupid dragon! How come you didn't know that your dragonfire was useless against divine light?"

Prika growled at Nege. "Because I've never run into divine light before? What do you want from me? Do you think I should know everything because I am a dragon? We aren't all-knowing beings, you know."

Hal shook his head. "Your bond must be very weak if this is how you two treat each other under stress. True Dragon Rider pairs don't hit or insult each other even when we are troubled. We treat each other with respect because we are equals."

"Silence, you insolent fool," Nege said. "What would a

farm boy like you ever know about something as complicated as—"

The cage suddenly glowed brighter than before, making Nege and Prika cry out in pain as the light seemingly hurt them. They struggled against the light for a moment before suddenly collapsing onto the floor of the cage, apparently having lost the will to live.

Anija bit her lower lip. "Are they—?"

Hal shook his head. "They're not dead, if that's what you are asking. Although I imagine they probably wish they were."

Before Anija could say anything to that, she heard the flapping of wings all around them and looked to see where the noise was coming from.

The remaining Glacian Riders had apparently disengaged from their battle with the Malarsan Riders and now surrounded Hal, Keershan, Anija, and Rialo on all sides. Anija did not see the Malarsan Riders anywhere, making her wonder if they had been defeated.

If so, that was not good for their odds of winning this fight, much less surviving.

"What did you do to Nege?" demanded one of the Glacian Riders, a veritable mountain of a man wearing a mask that obscured his face as he rode upon a crimson-colored dragon.

Hal gave the Rider a casual look. "I simply put her and Prika to sleep. They will be fine. You should worry more about yourselves than them."

"Oh, yeah?" said another Rider, a woman with an annoyingly high-pitched, nasally voice, clutching the reins of a white-and-brown dragon. "Why's that?"

Hal's eyes glowed. "Because we will do far worse to you

if you don't immediately retreat all the way back to the Northern Circle and cease this pointless invasion of our kingdom."

"Retreat?" the male Glacian Rider repeated. "Why in the world should *we* retreat? We have you outnumbered and overpowered. Sure, you took down our war balloons, but don't you know that we are the next evolution of Glacian air warfare?"

"Yeah," the female Glacian Rider said. "Kryo Kardia told us so himself. We're faster, stronger, and all-around better than those dinky old zeppelins. You'd better think twice before picking a fight with all of us at once."

Anija pursed her lips. She hated their arrogant attitude, but at the same time, it was not entirely misplaced. After all, the Glacian Riders still had them outnumbered. Even if Hal and Keershan had indeed received some mysterious new power boost from the gods, that did not guarantee victory against the Glacians.

Yet Hal and Keershan looked entirely unperturbed by the presence of the Glacian Riders. Mostly, they looked annoyed and impatient.

"You Glacian Riders talk a lot, you know that?" Keershan said, gazing around at them. "You should do less talking, more observing."

"Observing?" said the male Glacian Rider. He laughed. "What is there to observe? Two against twelve is not exactly hard to observe."

Hal frowned. "Two against twelve, you say? I don't know. I think it's more like fifty against twelve."

Confused looks appeared on the faces of the Glacian Riders before the sounds of dozens of pairs of wings beating the air could be heard.

And then what looked like the entirety of the Dragon Rider Order rose up around them, completely surrounding the Glacian Riders. The Glacian Riders and their Steeds looked around in alarm at the huge number of Malarsan Riders. Even Anija was surprised to see the cavalry had arrived, wondering when they could have all gotten here.

Probably around the same time that Hal and Keershan did, Rialo said. *I felt a mental command from Keershan go out to all of the Dragon Riders a few minutes ago. Even I felt the pressure to obey and I am already here.*

I didn't feel any mental commands from anyone, Anija said. *Are you sure about that?*

It must have only been sent out to the dragons, then, Rialo said. *As for how Keershan managed that, I don't know. I didn't even know it was possible.*

Anija bit her lower lip. *Another one of the new powers that Hal and Keershan apparently pulled out of nowhere. I feel like they've been holding out on us.*

Or their powers actually are new, Rialo said. *Although I wonder how and where they got their powers.*

Anija shook her head. *Maybe from the gods? Remember, Hal and Keershan went to the Abode of the Gods to get help dealing with Kryo Kardia. Could this be what the gods have given them?*

That was the main reason Anija was surprised to see Hal and Keershan again. The two of them, along with a Snow Witch named Boca, had traveled to the Abode of the Gods a month or two ago to request aid from the gods in defeating Kryo Kardia. Hal, Keershan, and Boca had been gone without contact for so long that Anija had almost forgotten about them.

Of course, that wasn't entirely true. Anija could never forget about Hal or Keershan. Still, Anija had not expected to see them back so soon, especially not in this manner. Although she supposed she couldn't complain, seeing as Hal and Keershan alone had turned the tide of battle in their favor in less than five minutes.

"Where did all of these Riders come from?" the masked Glacian said, clutching the reins of his Steed as he gazed around at the Malarsan Riders on every side.

"It doesn't matter," Hal said shortly. "The point is that you are the ones who are now outnumbered and over-powered."

The nasally-sounding woman glared at Hal. "We won't surrender, if that's what you are expecting us to do. We will fight to the very bitterest end, just as His Majesty ordered us to. We will even give our very lives for the cause, for we are loyal soldiers of the glorious Glaci Empire."

Hal raised an eyebrow. "I never said we were going to fight or kill you. All of you may go except for Nege and Prika."

Anija's jaw dropped. "What? Hal, you're just letting the Glacian Riders go when we have them right where we want them? Are you out of your bloody mind or something?"

Hal gave Anija a hard look. "Thank you for leading the Riders in our absence, Anija, Rialo, but Keershan and I will be taking over again."

What a polite way to tell us to shut up, Rialo thought.

More like a passive-aggressive way, Anija replied. *Seriously, Hal and Keershan are usually way nicer than that. Did their new powers make them jerks or something, too?*

Even the Glacian Riders looked stunned by Hal's commands, with the masked Rider saying, "You're letting us go? Just like that?"

"Just like that," Keershan said with a nod. His eyes

darted to the caged Nege and Prika. "Except these two. They're staying."

"What if we fight you for them?" said the masked Rider, pointing his sword at Hal and Keershan. "Nege is not only one of Kryo Kardia's daughters, but my baby sister as well."

Hal narrowed his eyes. "What's your name, Rider?"

The masked Rider sat up a little straighter in his seat, as if proud of who he was. "Prince Compe Kardia. The first and oldest son of Kryo Kardia. And the second Dragon Rider of the Glaci Empire after Kryo Kardia himself."

Hal nodded. "Thanks for giving us your name, Compe. And you can try to save your sister if you want. I would just ask that you think that through very carefully, because the odds of defeating us are not in your favor, to put it mildly."

Compe scowled, but the other Glacian Riders looked at him. It was clear that Compe was the leader of the Glacian Riders, or seen as such by them. Anija expected that the others would go along with whatever Compe decided to do.

Finally, Compe lowered his gaze from Hal and Keershan and said to the other Glacian Riders, "Fellow servants of the emperor, let us go."

"Are you saying we are going to retreat?" the nasally sounding woman demanded, her voice becoming near incomprehensible as she got angrier. "But Princess Nege is—"

"She and Prika will remain safely in our custody," Hal said. "We promise that we will not inflict harm or injury on either of them so long as they remain in our custody."

Compe met Hal's eyes. "Will you return them at some point?"

Hal met Compe's gaze without hesitation. "Do you

want to keep asking stupid questions until I change my mind or not?"

Anija whistled. That was a good one, although she didn't say that aloud. She wanted to make sure that the Glacian Riders didn't try anything funny.

At the same time, however, Anija was still annoyed at Hal for letting them go. She saw no reason why they couldn't take all of the Glacian Riders as their prisoners, especially since they decisively outnumbered them.

"We can still fight," said the nasally voiced woman. "Fight for Nege, fight for Prika, fight for—"

"And to what end, Sija?" Compe interrupted. "Even if we fought to the death here, we'd merely be giving up our relics to the Malarsans. And you know how Kryo Kardia feels about losing relics."

Anija found it interesting that Compe did not refer to Kryo Kardia as 'Father' like Nege did. She wondered if that signaled anything about Compe's relationship with his father or if she was simply overthinking things a bit too much.

Compe's point must have been valid because Sija did not argue. She simply grumbled something under her breath about how embarrassing this whole situation was. Anija could not help but smirk at Sija, though she turned her attention back to Hal and Compe.

"A wise choice, Prince Compe," Hal said. "But before you leave, I have a message I want you to deliver to your father."

Compe cocked his head to the side. "And what message might that be, Captain Norath?"

Hal pointed his sword at Compe. "We are coming for you soon. Get ready."

Sija hissed. "How dare you threaten His Majesty in our presence! We—"

"That is enough, Sija," said Compe shortly, interrupting Sija. He looked at Hal. "Your message has been received. I will ensure that it gets to the emperor right away."

With that, Compe and his dragon flew straight up into the air, outside of the circle that the Malarsan Riders had formed around them. The other Glacian Riders joined him, albeit reluctantly, with Sija in particular throwing Anija and the others a death glare as she flew away.

Anija watched the Glacian Riders as they flew away, until they soon disappeared into the distance, leaving Anija and the rest of the Malarsan Riders floating around Nege and Prika.

Then Hal looked around at everyone and said, "Dragon Riders of Malarsan, let us go back to Mysteria." He gave the unconscious Nege and Prika a hard look. "We have some prisoners to interrogate."

Chapter Three

THE AFTERMATH OF THE BATTLE TOOK SOME TIME TO CLEAN up. Particularly, the presence of the crashed war balloons meant that many of the trees on the border had caught fire, forcing the Dragon Riders and ground troops to work together to put out or contain the fires. Fortunately, by the time the battle was over, rain clouds had already formed in the sky, helped along by the few water mages who had joined the battle.

As for Nege and Prika, Hal and Keershan took the princess and dragon to Mysteria, escorted by Anija, Rialo, and all of the other Dragon Riders. As was expected, nearly everyone in Mysteria was overjoyed to see Hal and Keershan's return, with the streets becoming packed with humans and dragons alike as the pair flew over the town.

But neither Hal nor Keershan lingered to chat with the people of Mysteria. Instead, Hal told Anija to gather the rest of the council for an emergency meeting, which was fine by Anija. She'd expected that they would need to hold an emergency meeting whenever Hal returned anyway.

And fortunately for them, the entire council just so happened to be in Mysteria, so it was easy to gather everyone together.

Instead of meeting in the headquarters of the Dragon Rider Order, however, Hal and Keershan insisted that they hold their meeting inside the Forgotten Temple. That seemed like an odd location to Anija, given how it was less secure than the headquarters, but Rialo liked it because the Forgotten Temple was big enough for even a full-grown dragon to enter without making it feel cramped.

Thus, less than two hours after Hal and Keershan's dramatic arrival and defeat of the Glacian Riders, Anija and Rialo found themselves inside the main room of the Forgotten Temple, along with the other members of the council. They stood in front of the painting on the wall at the end of the lobby which depicted the original Dragon Riders' last stand against the Nameless One, the sound of the rain outside growing louder as time went on.

"You captured one of the Glacian Riders?" Surrels said, looking in astonishment at Hal and Keershan.

Hal stood in front of the painting, while Keershan sat by his side, the two looking quite at ease despite the tension in the air. "Yes. Anija and Rialo can confirm it."

"They definitely did," Anija said with a nod. "We saw them silence that arrogant princess with our own two eyes. Or four eyes, I guess, if we want to be literal."

Fralia, the archmage of Malarsan, shook her head. She stood closest to Hal out of all of the council members other than Keershan, watching him with keen interest from behind her glasses. "I can't imagine Kryo Kardia will be happy about that."

"He almost certainly will not," Hal said, folding his

arms in front of his chest. He was still glowing with the same divine light as before, although it was less intense now that they were no longer in battle. "Nor will he like the message we sent to him, either."

"What did you tell him?" Wilme said. She was an elderly woman and current head of the Dragon Rider School, standing beside Anija and Rialo, raising an eyebrow.

"We told him we are coming for him," Keershan said simply. "Which is true, because we are."

General Surrels, general of the Malarsan Army, gave Hal and Keershan a doubtful look. "Is that why you are here in Malarsan, rather than in the Northern Circle? Not that I am unhappy to see you two again or anything, but you do remember that Kryo Kardia is a little farther north, right?"

Hal looked at Surrels. "We know that. But if we are going to end this war before it gets any worse, then will need help to kill Kryo Kardia. Take him out and the Glaci Empire will fall."

Anija pursed her lips. "Didn't the White Foxes say that same thing? And look what happened to them."

Keershan shook his head. "We won't repeat the mistakes of the White Foxes. Thanks to the gods, we now have the power we need to kill Kryo Kardia."

"I was going to ask about that," Surrels said. "You two look divine, if that is the right word to describe you. Exactly what did the gods give you and how did you get it?"

Unless Anija's eyes were playing tricks on her, she thought she saw Hal and Keershan exchange worried looks with one another, as if Surrels had just asked a question they really didn't want to answer.

But then Hal looked at Surrels, all hesitation in his face and body lost, and said, "We completed a difficult challenge that only a handful of mortals have ever finished. By doing so, we proved to the gods that we were worthy of the power we asked of them and so they gave it to us."

"I'd say," Anija said. "You two practically look like gods yourselves."

Hal chuckled. "Don't get carried away by our appearance. Keershan and I are still very much mortals. We may be stronger than most mortals, but we aren't gods."

Anija found it interesting how Hal emphasized their mortality so much. She especially found it interesting how eagerly Keershan nodded in agreement with Hal's statement. She supposed it might just be that Hal was telling the truth and Keershan was agreeing with him, but …

I think Hal is lying, Rialo said mentally. *Or at least not telling the whole truth.*

Anija resisted the urge to glance at Rialo. *What makes you say that? Did Hal say something that tipped you off?*

Not Hal, Rialo said. *Keershan. He's my younger brother. I know him better than anyone, and I can tell that he and Hal are hiding something from us. Something important that they don't want us knowing for some reason.*

Should we press them on it now? Anija asked.

Rialo shook her head very slightly. *No. I don't think they are hiding anything nefarious from us. It might just be something difficult to share, something they might not know how to tell us. I'm sure they will tell us when they are ready.*

Anija pursed her lips. She hoped that Rialo was correct. Although she trusted Hal and Keershan with her life, the truth was that Anija did not like it when people kept secrets from her.

I suppose I am one to talk, Anija thought, glancing around at the others. *It's not like I've always been upfront with everyone about my past or my secrets, although I like to think I've at least gotten better at being honest with my friends.*

"Where is Princess Nege, anyway?" Fralia asked, looking around the temple. "I don't see her."

"I ordered the other Riders to take her and Prika to a cave in the Tops," Hal said. "Since Mysteria doesn't have any prisons, the mountain caves are the only places where we can safely keep prisoners."

"I see," Surrels said. "And how long, exactly, do you intend to keep Nege and Prika around?"

Hal shook his head. "Until they tell us what we need to know about Kryo Kardia. I believe they both hold critical information about the Glaci Empire that we can use to our advantage."

"Makes sense," Rialo said with a nod of her head. "If she's one of Kryo Kardia's daughters, then logically, she must be very close to Kryo Kardia. She probably knows many secrets of the Glaci Empire."

"Exactly," Hal said. "Keershan and I will handle the interrogation process. In the meantime, how has the war with the Glaci Empire been going?"

"Barely," Surrels said with a shrug. "Most of the battles have been minor border skirmishes with Hosar. The fact that they sent their Riders and Steeds is a new development and probably means Kryo Kardia is taking the war more seriously."

Hal nodded thoughtfully. "Perhaps. It's interesting to me because the Glaci Empire is known for its doctrine of total warfare."

"Total warfare?" Anija repeated. "What does that mean?"

"Simple," Keershan said. "Total warfare is a Glacian war doctrine wherein the Glaci Empire tries to totally dominate and destroy the opposition during war. As I said, simple."

"That doesn't sound like how they have approached us so far," Surrels said, folding his arms in front of his chest. "So far, all they've really done is, like I said, sent war balloons to do hit-and-run attempts on our border. Why are they holding back?"

Hal stroked his chin. "I don't know for sure, but if I had to guess, I'd say that not all is well in the Northern Circle."

"You mean the Fracturing?" Anija asked. "Kryo Kardia did look pretty awful the last time I saw him."

"Possibly," Hal said, "but I am more thinking of any unrest in the Glaci Empire. Although we saw the empire crushed the White Foxes, I sincerely doubt that they managed to destroy *all* rebel sentiment."

"You think that Kryo Kardia is dealing with an uprising at home?" Fralia said. "And that's why the Glacians have been going easy on us so far?"

Hal shrugged. "I think it's likely. The other possibility is that he is testing us."

"Testing us?" Rialo said with a snort. "Doesn't he already know our potential, thanks to his spies?"

Keershan shook his head. "Kryo Kardia doesn't know *everything* about us. He probably doesn't want to do things in a hurry and underestimate us."

"Those theories are all fine and well, but do you know what I think the real reason for Kryo Kardia's hesitation is?" Surrels said. He jerked a thumb in a vaguely westward direction. "Tipjok."

Anija furrowed her brow. "Tipjok? You mean that country to the west?"

Surrels nodded. "Yes. We know that the Glaci Empire has been trying to conquer it. From a military perspective, it would seem like the empire is fighting two wars on two different fronts, which naturally stretches their resources very thin."

"In other words, the Glaci Empire may lack the manpower necessary to perform total warfare on us," Wilme said.

Surrels gave her the thumbs up. "Precisely. You would make a good military strategist yourself, Wilme, if you don't mind me saying so."

"In any case, this works out for us because it gives us time to breathe and plan our next course of action," Hal said with a nod. "Our first step should be to make Nege and Prika talk. After that, Keershan and I will travel back north to confront Kryo Kardia."

Anija raised an eyebrow. "By yourselves?"

"We're the only ones who can stand against Kryo Kardia in a straight fight," Keershan said. "While we appreciate you guys' willingness to help, in the end, it has to come down to us. It has to."

That sounded awfully patronizing to Anija. "You do realize we aren't pathetic little weaklings who can't fight for ourselves, right?"

"Bickering won't get us anywhere," Fralia said before Hal could speak. She rubbed her forehead. "Hal's right. Our first order of action should be to interrogate Nege and

Prika. After that, then we can decide what to do based on the information they give us."

Hal scowled, but apparently did not seem to want to fight Fralia's point. "Fair enough. Perhaps Nege and Prika will have information that could help us defeat Kryo Kardia."

Anija cocked her head to the side. "By the way, Hal, did you know that Old Snow is——?"

"Dead," Hal finished for her. "Yes, I did. Keershan and I heard about it on our way here. Where was he buried?"

"In the royal graveyard in the capital," Surrels said, folding his arms behind his back. "Are you going to visit his grave?"

Hal bit his lower lip and looked away. "Maybe later. Right now, we have more pressing matters to deal with."

Now that was suspicious. Hal, Keershan, and Old Snow had been close friends for a while. Anija had expected Hal and Keershan to be completely broken over Old Snow's death and to want to visit his grave to at least pay their respects.

Instead, however, neither Hal nor Keershan seemed particularly surprised or bothered by Old Snow's demise. Did they really feel nothing at all? That seemed weird to Anija. It confirmed to her that something had changed about those two for sure, even if she wasn't entirely sure what just yet.

And it's not just their appearance, either, Anija thought.

"What happened to the Snow Witches?" Rialo said. "I seem to recall you said you traveled to the Abode of the Gods with the Snow Witches of the Wastes."

Hal put his hands in his pockets. "Boca did indeed travel with us to the abode, but we went our separate ways afterward. I believe she and her sisters are staying in the Northern Circle to, and I quote, 'give Kralot hell.'"

"What the heck is a Kralot?" Surrels said, cocking his head to the side.

"It's a Glacian word meaning 'orphan' and is apparently Kryo Kardia's real name," Keershan said. "The Snow Witches tend to call him by that name because that was the name they gave him when they raised him."

Anija shook her head. "Who cares about Kryo Kardia's backstory? I'm more interested in what the Snow Witches are doing."

"They were very vague," Hal said. He looked around again, curiosity on his face. "By the way, where is Lom, the Relic Crafter? Is he still around?"

Anija pointed at the floor under their feet. "He should be in his workshop right now, working on ... well, I'm not sure what, but he's working on it."

"Excellent," Hal said. "Keershan and I will need to speak with him about something later. For now, why don't we go interrogate Nege and Prika?"

"So soon?" Surrels said. "Why don't you guys take it easy for a bit? You've been gone for over a month. Don't you want to catch up with everyone, maybe have a good meal first, and then get to work?"

Hal whirled on Surrels, his body positively shining with divine energy. "There's no time to sit back and relax, Surrels! Kryo Kardia will probably strike again at any moment. Regardless of whatever is going on in the Northern Circle, we have to be proactive. We have to end this war *now*."

Anija was taken aback by Hal's surprisingly emotional response.

Surrels, too, looked taken back by Hal's response, a slightly puzzled expression on his face. "I understand the importance of killing Kryo Kardia, but surely you still have some time to rest and relax. We just want to make sure you guys are taking care of yourselves, after all."

Hal continued to glare at Surrels before taking a deep breath and stepping back. The shining aura around his body fading, Hal said, "Sorry. You're right. Perhaps tonight we can have a feast to celebrate our return. But tomorrow morning, we'll need to start interrogating Nege and Prika. Okay?"

Everyone nodded, which Anija sensed had to do with the fact that everyone was a bit too afraid of Hal to want to argue against him. Even Rialo looked at the Dragon Rider warily.

Hal seems way more intense than he normally does, Anija said to Rialo via their bond. *Do you think that his new godly powers have anything to do with it?*

Perhaps, Rialo said. *On the other hand, he is correct that we need to interrogate Nege and Prika at some point. And the sooner, the better. Although I must say, I am looking forward to that feast tonight.*

Wilme raised a hand suddenly. "I will speak to the town chefs and see what we can come up with on such short notice."

Keershan licked his lips. "I hope there is plenty of cooked lamb. Lamb is my favorite."

"I'm sure the food will be good, whatever it is," Hal said. He glanced at Surrels. "By the way, Surrels, how is the new king of Malarsan doing? Stebo, I heard his name was?"

Surrels pursed his lips. "Technically speaking, Stebo isn't actually king yet."

"What?" Anija said, whipping her head toward Surrels. "But I thought he's Old Snow's son, isn't he? Doesn't that automatically make him the king of Malarsan?"

Surrels rubbed his arm. "Stebo is too young to be officially crowned king just yet. Thus, Regent Akei, a noble who is a distant relative of Old Snow, is currently ruling until Stebo is of age."

"Akei?" Hal repeated. "I've never heard that name before. Is he a good leader?"

"So far, yes," Surrels said. "Certainly more trustworthy than Tenka. It helps that he's more directly related to Old Snow than to Marial, so he's probably not conspiring with demons to take over the kingdom. Probably."

Hal scowled. "I can't believe the demons tried to make a comeback. One of these days, Keershan and I will have to hunt down every last one of those demons ourselves, just to make sure the kingdom is free of their taint."

"Worry about that later, Hal," Surrels said. "For now, why don't we all go and get ready for tonight's feast? That sounds more fun than sitting around sharing updates."

Hal nodded. "Good idea, Surrels. Keershan and I will stay here. We need to speak with Lom concerning a few things first."

"I will go and speak with the town chefs," Wilme said with a bow. "I don't know what we will be having tonight, but I am sure lamb will be on the menu, at least."

Both Keershan and Rialo looked pleased by Wilme's statement, although Anija wasn't. She still didn't understand why dragons loved lamb so much. It seemed like it was their favorite type of meat, which made no sense to her because beef and chicken were far superior.

But Anija had bigger things to worry about than the meat preferences of dragons.

Such as what Hal and Keershan are hiding from us, Anija thought, looking at the two of them as they talked with Surrels and Fralia. *And why they are hiding it from us.*

Chapter Four

"You do know we'll have to tell them the truth eventually, right, Hal?"

Hal paused in the stairway, looking over his shoulder at Keershan. The small dragon was right behind him, wearing a frown on his face.

"What truth?" Hal said, turning away from Keershan and resuming his walk down the stairs. "We've told them what they needed to know. We completed the challenge. We got the power of the gods. We are going to use said power to kill Kryo Kardia and end the war. That's all they need to know."

"Or all that *we* decided to tell them?" Keershan said, walking by Hal's side in the wide staircase now. "I could tell that my sister and Anija were onto us. They know we're holding back important information from them, even if they don't know what it is or why."

Hal sighed. "And we agreed not to tell them because it will just create more confusion and chaos. Remember? This is the path we chose."

"But it's not the path we have to stay on," Keershan argued. "Sooner or later, they will either figure out what actually happened in the challenge or we will have to tell them. We can't hide everything from them forever."

Hal stopped again and looked at Keershan. "And we won't. I promise, we won't. But it wouldn't be wise to tell them now. You remember what Old Snow told us."

Keershan clicked his teeth together. "I don't remember him telling us to keep secrets from our friends, even if we have legitimate reasons for keeping those secrets."

Shaking his head, Hal said, "But he did tell us to be circumspect about who we shared our powers with. If the others knew the full extent of our abilities—and the decisions we had to make during the challenge to get these powers—that would distract them from the war with the Glaci Empire. This is for their own good, and for ours."

Keershan licked his lips. "If you say so. I still don't feel good about it."

"Neither do I," Hal said with another shake of his head. "But it is for the greater good. Now let's keep going. We need Lom's help."

With that, Hal resumed walking down the stairs to Lom's workshop. He heard Keershan walking behind him, although he sensed Keershan's displeasure as easily as if it was his own.

Mostly because it was, thanks to their bond.

And, despite himself, Hal could not help but think back to the challenge, to the day when his and Keershan's lives changed forever, although they did not yet know it at the time.

One month ago...

Hal could hardly believe his eyes. When he had stepped through the door of the abode, Hal had not been sure what he had expected, exactly. Gotcham Nubor, the king of the Gods, had kept the details of the challenge a secret from him and Keershan. The two were supposed to go in blind and handle whatever obstacles the challenge threw at them.

Thus, Hal was deeply surprised when he saw Old Snow, king of Malarsan and, more importantly, his close friend and mentor, standing in the grassy, windswept plains of Lamb's Hand. The sun shining overhead caused the stalks of wheat below to look like they were made out of solid gold. In the distance, Hal could see the town of Lamb's Hand itself, the way it looked before the demons burned it down and left nothing standing and nothing living. Even the air smelled of sweet wheat and summer evenings, bringing back many of Hal's childhood memories of growing up in the country before becoming a Relic Hunter for the kingdom and, eventually, a Dragon Rider.

But mostly, Hal's attention was on the aged, bearded king before him. "Old Snow? What are you doing here? How did you get to the abode?"

"Maybe that isn't actually him, Hal," Keershan said, narrowing his eyes. "Some of the oldest legends I've read mention a 'challenge' of the gods that says the challenge creates illusions to fool mortals unworthy of the power of the gods."

Old Snow laughed. "Ha! I am so pleased to see that you are as studious as ever, Keershan. And you, Hal, are as brave and strong as you always have been."

Hal eyed Old Snow carefully. "You seem pretty realistic for an illusion."

"That is because I am no illusion, Hal, Keershan," Old Snow said. He patted his chest. "I am as real as you two are, if in a different sense."

"What does that mean?" Keershan said. "And how can this even be possible? You were back in Malarsan the last time we saw you. If you really are real, then why did you come all the way here?"

Old Snow frowned. "Technically, I didn't. It is you who came back to me."

Hal looked around at Lamb's Hand in surprise. "Do you mean that the door took us back to Malarsan? Do we have to complete the challenge here?"

Old Snow shook his head. "None of this is real. The legends that Keershan mentioned were partially accurate. This is merely a recreation of your childhood memories of your hometown growing up. That is why everything looks much nicer and more pleasant than it does in real life."

Hal furrowed his brow. "So the town isn't real, but you are."

"Exactly," Old Snow said. "Clear as mud, yes?"

Keershan scowled. "That still doesn't explain how *you* got here, Old Snow, or what you meant when you said *we* came to *you*."

Old Snow sighed. "I was killed in the mortal realm, murdered by my own nephew, Tenka."

Hal's jaw dropped. "What? When? We haven't heard of this."

Old Snow shook his head. "It happened while you were away. Tenka manipulated Surrels into killing me so he could ascend to the Throne and become the new king of Malarsan."

"Did it work?" Hal said.

Old Snow shook his head again. "Fortunately, no. Our friends managed to stop Tenka before he could ascend to the Throne, but they weren't able to save me from dying. Thus, I have moved on to the spiritual realm, where all the dead go when we die."

Hal scratched the back of his head. "So is this place the spiritual realm, then? Does that mean we are—"

"No," Old Snow said. "You two are very much still alive. This place, however, is one of the few places in the mortal realm where the mortal realm and the spiritual realm overlap. Here, you are as likely to run into the departed as you are into living flesh-and-blood human beings."

Hal looked around eagerly. "Does that mean that my dad might be here?"

Old Snow stroked his beard. "Maybe. I haven't seen him or anyone else around. To be fair, however, the after-life is a vast place. He could be on the other side of the afterlife for all I know. The same goes for your father, Keershan."

Hal's shoulders slumped. When Old Snow mentioned that the dead lived in this place, Hal had hoped that his dad, who had perished fighting dragons in the Dragon War, might be here, too. Evidently, however, Hal should not have gotten his hopes up. He felt similar disappointment coming from Keershan, even though the dragon did not show it on the outside.

Keershan frowned. "So what is this? Just a giant cosmic coincidence that we ran into you here?"

Old Snow tapped the ground with his staff. "No. I am the keeper of the challenge, chosen specifically because of my relationship with you two. My job is to oversee the completion of the challenge and report back to the gods about your progress within it."

"But that still doesn't explain why *you*, in particular, are the keeper," Keershan said. "Not that I am unhappy to see you again, but I don't know why they didn't just choose a random person to do the job instead."

"A fair question," Old Snow said. "The answer is that the challenge is not merely about overcoming obstacles or solving puzzles, though you will do a fair bit of both during it. The gods are also testing your character and your moral compasses. And they need someone who knows you two quite well already to judge you accurately."

"Well, you know who we are and how good we are already," Hal said, putting his hands on his hips. "Why not simply report your opinions to the gods and ask them to give us the power? I mean, surely we're worthy of the power after saving the world from the Nameless One already, right?"

Old Snow shook his head. "I'm afraid it's not that simple. The gods will not simply take the word of one or two or even a hundred witnesses before granting someone their power. They want to see for themselves if you can pass *their* tests, which are different from the kind of tests that you may have experienced in the mortal realm. You must pass a series of such tests in order to prove your worth to the gods."

Hal scowled. "Why all this just for the power of the gods? Okay, that may be a stupid question, but the gods themselves have already acknowledged that Kryo Kardia's threat to the world is real. Why not give us a simpler test?"

Old Snow gave Hal and Keershan a slightly exasperated look. "Because, my boy, this test is not merely to determine if you and Keershan are worthy of wielding the power of the gods. This is about something much more."

"What could be more than that?" Hal demanded.

Old Snow smiled slightly. "Godhood, of course."

Keershan gasped. "You don't mean—?"

"I do," Old Snow said with a nod. "I do very much mean that."

Hal frowned. "Even though Keershan and I have a strong bond, I have no idea what you two are talking about."

Keershan looked at Hal urgently. "We're talking about the true purpose of the challenge, Hal. It's not just about giving us the power to defeat Kryo Kardia. It's not even really about defeating Kryo Kardia at all."

"Then what *is* it about?" Hal said. "Wasting our time?"

Old Snow shook his head again. "No. The true purpose of the challenge is to determine whether you two are worthy not merely of wielding the power of the gods, but of becoming gods yourselves."

Chapter Five

"WE ARE SUPPOSED TO BECOME GODS?" HAL SAID, narrowing his eyes. "I don't understand. Mortals can't become gods. Can they?"

Old Snow scratched his beard. "Actually, yes. It's very rare, as you might imagine, but it is entirely possible."

Hal shook his head. "I don't understand. I thought that the gods have existed since the beginning of creation itself. How, then, can a mortal become a god?"

Old Snow tapped the ground with his staff. "You know that gods can be killed, yes?"

Hal nodded. "Of course. We killed the Nameless One ourselves."

"And we also saw Shirataka's untimely murder by Vilona," Keershan added. "Although technically, I suppose that was a murder by a *demi*god and not a mortal. The principle still applies, though."

"It most certainly does," Old Snow said. "I am glad you are aware of this fact. But have you ever wondered what happens to the domains of the gods who are killed? Who controls them and watches over them? What happens to their followers? How said god is even replaced?"

Hal scratched the back of his neck as a soft breeze blew through, sending the wheat stalks shifting below. "I haven't, actually."

Old Snow pointed at Hal. "That's because it rarely happens. But when it does, the gods need to find a replacement for said deity. Upon death, the domains of a deceased god will automatically fall under the control of Gotcham Nubor, who I am sure you two already know by now. But Gotcham Nubor cannot control their domains forever, so he must find a replacement for the slain god in order to ensure the balance of the universe is correct and that he is not burdened with more work than he can deal with."

"More work than he can deal with?" Keershan said. "But he's the king of the Gods. Shouldn't that make him powerful enough to handle anything?"

Old Snow stroked his beard. "Gotcham Nubor is not all-powerful, despite being the king of the Gods. He doesn't have limitless power even if he is more powerful than the average deity. He can be overwhelmed, and if Gotcham Nubor were to be overwhelmed, the results would be quite catastrophic for the world."

"So the challenge is meant to test to see if we are worthy of becoming gods?" Hal said. "That's crazy to think about."

"Not just any gods, but the new gods of light," Old Snow said. "Since Shirataka's murder, the domain of light is currently lacking a god to control and oversee it. If you complete the challenge satisfactorily, then you two will be eligible to ascend to godhood yourselves and take control of the domain of light."

Keershan's jaw dropped open. "Wow! That's incredible. I never thought I'd get a chance to become a literal deity. I didn't even know that was possible."

Hal held up a hand. "Hold on, Old Snow. You said this has happened before. Who was replaced before Shirataka?"

"Why, the Nameless One, of course," Old Snow said. "I do not know the details of his replacement, but my understanding is that after the Nameless One's fall from grace, the gods chose a mortal to take over his domain. The Nameless One was the god of shadow before his corruption, so the new god of shadow was once a mortal who completed the challenge. This happened shortly after the Fall, from what I have been able to gather."

"We didn't see the god of shadow while we were in the abode," Hal said. "Admittedly, however, there were a ton of gods there, so perhaps we just didn't recognize him."

"If you complete the challenge, then you will almost certainly get a chance to see him when you return to the abode," Old Snow said. "So I wouldn't worry about that. I would worry about the challenge, which will be difficult enough for you two by my estimation."

"What if we don't want to become gods, though?" Hal said. "What if Keershan and I just want to stay mortal and only use godly power to defeat Kryo Kardia?"

Old Snow shook his head. "That isn't possible, I'm afraid. If you successfully pass the challenge, then you have to go forward with godhood, regardless of how you feel about it. Didn't Gotcham Nubor explain this to you before you started?"

Hal shook his head. "No, although now I'm starting to think that Gotcham Nubor didn't tell us a lot of things."

Old Snow pursed his lips. "That is disappointing, but at least you know now."

Hal nodded, although inside, he was furious at Gotcham Nubor for not revealing the true purpose of the challenge to them before they'd accepted it.

Gotcham Nubor probably is desperate for someone to replace Shirataka as soon as possible, Keershan said mentally. *Given Old Snow's explanation about how balance in the universe works, I can only imagine that he doesn't want to risk unbalancing the world by controlling her domain any longer than he has to.*

Even if that is the case, that doesn't change the fact that he left out important information that we could have used to make an informed decision, Hal said. *Surely you must be as upset about that as I am.*

I am, Keershan said. *But there's no point in getting upset about it now. We just have to move forward and hope for the best. And hey, becoming a god doesn't sound too bad, in my opinion. Could even be fun. I could finally live long enough to read all of the old books I want to read.*

Hal, still not as accepting of this situation as Keershan was, looked at Old Snow again. "But we don't want to become gods. We want to have the power to stop Kryo Kardia. Can't the gods merely bless us with their power temporarily or something?"

Old Snow shrugged. "They could, I suppose, but they clearly did not, perhaps because Gotcham Nubor really wants to replace Shirataka as quickly as possible."

"That's what I told Hal," Keershan said. "But Hal didn't listen."

"Because it's unreasonable," Hal said. "If we become gods, we will have to live in the abode like the other gods. We won't be able to see our friends or families ever again."

"True," Old Snow said. "And I do think it was wrong of

Gotcham Nubor to leave out that crucial bit of information when he explained the challenge to you. But as I said, it's too late to back out now. The only way out now is to either complete or fail the challenge. There are no other options."

"What if we intentionally failed the challenge?" Keershan said. "Would we still be able to get the powers of the gods?"

Old Snow frowned deeply. "Intentionally throwing the challenge would be a good way to get on the gods' bad side. Forever. I wouldn't do it if I were you."

Hal scowled. He tried to see a way around this but couldn't. He had not signed up to become a god or take Shirataka's place as the god of light.

On the other hand, if Hal and Keershan did not complete the challenge, then it sounded like they would not get any blessings from the gods at all. And they needed the blessings of the gods if they were going to stop Kryo Kardia from invading Malarsan and conquering the world.

That left them with no choice but to accept the challenge and complete it to the best of their ability. Even if that meant sacrificing their own mortality, they would have to do it. Hal just hoped that perhaps later they would find out a way to get around the part about becoming gods.

With a frustrated sigh, Hal said, "Fine. We will do the challenge. And we will complete it."

"Good to hear," Old Snow said. "I know how frustrating this is, but in the end, you have to do it."

"I know, I know," Hal said with a wave of his hand. "Let's just move on with it. What's the first challenge?"

Old Snow gestured at the town below. "Your first obstacle is in your hometown."

"And what is our first obstacle?" Keershan asked.

Old Snow winked at them. "You will have to go down there and find out for yourselves. I, unfortunately, am not allowed to tell you what the first obstacle is."

"But you're the keeper of the challenge," Hal said. "And, more than that, a good friend of ours. Why wouldn't you tell us what the first obstacle is? Or at least give us a hint so we aren't going in totally blind?"

Old Snow pursed his lips. "The purpose of the challenge is to reveal insights into your character that you yourself may be unaware of so the gods can see you two as you truly are and not just as I say you are. Each obstacle you face in the challenge must be a secret so you cannot prepare for it or do anything to alter it."

"We could alter the obstacles if we knew what they were?" Keershan said.

Old Snow held a finger up to his lips. "I cannot tell you more than that, other than you must use all your wits, strength, and knowledge to handle them. If you complete the challenge and complete it to the satisfaction of the gods, then you will get the power you seek and even ascend to godhood."

"And what happens if we fail?" Hal said. "What then?"

Old Snow shrugged. "Then you will be kicked out of the challenge and will not be allowed to try again."

"We don't get a second chance?" Keershan said.

Old Snow nodded. "Correct. All challengers, which is what you two are, get only one chance to succeed. If you do not pass it the first time, then you will not be given another chance."

"Seems kind of harsh," Keershan said, "especially if the gods are as desperate for a replacement for Shirataka as you say they are."

"The challenge is seen as the final judgment for whether mortals like you are worthy of the power of the gods or not," Old Snow said. "There are no second chances in final judgments. There is only failure or success. And I wish you nothing but the best."

With that, Old Snow's form disappeared, leaving Hal and Keershan standing by themselves in the illusionary wheat fields of Lamb's Hand.

Hal sighed and looked down at the town below. "Looks like we will have to go down there to overcome the first obstacle."

Keershan spread his wings out behind him. "Should we fly? It would be faster than walking."

Hal shook his head. "No. It's not that far. Walking won't hurt us."

With that, Hal walked down the hill, Keershan by his side. Neither of them said anything, but they were both thinking the same thing: They had not signed up to become gods.

Chapter Six

"Are the people of Lamb's Hand blind," Keershan said as they walked through Hal's hometown, "or are they just really polite?"

Hal looked over his shoulder at Keershan in confusion. "What do you mean?"

Keershan gestured with a claw at the townspeople walking around them. "I mean, there's a freaking dragon in the middle of the street and not a single person here has even commented on my appearance or even looked at me for that matter. It feels strange."

Hal gazed around the street they stood on. Keershan had a point. Despite both of them taking up a considerable portion of the street, the townspeople of Lamb's Hand paid no attention to either Hal or Keershan. In fact, they seemed to be deliberately ignoring them, like they didn't even exist. The only hint that the townspeople even seemed to notice their existence was how they would walk around Hal and Keershan, but other than that, they might as well not have existed for all the attention that the townspeople paid to them.

Hal sighed. "I don't know, but you have to remember that this is just an illusion. These people aren't even real. If they aren't reacting to your presence, it's probably not because they are either polite or blind. It's probably because they aren't even real."

Keershan huffed. "I guess. It still feels strange, however, to be treated like I don't exist."

"Maybe that's the obstacle we have to overcome," Hal said, glancing around the street. "Perhaps the gods are testing us to see how we react to being treated like nobodies. If so, I wonder if we are doing well or failing miserably."

Keershan shook his head. "I severely doubt that this is a test. Surely we would know if this was part of the challenge. It wouldn't be fair otherwise."

Hal raised an eyebrow. "Would we? I'm not so sure. Old Snow didn't give us much to work with back on the hill. He didn't even say how we would know we found the obstacle. He just told us it was somewhere here in town, and even that, I feel, might have been pushing it in terms of hints he could give us."

"Old Snow isn't allowed to give us hints, remember?" Keershan said. "I'm sure he would have given us more information if his hands weren't tied."

It was Hal's turn to huff. Turning away from Keershan, Hal said, "Right. Let's just keep looking. We're bound to find the obstacle eventually. Lamb's Hand isn't a very big town."

With that, Hal resumed walking, but he did not look to see if Keershan was following him. He was caught up in his own thoughts.

They had been walking around Lamb's Hand for about thirty minutes now, and they hadn't run into anything that Hal would describe as an obstacle in a divine challenge. He had seen only people he knew back in the real world, farmers taking their animals to market, and children playing in the streets, among other ordinary things.

Nothing that unusual or out of place in the town, in other words.

But oddly, anytime Hal tried to look directly at another person's face, their facial features would become blurry for some reason. It was like there was a filter or something in place to make sure that he could not see them clearly. He didn't know how else to describe it. It was like the illusion did not want him to recognize or interact with other people.

It left Hal feeling very alone, aside from having Keershan at his side. Every time Hal thought he recognized someone, he would find it impossible to see their faces. And all of his attempts to stop people in order to chat with them had proved fruitless as well, because Keershan wasn't the only person the inhabitants of Lamb's Hand were ignoring. They were ignoring him, too. Even touching them wouldn't get a reaction out of them.

Hal suspected the odd appearances and behaviors of the townspeople were connected in some way to the challenge or to the illusions conjured by the challenge, but for the life of him, Hal could not figure out how. Maybe it was just meant to creep them out.

If so, it was working very well.

"Do you think we're under a time limit?" Keershan said, his voice snapping Hal out of his thoughts. "Like, if we don't complete the first obstacle in a certain amount of time, we will be kicked out of the challenge entirely and automatically fail it?"

Hal shook his head. "I doubt it. Old Snow didn't say anything about a timer or deadline. I suspect we can stay here as long as we want or until we complete or fail the challenge."

Keershan sighed. "Then I guess we're going to be here for a while, huh?"

"Hey, you two!" a female voice suddenly called out. "What are you two doing here?"

Hal and Keershan stopped and looked over their shoulders to see a young woman who neither of them recognized running toward them. The young woman came to a stop several feet away from them, putting her hands on her knees and panting slightly as she glared at them.

The young woman appeared to be in her late teens or possibly early twenties. Her long blonde hair was tied up in a neat bun and she wore a simple brown dress with a black jacket, giving her a very humble appearance. Her skin was painfully pale, however, and her eyes were a shocking green that Hal found difficult to ignore.

"Hal, who is that?" Keershan whispered to Hal. "Someone from your hometown?"

Hal shook his head. "No. I don't recognize her. She's a total stranger to me."

"What are you two whispering about?" the young woman demanded. She rose to her full height, although given how short she was, it wasn't a very impressive sight. "It sounds like you are talking about me. Are you talking about me?"

"No, of course not," Hal said, quickly exchanging guilty

looks with Keershan. "We were just, um, trying to find our way to the market."

"Yes," Keershan said. "We are, um, lost."

The young woman eyed them skeptically. "If the marketplace is what you are looking for, it's in the other direction."

The young woman thrust her thumb over her shoulder. "Keep going that way. Once you see the farm animals being penned up and sold, you'll know you've found the right place."

"Thanks," Hal said, "but why did you stop us in the first place, Miss—?"

"Erla," said the young woman. "As for why I stopped you, it's because you two are clearly newcomers. I've never seen either of you around here before. Especially the dragon."

Hal frowned. "I grew up here. I know everyone here. I don't recognize you."

Erla eyed Hal even more skeptically than before. "If you grew up here, then how come you needed me to tell you where the marketplace is? That doesn't sound like someone who grew up here. That sounds like someone from out of town. Unless you're lying about that, that is."

She's got you there, Hal, Keershan said mentally. *You should have kept with the out-of-towner lie.*

But I just got so offended that she accused me of not being from around here, Hal said. *Not my fault she's rude, although I guess you have a point. Maybe she's part of the challenge.*

Clasping his hands together, Hal said, "Okay, I see what is going on here."

"What do you mean?" Erla said, raising a questioning eyebrow.

Hal pointed at Erla. "You're clearly part of the challenge, maybe even part of the first test. I don't know exactly what you are testing us about, but whatever it is, we are ready to do it."

Erla scowled. "The world doesn't revolve around you two. I have no idea what this 'challenge' thing is, but it clearly has nothing to do with me. Try that line on another girl."

With that, Erla turned and marched away from Hal and Keershan, prompting Hal to shout, "Wait! Don't leave us. We still need help finding the first obstacle of the challenge!"

"Find it yourself!" Erla replied irritably over her shoulder. "Or try another girl who is way more naive than me!"

With that, Erla disappeared into the crowd of people, vanishing among them like a ghost in the wind.

Keershan sighed. "If that was the first obstacle, I don't know if we passed it or not."

Hal scowled. "That woman is clearly part of it. Why else would we be able to interact with her if she wasn't connected to the challenge in some way? I doubt she's the full obstacle herself, but maybe she could lead us to—"

A woman's scream interrupted Hal, causing him and Keershan to look in the direction from which it came.

It was the same direction that Erla had gone.

Chapter Seven

HAL DID NOT HESITATE TO RUSH DOWN THE STREET, PUSHING past and through the walking townspeople with Keershan by his side. Although he had no way of knowing who the screaming woman was, Hal recognized the general meaning of the scream quite well. Someone was in trouble.

And that same someone needed their help.

"Who do you think is screaming?" Keershan yelled as they ran. "Do you think it was that Erla lady from earlier?"

Hal pointed down the street as they ran, ducking his head to avoid slamming into an overhanging sign of a shop they passed. "No idea, but the screaming is getting louder, so we must be getting closer. Just a little bit further and—"

"Help!" a much closer female voice called out. "Please, help me! Anyone!"

Skidding to a stop at the mouth of an alleyway, Hal turned to look down the alleyway.

Erla was backed against a wall at the end of the alley, menaced by two thugs who seemed to have more brawn than brains between them. One of the thugs had a knife, while the other wore brass knuckles on his fists that were spiked.

"Or maybe the screaming *isn't* from Erla," Keershan said, peering into the alley with Hal, a frown on his face. "What are the odds of two women being in danger at exactly the same time?"

Hal nodded. "Agreed. It's weird. This must be part of the challenge."

Before Hal or Keershan could enter the alley, however, that same scream from before blared again, causing them to whip their heads in that direction in surprise.

"There are definitely two women screaming for help," Hal said. "This definitely has to be part of the challenge. It has to."

"But who should we help?" asked Keershan. "We can't be in two places at once. What if we pick the wrong woman to save and fail the challenge?"

Hal thought quickly. Keershan was right. They couldn't be in two places at once. Yet Hal did not want to pick and choose who to save and who not to save. Even if this wasn't part of the challenge, a part of Hal hated the idea of abandoning innocent people who were in danger, even if the innocent people were merely elaborate illusions and not true flesh-and-blood human beings.

Then an idea occurred to Hal and he clapped his hands together. "Okay, Keershan. We'll split up. You can go and save the other woman. I will stay here and save Erla from these thugs."

"You want us to split up?" Keershan questioned. "Are you sure that is wise?"

Hal nodded. "Yes. This way, we are almost guaranteed to pass the test no matter who we save. Plus, I've fought enemies far tougher than a couple of street thugs before. I can take care of myself."

Keershan gave Hal one last skeptical look before nodding. "All right. You make a good point. But if you need help, let me know."

With that, Keershan flapped his wings and took off into the air toward the sounds of the screaming. No doubt Keershan wanted to lower the amount of time it took to reach the source of the screams as much as possible, hence why he flew.

But Hal paid little attention to that. He just drew his sword and ran into the alleyway, shouting, "Hey, you two! Pick on someone your own size for a change."

The two thugs stopped advancing on Erla and turned around to face Hal. They were even uglier than Hal thought. The first thug had scars all over his face while the second thug looked like he'd had his face violently reconstructed by a dragon recently.

And both of them did not show any fear toward Hal as he approached them.

"Who the hell do you think you are, loser?" said the first thug, who had a slight lisp to his words. "Some kind of hero?"

"I'll let the lady decide that," Hal said, coming to a stop. He pointed his sword at the thugs. "If you step away from the woman and never bother her again, I will let you both walk out of here on your own feet."

"And if we don't?" said the second thug with a sneer. "What will you do then?"

Hal frowned. "I'll get really violent and I don't think you guys want to see me when I get really violent."

The two thugs exchanged puzzled looks with each other

while Erla, still cowering behind the men, raised her head slightly, a surprised look on her face. "Wait, aren't you the out-of-towner I just saw earlier? What are you doing here? Where is your dragon?"

"I don't need a dragon to deal with these two chuckle-heads," Hal said, gesturing at the thugs. "As for why I am here, I just don't like seeing a couple of bullies treat a woman this way."

"Think you're some kind of chivalrous knight, do you?" said the second thug. He slammed his fist into his other hand. "You'll be really fun to beat."

The second thug shot toward Hal far faster than Hal had expected him to.

But Hal, drawing on his bond with Keershan, was faster still.

He leaped to the side, neatly avoiding the second thug's fist, before slashing with his sword. Hal's sword slashed diagonally across the second thug's chest, causing blood to start pouring from it as the second thug howled in pain.

Hal then followed up the blow with a kick to the chest, aiming for the wound he'd just created. The second thug fell over onto the street with a loud *crash*, blood pooling underneath him, his fingers twitching as he lay defeated underneath Hal's boot.

Hal looked up at the other thug, spinning his sword the whole time. "Do you want to rumble with me next and end up like your friend?"

The first thug scowled. "My 'friend' was a weakling. I'll give you the pounding you deserve and then resume mugging this pretty lady. By the way, call me Knife."

Hal frowned. "Knife? Is that supposed to be a nickname or something? If so, it's a terrible one."

Knife chuckled. "I don't care what you think about my nickname, mostly 'cause you ain't gonna live long enough to think about it."

Hal, expecting Knife to rush forward, raised his sword defensively.

Instead, however, Knife threw his dagger straight at Hal's face. The dagger flew through the air straight and true, forcing Hal to knock it out of the air to avoid getting stabbed in the face.

But the dagger, it turned out, was just a distraction. Knife rushed forward and slammed his shoulder into Hal's gut, making Hal gasp in pain and stagger backward. Hal tried to slash at Knife with his sword, but Knife caught his wrist and twisted it, forcing Hal to drop his sword onto the street with a clatter.

"What's the matter, hero?" Knife sneered at Hal, tightening his grip on Hal's wrist. "You don't look so brave anymore now that you don't have that fancy sword of yours."

Hal hated to admit it, but Knife had a point. Hal had underestimated Knife's intelligence and strength. He bet that Knife could snap his wrist without even thinking about it.

But Knife failed to realize that Hal did not need his sword to utterly take him down.

Channeling dragonfire through his body, Hal heated up his arm. Knife screamed and let go of Hal's wrist, clutching his burning hand. Shaking his wrist, Hal kicked Knife in the gut, sending Knife staggering backward.

With Knife distracted, Hal bent over and picked up his sword. Rising to his feet, Hal swung his blade at Knife's face, aiming to cleave the thug's head in two.

But Knife drew two daggers from nowhere and blocked Hal's sword with a *clang*. Surprised, Hal struck again and again, but no matter how many times he tried to hit Knife, the thug would just block his attacks with his daggers.

"Come on," said Knife, grunting under every blow from Hal. "You gotta do better than that if you're going to save the girl."

Hal said nothing to that, mostly because he was trying to see a weakness in Knife's defense. It seemed like Knife was doing his best to avoid giving Hal any openings to take advantage of, which spoke to Knife's intelligence and combat skills.

So Hal feinted. He slashed his sword toward Knife's face, forcing Knife to raise his daggers to block the attack.

Only for Hal to stop and fire a dragonfireball at Knife with his free hand.

The dragonfireball slammed into Knife's stomach, sending him flying backward. Erla dove out of the way to avoid Knife, who crashed into the wall that she'd been standing in front of with enough force to crack it. Knife fell face-first onto the grimy street, twitched once or twice, and then stopped.

Lowering his smoking hand, Hal said, "Looks like I *did* do better than that."

"What was that?" Erla said, looking at Hal in confusion. "You shot fire from your hands. Are you a mage or something?"

Hal shook his head. "Not exactly. Are you all right?"

Erla rubbed her arm. "I'm fine. Those idiots didn't lay even one finger on me. I probably could have saved myself, honestly."

Hal grinned. "Sure you could have. Anyway, I'm glad I

saved you. I'm going to go check on my dragon now and see how he's doing with the woman he's—"

Suddenly, Keershan's voice blared in Hal's mind, saying, *Hal! It's a trap! Get out of there now!*

"A trap?" Hal said aloud without realizing it. "What is the—"

Hal felt a sharp, biting sensation in his gut and looked down to see a knife embedded in his stomach.

Looking up, Hal found himself staring into the smirking face of Erla, showing very pointed, inhuman teeth.

"I'm the trap," Erla said. "And you just fell for it."

Chapter Eight

SURRELS DID NOT KNOW WHY HE HAD TO INTERROGATE A spoiled princess and her dragon tonight while everyone else got to enjoy a feast.

Probably because you volunteered for the job, idiot, Surrels told himself as he walked down the line of cells. *Should have gotten Wilme or someone else to do it instead. I'm sure Wilme would make an excellent interrogator. She has the iron will to do it and is pretty scary.*

Although the original plan had been to throw a huge party to celebrate the return of Hal and Keershan to Malarsan before making either Nege or Prika talk, Surrels had decided that he couldn't wait until tomorrow to interrogate Princess Nege. The information she had on Kryo Kardia's plans and movements was too valuable to ignore for long. He'd even discussed it with Wilme and Fralia, who agreed that this was probably the best time to try it.

The likely culprit was Surrels's military and Black Soldier instincts. He had been a foot soldier in the Malarsan Army as a young man before transferring to the

Black Soldier Corps, a selective group of elite soldiers who carried out covert jobs for the Malarsan royal family. He'd performed a number of interrogations over the decades in that position, even if he didn't specifically remember most of them thanks to the constant memory wipes that he and his fellow Black Soldiers had undergone for security reasons.

But Surrels had not forgotten the various interrogation skills and knowledge he'd picked up during that time.

I suppose I wouldn't have made such a good Black Soldier if I forgot all of the talents and skills that had made me valuable to Queen Marial in the first place, Surrels thought ruefully. *Unlike my memories of my wife and children, of course, which I didn't need to remember in order to be a good Black Soldier, although I certainly needed to remember them in order to be a good husband and father.*

Surrels had spent a lot of time over the last year or so trying to regain his memories of his family and his life before he became a Black Soldier. He'd recovered a lot of them and even reconnected with his estranged children, but he still didn't remember all of it, a fact he was all too aware of. It was quite frustrating.

But Surrels's personal quest to regain his memories had gone on the back burner for now. Since Kryo Kardia declared war on the kingdom of Malarsan about a month ago, Surrels had been working nonstop to make sure the Malarsan Army was in good shape to deal with any attacks from the Glaci Empire.

And unfortunately, it wasn't. The end of the Dragon War in Malarsan over a year ago now had led to the government diverting funds from the military to funding things like infrastructure, magical research into non-combat uses for magic, and more. It had seemed like a good idea at the time when peace had been on the horizon, because no one had expected a war with the Glaci Empire, but that decision was certainly coming back to bite them in the butt.

At least the current regent is a former soldier himself, Surrels thought. *He understands the importance of having a strong army and military, especially in the middle of a war you didn't start.*

The current regent of Malarsan, Regent Nobyd Akei, was the closest living adult relative to the Malarsan royal family. He was currently serving in place of Stebo, the young son of King Rikas and Queen Mariel, who wouldn't be old enough to rule as king himself for another decade at least.

In the meantime, Regent Akei was the most eligible ruler thanks to his distant relation to King Rikas. Surrels thought that Akei was some kind of distant third cousin on King Rikas' mother's side of the family, but either way, Akei had won a landslide vote from the nobles last month shortly after the demise of Hojara Tenka, the only other living adult relative of the royal family, who had been killed by demons after attempting to take the throne himself.

And good riddance, Surrels thought with a shudder. *That man would have been even worse than Marial. Fitting that they were related to each other.*

One of Akei's first acts, in fact, had been to focus on rebuilding the army and the kingdom's military focus due to the war with the Glaci Empire. Still, it would take a long time, Surrels knew, before the Malarsan Army would be anywhere near close enough to challenge the might of the Glaci Empire. It helped that Akei had served in the army during his twenties and so understood the importance of a strong military, especially in times of war.

Yet even at its height, the Malarsan army hadn't been

anywhere near as big or powerful as the military forces of the Glaci Empire. True, they had Dragon Riders now, but so did the Glaci Empire, and the Glaci Empire had had a lot more time to bolster its forces in preparation for this conflict than they had. That didn't even take into account the Glaci Army or their own mages or the war balloons, for that matter.

All in all, this is exactly why we need every bit of information we can get about the enemy's movements and plans, Surrels thought, stopping in front of the only occupied cell in the entire dungeon, though there were cells on both sides of the hallway. *And why I am here tonight.*

Surrels knocked on the metal bars of the cell. "Anyone awake in here?"

A loud groan came from the cot, and a feminine form, half-tangled in the blankets, sat up. Princess Nege Kardia glared at Surrels,.

"Who are you and why are you interrupting my important beauty sleep?" Nege demanded. "It's bad enough I don't have my snow duck feather bed to sleep on. Now I have ugly old men like you bothering me, probably for dirty reasons."

Surrels shook his head. "Unlike your people, we don't rape prisoners if that's what you mean. I'm here to make you talk."

Nege looked away from Surrels. "No. And where is Prika? I can sense he is still somewhere in town, but it's difficult to feel him since you dumb Malarsans took away my relic."

Surrels nodded. That had been his suggestion when Nege had been captured and brought down here earlier today. Although the Dragon Riders were powerful, they were significantly weaker if separated from their dragon, and even weaker than that when they didn't have their relics. Nor did Surrels feel bad about taking her relic, seeing as it had probably been stolen from *them* in the first place, because most of the Glacian relics had belonged to them before a traitor in the order had stolen and sold them off. They were just rightfully taking back what was theirs.

"Your dragon is being kept in another part of town," Surrels told her. "He's perfectly safe, if you are worried about him."

Nege pouted. "Not really. I only want to know where he is because he's my only ticket out of here. And Father would be very upset if I returned without my relic or Steed."

Surrels raised an eyebrow. Although not a Dragon Rider himself, Surrels understood that the bond between Rider and Steed was incredibly close, in some ways even closer than a marriage relationship between a man and a woman. Riders and Steeds were often willing to die for each other, yet Nege acted like Prika was more like a glorified pet than a partner she would spend the rest of her life with.

Daddy probably only made her a Dragon Rider to make her happy, Surrels thought. *And if the rest of the Glacian Riders feel similarly about their Steeds, then perhaps they aren't as dangerous as I thought. Just spoiled and selfish.*

Nege glared at Surrels. "You aren't even a Rider yourself. What are you even doing here?"

Surrels started. "How did you know I'm not a Rider? I didn't tell you that."

Nege snorted. "It's obvious. For one, you clearly don't have a relic of your own. And secondly, you just lack the aura that we Riders have. It's difficult to put into words, especially words that a non-Rider like yourself would understand."

Surrels folded his arms in front of his chest. "I'm more versed in Dragon Rider lore than you think, but that knowledge probably won't be helpful or necessary here. As I said, I am here to make you talk."

Nege gasped. "You are going to *interrogate* me? Like I am some sort of common prisoner?"

Surrels gave Nege a dry look. "Yes, because you *are* a prisoner, albeit not a common one."

Nege stood up, her hands balled at her sides. "If you dare to lay even one finger on me—"

"With luck, I won't," Surrels said. He tapped the bars. "There are ways to make prisoners talk even without using violence or physical force."

Nege cocked her head to the side. "How so? Are you going to use your weak Malarsan magic on me? You don't seem like a mage."

"I'm not a mage," Surrels said. He frowned. "I am—no, I was—a Black Soldier. I interrogated a lot of prisoners in my time, including dragons."

Nege did not show any fear, although Surrels could tell that he'd rattled her with *that* particular revelation. "You, a mere human, have interrogated dragons? As in, full-size adult dragons that could eat you like a snack?"

Surrels ran a finger along the bars. "Only after they'd been subdued by the Army and with assistance from trained war mages, of course. But the truth is, the dragons wouldn't have talked during the Dragon War if not for my unique methods of interrogation."

Surrels was telling the truth. Although he had no

specific memory of which dragons he had interrogated during the Dragon War, Surrels had indeed interrogated some. Not very many, because the official policy of the kingdom at the time had been to kill all dragons, but every now and then the army would capture a dragon that needed to be made to talk. Or, even more rarely, a dragon would willingly come to the army with information it wanted to sell to the kingdom in exchange for personal gain.

That, of course, never worked out for the dragon, as any dragon dumb enough to approach the army was almost always killed. And those who were not killed right away, of course, were interrogated harshly by Surrels and his fellow Black Soldiers to get every last drip of information about the Clawfoot Clan's movements out of them.

Nege's calm facade was cracking now. She sat back on the cot and pulled her blankets tightly around herself. "This is a war crime. I am not just a soldier, but actual royalty. You can't treat me like this."

Surrels cocked his head to the side. "Why not? Although you might be royalty, you are also a combatant who willingly put yourself on the field of battle. That means you're as much a soldier as anyone in war is. And besides, I said I wasn't going to torture you, so I'm not sure what you are so worried about."

Nege gulped. "I'm not worried about what *you* will do to me. I'm worried about what Father will do once he finds out I gave you critical information about our military's plans and strategies."

Surrels frowned. "What if I guaranteed you that we would keep you and Prika safe and sound if you would agree to talk? We will make sure that your father doesn't get a chance to unleash his wrath on you if you just tell us what we want to know."

Nege shook her head. "You can't promise that. No one can. My father is the most powerful man in the world. When he decides someone needs to die, that person *dies*."

Surrels smirked. "Like Hal, Keershan, and Anija? I understand that he tried to kill them, but they're still alive. At least, they look alive to me, anyway."

Nege pulled her blankets up to her chin. "Why else do you think Father declared war on your pathetic little kingdom? In all of my years of life, I have never seen Father as angry as he was on that night. He punished everyone who had anything to do with trying to stop your friends from escaping. He almost punished me, even, and he never punishes me."

Surrels furrowed his brows. Although Surrels knew that Kryo Kardia was not winning any father-of-the-year awards anytime soon, he was surprised to hear how angry the emperor of the Glaci Empire could get. And he didn't think Nege was lying, either. That fearful look was too genuine for her to fake. She wasn't that good of an actress in Surrels's opinion because that would require effort on her part, and Nege had clearly never worked a day in her life for anything.

"Like I said, we won't punish you if you agree to help us," Surrels said, wrapping his hands around the bars of the cell. "Unlike Kryo Kardia, we don't punish our allies. We don't even punish our enemies, at least not as badly as your own father treats you and his servants, apparently."

Nege shook her head again. "You don't understand. Father will *know* if I talk. And if Father finds out I said anything, anything at all, you won't be able to stop him. I've seen him kill children who disobey him before. I've always been a good girl. I don't want to die."

Surrels raised an eyebrow. "Die? Your father won't actually kill you, will he? You're one of his Riders, not to mention his favorite daughter."

Nege shuddered. "It doesn't matter. Father has gone off the deep end ever since your friends escaped him. I won't tell you anything."

Surrels gripped the bars tighter. "As I said, we can protect you. We can treat you even better than your father. Trust me. We aren't like him. We're not petty or cruel."

Nege bit her lower lip. She seemed torn. She was probably weighing her odds of telling Surrels what he wanted to know versus the odds of Kryo Kardia learning of her betrayal and punishing her. It was probably the hardest that she'd ever had to think in her life, or so Surrels assumed, as she did not seem particularly intellectual to him.

Finally, Nege said, "All right. I will answer your questions. Just don't hurt me or Prika, okay? And *don't* tell Father."

Surrels put a hand over his heart. "I swear by the names of the gods that I won't tell your father about your agreeing to work with us."

A soft chuckle suddenly echoed in Surrels's ear. "That's good. Because you won't live long enough to tell anyone anything, Malarsan."

Surrels whirled around just in time to get punched in the face by someone. He crashed into the bars of the cell and, despite being dazed, jumped to the side to avoid another punch. This punch actually bent the bars upon impact, causing Nege to shriek, but Surrels paid no attention to that. His eyes were on the figure standing a few feet away from him.

Surrels had never seen a more colorfully dressed assassin. Clad in yellow-and-red robes, the figure looked more like something one might see at a festive circus than deep in the dungeons of a mountain town. Energy seemed to crackle along the figure's robes as he pulled his fist back, which now smoked like it had been on fire.

Nege's eyes widened. "Crap. It's him."

Surrels reached for his sword. "Him? Who—?"

But Surrels did not feel the familiar wooden hilt of his sword. He looked down at his belt only to see his sword was missing.

"Looking for this?" said the mysterious figure.

Surrels looked up in time to see the mysterious figure holding up his sword with both hands.

Before snapping it cleanly in half over his knee.

Chapter Nine

THE ROBED FIGURE TOSSED BOTH HALVES OF THE SHEATHED sword in Surrels's direction. The pieces clattered harmlessly on the stone floor at Surrels's boots, but Surrels was not looking at them. He was staring at the robed assassin, realizing that anyone who could bend bars with a fist and break a solid metal sword cleanly in half over their knee had to be stronger than him.

And way, *way* outside of his league.

"Who are you?" Surrels said, wishing he had brought another weapon with him, but his sword was the only weapon he carried with him on a regular basis and it was now currently in halves at his feet.

The robed figure, whose face was partially hidden by his robes, cocked his head to the side. "I am Inquirer Ronix, vice inquirer of the inquirers of the Glaci Empire. And Kryo Kardia's most trusted problem-solver."

"Inquirer—?" Surrels repeated. "Like Dedeket?"

The robed figure sneered. "Don't compare me to that fool. He believes the secret to winning His Iciness's approval is through flattery and ego-stroking. I, on the other hand, know that His Majesty values results over anything else. And I fully intend to show him the best results."

"So you're another inquirer," Surrels said. "I had no idea there were more of you."

"There are over a hundred of us," said Ronix. His eyes shifted toward Nege. "But only a handful of us are entrusted with missions as important as this."

Ronix suddenly drew a vial from his robes and tossed it between the bars of Nege's cell. The vial smashed into pieces when it landed, creating a huge cloud of sickening pink gas that slowly started to expand in Nege's cell.

Nege was crying now, backing up against the back wall of her cell. "Don't do this, Ronix! I didn't tell the Malarsan anything. I—"

"But I heard you agree to his demands," said Ronix. "And you know how His Majesty feels about traitors. Especially traitorous children like yourself."

Nege glared at Ronix. "Father will never believe you! You have no proof of my betrayal."

Ronix blinked. "I don't *need* proof. His Majesty trusts my word more than yours, as it is less likely to be colored by irrational girlish feelings and a desire to make yourself look good. Yet even if he didn't, I have proof enough right here."

Ronix blinked again and twin beams shot out of his eyes. The beams created an image of Nege's face in midair, repeating the same words she had said to Surrels just a few seconds ago. The real Nege's skin became even paler as she heard her own words repeated right in front of her eyes.

"What kind of magic is that?" Surrels said.

Ronix blinked once more, and the image vanished. "A

highly advanced version of memory magic that your
Malarsan mages only read about in books. It is a way of
projecting my memories in a way that other people can
hear and understand."

Nege gaped. "But Father sent you to rescue me,
didn't he?"

Ronix held up two fingers. "Your father gave me two
missions, dependent entirely on your own actions. If you
shared our plans with the enemy, then I was to kill you
dead. If, on the other hand, you did not tell them anything,
then I was to save your life and bring you back to the
Northern Circle. Guess which mission I am going to
complete tonight."

Nege had broken down crying now. Between being
abandoned by her father and now about to be killed by that
lethal pink gas, Surrels did not blame her for having the
reaction she did. He certainly thought that Kryo Kardia
was a pretty terrible father for doing that to one of his own
children, even if it was a brilliant strategic move that would
protect the Glaci Empire's secrets.

"And do not worry," said Ronix. "That gas won't kill
you right away. Once you inhale it, the gas will first freeze
every nerve in your body, and then slowly burn your organs
from the inside. It's quite deadly and there are no known
cures for it, so I would suggest not inhaling it if you desire
to keep living."

Surrels scowled at Ronix. "Have you forgotten about
me already? I'm not going to let you kill her, not if I can
help it."

Ronix gave Surrels an unimpressed look. "General
Surrels Megat, General of the Malarsan Army, and former

Black Soldier. You are even weaker in person than the description of you from the briefings I reviewed."

Surrels raised his eyebrows. "How do you know who I am already? I haven't even told you my name."

Ronix chuckled. "I am an inquirer. Knowing things is what we do. And I know much about you, having spent the last month working closely with the empire's mythkeepers to gather as much intel on you and the other members of Malarsan's council as possible in preparation for this mission."

Surrels bit his lower lip. This wasn't good. Although Surrels had no special skills that he thought would be immediately useful in this situation, he still hated that Ronix knew more about him than Surrels knew about him. It made Surrels feel unsafe and vulnerable, which was probably Ronix's goal.

"Then surely you must know about my own assassination skills," Surrels said. "I have killed a lot of people in my time, including people far stronger than you."

Ronix shook his head. "You haven't even *seen* someone like me before. But very well. His Majesty ordered me to kill anyone who got in the way of my mission. And you are clearly trying to get in the way, so I will have to deal with you myself."

Ronix stomped his foot on the ground. The temperature in the dungeons suddenly dropped by thirty degrees, or so it felt to Surrels, whose teeth immediately started chattering in his mouth uncontrollably. "What—? What is going—?"

Surrels was interrupted by a wave of ice erupting from the soles of Ronix's feet. The ice covered the floor of the dungeons in an instant, causing Surrels to slip. He quickly grabbed onto the bars of another cage for support, although it wasn't very supportive, his legs barely able to find any footing in the vast ice that now covered almost everything.

"First rule of combat," said Ronix, raising one finger. "Controlling the battlefield is ninety percent of victory."

Without warning, Ronix rushed along the ice toward Surrels as smoothly as a ghost along the wind. Ronix slammed his fist into Surrels's gut, causing Surrels to let go of the bars and collapse onto the floor. Even as Surrels fell, however, Ronix slammed his boot into Surrels's stomach, sending Surrels sliding across the floor and into the wall on the other side.

Gasping for breath, Surrels looked up in time to see Ronix rushing toward him. Ronix raised his right leg, revealing a wickedly sharp blade on the sole of his boot, which was probably what allowed him to skate across the ice so easily.

And it was coming straight toward Surrels's face.

Surrels managed to push himself off the wall, however, in the other direction. But Ronix, displaying incredibly fast reflexes, quickly changed directions, lowering his foot onto the skate while stretching out his hand to catch the wall and stop himself before he could crash into it.

Coming to a stop in front of the bars of another cell, Surrels gazed up at Ronix, his heart pounding. "You're fast."

Ronix cocked his head to the side. "Is that all? How disappointing for your last words."

Ronix shot toward Surrels again, this time moving even faster than before. Surrels knew there was no way he could keep up with Ronix's speed or maneuverability.

So he didn't.

Instead, Surrels pushed himself forward toward Ronix. The inquirer's eyes widened in surprise, clearly not expecting this move, before Surrels barreled into Ronix's legs and knocked the inquirer down on the ground.

The inquirer collapsed onto the floor beside Surrels, and before he could react, Surrels was on top of Ronix, punching him in the face as hard as he could. His fists were slightly buffered by Ronix's thick robes, but he could still feel his knuckles slamming into a chin and other facial features, as well as hear Ronix's groans of pain as he attacked him.

"Not so fast now, huh?" Surrels said in between punches.

But Ronix suddenly caught his fists and twisted, causing Surrels to cry out in pain. Ronix then shoved Surrels off of him and, jumping to his feet, slid away from Surrels, putting some distance between them.

Panting slightly, Ronix said, "You are a worthier foe than I expected. Normally, most non-Glacians have no idea what to do when they find the floor frozen under their feet, but you figured out the weakness in my strategy fairly quickly."

Surrels, rolling onto his hands and knees, gazed up at Ronix defiantly, ignoring the blood dripping from the corner of his mouth. "It's an impressive trick, to be sure, but you Glacians still have to operate by the same laws of physics that the rest of us do. Falling over onto an icy stone floor is no safer for you guys than it is for 'inferior' Malarsans like myself."

Ronix nodded. "I see now why you are the general of the Malarsan army. I would most certainly not want to face you on a proper battlefield. I feel like you would be a dangerous opponent."

Surrels narrowed his eyes. "Thanks, but you do realize that you're wasting a lot of time by talking to me, right? Any minute now, someone from above will come down to check on me and Nege. I told the others where I would be and how long I expected it would take me to interrogate Nege. That time has definitely passed."

Ronix chuckled for a moment before breaking into full-on laughter. His mad laughter echoed in the dungeons, making the hair along Surrels's arms stand up and even causing Nege to pause her crying to stare at Ronix in fear.

"What are you laughing about?" Surrels demanded. "What is so funny about this situation?"

Ronix, his laughter dying down, gave Surrels a look he did not like. "Your faith in the ability of your friends to save you. You're assuming they will even have time to do so."

Surrels raised an eyebrow. "What do you mean by—"

A muffled *boom* shook the ceiling of the dungeons, cracking the ice along the ceiling and sending small bits of ice falling onto the floor. The sound startled Surrels, who looked up at the ceiling in confusion and worry.

"What was that?" Surrels said.

Ronix cocked his head to the side. "The distraction, of course. But if I were you, I would worry more about how you are going to beat me than how your friends are doing. It is the one thing, the only thing, you can control."

Chapter Ten

THE EXPLOSION IN THE CENTER OF TOWN DREW ANIJA'S attention immediately. She and Rialo had been in the process of helping set up tables for the celebration feast when a deafening *boom* exploded through the town, instantly drawing the attention of her, Rialo, and the other people with them to the center of the town. A column of smoke rose from the center of Mysteria into the darkening night sky, still quite visible despite the dimming light from the setting sun.

"What was that?" said an earth mage, who Anija recalled was named Proe, standing a few feet from her. He gazed up at the sky with a puzzled expression on his face. "An explosion?"

Anija, her danger senses kicking in, didn't even need to exchange looks with Rialo. They knew they were under attack.

"Everyone, stay here!" Anija said to Proe and the other soldiers and mages who had paused setting up things for the feast to stare at the column of smoke rising from the town square in the distance. "Rialo and I will investigate the blast."

"Are we under attack?" a soldier who looked like he was barely out of his teens asked, a fearful expression on his face. His hand rested on the hilt of his sword.

"We'll see," Anija said.

With that, Anija climbed onto Rialo's back before the dragon took off into the air, flapping her mighty wings as hard as she could, the wind making Anija's hair billow out behind her.

I do not like that explosion, Rialo thought as she and Anija flew through the air. *I do not like it at all.*

Not a fan of the random explosion, either, which I doubt is part of the celebrations, Anija thought. *Where are Hal and Keershan?*

Still talking with Lom in his workshop, I believe, Rialo replied. *Why?*

Anija scowled. *Because I think we are under attack.*

Anija and Rialo were not the only ones to respond to the blast. At least a dozen other Dragon Rider pairs, including Lieutenant Ragnol and his Steed, Dinne, had responded, flying in circles around the column of smoke. Anija did not understand why none of them had landed until they got close enough to see the damage left by the blast.

A massive spiked icicle stood in the middle of the crater created by the explosion, smoke and cold air wafting off it in equal measure. The town square had been completely pulverized, leaving little more than piles of destroyed rubble and chunks of ice everywhere. Even from a distance, Anija could feel the freezing air rising from the icicle's surface.

Combined with the stench of the smoke, it created a scent Anija had never quite smelled and hoped to never smell again for as long as she lived.

"What happened?" Anija shouted to Ragnol when she and Rialo got close enough. "A war balloon attack?"

"We're not sure," Ragnol said, raising his voice to be heard over the wind and flapping of dragon wings. "Town scouts do not report seeing any Glacian war balloons in the area or over the town. There's no way they could have sneaked past our guards without being seen, even with magic."

"What about casualties?" Rialo asked. "Was anyone injured or killed?"

"Not that we have seen," Ragnol said, "but the explosion just happened, so we are still investigating it."

Anija scowled. That wasn't good. Although she did not see any bodies in the wreckage below, she still hoped that no one in the town had died. The thought of anyone dying, especially under her watch, was enough to make her almost too angry to think.

Calm yourself, Anija, Rialo told her. *We must remain in control of our emotions if we are going to get to the bottom of this.*

I know, Rialo, I know, Anija said, *but you have to admit, this is enraging just to think about it.*

Aloud, however, Anija gestured at the gigantic icicle and said, "This is clearly the doing of the Glacians. If *they* didn't drop one of their ice bombs onto the town, then where else could it possibly have come—"

Crack.

A thick crack formed in the center of the icicle, running all the way down to its base. The crack grew wider and wider, until both halves of the icicle fell to either side of the town square with a loud *bang*.

Anija gaped when she saw what had been left behind. "What *is* that thing?"

Rialo grimaced. "I have no idea. Nothing in dragon lore has even described such a monster before."

Because the creature sitting in the town square, right where the icicle had once stood, was indeed a monster. Curled up with its arms and legs around its body, the creature's actual appearance was difficult to discern, although Anija could tell it was definitely alive. A soft purple light glowed within its chest, which Anija assumed was some kind of heart or energy source.

"Whatever it is, we should kill it before it starts moving," Ragnol said, raising his sword. "Even if it's not an ice bomb, it's obviously a Glacian weapon. We must—"

Crack.

The creature started to unfold. Two tall, strong legs lifted up its round body, from which a long tail curled out to its full length. Twin short, almost stubby arms reached out from its body, and finally, a large head that reminded Anija of a dragon head formed on top of its short neck. Thick, icy frills ran from the back of its neck all the way down the length of its tail, which ended in a spiked sphere that looked like the head of a mace.

"Holy shit," said another Dragon Rider nearby in disbelief. "What is that?"

"It looks like a wingless dragon," Ragnol said. "But that can't be possible because all dragons have wings."

"Whatever it is, it's probably dangerous, and we need to kill it before it kills anyone in town," Anija said. She raised her voice. "Everyone! Fire dragonfire at the Glacian weapon on my command. Three ... two ..."

The Glacian monster's eyes cracked open, and staring at Anija, it opened its mouth and unleashed a beam of cold energy at her and Rialo.

Rialo banked to the left at the last moment, just barely avoiding the cold beam that sliced through the air like a knife. The other Dragon Rider pairs scattered as well, flapping their wings and soaring through the sky to avoid the monster's attack.

Even Anija had to admit that the Glacian monster was huge. It towered over every other building in town except the Forgotten Temple, dwarfing even the dragons. Its head whipped this way and that, however, no doubt trying to decide which Dragon Rider pair to go after first.

Let's help it make that decision, Rialo, Anija said.

Rialo growled approvingly. *With pleasure.*

Rialo darted toward the wingless ice dragon and unleashed a stream of dragonfire toward it. The wingless dragon cried out in pain as the dragonfire washed over its form.

But then the wingless dragon swung its tail at Rialo, forcing Rialo to cut off her dragonfire and bank upward at the last second. The wingless dragon's tail slammed into a nearby building, smashing in the roof and causing its inhabitants—a young human family—to flee onto the streets, screaming.

There are too many pedestrians and citizens here, Rialo said. *We need to lure this thing out of town.*

Good point, Anija said.

Raising her voice, Anija shouted, "Ragnol! Take half of

the pairs and evacuate the town square. The rest of us will lure this thing out of town or kill it."

Ragnol and Dinne did not argue with Anija's orders. They merely peeled off from the attack, along with five other Dragon Rider Pairs, leaving only six Dragon Rider pairs to take on the wingless dragon. The wingless dragon, however, seemed to be paying little attention to that, for its big eyes had fixed on the Forgotten Temple.

With a grunt, the wingless dragon made its way toward the Forgotten Temple, each fall of its huge feet shaking the town itself.

"We can't let it get to the temple!" Anija yelled. "Everyone, Dragon Formation A!"

Anija was pleased to see that all of the pairs she was working here with knew exactly what Dragon Formation A was. It meant she was working with some of the more experienced Riders.

As part of training the new generation of Dragon Riders, Hal, Keershan, Anija, and Rialo had been forced to come up with training exercises and group strategies for the new Dragon Riders. Using a mixture of knowledge gleaned from old legends and stories about the Dragon Riders and their own battle experience, they created a variety of techniques and strategies that groups of Dragon Riders could use in combat.

Dragon Formation A, however, just so happened to be Anija's favorite, because it was quick, simple, and, best of all, highly effective in dealing with a single powerful enemy.

Such as a giant wingless ice dragon, for example.

The six pairs of Dragon Riders flew in a circle around the wingless dragon and immediately started pouring dragonfire on its body. Streams of red-hot dragonfire hurtled from the mouths of the Steeds as they circled the wingless monster, moving in a clockwise pattern to ensure that they did not run into each other or slow down.

And it was working. The wingless dragon's progress through the town had slowed to a crawl, and then it stopped entirely. Whining cries came from the wingless dragon's mouth, the monster likely in immense pain from getting burned by so many dragons at once.

That's right, you big ugly monster, Anija thought, smiling triumphantly as the beast's skin started to melt. *Keep crying. I'm sure mommy will be by any minute to save you. Not.*

Anija's triumph, however, was short-lived, because the purple light in the wingless dragon's core flashed.

And the spikes on the wingless dragon's back exploded off its body toward the Dragon Rider pairs.

Rialo, as usual, managed to bank out of the way, as did a couple of other pairs. But the remaining three weren't so lucky, with their wings being grazed or even pierced by the flying spikes, thus forcing them to land in town to avoid crashing to their dooms.

With the Dragon Riders now temporarily distracted, the wingless dragon resumed its stomping through town toward the Forgotten Temple. Even before Anija's startled eyes, the wingless dragon's skin began to freeze over again, quickly healing what little damage they had managed to inflict on it in the first place.

"That thing can heal itself?" Anija said in disbelief, watching the beast march through town as if on a mission.

"We need to take out its core," Rialo said, "which appears to be that purple light in its chest. That seems to be the source of its power."

"Good idea," Anija said, "but how are we supposed to

get inside its body when it is so big and it isn't letting us get close enough?"

Rialo scowled. "Not sure, but we might need to try melting its skin. If we can melt it enough, we might be able to strike its core, and therefore kill it."

Anija bit her lower lip and looked around at the smaller number of Dragon Riders they had. She doubted three dragons would be enough to melt that thing's skin, and that didn't take into account that the monster obviously did not want to have its skin melted. Yet she could not see any other option unless they summoned more Dragon Riders, which they had no time to do. They would just have to make do with what they had, even if it wasn't very much.

"Riders and Steeds!" Anija called out. "We're going to aim for the purple core in its chest! Do whatever you must to take it out!"

Anija was pleased to see the remaining Riders immediately act on her orders. They flew toward the wingless dragon, keeping a good distance from it while occasionally pelting the monster with fireballs. This forced the wingless dragon to once again stop and spew ice energy at them, although the Steeds were too swift for any of its attacks to hit.

The others are keeping it distracted, Rialo said. *What do you think we should do?*

Anija gripped the hilt of her sword tightly in her hand. *What else? We kill it dead. And I have a great idea of how to do that.*

Rialo growled. *No. I won't let you put yourself in danger.*

Do we have any choice? Anija demanded. *That thing will destroy the whole town if we don't take it down now.*

Rialo growled again, but said, *Fine. Do it. But if I feel you are in danger at any point, I will save you. Got it?*

Of course, Anija said. *Now let's do it!*

Rialo flapped her wings and shot toward the wingless dragon, which was still distracted by the other three Rider pairs who it had not yet taken down. The wingless dragon alternated between shooting its back spikes and unleashing more ice beams at them, but again, the remaining Riders avoided getting hit.

As a result, the wingless dragon was far too focused on the other Riders to notice Anija and Rialo drawing closer and closer to it.

Closer, Anija thought as Rialo's wings flapped furiously. *Closer. Closer.*

In a second, Rialo flew directly over the wingless dragon, at which point Anija did what she had been planning to do all along.

She jumped off of Rialo's back and fell toward the wingless dragon below. As Anija fell, she channeled dragonfire through her sword, causing it to blaze with pure flame in the cold air radiating off the wingless dragon.

Allowing Anija to land on its back and drive the blade of her sword into its back.

The ice of the wingless dragon's body hissed as her flaming sword bit into it, burning hotter and hotter against the sheer cold of the monster. Anija herself had to redouble her grip on her sword, doing her best to maintain her footing on the rapidly melting ice.

The wingless dragon roared in pain as Anija dug her sword deeper and deeper into its back. But Anija paid no attention to its screams of pain. She just drove her sword as deep into its back as she could, creating a bigger and bigger hole.

In fact, Anija was so focused on deepening and

widening the hole that she'd made that she almost didn't notice the huge shadow fall over her. But Anija had just enough self-awareness left in her to gaze up.

And see the open maw of the wingless dragon coming straight down toward her.

Chapter Eleven

BUT ANIJA LET GO OF HER SWORD'S HILT AND JUMPED backward at the last possible second. The wingless dragon's head—twisted backward with its suddenly elongated neck—succeeded in biting only air as Anija barely avoided its sharp teeth.

Unfortunately, Anija also lost her balance completely and slid off its back. She plunged to the streets of Mysteria below, crying out in alarm.

But Rialo suddenly dove underneath Anija, catching her on her back before banking upward back into the sky away from the wingless dragon.

"That was insane!" Rialo cried out as they flew. "And far too close for my liking!"

Panting hard, Anija brushed her hair out of her face, a big grin on her face as adrenaline rushed through her. "Was it any riskier than when we dive-bombed that magical barrier at the end of the Dragon War?"

Rialo grunted. "I didn't like that, either. You humans

have absolutely no sense of self-preservation. It's a miracle your species has made it this far without dying."

Even through Rialo's scolding, Anija could tell that her Steed was more happy that she was still alive than anything. And was perhaps more impressed with Anija's gutsy plan than she initially let on.

Then an ice spike flew out of nowhere and struck Rialo's right wing. Rialo roared in pain and immediately started descending toward the town. Anija clung on for dear life as Rialo tried to bring them in for a soft landing.

Rialo crashed on the rooftop of a home, cracking it but not destroying it. Anija almost bit her tongue in two from the impact, every bone in her body rattled by the crash landing, although she was not injured. She could, however, feel the pain from Rialo's injured wing through their bond, a soft, throbbing pain that made her wince.

"Rialo, are you okay?" asked Anija.

Rialo growled. "My wing will be fine, but it may take some time to heal. At least I managed to get us a safe landing place."

A towering shadow suddenly fell over them, causing Anija to look over her shoulder and grimace. "Um, you might have spoken a bit too soon there, Rialo."

The reason Anija said that, of course, was because the wingless dragon now towered over them, glaring down at them with hateful purple eyes. It opened its mouth, no doubt about to unleash another ice beam on them and kill them both in one blow. Anija could have avoided the blast, but that would have required abandoning Rialo, which she definitely wasn't going to do.

But Anija did not need to abandon Rialo, nor did the

wingless beast get to unleash its deadly ice beam on them and kill them both.

Instead, the other three pairs of Dragon Riders soared over the wingless dragon and breathed dragonfire onto its back. Specifically, they aimed at the hole that Anija had partially carved out already, blasting it again and again with their fireballs, deepening and widening the hole with each strike.

The wingless dragon roared in pain. It twisted its head around to try to get them, but Anija shot her own fireball at its face. The fireball exploded in the wingless dragon's face, causing it to look back at Anija and Rialo.

The wingless beast now seemed confused. Between the Riders attacking its back and Anija and Rialo attacking it from the front, the wingless beast was clearly not sure who to attack. It growled and snarled, but every time it tried to focus on one group, it would get attacked by the other.

Anija smiled. *We've got it on the rocks. Just a little bit more and then we'll reach its core and kill it.*

Finally, after several more attacks, the back of the wingless dragon was wide open. The wingless dragon, seemingly aware of its own fragility now, tried to run, but it didn't get far before one of the Dragon Riders launched one last fireball at the core.

And struck it.

The wingless dragon blew up, sending huge chunks of ice flying everywhere. Anija took cover under Rialo's wings as the remains of the wingless dragon flew in every direction. She felt chunks of ice slamming into Rialo's wings, but she tried to ignore them. She did her best to keep her head down until she no longer heard the ice going everywhere.

"Is it safe to come out?" Anija asked Rialo.

"Yes," Rialo said. "Although it doesn't look pretty."

Peering out from underneath Rialo's wing, Anija grimaced.

Rialo wasn't kidding. The remains of the wingless dragon had smashed into most of the nearby buildings. A particularly thick chunk of ice, which partially resembled one of the wingless dragon's teeth, lay directly in front of them, cold air floating off it. It felt even colder up close, although nowhere near as cold as the wingless dragon itself had felt not too long ago.

People were starting to spill out of the buildings now. Most of the people looked around at the destruction with confusion in their eyes, while others looked more fearful and still others seemed shocked. Not that Anija could blame them. She barely understood what had just happened, too.

Taking a deep breath, Anija stepped out from underneath Rialo's wing and said, "All right. Looks like big, mean, and ugly is dead. Good job, guys!"

Anija said that last sentence to the Riders flying overhead, who gave her the thumbs up before flying off. No doubt they were going to check the rest of the town to make sure that the Glacians hadn't left any other 'presents' for the Mysterians to find.

Anija turned toward Rialo, a concerned look on her face. "What about your wing? Do you think we'll be able to heal it?"

Rialo grunted again and rose to her feet. "Yes. It's already healing thanks to our bond. See?"

Rialo gestured with her head toward her right wing, the hole in it already closing even before Anija's eyes. "The injury wasn't as bad as it could have been."

Anija sighed in relief. "I'll say. Although I'm still trying to figure out where that wingless dragon even came from. And why they sent it."

"It did go down rather easily once we figured out its weakness," Rialo agreed. "Almost like it was a distraction."

"A distraction?" Anija repeated. "From what?"

"Vice-Captain Anija!" Ragnol's voice suddenly rang out, coming from the streets below. "You need to see this!"

Anija ran over to the edge of the roof they had landed on and peered over the side. Ragnol and his Steed, Dinne, stood in the street below, standing in front of some kind of strange glowing purple stone. The other Mysterians gave the stone a wide berth, many of them eyeing it with a mixture of curiosity and fear.

Hopping down from the roof and onto the street below, Anija walked over to Ragnol, frowning. "What did you find, Lieutenant?"

Ragnol gestured at the purple stone at his feet. "This strange purple rock. It's glowing the same shade of purple that the core of the wingless dragon had."

Ragnol was right. The softly glowing stone did resemble the light from the wingless dragon. It radiated cold energy that made Anija shiver slightly, despite her bond with Rialo giving her strong internal heat.

"Maybe that is what powered the monster?" said Dinne, cocking his head to the side. He gazed up at the sky. "This was where the wingless beast stood, after all. When it exploded, its core probably fell to the streets."

Anija nodded. She knelt before the cold stone, reaching out to it with one hand. "You are probably right. I'll take this to Fralia and the others and see what they think. Fralia may know something about it."

Anija wrapped her fingers around the stone and in the

next instant, found herself in a completely different environment.

Anija was kneeling on the top of Kryo Kardia's citadel in the Northern Circle. Jerking her hand back, Anija rose to her feet, slowly rotating on the spot, taking in her new surroundings with big eyes.

"What the—?" Anija said. "How did I get back here?"

"How, indeed," said a familiar ice-cold voice behind her. "Although I think I may have an idea."

Anija whirled around to find herself face-to-face with the very last person she wanted to see right now.

Emperor Kryo Kardia himself stood on the opposite side of the flat rooftop, clad in his ice-like armor, glaring at her with cold purple eyes.

Chapter Twelve

TEN MINUTES BEFORE THE WINGLESS DRAGON'S ATTACK ON Mysteria.

Hal knocked on the door to Lom's workshop, causing the familiar high-pitched, if slightly irritated for some reason, voice of Lom on the other side to say, "Come in! Door's unlocked."

Opening the door, Hal stepped through and looked around at the workshop. The last time he'd been here, the workshop had been dusty and abandoned.

But now, it was full of piles of junk, parts, tools, and various things that Lom the Relic Crafter had likely made or started working on since moving into the space a couple of months ago. One wooden table off to the side was weighed down by a bunch of half-finished items that reminded Hal of relics, although he got the impression that they were something else entirely. The room smelled of oil and metal and other smells that one might expect in a workshop.

Most impressively, however, was that there was not a speck of dust anywhere that Hal could see. However messy the workshop might have looked now, Hal knew that it was cleaner than it appeared.

But Hal's attention was drawn to Lom. The four-armed Relic Crafter stood at the back of the room, hammering what looked like a large piece of armor with all four of his arms. The Relic Crafter paused, however, when Hal and Keershan entered the room and turned around to face them.

"Wilme, I told you I would have the Rider armor ready by—" Lom stopped speaking when he saw Hal and Keershan, his jaw dropping at the sight of them. "Hal? Keershan? Is that really you guys?"

Hal, cocking his head to the side, said, "Hi, Lom. It's really us. But what were you saying about Wilme?"

Lom shook his head, dropping his hammers into the loops on his leather work apron with surprising grace and fluidity. "Never mind. Wilme's just been on me recently for not making armor fast enough for the Riders. She can be a very cruel taskmaster when she wants to be, that woman. I don't know how you live with her."

Hal nodded. "That sounds like Wilme. Didn't realize you were making armor for the Riders, though. I thought you Relic Crafters didn't make weapons."

Lom moved all four of his shoulders in something like a shrug. "We try not to, but sometimes, we have no choice. Besides, armor is technically not a weapon, but more like a defensive tool that people use to keep themselves safe from others who would harm them. It doesn't violate the Relic Crafter oath that we all swore to follow."

"That seems like a very fine distinction to me," says Keershan.

"Well, it makes sense from a Crafter's point of view," said Lom. He clapped his hands together, smiling. "But this is so unexpected! I didn't know you guys were back in town."

"You didn't?" Hal said. "Didn't anyone tell you?"

Lom shook his head again. "Nope. I tend to spend most of my time down here. I'm barely aware of what is going on in the world or even just in Mysteria most of the time. I kind of prefer it that way, honestly, because there's just too much going on that just ends up distracting me from my work. And I really need time to focus if I am going to make anything worthwhile."

"Guess that makes sense," Hal said. "I am pleased to see that you have adapted well to Malarsan already. I was a bit worried when we sent you with Anija that you might have trouble adjusting to a new country."

Lom nodded eagerly. He gestured at the workshop. "The transition has honestly been easier than I expected thanks to this workshop, although your friends are pretty nice, too, much nicer than the Snow Witches. Aside from the ever-present threat of the Glaci Empire invading the country, I feel right at home."

Hal frowned. "Yes, the invasion is a big problem. One we hope to solve soon."

Lom nodded again. "Anyway, this is great! Did you succeed in getting the power of the gods? Obviously, you must have, because you two look quite godly—"

Lom stopped speaking. He looked from Hal to Keershan and back again, realization slowly dawning on his face. "Oh. That's unfortunate."

"What's unfortunate?" asked Keershan. "Do we look weird?"

Lom lowered his head to his chest. "No. I just know that you guys are gods now, which means a lot of changes have happened to you since we last spoke. And far more will happen later, I assume, once you do what you came here to do."

Hal started. "How did you figure that out just by looking at us?"

Lom raised his head again, giving them a mournful look. "We Relic Crafters are closer to the gods than most mortals. We're familiar with the challenge of the gods, which only mortals who seek to become gods undertake. Your divine energy reminds me too much of the gods themselves to merely be a temporary power boost given to you by the gods. It's a logical conclusion."

"We were tricked," Keershan said, clawing at the floor. "Gotcham Nubor didn't tell us we'd become gods if we completed the challenge, but by the time we learned that, it was too late for us to back out. So we had to go forward with the challenge and complete it regardless."

Lom sighed and turned back to his worktable, which he began cleaning up. "Yeah, that sounds like Gotcham Nubor. He was always a very pragmatic deity, although I suppose one has to be if one is the king of the Gods and in charge of the whole world and everything in it."

"You sound like you know Nubor personally," Hal said.

Lom put a piece of metal on a shelf over his table. "I did. He wasn't exactly a *close* friend of mine, but he and the leader of the Relic Crafters communed regularly. As a Relic

Crafter in training under our leader's mentorship, I got to see the king of the Gods on a regular basis."

"So you know how tricky he can be," Hal said. "Why didn't you warn us?"

Lom glanced over his shoulder at them. "I thought Boca would warn you. Where is she, by the way?"

"Back in the Northern Circle keeping an eye on the Glaci Empire, along with her sisters," Hal said. "But no, Boca didn't warn us about him, either, or the tricks he'd play on us."

Lom raised an eyebrow. "That's interesting. Did a god die or something? Is that why you guys had to complete the challenge?"

Hal nodded. "Yes. Shirataka, the goddess of light, was murdered in the abode. We are now the new gods of light."

"And that's why you look so sad," Lom said. "You know that after you deal with Kryo Kardia, you two will have to go and live in the abode away from your friends and family forever, right?"

"That's surprisingly insightful coming from you," Keershan said, "but yes, that's why we're sad."

Lom nodded. "Thought so. The Ancient Laws forbid mortals and gods from living side by side, and given your newly granted immortality, you will inevitably outlive everyone you've ever known or loved. Have you told any of your friends yet?"

Hal shook his head. "No, we haven't. We aren't sure how."

"You're afraid you'll hurt them," Lom said. He pulled out a rag from his utility belt and wiped down the surface of the worktable. "Which is understandable. Your friends probably would miss you if you went to the abode."

"Exactly," Hal said. He rolled his shoulders in frustration. "But we don't know how to get out of this situation, if it's even possible."

Lom shrugged again. "Unfortunately, I don't know if it's possible for mortals who become gods to once again become mortal. I am pretty sure the transformation is irreversible, mostly because I've never heard of anyone successfully reversing it before."

Hal sighed. "It doesn't matter, I guess. We'll live with the consequences of our actions. We really came down here to ask you to make us something."

Lom paused and looked over his shoulder. "What do you need?"

"A weapon," Keershan said. "During the challenge, we learned that to kill Kryo Kardia, we'll need a weapon even stronger than the Final Relic. Have you heard of the Soul Slayer?"

Lom tilted his head to the side. "I have, yes. But it's just a legend."

"Not according to the people we spoke to in the challenge," Hal said. "According to them, the Soul Slayer is a weapon that can kill even the undead. Supposedly, the Soul Slayer *did* exist at one point but was destroyed due to how dangerous it is."

Lom bit his lower lip. "That's putting it mildly. The Soul Slayer is probably the single most dangerous weapon that the Relic Crafters have ever made and I can't make it for you."

Hal scowled. "Why not? Are you incapable of making it?"

Lom shook his head. "No. I could rebuild it if I wanted to. When I say 'I can't,' I mean that I would violate the

Relic Crafter oath that all Relic Crafters swore to follow after the Fall. That is to say, I would get in trouble with my fellow Crafters. Big time."

"Why would it violate your Relic Crafter oath?" Keershan said. "We just want to use it to kill Kryo Kardia. We aren't planning to use it for any nefarious purpose."

"Your motives for wanting it don't matter," Lom replied with surprising bluntness. "The Relic Crafters have decided that the Soul Slayer must never be made again for any reason. You'll just have to find another way to defeat Kryo Kardia. The consequences are far too severe, and I really don't want to get into the exact reasons why right now, although I am sure you already know them."

"But Kryo Kardia needs to be stopped," Hal insisted. "Even with our godly powers, the only way to stop him is with the Soul Slayer."

"And not to make light of your oath to your fellow Relic Crafters, Lom, but how would any of them ever know about your involvement in the creation of the Soul Slayer if you don't tell them?" Keershan said. "I was under the impression that you Relic Crafters have remained largely isolated from one another over the last five thousand or so years since the Fall."

Lom nodded. "True. I haven't spoken to another Relic Crafter in an age and a half. But you don't understand how Relic Crafter oaths work. Let me show you."

Lom suddenly unbuttoned the front of his shirt with his four hands and pulled it open, revealing his thin, small chest...

With an image of a hammer carved into it.

Hal grimaced, though did not look away. "Who did that to you?"

"I did it to myself," Lom said, gently running a finger along the image's outline against his skin. "Every Relic Crafter has a similar scar somewhere on their body, usually on their chests or back. To make a complicated ritual overly simplistic, this scar is created by magical weapons, which bind our blood to an oath we swear. Should I make your weapon for you, every single Relic Crafter in the world would instantly know."

"And then what would happen?" asked Keershan. "Would you die?"

Lom shuddered. "You don't want to know. Let's just say that the wrath of the Relic Crafters would make the Glaci Empire look like a joke and leave it at that."

Hal cocked his head to the side. "So you really can't make the Soul Slayer for us."

"I am sorry, but I cannot," Lom said as he buttoned up his shirt. "Not without making things infinitely worse for all of us." He gave Hal and Keershan a hard look. "And while I trust you two with my life, the Soul Slayer is something better off forgotten in the annals of history. Unless you *want* to cause untold suffering, that is."

Hal's hands balled into tight fists. "But this is the only way to do it. We were told so during the challenge by Old Snow."

Lom shrugged. "Again, the answer is no, Hal. It's too risky."

Anger flowed through Hal's body and he stepped forward, divine energy radiating off him. "You *will* make the Soul Slayer for us, Lom."

Lom raised a defiant eyebrow. "That doesn't sound like the Hal I know."

"Because I am not," Hal said. He gestured at Keershan.

"And neither is Keershan the same. Not after what we've been through."

Lom folded his arms in front of his chest. "So that's it? You get one taste of godly power and now you decide to become a big bully like the rest of them?"

Hal hesitated. "We're not bullies. We're just—"

"Making impossible demands of people despite knowing that the consequences are that severe?" Lom finished for him. "You're right. You're not bullies. You're tyrants."

Hal bit his lower lip. He was impressed by how Lom stood up to him, even though Lom was nowhere near as powerful as he was right now. With a thought, Hal and Keershan could easily wipe out Lom from existence with their newfound godly power.

And that, right there, was when Hal realized that Lom was right.

Pushing his divine anger down, Hal stepped back. "I'm sorry, Lom. I got carried away."

Lom nodded, though he still didn't look happy himself. "I understand. Like I said, I wish I could make the Soul Slayer for you, but I can't."

"Then I guess we might as well go back to the surface," Keershan said, glancing over his shoulder. "I'm sure that the others are still waiting for us. We do have a celebratory feast to get to, after all."

"Sounds good," Lom said, "but before you go, I do have *something* I can give you."

Hal gave Lom a puzzled look. "And what would that 'something' be?"

Lom glanced around quickly, almost like he was afraid of someone eavesdropping on them, before pulling something out of his pocket and holding it out to Hal. "Take this."

Hal took the object in Lom's hand and turned it around in his hand.

It was a small silver ball inscribed with markings that Hal didn't recognize in the slightest. About the size of a small orange, the sphere was warm to the touch and felt completely smooth despite the inscriptions on it. "What is this?"

"It's a Relic Crafter sphere," Lom said. "Show it to any Relic Crafter and they will know you can be trusted."

"I see," Hal said, "but I don't see how this will help us defeat Kryo Kardia or get the Soul Slayer."

Lom pursed his lips. "Although the Relic Crafters as a whole are against making weapons, not all of us agreed to take the oath. Some, valuing their freedom over the common good, decided to go their own way and design weapons that they sell to the highest bidders."

Hal gave Lom a puzzled look. "Are you telling us to locate such Crafters and ask them to make the Soul Slayer for us?"

Lom shook his head. "I'm not telling you anything. Technically. The information is yours to do with as you see fit."

Hal frowned. He had underestimated the Relic Crafter, who he had originally thought of as an intelligent and creative, if cowardly and fearful, maker of relics.

Now, however, Hal was starting to realize that Lom had not survived for over five thousand years on his own by luck alone. The Relic Crafter was craftier than he appeared.

Before Hal could ask for further clarification on what Lom meant, however, the ceiling of the workshop shuddered, causing Keershan to say, "What was that? An earthquake?"

Hal immediately raised his senses, focusing on his hearing. That was when he heard, somewhere above them but well within the borders of Mysteria, a roar similar to, but in important ways different from, that of a dragon.

"Mysteria is under attack," Hal said as he slipped the sphere into his pocket. He gave Lom a grateful look. "Thank you for your help, Lom. I appreciate it."

Lom raised an eyebrow. "How did I help you? I didn't even make the weapon you asked me to make for you."

Hal smiled. "But you did help in other ways."

With that, Hal and Keershan rushed up the stairs, hoping against hope to make it back to the surface in time to deal with whatever was attacking their town.

Even as they ran, however, Hal's mind flashed back to the first obstacle in the challenge, along with how close they had come to almost failing it completely.

Chapter Thirteen

ERLA'S BEAUTIFUL FACE WAS NOW STUCK IN A WICKED SCOWL that made her look positively demonic to Hal. She twisted the knife in his gut, causing Hal to gasp and double over.

Only to slam her fist into his face, sending Hal falling over onto his back onto the street. Slamming down onto the street, Hal grabbed his bleeding stomach, feeling the hot blood flowing like a river down his clothes. He'd been stabbed before, but somehow, this stabbing felt worse than any previous stabbing he had suffered.

"What's the matter?" asked Erla mockingly, standing over him while twirling her bloody knife in one hand. "Can't the big, bad Dragon Rider handle a little stabbing?"

Hal coughed and glared up at Erla. "Your knife."

"What? You mean this tiny little thing?" Erla said. She laughed. "I suppose I did coat it with viper poison, a potent poison that paralyzes the victim. It's not lethal—not in small doses—but it doesn't need to be. That's where I come in."

Erla drove the heel of her foot into Hal's stomach, right

where she'd stabbed him. Hal cried out in pain and doubled over again, but he could barely move his arms to push Erla away. He could, however, feel the heel of her shoe digging into his wound just fine.

"I can't believe you fell for that trick so easily," Erla said. "I knew you were the heroic type the minute I laid eyes on you. Didn't realize you were the stupid type, too."

A groan to his left caused Hal to flick his eyes in that direction. The first thug, the one with brass knuckles on his fists, was coming to already. His beady eyes opened as he stood up, rubbing his head where Hal had struck him before.

"Ugh," said the first thug, rubbing his head. "That hurt."

Erla cast a condescending glance in the first thug's direction. "Knuckles, my brother, you really are good at stating the obvious, aren't you?"

Hal blinked. "Brother—? He's your brother?"

Erla nodded. She jerked her knife over her shoulder at Knife, who was coming to himself. "And so is he. I know it's hard to believe, given how completely different we are in appearance, personality, intelligence, and general competence, but it's true. We're siblings."

Knuckles, which was apparently the name of the first brother, rose to his feet, glaring at Erla. "Competence? You nearly blew our plan earlier by running into 'em before we was ready."

Erla gave Knuckles a disparaging look. "And you got yourself knocked out by a mere mortal. What does that say about you and Knife?"

"Can you two stop fighting, please?" asked Knife as he

walked up to them, rubbing his hands together anxiously. "What if Mom hears us?"

"Mom told us to make sure these two didn't complete the challenge," Erla said, gesturing at Hal. "Although I have no idea where his dragon is."

Hal looked from Erla to Knife and Knuckles and back again, frowning deeply. "Who … are … you … people?"

Talking was hard for Hal, mostly because of the viper poison coursing through his veins and the intense pain from Erla's foot in his wound.

"We're what you mortals might call demigods," Erla said. She cocked her head to the side. "Specifically, we're the children of Medusok, goddess of deception and lies."

"And Mom doesn't like it when we fight each other," Knife added.

"Mom's a liar, dummy," Knuckles replied, punching Knife in the arm. "What, do you also believe her when she tells you that you're her favorite?"

Knife's eyes widened. "You mean I'm not?"

"Obviously," Erla said. She looked down at Hal again. "Knife, unfortunately, didn't get any of Mom's intelligence or cunning, as you can tell."

Knife fell into an embarrassed silence, although he did not argue with his sister about that. Hal got the impression that Erla was the oldest and the other two were younger, if not twins.

In any case, Hal did not care about the birth order of the demigods. He cared about winning the challenge in the long run and, in the short run, surviving here.

"What is your role in the challenge?" Hal asked.

"Easy," Erla said, flipping her dagger in her hand again. "Our role is to test the cunning of challengers. If you are to ascend to godhood, then you will need to prove that you can discern between true problems and false ones."

"What separates mortals from gods—other than every-thing else—is the gods' ability to discern between truth and lies easily," Knuckles added. "Mortals are often fooled by appearances, but gods are often not. It takes a lot to fool a god, so we want to make sure you can't be easily tricked yourself."

Hal, thinking about how Vilona had tricked the entire abode into thinking that Hal and his friends were respon-sible for the death of Shirataka, disagreed that the gods were less prone to believing tricks and lies than mortals, but he was in no position to debate that with them. Every second he spent lying here letting Erla kill him was another second that his wounds would get worse and become infected.

Assuming they don't kill me outright, that is, Hal thought, *although that seems like the most likely endgame for them.*

Erla stopped flipping her knife. "Anyway, you clearly failed to see through our deception, so I would humbly argue that you failed, and failed quite miserably at that. Hence why we are going to take your sorry excuse for a mortal life right now."

Knuckles licked his lips. "Man, it's been ages since we last got to kill a mortal. This is going to be fun."

Hal gulped. He would have fought them off himself, but with his body still paralyzed, he couldn't do anything except lie there helplessly. He was at the mercy of these demigods, and they knew it. This was going to be very tough, if not impossible, for Hal to get out of.

Yet Hal did not let himself panic. However much he

may have wanted to, Hal knew that panicking would not get him anything except more mockery from the demigods.

But it might also get me something else.

Hal, putting on his best frightened face, said, "Please don't kill me! I beg of you! Spare my sorry mortal life!"

"Wow," Erla said with a smirk. She glanced at her brothers. "He's begging now. Isn't that just pathetic?"

Knuckles giggled. "It sure is." He put his hands on his hips and sneered at Hal. "Beg all you like, mortal. Beg until your final breath, but I can assure you that begging won't get you anything except a much more painful and drawn-out death."

"Yeah," said Knife, who was now playing with his own daggers. "I can't wait to gouge out your eyes."

Erla slapped Knife on the head. "I'm going to gouge out his eyes, idiot. You can have his liver."

"But gouging out eyes is so much more fun," said Knife, almost whining like a child. "Why do you always get the fun parts?"

"I'll take his tongue," said Knuckles, cracking his knuckles. "They always make a very satisfying ripping sound when you remove them with your hands. And human tongues, fortunately, aren't very slick, so I ought to get a good grip on it."

Hal, his lips trembling in what he hoped was a convincingly crude approximation of fear, said, "Please don't gouge out my eyes or rip out my tongue. I promise, I will do anything in order to live. Anything at all."

"Sorry, but you don't have anything we could want," Erla said with a shake of her head. "Right, brothers?"

"Right, sister," said Knuckles. "What could a simple mortal like you ever give divine beings like us, anyway?"

Hal suddenly felt a familiar presence close at hand and smiled despite the pain from his injuries. "A hard time."

Without warning, Keershan flew over the top of the buildings overhead, spewing dragonfire from his mouth. The dragonfire washed over the demigods, showering them in flame and making them scream in pain and surprise.

But Keershan wasn't done yet. He swooped down into the alley and, landing on the street hard enough to crack it, swung his tail at the demigods, striking all three of them in one blow. The impact of the blow sent the three demigods flying backward. They crashed into the back wall of the alley hard enough to smash through it completely, causing chunks of stone and brick to fall on top of them in addition to the dragonfire still clinging to their skin.

Their screams were quite painful.

But Hal did not care. He looked up at Keershan and gave him an expression closer to a grimace than a smile. "Thanks for the save, but the poison and my wound."

Keershan winked. "No problem, Hal. Let me help you."

Suddenly, Hal felt Keershan's healing energy flowing through their bond into his body. The healing energy drove away the paralysis caused by the viper poison and closed his bloody wound, cleaning it as well as healing it.

In seconds, Hal felt back to normal, if a bit more exhausted than he usually did. He took a deep breath and sat up, rubbing his newly healed stomach. Not for the first time, Hal was grateful for his bond with Keershan, as it had saved him more than once over the last year and a half they had come to know each other. "Thanks."

"No problem," Keershan said. "I got here as fast as I could, but I ran into some problems myself."

Hal nodded. He had been too busy dealing with the demigod trio to pay attention to his bond with Keershan, but he'd been vaguely aware of Keershan's own challenges in the back of his mind. "Good to know. What happened?"

"The woman I saved had gotten trapped under a fallen cart," Keershan explained. "None of the human men who tried to help her were able to do so. It took a lot of convincing from me before they allowed me to help, and even then, I am pretty sure they didn't trust me one bit until the woman was free."

Hal rose to his feet, leaning on Keershan for support, because despite being healed, he was quite exhausted. "Sounds like you had it easier than I did. I almost got killed by those three."

Keershan grimaced. "I know. I didn't realize we could die here. I thought that if we failed the challenge, we'd just get kicked out and have to leave."

"Death is always a possibility in the challenge, dragon," came Erla's voice from within the hole in the wall, although she sounded far hoarser than before. "And an inevitable for those who are unable to handle the risks of the challenge."

Three figures emerged from the hole in the wall. They must have been Erla, Knuckles, and Knife, but now, they did not look even remotely human.

Rather, they looked like three thin ghouls, their skin whiter than snow, bulging black eyes sticking out of their skulls. Erla still had a vaguely feminine form in comparison to her siblings' more masculine bodies, but Hal would not have mistaken any of them for human in their current ghastly states. The scent of burned skin hung in the air as well, making Hal's stomach churn.

"What happened to you guys?" Hal said. He picked up

his fallen sword and held it before him defensively. "You look hideous."

"Dragonfire melted away the fake human skins we'd been wearing to lower your guard," Erla said, her voice deeper and hoarser now. She took a step forward, her joints cracking from that movement alone. "This is how we truly look. Only dragonfire and divine fire can burn away the fake skins we wore, hence why we now look the way we do."

Hal grimaced. "And here I thought you looked rather cute before. Good thing I didn't try to ask you out."

Erla sneered. "For that comment alone, Rider, I will make sure your death is extra painful and excruciatingly slow."

Hal gripped the hilt of his sword tightly. "If it's a fight you want, demigod, then we will be more than happy to give it to you."

Keershan nodded. "That's right. We're not afraid to rumble with you three. We've killed gods before. Demigods like you are a piece of cake."

"We will see who is the piece of cake and who isn't once we are done with you, mortals," Knuckles growled.

"Actually, neither of you will be seeing any of that," Old Snow's voice said above them suddenly. "Because the first part of the challenge is officially over."

A bright light abruptly shone down from above, making Hal, Keershan, and even the demigods cringe and look away. The light, however, did not last forever and vanished very quickly, allowing Hal and Keershan to look again.

Old Snow stood between them and the demigods, clutching his staff, a friendly smile on his face.

"The first obstacle is over?" Hal said, narrowing his

eyes. He exchanged puzzled looks with Keershan. "Did we win?"

Old Snow nodded. "Indeed! I can safely say that you two completed the first part of the challenge. Congratulations! You may now move on to the second part."

Chapter Fourteen

HAL DID NOT QUITE KNOW WHAT TO MAKE OF OLD SNOW'S pronouncement. He almost wondered if it was a joke because this seemed like too abrupt an end to the first part of the challenge. He had certainly expected more.

Keershan clearly thought the same thing because he said, "Are you sure about that, Old Snow? I thought we needed to defeat these three in order to continue the challenge."

Erla snorted. "We're children of *lies*, dragon. Did it not occur to you that we might have been lying when we said that this part of the challenge involved seeing through lies and deception?"

"Erla is correct, despite her rude attitude," Old Snow said before Hal or Keershan could respond to her arrogant comments. He gestured at the buildings around them. "The first part of the challenge requires saving the lives of mortals who are in danger. It tests the heroism and altruism of the challengers to see if they have a good heart or not. And fortunately, both of you passed with flying colors."

"Because Keershan saved that other woman?" Hal said, scratching the back of his head.

"Precisely," Old Snow said with a wink.

Keershan waved a wing at the demigods. "Then what is the purpose of these three? To mess with our progress?"

"In less crude terms, yes," Old Snow said. "Erla, Knife, and Knuckles are supposed to distract you. If you fell for their tricks, then you would have failed the challenge. If, on the other hand, you saw through them and knew they were fake, then your odds of success would have gone up immeasurably."

Hal frowned. "So we were this close to failing. Good thing we decided to split up when we did."

"That was indeed a wise move on your part," Old Snow observed. "Because you did not want to let any innocent people die or suffer, you decided to split up to try to save both at once. This despite the dangers splitting up might have posed to you. This reflected well on your sense of morality and righteousness."

"So gods need to be moral?" Hal said. "Is that one of the things we were being tested on?"

Old Snow nodded. "Of course. While the gods are not perfect themselves, it is of utmost importance for them to have higher standards than mortals. If the gods did not adhere to standards of their own, then we'd get more gods like the Nameless One, for example."

Hal pursed his lips but decided not to argue the point with Old Snow. Given what he'd seen of the gods so far, he wasn't exactly impressed with their 'morality,' although he supposed that they must have been better than they seemed given how only the Nameless One had fallen. He did wonder exactly what kind of moral standards the gods themselves adhered to, though.

Must include saving innocent people, Hal thought, *although given the problems in the world today, I wonder how good they are even at doing that.*

Keershan asked, "So what do we do next?"

"You will move on to the second part of the challenge," Old Snow said. He gestured at the demigods. "You three may leave now. Your help is no longer needed."

Erla, Knife, and Knuckles nodded. In a flash of light, the demigod trio was gone, leaving Hal, Keershan, and Old Snow standing by themselves in the now empty alleyway.

Hal, rubbing his belly where Erla had stabbed him, gazed at Old Snow. "How many parts does the challenge have, exactly? I don't recall you telling us beforehand."

Old Snow held up three fingers. "Only three. As I just said, you passed the first part with flying colors. The second part, I am afraid, will be much more difficult."

Keershan's wings drooped on his back. "And you can't give us any hints or tell us anything specific about the second part, right?"

"Correct," Old Snow said with a nod. "Although this time, it will be for a different reason than before."

Hal cocked his head to the side. "What do you mean?"

Old Snow stroked his white beard, clearly considering his next words very carefully. "The second part of the challenge is always tailored to the individual challengers and their personalities and foibles. Therefore, each second part is always different than the last, unlike the first and third parts, which are always the same no matter who the challenger is."

"So even you have no idea what the details of the next part are," Hal said. "That doesn't seem fair."

"None of it is," Old Snow replied, "but life isn't fair, so it is appropriate."

Hal scowled and looked around at the empty alleyway. He could still smell hay and wheat in the air, even though they were nowhere near the wheat fields of Lamb's Hand at the moment. "I still don't understand why we had to perform the challenge in a recreation of my hometown. It didn't seem to have an impact on anything."

Old Snow shook his head. "On the contrary, putting you in a place you are familiar and comfortable with caused you to lower your guard, if on a subconscious level. Had you been in a new, different, or unfamiliar place, you would have been more suspicious of the people around you, and therefore less likely to struggle to complete the challenge."

Hal put his hands on his hips. "In other words, it was just to make things more challenging for us."

Old Snow nodded. "Yes. Although you seem a bit upset."

Hal sighed. "That's putting it mildly. While we are stuck here participating in a challenge we didn't even want, Kryo Kardia and the Glaci Empire could be invading Malarsan. Our friends could be dying. And then what good would all of the godly power in the world do for us?"

"I don't mean to sound ungrateful, Old Snow, but I agree with Hal," Keershan said. "With how differently time passes between the mortal and divine realms, there's no guarantee the people we know and love will even be alive by the time we get back."

Old Snow stroked his beard once more, a thoughtful

expression on his face. "You both bring up fair points. And you aren't the first challengers to think so. But I can tell you that Malarsan is currently safe. Your friends are alive. You still have time."

Hal folded his arms in front of his chest and looked at Old Snow hard. "How can we know you're even telling the truth? If the demigods proved anything, it's that we can't trust everything we see here. How do we even know you are the real Old Snow and not an illusion conjured by the gods to trick us?"

Old Snow, to his credit, did not look offended by Hal's question. He simply sighed. "I suppose I can't prove that I am the real Old Snow, as the gods are as likely to know anything about you that I would. But I would ask you this question: Would a mere illusion spend this much time talking to you? You should have started the second part of the challenge already, but you have not."

Keershan started and looked around wildly, his eyes big as panic flowed through him. "We should have? Did we actually fail the first part and now we can't move on to the second part?"

"No," Old Snow said. "The reason you haven't moved on yet is because I am keeping you here for now. Because once the challenge ends, then I will no longer see you two again."

"You won't?" Hal said. "What will happen to you?"

Old Snow put a hand on his chest. "I don't know. I suspect I will return to the spirit realm where I was plucked from, but truthfully, I am not sure. But one thing I do know is that once I am gone this time, I will be gone for good."

Hal's shoulders slumped. "Great. Not only are we on a

deadline, but even you are on one. The gods really love giving us deadlines."

"So they do," Old Snow said. "But do not think of this time as a waste. Once you complete this challenge, you will, indeed, gain the power of the gods. You will be able to go toe to toe with Kryo Kardia, and even win. Although if you truly wish to tip the scales in your favor, then you must find the Soul Slayer."

Hal immediately looked at Keershan. "What is the Soul Slayer?"

Keershan frowned. "Why are you asking me? I didn't mention it."

"Because you usually know about old or forgotten history and myths," Hal said. "I suppose I could have used our bond to search your mind for the answer, but I know you like sharing your knowledge with people, so I figured I would just ask."

"Thanks for the vote of confidence, but I honestly have no idea what the Soul Slayer is, either," Keershan said with a shake of his head. "It's not a term I have run across in my research."

"That is because the Soul Slayer is not merely forgotten history," Old Snow said. "It is *deliberately* forgotten history. And perhaps for good reason, as the Soul Slayer was a dangerous weapon. I do not recommend its use lightly."

"Tell us what the Soul Slayer is, then," Hal said. "We're listening."

Old Snow leaned on his staff. "The Soul Slayer was a weapon crafted by the Relic Crafters some six thousand years ago."

"That's a thousand years before the Fall," Keershan

said in awe. "We don't even have records from before the Fall. How did you find out about it?"

Old Snow chuckled. "In the afterlife, you run into some interesting people and learn some interesting things. But to continue, the Soul Slayer was a sword capable of killing the souls of its victims. It could be used on the living, but also on the undead."

"Like Kryo Kardia," Hal said in realization. "So you are saying that we need to find this Soul Slayer weapon in order to kill Kryo Kardia?"

Old Snow shook his head. "You can't find it because, like I said, it was destroyed. But you can almost certainly find someone who can make it for you. Like Lom, your Relic Crafter friend."

"How do you know about Lom?" asked Hal. "You didn't meet him before your death."

Old Snow gave Hal a slightly deadpan look. "Recall what I said about talking to interesting people in the afterlife. I ran into his sister, a fellow Relic Crafter who died a while ago. She told me about him, and Gotcham Nubor mentioned to me that you and he were working together."

"Sounds good to me," Hal said, rubbing his hands together eagerly. "Between the power of the gods and the Soul Slayer, I'd say our odds of beating Kryo Kardia are very good."

Keershan's tongue flicked out of his mouth nervously. "Not to sound like a downer, but Old Snow, you mentioned that the Soul Slayer is *deliberately* forgotten history and that it was destroyed. I assume there is a good reason that that weapon no longer exists."

Old Snow pursed his lips. "There is. The Soul Slayer was one of the many weapons of antiquity crafted by the

Relic Crafters before they took the Relic Crafter oath of non-violence. Originally, it had been designed for a hero like you two, who needed it to destroy a villain who threatened the world. But then, when the villain was finally vanquished, the Soul Slayer was not satisfied."

"You talk about the Soul Slayer like it's a living thing in its own right," Hal said.

"Because, in a sense, it was," Old Snow said. "The Soul Slayer did not merely slay the souls of its victims, but absorbed them. Over time, the Soul Slayer constructed a 'soul' of its own, so to speak, designed from fragments and pieces of other souls. It then used its power over its wielder to influence him and turn him into the very villain he sought to defeat."

Hal shuddered. "So you're recommending we recreate this evil weapon because—?"

"Because it is the only way to ensure Kryo Kardia will never come back," Old Snow insisted. "In his undead state, Kryo Kardia cannot be killed conventionally. The only way to truly end an undead being is by destroying his soul. Otherwise, he will come back eventually and much worse than before. Given the threat that Kryo Kardia poses not just to Malarsan, but to the whole world, I consider this a reasonable measure to take."

"Assuming the Soul Slayer doesn't make *us* evil, anyway," Keershan said.

Old Snow shook his head. "That's why you need to be careful in its use. And in any case, that is all I can tell you about it for now. I can no longer hold back the second part of the challenge, so let it begin now."

Old Snow snapped his fingers.

And before either Hal or Keershan knew it, the area around them vanished into thin air.

And they found themselves above a vast, seemingly endless sea that they immediately plunged down toward, screaming their heads off as they fell.

Chapter Fifteen

SURRELS HAD NO IDEA WHAT KIND OF DANGEROUS distraction his friends on the surface were dealing with. He could only guess that, whatever it was, it would keep them distracted long enough for Ronix to kill him and Nege.

Ronix appeared to think the same thing, because he bent forward slightly, a wicked grin crossing his blue-skinned features. "Now that your friends are sufficiently busy, let's end this fight here and now. For the emperor!"

Ronix dashed toward Surrels, his skates letting him practically glide across the ice toward him. Ronix moved too fast for Surrels to dodge. The inquirer seemed to be picking up speed, going faster and faster.

Until a dragonfire ball flew out of Nege's cell and struck Ronix in the back. Ronix cried out in pain as the fireball exploded against his back, sending him careening to the side. Ronix slammed into the wall beside Surrels and immediately collapsed onto the ground in a pile of his own robes, smoke rising from his back, a pained groan emitting from his mouth.

Panting, Surrels heard the breaking of metal bars and looked toward Nege's cell to see an unexpected sight.

Nege had ripped open the bars to her cell, creating an opening for her to escape. She stumbled out, hacking and coughing, her skin an unnatural shade of light pink. The gas in the cell behind her, oddly enough, did not spill out, making Surrels wonder exactly what kind of magic that stuff was made out of.

Beside Surrels, Ronix groaned and rolled onto his back. He looked, not at Surrels, but at Nege, who now stood just outside her cell, her hands on her knees.

"Foolish princess," said Ronix. He gestured at Surrels. "You missed."

Nege shook her head. She seemed to be struggling to remain standing. "No. You were always my target, Ronix."

Rising to his feet—which Surrels considered impressive, given how he'd taken a direct hit to the back from dragon-fire—Ronix shrugged his shoulders. "Then this is treason."

"T-Treason is killing the daughter of your emperor because you have decided I am not sufficiently loyal to my own father," Nege replied. "Besides, now that I know what my father *really* thinks of me, I question whether I should be loyal to him at all."

"All who oppose the emperor of the Glaci Empire *will* perish," said Ronix. "Especially traitors like you."

Nege scowled. "I-I think you forgot something very important, Inquirer Ronix."

Ronix raised an eyebrow. "What would that be? Not that I need to know it. Given how obviously weakened you are by the pink gas, killing you still shouldn't take much time on my part."

Nege smiled. "I am not alone."

Ronix glanced dismissively at Surrels. "You are referring to General Surrels here, yes? He's in no shape to help you. He's even weaker than you are and he isn't even poisoned."

Surrels scowled. "I am not that weak."

Nege shook her head. "Let me correct myself: I wasn't talking about Surrels."

A puzzled expression crossed Ronix's face before a dragon roar blasted throughout the dungeon. Ronix looked around wildly, as did Surrels, who suddenly felt every bone in his body shake from the sound.

"A dragon—?" Ronix said. He looked at Nege. "Your dragon can't get in here. It's too big."

Nege smiled even more cruelly. "Prika doesn't need to enter this place in order to kill you."

Without warning, Nege looked at Surrels and yelled, "Into the cell behind you! Now!"

Surrels, not one to argue with a Dragon Rider who seemed to have a plan, immediately dove into the cell behind him just as Nege had told him to.

And not a moment too soon, either, because as soon as Surrels feet passed the threshold of the cell, a bright-red light suddenly filled the hallway of the dungeon. Ronix turned toward the exit, reaching for something tied to his waist.

But whatever it was, Surrels never got to see, nor would he ever know if it would have actually helped Ronix or not.

Because in the next instant, a wave of red-hot dragonfire rushed out of the exit. It washed over Ronix, covering him from head to toe in pure flame. Ronix yelled in agony before his screams abruptly cut off, the roaring of the flames drowning out any other sound in the cell. Surrels just rolled to the very back of the cell he was in, but even then, sweat broke out across his forehead and body as the flames of the dragonfire raised the temperature in the dungeons considerably.

A few seconds later, however, the seemingly endless stream of dragonfire cut off. The temperature in the dungeons immediately cooled, but it was still significantly hotter than it had been before. Still, Surrels felt safe enough to crawl to the entrance to his cell and peer outside.

The sight before him was nightmarish. The floor, walls, and ceiling of the dungeon hallway were completely blackened, filling the air with the stench of burnt stone and flesh. The bars of most of the cells were melted or warped, their own stench making Surrels's nose twitch.

Inquirer Ronix was little more than ash and bone now. Surrels wouldn't have even known it was Ronix if not for the pieces of yellow and red cloth that clung to his partially melted bones. His hair, skin, and much of his clothing had been completely burned away, leaving a bare skeleton standing on top of a pile of ash.

And before Surrels's eyes, Ronix's skeleton tipped forward and fell onto the floor with a soft *thunk*.

Nege, however, had survived. She looked no worse the wear, despite having been in the middle of the dragonfire herself. Surrels recalled that all Dragon Riders possessed a degree of immunity to dragonfire, at least when it came from their own dragons. If Prika, Nege's Steed, had breathed that dragonfire, then it made sense why Nege survived while Ronix did not.

Although Nege did not look that much better herself. She collapsed to her hands and knees, coughing and shuddering. Worried, Surrels rose to his feet and ran toward her.

He noticed that the dragonfire had also melted all of the ice that Ronix had put on the floor, meaning he could now safely move and run without worrying about tripping or slipping and sliding.

Reaching Nege in seconds, Surrels knelt beside her, putting a hand on her back. "Are you okay? Is the poison hurting you?"

Nege nodded shakily. "Y-Yes, but I think I will be okay. I got out before I could inhale too much of it, and my bond with Prika is healing my body. I should be fine."

Surrels nodded. He was quite relieved to hear that. As Nege was their most important prisoner, Surrels didn't know what they'd do if she died.

But also...

"Thank you for saving my life," Surrels told her. "I didn't expect it."

Nege spat onto the ash. "I wasn't trying to save your life. I was trying to save my own. And teach Ronix why I am a Dragon Rider and he is not."

Surrels glanced at Ronix's bones, biting his lower lip. "I'd say you got your point across quite well. Almost a little *too* well."

Nege growled. "One can never show mercy to traitors. If there's one thing Father taught me, it's that."

Surrels pursed his lips. "Speaking of your father, I assume you are willing to help us now?"

Nege looked up at Surrels, her eyes blazing with anger. "Help you? I want to kill Father myself now."

Surrels's eyes widened. "Uh, good for you. That's, er, quite the change in attitude."

Nege shook her head. "It's what Father deserves. He

sends someone to kill me, his favorite daughter. Why should I not return the favor?"

Surrels licked his lips. He wasn't unfamiliar with children who had bad relationships with their fathers—just look at his own relationship with his children—but even he was taken aback by how betrayed and angry Nege seemed to be.

Guess that's a good thing, Surrels thought. *It means she will be more likely to help us.*

"Cool," Surrels said, deciding not to discuss this with Nege any further. "Now that we have established that, why don't we go ahead and get you some help? I'm sure that you need it."

Nege brushed Surrels's hand off her body and stood up. "No need. What we really need to do is call another meeting of your council."

Surrels gazed up at the princess in confusion. "Why?"

Nege smiled coldly. "So I can spill all of Father's secrets to them, of course."

Chapter Sixteen

PRINCESS NEGE KARDIA SAT ON A STONE CHAIR IN THE middle of the Forgotten Temple's lobby, unbound. Her dragon, Prika, lay beside her, eyeing the council members with more than a hint of distrust and even hostility, an expression that Nege herself shared.

Surrels couldn't say that he and the rest of the council looked any friendlier, however. They stood in a half-circle in front of the temple's only entrance, partially because there was more room there than at the end of the lobby, partially in case Nege and Prika decided to try to make a break for it. Not that Surrels thought they would at this point, however. He still remembered how angry Nege had looked in the dungeons earlier when she talked about wanting to kill her father.

"So," Hal said, standing beside Surrels, arms folded in front of his chest. His glowing golden eyes fell on Nege. "You are willing to work with us to take down Kryo Kardia."

Before Nege responded, Surrels reflected on how difficult he found it to stand beside Hal and Keershan. He felt an almost overwhelming urge to get down on his knees and worship them. He didn't know where that urge came from, which was why he was able to fight it down, but he felt it nonetheless.

Maybe it's related to the power of the gods that they got from the abode, Surrels thought, doing his best to ignore the urge. *Still doesn't make any sense, though, seeing as neither of them are actually gods themselves. Perhaps it's just a side effect of gaining godly power.*

Nege nodded, a savage expression on her face. "Oh, yes. I will tell you everything I know, at least as it relates to the Glaci Empire's military strategy for conquering Malarsan."

Hal nodded. His eyes shifted to the right. "Can you also explain what happened to Anija?"

Everyone in the chamber looked over to the right, where Rialo sat, with Anija lying at her feet.

Surrels did not enjoy seeing Anija in her current state. She lay, seemingly comatose, on the floor. She clutched in her hands a glowing purple stone, but more worryingly, her eyes glowed that same purple color. She was still breathing, as far as Surrels could tell, so he was pretty sure that she wasn't dead yet, but Surrels worried for her health nonetheless.

Nege cocked her head to the side. "How did that happen?"

"After we destroyed the wingless dragon, Anija tried to pick up what we assume is its core," Rialo said, her voice tense. She was looking at Nege like this was all her fault. "Then she fell over and became as stiff as a statue. She is still alive, but even I can't reach her in her current state."

Nege raised an eyebrow. "You mean this woman

touched a core stone with her bare hands? And no one tried
to stop her?"

Rialo growled at Nege. "None of us have any idea what
a 'core stone' is, princess. How could we have known it
would do something like this if Anija touched it?"

Fralia, leaning against one of the pillars supporting the
ceiling, adjusted her glasses. "Wait, that's a core stone? Seriously? I've never seen one in real life before."

Surrels whipped his head toward Fralia in disbelief.
"You mean you knew what that thing was this entire time
and didn't tell us?"

Fralia shrugged. "I've only ever read about them in
books that don't have illustrations and aren't very good at
describing them. core stones are supposed to be a lot bigger
than that."

"Does anyone care to explain what a core stone actually
is?" asked Hal, tapping his foot impatiently. "Because Rialo
is right that the rest of us do not know."

Prika raised his head, his dark eyes darting toward
Anija. "A core stone is a rare magical object often used to
create golems. It can be infused with moulash, specifically
elemental moulash, to bring into existence a golem."

"Is that what that wingless dragon was?" asked Rialo.
"A golem?"

Nege nodded. "Yes, but this golem was clearly based on
the bones of the wingless dragons that once roamed the
Northern Circle back when it was the kingdom of Maya.
Father has always had a soft spot for those wingless dragons.
He loves making golems based on them, mostly due to their
sheer destructive power against unsuspecting foes."

"That checks out with what the books I read about
them said," Fralia said. "They are difficult to create because

they require an immense amount of moulash and are usually supposed to be handled with special equipment, right?"

"Right," Prika said with a nod. "Generally, you need magic-proof gloves or tongs to handle them safely, although most Glacian mages simply use air magic to move them around or transport them in sacks. Directly touching them with your bare hands is usually a good way to lose your hands or die, as the case may be."

Surrels scratched the side of his face. "But Anija is still alive and has both of her hands. She seems to be in a coma of sorts, although not a normal coma, that is for sure."

"There are other potential side effects from mishandling core stones," Prika said. "For example, the shock of touching that much magical energy at once might cause the victim to lose consciousness, although it's such a rare side effect that I don't think I've ever seen it happen before."

"Do you think the fact that Anija is a Dragon Rider might have something to do with it?" asked Keershan, gazing at Anija with concern in his eyes. "The bonds between Riders and Steeds can protect both parties from things that would ordinarily kill them."

"That is possible," Prika said, clicking his teeth together. "I believe Anija is the first Dragon Rider I am aware of who has ever directly handled a core stone. There's no telling what might happen to her at this point."

Surrels looked at Nege. "You wouldn't happen to have any special insight, would you?"

Nege shook her head. "That's Prika's job. Personally, I am more into punishing my enemies and teaching them a lesson than I am into learning about the intricacies of magic I don't practice and have no use for."

Surrels cocked his head to the side. Nege and Prika seemed to have a similar dynamic to Hal and Keershan, only Nege seemed far more dismissive of Prika than Hal was of his Steed. No doubt Nege's upbringing as royalty had something to do with that. She certainly wasn't the first member of royalty that Surrels had seen with a superiority complex.

But knowing that they needed Nege to share her information, Surrels said, "Is there any way we can help Anija?"

Prika tapped the floor with the claws of his front left foot. "The only solution I can think of is to have a mind mage do a deep dive into her mind. Either that or Rialo should use her bond with Anija to attempt to dive deeper into her mind and bring her out of whatever coma she is in. Didn't you do something similar back in the Northern Circle when we fought you?"

Rialo nodded. "I did. I managed to briefly take over Anija's body and disrupt Shadow Mask's control over it. As I've said, though, I've been trying to reach her through our bond but have not had much luck so far."

An idea popped into Surrels's mind and he looked at Hal and Keershan. "You two have divine power now, right? Can't you use some of that godly power of yours to help Anija?"

Hal pursed his lips. "Unfortunately, our divine power is mostly offense-based. We can heal physical injuries just fine, but mental issues, such as magic-induced comas, are outside of our ability to do."

"We tried already when we came up to the surface earlier," Keershan said. He lowered his head sadly. "We didn't have much better luck than Rialo did."

Surrels's shoulders slumped. "So she's going to be stuck like that, isn't she?"

"For now," Prika said. "As I said, there's no telling what will happen to her. She might recover. Or she might not."

"And frankly, I don't care either way," Nege said with a dismissive, practiced wave of her hand. "The woman's condition is of no relevance to our current objective of killing my father."

Hal gave Nege a hard look. "Anija is our friend. Keep talking about her 'relevance' and we'll show you just how 'relevant' *you* are to our plans."

Surprisingly, Nege appeared to deflate slightly at Hal's threatening words. That indicated to Surrels that Nege was indeed cowed by Hal's threats, which made sense. Given how divine both Hal and Keershan looked, Surrels did not doubt that Nege and Prika would not last long against them in a fight.

I bet she still remembers how Hal and Keershan alone swept the floor with her fellow Glacians and Riders yesterday, Surrels thought with a soft chuckle.

"Fine," Nege said. "I apologize for rudely dismissing the life of your friend. Now can we get back to the main subject? That is, spilling all of my father's secrets to you so you can go and kill him?"

Hal sighed. "I suppose that is as good an apology as we are likely to get. Go ahead. Tell us everything you know. And leave nothing out."

"Specifically, we'd like to know about his military strategies over the next month or so," Surrels said. He gestured north. "At the moment, we have been strengthening the northern border of Malarsan in anticipation of a northern attack, as that is where most of the current skirmishes have occurred."

"Then you are dead wrong," Nege said. "All of those border skirmishes have been distractions. The main attack is going to be from the east."

"From the east?" Fralia questioned. "But the Glaci Empire doesn't have any provinces to the east of Malarsan."

Nege snorted. "Until earlier this month when the forces of the Republic of Tipjok fell to our might. I was there when King Ores, king of the United Tipjokian Tribes, was personally beheaded by Father himself."

Surrels tensed. "Tipjok has fallen already? I thought they would hold out for at least a little while longer."

"That's the main reason why the Glaci Empire has only sent small groups to attack Malarsan so far," Prika said. "Emperor Kryo Kardia knew that you would be expecting a northern attack, so he encouraged that thinking by having the Glacian Army attack it just often enough to meet your expectations. The bulk of our forces have been dealing with the situation in Tipjok, which is now firmly under the control of the Glaci Empire."

Prika sounded more than a hint pleased with the result, although Surrels suspected it had more to do with pride than anything. Unlike the Clawfoot Clan of Malarsan, the Fang dragon Clan of the Northern Circle seemed far more war-like to Surrels. He suspected Prika simply enjoyed being on the winning side.

"As a result, Father has been building our forces in the east in preparation for a sneak attack on Malarsan," Nege continued. "The Glaci Empire normally prefers to slowly annex weaker countries over time by making them dependent on our aid for their survival. However, sometimes, as in the case of Malarsan, the best plan of action is swift conquest."

"Exactly," Prika said. "From the last strategic meeting we attended, the idea was to smash through the eastern border and make a direct beeline to the capital of Malarsan, conquering or destroying smaller towns and cities along the way. If everything goes as planned, then Malarsan will fall in two weeks."

Surrels's eyes widened. "Two weeks? That's insane. Aren't they expecting any resistance from us at all? Even if they did do their sneak attack without opposition, we'd rally eventually, certainly in time to protect the capital if nothing else."

Prika raised his right front claw and clicked two of his talons together. "We forgot to mention that it is actually a two-pronged attack. The bulk of the forces will invade from the east, but another smaller group will strike from the north. The northern strike force's job is to distract the Dragon Riders, who are largely concentrated in the northern part of your kingdom, while the eastern forces tear through the countryside on their way to the capital."

"And given how tiny your Army is in comparison to ours, it's a plan that is likely to work," Nege said.

Surrels did not know how to feel about this. Nege and Prika were right that it *was*, militarily speaking, a good plan. By striking from two directions at once, Kryo Kardia all but assured that the Malarsan Army, small as it was, would be unable to properly defend either the eastern or northern borders of the kingdom.

And given how the entire thing was supposed to be one big sneak attack, we wouldn't have even seen it coming, Surrels thought.

Although given how powerful the Glaci Empire is, I am not sure it does us much good even if we do know what to expect.

Fralia stroked her chin. "Let me get this straight. The Glacian Army will attack us from the east and the north, effectively dividing our attention and our forces, which will weaken us and make it even easier for them to conquer us."

"Precisely," Nege said.

Surrels gulped. "And when did you learn of this plan?"

"It has been in the making for months," Prika explained. "But this version is the one we heard at the most recent military meeting in the Northern Circle. Thus, it is the most up-to-date version of the plan, and therefore the one that the Glaci Empire will likely put into practice."

"I am not afraid," Rialo said. "Let your father send all of the armies of the Glaci Empire at us. We will crush them all."

"No, Rialo, we won't," Hal said with a shake of his head, drawing everyone's attention to him. "If the Glacians are allowed to put this plan into action, then that will spell the end of, not just us, but of the kingdom of Malarsan in general. The whole country will fall and we, as its leaders, will most likely be killed."

"Hal is correct," Keershan said with a nod. "This is a brilliant plan on Kryo Kardia's part. There's no way we can stop two invasions at once, not with our current manpower. It just isn't possible."

Surrels whistled. "And here I thought *I* was the cynical one, although I can't say I disagree."

"Then what *should* we do, Hal, Keershan?" Rialo demanded, glaring at them both. "Roll over onto our bellies and beg for mercy from Kryo Kardia? Give up and run away? Abandon the kingdom? Know that the Clawfoot

Clan will never abandon Malarsan, not under my leadership."

Hal returned Rialo's gaze without missing a beat. "We aren't going to run away, give up, beg for mercy, or do any of those things. We are going to kill Kryo Kardia."

"That is all well and good, Hal, but I think that is easier said than done," Wilme said, who stood beside Rialo. She gazed at Hal curiously. "You yourself have seen how powerful Kryo Kardia was and is."

Hal nodded. "I have. But the fact is, the White Foxes were correct. Kryo Kardia is the only thing keeping the Glaci Empire together. If we can slay him, then the empire will collapse."

"Hal is right," Nege said with a nod of her own. "The Glaci Empire likes to project strength to the outside world, but truthfully, we are weaker than we look. Although the rebellious forces of the White Foxes may have been crushed, that has done little to quell the rebellious sentiment forming among the provinces."

Prika grinned, showing his rows of teeth. "Many of which we have put down, but more keep coming every day. The only thing keeping a lot of the empire's population from doing anything is Kryo Kardia's existence. Should he die, the entire empire would destabilize. Provinces would break off. Nobles, lords, and Kryo Kardia's children would fight each other over the remaining scraps, and pure hell would reign across the empire."

"Such instability would definitely put an end to any military plans, too," Surrels noted. "But I must say, it disturbs me how eager you two seem to be to see your own empire fall."

Nege shook her head. "Our empire? Father has made it

clear that the Glaci Empire is his and his alone. We, his children, have no special place in his heart, not really. I knew I'd never succeed him as emperor, and I doubt any of my siblings would, either. What do I have to lose, really, by destroying it all?"

Surrels couldn't argue with that logic too much. He supposed that this was the issue with Kryo Kardia's parenting methods more than anything.

"That's all well and good," Fralia said, raising her hand. "But Hal, how are we going to kill Kryo Kardia? Are you going to go north again and try to assassinate him again like before?"

"No," Hal said. "Even with my godly power, the Northern Circle is too protected. Kryo Kardia could just sit back and wait for his forces to weaken me and Keershan, then swoop in to finish us off. No, we're going to challenge him to a trial."

Surrels cocked his head to the side. "A trial? What do you mean?"

Hal turned toward Surrels, a serious expression on his face. "A trial by combat. The winner's country will survive. The loser's will not."

Chapter Seventeen

ANIJA'S HEART POUNDED AT THE MERE SIGHT OF KRYO Kardia standing on the other side of the rooftop. And not in the fun, romantic way, either. Her heart pounded with the fear that she imagined a rabbit felt when finding itself face to face with a hungry wolf that licked its lips.

Kryo Kardia cocked his head to the side. "Well? Are you going to say anything? Or are you just going to sit there and stare at me?"

Anija shook her head. She immediately drew her daggers from the sheaths on her belt and held them up defensively. "I don't have anything to say to you that doesn't involve a lot of cussing."

Kryo Kardia rolled his eyes. "Is that how mothers in Malarsan teach their daughters to speak to their superiors? No wonder your insignificant country is such a backwater. Among civilized peoples, women are taught to treat their superiors with respect."

Anija narrowed her eyes. "I didn't have parents. I

learned how to address blowhards like yourself through trial and error."

Kryo Kardia raised an eyebrow. "You also are an orphan? Interesting. I, too, was abandoned by my parents when I was a babe. I had to learn much about the world by myself."

"What about the Snow Witches?" Anija said. "Didn't they raise you like their own son?"

Kryo Kardia scowled. "Do not speak of those women to me. Their understanding stopped at the borders of their little compound. Their lack of curiosity left them unable to envision the heights to which their magical power could take them. I have nothing in common with them."

It was Anija's turn to raise an eyebrow. "Are you sure about that? Because you still seem rather sensitive about being tied to them."

Kryo Kardia glared at Anija. "Keep talking and we will see exactly what kind of damage I can do to you from a distance, young woman."

Anija pursed her lips. "How did I get here? You said you had an idea about how I am here. Mind sharing your theory?"

Kryo Kardia folded his arms behind his back and began circling Anija in a very predator-like way. Although Kryo Kardia did not act like he was going to attack her, Anija nonetheless felt like a rabbit being circled by a wolf. She rotated on the spot to keep him in her sight, not wanting to risk Kryo Kardia leaving her vision.

"My 'theory,' although I consider it more like a fact, is that you touched the core stone of the golem I sent to destroy your little town," Kryo Kardia continued. "Normally, such a reckless, irresponsible action would have destroyed you outright. But seeing as you are a Dragon Rider with a deep bond to your Steed, I can only surmise that the magic of your bond protected your body and mind from the inevitable death which would have awaited you normally."

Anija narrowed her eyes. "So what does that mean? Other than I am not dead?"

Kryo Kardia glanced at Anija as he circled her. "What it means is that the core stone, which is infused with my own magic, somehow connected our minds together. I assume it is a temporary connection, seeing as it feels very weak. I imagine it will break on its own soon, although how soon, I can't say, as this is the first time I have experienced anything like this before."

"So we're in uncharted waters, magically speaking?" Anija said.

"More or less," Kryo Kardia said. He shook his head. "And I *hate* not knowing things. Although it does arouse my curiosity and makes me wonder how best to take advantage of this connection."

"If you are going to try to take over my mind and body, ask Shadow Mask how well that went when he did it," Anija said. She smiled. "Oh, that's right. You can't. Because he's dead."

"I have no illusions about my ability to take over your body, mind, and soul," Kryo Kardia continued. "Our connection is far too weak for me to even attempt to try something like that. But I think I can take advantage of this in another way."

Kryo Kardia suddenly appeared in front of Anija. He grabbed her head with both hands before she could react. She felt his icy, dead skin against her cheeks as Kryo Kardia forced her to look up at him and into his deadly purple eyes.

"Let's see what sort of information I can take from your head," Kryo Kardia said, "secrets of Malarsan that might help my plans to invade your pathetic little kingdom."

Anija, fear rising in her soul, did the only thing she could think of:

She raised her daggers and stabbed Kryo Kardia in the chest as hard as she could.

To her surprise, the attack worked. Kryo Kardia grunted and let go of her head, staggering away from her while clutching his chest wounds. Slick black blood leaked from his wounds, its acidic stench filling the air, although it did not look like much blood to Anija.

Kryo Kardia raised his bloodstained hands up, disbelief on his face. "You actually hurt me."

Anija nodded, holding up her bloody daggers. "Guess in this place, we are on even footing. Feel free to get close if you want, though. I think I missed a spot."

Kryo Kardia glared at Anija but did not take up her offer. That was good. It meant that he had also realized how foolish it would be to fight her here. That made Anija feel rather proud of herself.

"I underestimated the strength of your mental defenses," Kryo Kardia said slowly. "Given how much mental anguish and strife you have had to deal with, it only makes sense that your mental boundaries would be strong. That does complicate things for me, though I am not so foolish as to make the same mistake twice."

Anija smiled again. "So you are capable of learning, after all. I thought you were too proud to admit you could make a mistake."

Kryo Kardia smiled, however, an expression that was not at all fitting for his corpse-like face. "I wouldn't have gotten to where I am if I could not admit, even if only to myself, my failures. But even when I briefly touched you, I saw something in you that I don't think even you know about."

Anija furrowed her brow. "What the heck does that mean? I know myself quite well, thank you very much. There's nothing hidden in my mind that I am not already aware of."

Kryo Kardia shook his head. "On the contrary, most people don't know themselves nearly as well as they like to think that they do. Every person has aspects of themselves shrouded in mist, lying in the darkness. In some cases, it has been forgotten, often deliberately so. Other times it was never known in the first place, but has always been there, waiting to be discovered."

"Stop talking in riddles like some kind of lame traveling bard," Anija said. "What 'secrets' about myself am I supposedly unaware of? And how do I know you aren't just lying?"

Kryo Kardia chuckled. "Don't take my word for it. See the memory I glimpsed myself. A memory of a long time ago, one you have since forgotten."

Kryo Kardia waved his hand. Without warning, the mindscape around them disappeared, leaving Anija and Kryo Kardia standing by themselves in total darkness.

At first, Anija thought this was another mental attack by Kryo Kardia. She felt cold wind rush by her, almost like they were flying through the air.

Then the world materialized around them again and the two were floating in midair in the middle of the night, the full moon shining down upon them. It took Anija a moment to gain her bearings again, but when she did, she was surprised by what she saw.

It was the Desolate Tops, the current home of the town of Mysteria, and the birthplace of the original Dragon Rider Order. It was a place Anija was very familiar with at this point, although this memory did not seem to be recent as she could not see Mysteria.

And a small group of travelers crossed the border from Hosar to Malarsan, carrying with them a small redheaded baby who Anija instantly recognized.

It was herself as a baby.

And that woman holding her ... that woman had to be her mom, who she had never known.

Chapter Eighteen

ANIJA LOOKED BACK AT KRYO KARDIA FLOATING BESIDE her, his arms folded behind his back. "What is this? An illusion of yours?"

Kryo Kardia shook his head. "Not an illusion. A memory. One of yours, specifically, from when you were but a little babe, barely conscious of your surroundings."

Anija looked down at the caravan of travelers below, visible thanks to the brilliant rays from the moon overhead. "But how could I remember this much? If this was my memory, I would think it would be much fuzzier, given how bad babies' memories are. I don't even remember what being a baby was like."

Kryo Kardia shrugged. "The memories of babies and children, in my experience, fade primarily due to age. If pressed, an adult's mind can recall more details and information than they realized they had, even from their youngest days. Little children's developing brains often pick up more details than even their own parents realize."

Anija pursed her lips again. "So this is a memory of my childhood. And those people down there ... are they my parents?"

Kryo Kardia nodded. "So it would appear. Want a closer look?"

A blink of an eye later, Anija and Kryo Kardia were on the ground, near the caravan. Now that they were closer, Anija could see the caravan and its travelers much better, even through the darkness of the night.

Half a dozen wagons drawn by strange creatures that looked like a cross between a goat and an elephant rumbled along the faint stone road that connected Malarsan to Hosar. The wagons appeared to be in rough shape, mostly due to weather, Anija guessed, although she saw a few rips and tears in the cloth coverings that indicated that they must have been attacked at some point.

But even more interesting was the skin color of the travelers.

They were the familiar blue skin color of the Glacians themselves.

That included the woman holding baby Anija, who did not have blue skin for some reason, in her arms. The woman, who Anija assumed was her mother, bore a striking resemblance to Anija herself, aside from the blue skin. They even had the same hair color and style. If Anija hadn't known any better, she might have assumed that the woman was herself painted blue.

The wagons came to a stop in a small clearing at the foot of the Desolate Tops. A man with a thick mustache and broad shoulders hopped out of the lead wagon and yelled, "Everyone out! We are camping here for the night.

We will resume the journey first thing tomorrow morning. Praise be to the gods!"

"Praise be to the gods!" the other members of the caravan repeated in unison, like a practice chant.

Anija did not quite understand what their chant meant, but she noticed Kryo Kardia's expression harden when they said it. Clearly, it was not a phrase he was fond of for some reason.

Immediately, other blue-skinned Glacians poured out of the wagons, although they were a sorry-looking bunch. Their clothes were ripped, torn, and sewn hastily together in several places, lacking the normal color and flare that Glacians usually had. More than one person sported a bandage over a wound somewhere on their body, including a young man with a patch over his left eye. Only Anija's mother and baby Anija herself seemed unharmed, probably because a young mother and her child were not meant to be on the front lines of whatever battles the caravan had clearly fought to get this far.

"Are these Glacians?" asked Anija, looking at Kryo Kardia again.

Kryo Kardia scowled deeply. "Not anymore. If they are who I think they are, then I should have destroyed them when I had the chance."

Anija raised an eyebrow, but before she could dig deeper into what Kryo Kardia meant, she heard the baby crying. Looking at the caravan where her mother was, Anija saw her mother trying to comfort baby Anija, speaking softly to her in the Glacian language.

The broad-shouldered, mustached man from before, who Anija assumed was the leader of the caravan, walked down the line of wagons to Anija's mother and baby Anija. "Is baby Kiri doing well?"

"She's fine, Arom," said Anija's mother over the cries of her baby self. "She is just very tired from the long journey."

Anija narrowed her eyes. "Why are they calling me Kiri?"

"It is probably the name they gave you before you were adopted by the Dark Tigers," Kryo Kardia said. He chuckled. "A fitting name, too, because 'Kiri' is an old Glacian word meaning 'loud,' although it can also mean hope. Which all but confirms who this particular band of travelers is to me."

Kryo Kardia said that last sentence with absolute venom in his tone, giving Anija the impression that, whoever these people were, Kryo Kardia was not exactly their biggest fan. It just made Anija all the more proud of her parents. Whatever they'd done to piss off Kryo Kardia had to be good if he was still this upset years later.

Arom reached up and patted baby Anija's head. "There, there, girl. We're in safe territory now. Our enemies are not going to touch us here."

"Are you sure about that?" asked Anija's mother, her eyes darting around the dark trees around them, although a few of the caravanners had already set up campfires for the night. "I've heard rumors of bandits in these parts of Malarsan."

Arom shook his head. "There are no bandits here. And even if there were, they would take one look at our blue skin and run. It is well known that Malarsans are very wary of outsiders, especially Glacians." Then he winked. "Besides, I'd never let any harm come to you or our baby. Trust me on that."

Anija gasped. Not only was she finally seeing her mother, but now she even knew what her father looked like. Looking closely, Anija could even see that they had the same eye color, although they looked very different aside from that. Her heart unexpectedly tugged at the sight of both of her parents showing her such affection when she was so little.

"You seem emotional," Kryo Kardia said, cocking his head to the side.

Anija took a deep breath and gazed up at Kryo Kardia. "Shadow Mask told me that my parents had abandoned me at birth. He told me that they hadn't cared about me. I always believed him until now."

Kryo Kardia raised an eyebrow. "You believed that liar?"

"I had no choice," Anija said. "I didn't have any information to contradict anything he told me. Now I wonder what really happened to my parents."

Kryo Kardia smirked. "Watch and find out."

Anija frowned deeply, not at all sure she liked Kryo Kardia's smirk. She recalled that he'd already glimpsed this memory of hers, which meant he already knew how it ended.

And his glee did not bode well for her parents.

Turning her attention back to the memory, Anija heard her mother say, "I hope you are right, Arom. Although if the Malarsans are as wary of outsiders as you suggest, then I wonder if they will welcome us or not."

"I believe that they will," said Arom. He glanced toward the peaks of the Desolate Tops, visible under the moonlight overhead. "Though the Malarsans are a proud people, their monarch, King Rikas, is said to be wise and compassionate to all, even to foreigners. Once we reach the capital and lay out our case to him, I am sure that King Rikas will help us."

"I pray to the gods that you are correct," said Anija's mother. She sighed. "I should get little Kiri to bed. It is too late for her and for us."

Arom smiled. "Sounds good. I will join you as soon as we are done setting up camp and have secured the area. I will probably take the first—"

A scream of terror suddenly broke the quiet night air, interrupting Arom and making him and Anija's mother look around in alarm. Baby 'Kiri,' as Anija's baby self was called, resumed crying, forcing her mother to try to quiet her down again.

"What was that awful sound?" asked Anija's mother fearfully.

Arom scowled, already reaching for a sword at his side. "No idea. It sounded like—"

"Captain!" a young man's voice called out. "We are under attack!"

A young Glacian man who couldn't have been older than eighteen or nineteen rushed up to Arom. With him came a handful of other young Glacian men who seemed to be the caravan's guard, based on the weapons they held and the scars on their faces and bodies.

Arom turned toward them, a questioning expression on his face. "Under attack? By who?"

"We don't know," said the young man, fear and frustration mixing together on his face. "Pepea was found with several knife wounds in his chest and his throat slit. He was dead when we found him."

"Bandits?" Anija's mother asked fearfully.

Arom scowled. He drew his sword and said, "If it's

bandits, then we will teach them what happens when you attack the Warrior Monks of the Lower Northern Circle! Get all able-bodied men armed. We will not let this crime go unpunished."

The young men nodded and ran off, yelling at the other wagons, although they didn't really need to. Glacian men both young and old hopped off of their caravans, swords and other weapons in hand, and formed a loose but strong circle around the wagons.

Arom looked over his shoulder at Anija's mother and Kiri. "Erpa, stay here. Keep Kiri safe."

Erpa, apparently the name of Anija's mother, gulped and just hugged Kiri closer to her chest.

Anija pursed her lips. "Who is attacking them?"

"Wait and see," Kryo Kardia said. "They should be showing themselves soon."

Another scream of pain and terror filled the air, and one of the young men who formed the circle collapsed, an arrow sticking out of his throat.

To their credit, the Warrior Monks did not break their defenses. They simply tightened their circle while a handful of them grabbed the dead young man and dragged his body away from the front lines.

Even so, Anija could easily see them trembling, especially the younger, less experienced ones. The older Monks appeared calmer, but even they clutched the hilts of their swords with more rigidity than expected.

Arom stepped forward, holding his blade above his head, and shouted, "Show yourself, cowards! This is not the way of honor."

No response. Not surprising. So long as the attackers kept silent, they had the advantage. It meant that the

Warrior Monks would be unable to mount an effective defense. Indeed, Anija was already spotting holes in their defenses that any intelligent fighter could take advantage of.

Not that Anija noted that with any happiness, however. She just hoped that this would not end the way she expected it to.

A single *twang* filled the air and a bright bolt of fire—really an arrow set on fire—crashed on top of the wagon in front of Erpa's wagon. The wagon instantly caught fire, forcing the women and children who had been inside it to jump out and run for safety.

Unfortunately, the presence of the burning wagon meant that some of the Warrior Monks had to break off from the circle to try to put out the fire. Although the circle tightened once again, Anija knew this was exactly the break that the mysterious assailants had been waiting for.

More cries of pain and fear filled the air as more Warrior Monks fell to the ground, their throats slit or arrows sticking out of their heads. A handful of the more cowardly Warrior Monks fled into the trees screaming their heads off, only for their screams to be abruptly cut off by the sounds of iron slashing flesh.

Soon, absolute chaos reigned over the caravan. More wagons caught on fire as the fire from the first wagon spread, despite the best efforts of the Warrior Monks to douse said fires. But it wasn't enough. They didn't have nearly enough water to put out the flames, which meant it was inevitable that the wagons would all burn down.

Save, that is, except for Erpa's wagon, which was far away enough from the rest of the caravan to avoid catching fire. Erpa, Kiri in her arms, had already retreated into the relative safety of the wagon, going all the way to the back of the wagon. She clearly was trying to hide among the dozens of boxes and crates full of supplies, as the wagon's interior was very densely packed. Anija doubted that it would be that hard for someone to find her if they really wanted to, though.

And because this was Anija's memory, that meant she could no longer see what was going on outside of the wagon. She and Kryo Kardia found themselves inside the wagon with Erpa, although she obviously did not notice them.

Kiri was crying, while Erpa did her best to calm her. It pained Anija to see just how frightened her mother was. And it filled her with anger knowing that these attackers, whoever they were, were killing innocent people.

That was when a silhouetted figure appear in the mouth of the caravan. The figure in question was clearly not any of the Warrior Monks. He appeared to be one of the attackers, although Anija could not quite make out his appearance. Something about his outline, however, seemed vaguely familiar to her, even though she could not place where she might have seen him before.

Erpa, obviously, noticed the man as well. She clutched Kiri closer to her chest and said, "Please ... don't kill my baby ... she's special ... innocent ..."

The assailant flipped a dagger in his hand and took a step into the caravan. "Innocent? Not according to the contract that my guild took. It said that every single one of you Warrior Monks is a Glacian outlaw. I assume that includes the babies."

Anija felt her heart stop. Even before the assailant stepped into the light of the candle on the box in front of

Erpa, revealing his physical appearance, there was no way in hell that she would ever forget that voice.

It was the voice—and physical appearance of—Shadow Mask, the late leader of the Dark Tiger Guild, and the man who had raised Anija in the absence of her parents.

Chapter Nineteen

SHADOW MASK LOOKED MUCH THE SAME AS ANIJA remembered him, although he had a younger, fresher attitude about himself that told Anija this had happened many years ago.

Yet for all that, Shadow Mask still wore that same horrible, evil mask, his eyes glinting from within as he approached Erpa and Kiri.

Anija stepped forward to stop Shadow Mask, only for Kryo Kardia to put a hand on her shoulder and say, "Don't. You can't. It's a memory. You can't change the past."

Anija hated to admit it, but Kryo Kardia was right. That did not change her desire to punch Shadow Mask directly in his ugly mask, however, even if this was a younger version of the same Shadow Mask who was already dead in the present.

"You don't understand," said Erpa. "We aren't criminals. We are a persecuted minority, seeking protection from Kryo Kardia's oppressive rule."

"Do I look like someone who gives a damn about persecuted minorities and your foreign politics?" Shadow Mask asked, still flipping his dagger as he stepped over a small box. "All I care about is getting paid for my contract. And until every single one of you Warrior Monks is dead— women and children included—I won't get paid a penny from the man you are running away from."

Anija looked at Kryo Kardia in horror. "You mean you hired the Dark Tigers to kill my parents before?"

Kryo Kardia gave Anija an unimpressed look. "I put out a general bounty on their heads that anyone could take up. So I did not hire them, specifically, although this is the event that put them on my radar, so to speak. Now shush and keep watching. We're about to get to the fun part."

Before Anija could tell Kryo Kardia where to shove it, Erpa said, "If it's money you want, you can have it. We have money. Not a lot of it, but we have some. Take our money, our food, water, caravans, even the clothes off our backs. Just spare us."

Shadow Mask actually stopped and looked at Erpa with a rather dismissive expression. "You are clearly a bunch of poor refugees barely worth half the price of the generous bounty on your heads. It is more profitable for me and my men to kill you and your fellow travelers than it is to take whatever meager coin you happen to scrounge up from your pockets and purses."

Erpa bit her lower lip. "But I was once the God Emperor's favorite consort. I can get you anything you want."

Shadow Mask laughed. He looked around at the wagon in which they stood. "Anything I want? Do you mean any of these worthless little trinkets or the stale bread and stagnant water you have no doubt been using to keep your bodies functioning? And your relationship with Kryo Kardia matters little to me."

To Anija, however, it did matter a great deal. But she did not ask Kryo Kardia about it, at least not yet. She sensed that she would get the answers to the questions bubbling up in her mind soon enough.

Shadow Mask resumed walking toward Erpa and Kiri, clutching his knife in his hand. "Now, because I dislike wasting time, I will put you and your baby out of your misery very quickly. Trust me, you won't even feel me slit your throat. Nor will your baby."

Erpa's lips trembled. She backed away as much as she could, but there was nowhere for her to hide, and Shadow Mask blocked her only escape route. Kiri kept crying.

But then Erpa suddenly said, "Wait! Kiri isn't my daughter."

That statement hit Anija like a sledgehammer to the face. She didn't quite understand it.

Shadow Mask stopped again, now less than three feet from Erpa and Kiri. He looked down at her, still unimpressed. "Why should I care that you cheated on your husband?"

Erpa's lips trembled more violently, but she still managed to say, "Because Kiri's actual father is Kryo Kardia."

Shadow Mask froze. His eyes darted to Kiri, who was still crying as loudly as ever.

Anija also stared at her younger self, but her mind raced with questions. Her father was actually Kryo Kardia? That made no sense. Was Erpa lying just to save her and Kiri? That was the only explanation that Anija thought reasonable.

Or rather, the only one she *wanted* to think was reasonable. The implications of the only other explanation made her ill just thinking about it.

Anija deliberately chose not to look at Kryo Kardia, however, or ask him any questions. She just watched the memory playing out before them much more closely than before, waiting—and hoping—that her mother had a good explanation for that statement.

For a while, the only sounds were the screams of terror from the refugees outside, the crackling of flames, and Kiri's own crying.

Then Shadow Mask said, in a low voice, "This child is the daughter of Kryo Kardia?"

Erpa nodded shakily. "Y-Yes. Kryo Kardia accidentally got me pregnant. When he found out, he wanted me dead. But I didn't want me or my daughter to be killed, so my husband, our clan, and I formed our caravan and escaped the Northern Circle before his soldiers could get us. We have been on the road ever since."

Anija knew Shadow Mask well enough to tell when his mind was putting the pieces together. "That explains the unusually high bounty Kryo Kardia had put on your heads. I assumed he simply was very prejudiced against your little group of refugees for racial or political reasons. But if you are the mother of his secret child, then that makes much more sense."

Erpa gulped. "I am glad you understand. Kryo Kardia does not want his consorts to have children. He sees her as a potential threat to his power. That's why he wants us wiped out. He wants to eliminate any threats to his rule, even if said 'threats' are harmless babies."

"Fascinating," said Shadow Mask thoughtfully, tapping

his chin. "This does indeed change things. Actually, that is an understatement. This changes *everything*."

Hope flashed in Erpa's eyes. "Are you going to spare us?"

Shadow Mask lowered his knife. "I am going to spare —"

"Leave my family alone, assassin!" Arom cried out behind Shadow Mask.

Arom appeared in the wagon entrance and jumped toward Shadow Mask. He brought his sword down on Shadow Mask's back, clearly aiming to take out the assassin in one blow.

And for a moment, Anija thought he just might. The wagon was a very enclosed space with little room in which to move among the supplies. Even Shadow Mask, as agile as he was, would have trouble avoiding an attack at close range like that.

Unfortunately, Arom tripped over a small box—the same one Shadow Mask had stepped over earlier—and staggered forward. His sword barely missed Shadow Mask's back.

And Shadow Mask whirled around and stabbed Arom directly in the throat.

Erpa screamed.

Kiri cried.

Arom tried to scream, but couldn't. He just gasped, blood rushing down the front of his shirt, staring at Shadow Mask with huge eyes.

Shadow Mask, by contrast, was silent as the grave. He pulled his dagger out of Arom's neck and kicked him in the chest. Arom collapsed onto the floor of the wagon, twitched once or twice, and then became very still.

Erpa was sobbing now, holding Kiri closer to her chest than ever. Anija herself felt tears coming on, tears she struggled to hold back. She almost felt like a powerless baby herself, seeing her father—even if just her stepfather—die like that.

Shadow Mask, however, simply turned around and wiped the blood off his dagger. "That was a close one. Good thing this packed wagon wasn't very well-organized. Otherwise your husband might have actually killed me."

Erpa gulped. "B-But you said you would spare us."

Shadow Mask chuckled. "I didn't get to finish my sentence, remember? I meant to say that I would spare the *baby*. Not you, not your husband, not anyone else."

Erpa gasped. "Why? Why would you be so cruel, even knowing the truth?"

Shadow Mask flipped his dagger again. He walked up to Erpa, who just stared up at him in fear.

"Why?" said Shadow Mask. He glanced at Kiri. "The baby could be useful blackmail at some point, should Kryo Kardia or the Glaci Empire ever decide to make themselves trouble for my guild. By taking the girl and raising her as my own, I will have a weapon that even Kryo Kardia fears and one he won't even realize exists until it's too late."

"But the bounty specifically said that you have to kill everyone in the caravan to get the reward," Erpa said. "Including the children. Kryo Kardia won't give you even one coin if you keep Kiri alive."

Shadow Mask sneered at Erpa. "Do you think Kryo Kardia himself will personally come to the wilderness of a backwoods country like Malarsan just to verify the death of the baby? No. All I will need to do is send your corpse back to the Northern Circle with a nice note explaining how I killed you and everyone else and then I will get both that nice bounty *and* the baby. A winning situation for myself, don't you agree?"

"It's monstrous," said Erpa. "It's evil. It's—"

Shadow Mask's knife flashed across Erpa's throat too quickly even for Anija's eyes to follow.

Erpa, blood pouring from her throat, fell onto the floor of the wagon. She dropped Kiri, who rolled along the floor, crying all the while.

But Shadow Mask, blood still dripping from his dagger, bent over and picked up Kiri. Cradling her in one arm, Shadow Mask said, in what he undoubtedly thought was a comforting tone of voice, "There, there, young one. No need to cry. Soon, you won't even remember any of this. Just think of how valuable you will be to me going forward."

Of course, baby Kiri kept crying. Shadow Mask simply shook his head, turned, and walked out of the wagon, stepping over both of Kiri's dead parents on his way out.

And then, in the very next instant, Anija and Kryo Kardia were standing atop the citadel in the Northern Circle again, the cold night air biting at Anija's exposed skin.

Anija barely paid attention to that, however. She slowly turned toward Kryo Kardia, her hands shaking. "Is it true?"

Kryo Kardia put his hands on his hips. "That you are actually my daughter? I do not know."

Anija blinked, feeling tears well up in her eyes. "What? How do you *not* know? My mother sounded so certain that you are my father."

Kryo Kardia glanced out over the gleaming city below.

"As your mother implied, I have many consorts and wives, and your mother was one. She was also my favorite, although I do rotate through them on a fairly regular schedule to avoid boredom, of course."

Anija sniffled. "Did you ever get any of them pregnant?"

Kryo Kardia shook his head. "Of course not. All of my children are adopted. I do not want any blood relatives who may think I owe them something. I take careful measures not to get any of my consorts pregnant. And I am pleased to say, in all of my years of living, that I never have gotten anyone pregnant, except possibly for your mother."

Anija gulped. She was angry but also curious. "You make it sound like you aren't sure."

"I am sure of many things, but not this," Kryo Kardia said. "A few weeks after an engagement with your mother, I learned she was pregnant. Due to the timing, I had to assume that the baby was mine."

Anija narrowed her eyes. "But couldn't I have been Arom's child? And how did my mother have a husband if she was your consort?"

Kryo Kardia gave Anija a look like she'd just asked the single dumbest question in the world. "The job of a royal consort is to amuse and provide pleasure for me. She can be married to another man for all I care, so long as her marital duties do not interfere with her consort duties. Your father was also a servant of mine, a junior sergeant in the Glacian Army, so he was often on the front lines for months at a time. He was away on war business during the time your mother got pregnant, and seeing as she slept with no one else other than me and her husband, the only logical conclusion is that I am your father."

Anija shook her head. "But you're an undead thing. How can you impregnate a living woman?"

"As I said, I do not know," Kryo Kardia said. "It's possible your mother was lying and had indeed gotten pregnant from someone else. She could have been trying to use you to blackmail me, probably to get out of being my consort. She was madly in love with her husband and no longer wanted anything to do with me. That would be motive enough for her to lie to me."

"Yet you ordered their deaths—and mine—anyway," Anija said. "Why?"

Kryo Kardia folded his arms behind his back. "Insurance. Although I could not be certain that you were my daughter, I also did not survive this long by taking needless risks. Under the guise of hating her people, the Warrior Monks, I put out a bounty on their heads to make sure they would not be safe even if they escaped the borders of the Glaci Empire. That the Dark Tigers were the ones who ultimately fulfilled the bounty, at least partially, is more due to luck than anything."

"So you never realized that I was still alive?" Anija said. "Even though you never saw my body?"

Kryo Kardia shook his head again. "I didn't even see your body. Shadow Mask did, however, send me the head of your mother as his way to prove that he wasn't lying. I assumed that Shadow Mask, ignorant of the real reason I wanted your mother dead, would have killed you, too. Hence why I never bothered to send any of my inquirers to confirm your death."

Anija's mind raced at the implications of this statement. "So that means that Shadow Mask actually … actually …"

"Saved your life?" Kryo Kardia finished for her. "So it

would appear. Although he took the lives of your parents, he allowed you to live on to this very day. Ironic, isn't it?"

Anija bit her lower lip. She didn't say anything just yet, mostly because she was still processing that revelation herself.

On one hand, Anija finally knew what had happened to her parents. Although it was not something Anija had obsessed over, it was something that had always been at the back of her mind over the years. She had once asked Shadow Mask about it, only to be told that her parents had abandoned her in the woods at a young age and she would have died if not for Shadow Mask's intervention.

The twisted part was, that answer had only been *half* wrong. Shadow Mask could have easily killed her along with her parents, but he chose not to.

On the other hand, Anija had only ended up parentless because of Shadow Mask. If Shadow Mask and the Dark Tigers hadn't killed her mother and stepfather, then Anija's life would have turned out drastically different. And probably better, given all of the trouble that the Dark Tigers had caused for Anija throughout her life.

But in the end, Shadow Mask was dead. He'd already faced justice for his crimes, so Anija found it difficult to actually be angry with him for this. It just made her hate him all the more, although given how she already hated him a great deal, that wasn't much of a difference to Anija.

The bigger revelation, however, was the possibility that Kryo Kardia was her actual father. It still seemed unlikely to her, but at the same time, Kryo Kardia's own uncertainty about it made her anxious. The emperor of the Glaci Empire always seemed so sure of everything else.

If even *he* wasn't sure if Anija was his daughter or not. Anija did not know how to feel about that.

Kryo Kardia bent from the waist toward her, his cold breath washing across her face. "This is why I wanted you to see this memory. I wanted you to realize that we may be closer than you think."

Anija stepped away from Kryo Kardia purely out of instinct, her daggers flashing into her hands. "Don't get any closer."

Kryo Kardia stood up straight again, an amused expression on his face. "Don't be so defensive, Anija. Although I have a feeling that we will be seeing each other again very soon."

With that, Kryo Kardia's form dissipated into a white mist, blown away by a strong gust of wind that came out of nowhere.

As for Anija, she just stood, shivering in the coldness of the night, as her environment slowly faded into blackness.

And then she woke up on a solid stone floor, surrounded by her friends, and screamed.

Chapter Twenty

"You are going to challenge Kryo Kardia to a trial?" Fralia said. "Excuse me for asking, Hal, but what *is* a trial?"

"Something very foolish, I imagine," Wilme said dryly, brushing a strand of white hair out of her face.

Hal gave Wilme an annoyed look. "It's not as foolish as you might think. A trial by combat is an ancient ritual that used to be much more common in Malarsan than it is today. It predates the Dragon War and even the Fall."

"We learned about it during the challenge," Keershan explained. "Thousands of years ago, when rival nations or tribes went to war against each other, one way to resolve said conflicts was through a trial by combat. In this ritual, both sides in the war would pick their strongest champion to represent their army to duel the opposing nation's champion."

Hal nodded. "The winner of the trial would essentially bring the war to a close. It was considered a safer, quicker, and less costly way of resolving differences between warring nations than outright war. After all, the only casualties were whoever lost, rather than hundreds or even thousands of soldiers whose lives would otherwise be lost."

Surrels stroked his chin. "I seem to have heard about it from some of the Malarsan Army historians I learned from during my early days as a soldier, but I didn't know that much about it."

"Personally, I think it is destined to fail," Rialo said. "There is no way in hell that Kryo Kardia would ever agree to duel with you one on one, especially if it means losing the chance to conquer Malarsan."

"I have to agree with Rialo on this one, Hal," Fralia said, rubbing her hands together anxiously. "Kryo Kardia is a madman. We know the Glaci Empire has the power to destroy us, so he must know that as well."

"Actually, I think Hal and Keershan's plan is probably your best bet at survival," Nege said.

Everyone whipped their heads toward Nege, including Hal and Keershan.

"You mean you think that Kryo Kardia *would* be willing to duel Hal in a one-on-one duel to the death?" asked Surrels skeptically. "Even though there is a possibility he might lose?"

Nege nodded. "You don't understand Father the way that I do. He's a proud but pragmatic man. Haven't you ever wondered why the Glaci Empire, despite having the biggest and strongest army in the world, prefers to subdue nations by making them dependent on aid than through force?"

Fralia shook her head. "Not really. I just assumed that Kryo Kardia wanted to look good."

Prika snorted, smoke shooting out of his nostrils. "Kryo

Kardia doesn't care about looking good to anyone. The real reason he does it, as Nege implied, is because war is costly. Conquering even a small nation like Malarsan requires expending a lot of resources. Even if the outcome is inevitable, the losses would take years to recoup, even using the vast resources of the empire as a whole."

"Haven't you noticed how long it has taken Tipjok to fall?" Nege said. "And Tipjok is, in my opinion, a much weaker nation than Malarsan, which has an entire order of Dragon Riders ready to fight and defend it. Not to mention Hal and Keershan's obvious godly power-up, which Father is likely all too aware of right now."

Hal gestured at Nege. "Nege is right. I don't doubt that Kryo Kardia will agree to fight us. It would definitely be quicker and easier than his current two-pronged invasion approach while also giving us a fighting chance at saving the kingdom."

"And if anyone should know Kryo Kardia well, it would have to be Nege," Keershan said, gesturing at her with one of his wings. "She's his daughter, after all. She should know him much better than we do."

Nege scowled and looked at the floor. "I thought I knew him well, at least until he sent one of his inquirers to kill me and Prika. Although I suppose even that is in line with how he raised us. He always made it very clear what would happen to any of us who betrayed him."

Hal sensed a lot of pain and sadness in Nege when she said that. It made him wonder exactly what kind of child-hood she had. Growing up as the daughter of the most powerful man in the world undoubtedly came with perks and privileges that had probably made her life as smooth as butter.

On the other hand, Hal had firsthand experience with the cruelty of Kryo Kardia. That he had sent an assassin to kill her, even before knowing if she would betray his trust or not, told Hal all that he needed to know about Kryo Kardia's parenting methods.

I am glad that my parents didn't raise me that way, Hal thought. *They were not rich or powerful like Kryo Kardia, but they loved me, and that's worth more than all of the money and power in the world.*

Even my parents weren't that bad, Keershan agreed, *even though they did exile me for the crime of liking books too much.*

Hal, looking around at the council again, said, "Now that we have laid out all of the reasons for doing this, does anyone object to my plan?"

No one in the council spoke up. Even Surrels, who wore a deeply skeptical look on his face, remained quiet. Hal could only guess that no one had a better plan, so no one bothered to object.

That was when Anija suddenly sat up screaming, dropping the core stone onto the floor. Everyone looked at Anija in surprise, including Rialo, who bowed down closer to Anija and said, "Anija! Can you hear me, Anija? Anija?"

Anija, however, kept screaming. Her eyes seemed distant and unfocused, like she was staring at something horrifying in the distance that only she could see.

"Rialo, what's wrong with Anija?" Hal asked, taking a step toward her.

Rialo shook her head. "I-I am not sure. I am using our bond to enter her mind, but there's so much fear and pain in there that it's difficult for me to get a read on what has upset her so badly. I can't reach her."

Hal bit his lower lip. "Maybe I can."

Hal ran over to Anija and put a hand on her head. Using his godly powers, Hal closed his eyes and tried to connect with Anija.

Normally, Hal would have tried to expand his bond so that Anija could become part of it. Although bonds between Riders and Steeds were often reserved for the two of them alone, it was possible for more people to join a bond if allowed.

But Hal, no longer just a Dragon Rider, used something much more powerful. Drawing upon the divine energy flowing through his being like blood, Hal bypassed Anija's bond entirely, directly sending soothing energy into her mind and soul. It felt like pouring cold water on a burning bush.

But it worked. In seconds, Hal felt Anija's fear and pain dissipate entirely, and Anija herself stopped screaming. She was, however, shivering uncontrollably, like Hal had literally poured ice-cold water over her head, even though she was physically dry.

Removing his hand from her head, Hal said, "Anija, are you all right? Can you hear us now?"

Anija, trembling, looked up at Hal with wild yet tired eyes. "Hal? Is that really you? Where ... where am I? What happened?"

Hal gestured at the core stone at her feet. "You picked up the core stone of that wingless dragon that Kryo Kardia had sent to destroy Mysteria. After that, you lost consciousness, so we don't know what happened to you during that time."

"Can you remember, Anija?" Keershan asked, having approached her right behind Hal. "What did you see?"

Anija took a deep, shuddering breath. "I saw... I don't

remember what I saw. It was horrifying, however. That is all I remember of it."

Although Anija sounded sincere, Hal noticed the way that Anija and Rialo shared a quick glance with each other. He dismissed it, however, as their bond reconnecting. No doubt Anija and Rialo were trying to reestablish their bond, which would definitely help Anija calm down.

"Well, I am glad you are okay," Hal said, "because we are going to need everyone on board if our current plan to take down Kryo Kardia doesn't work."

Anija narrowed her eyes in confusion. "What plan? No one told me about any plans to take down Kryo Kardia."

Hal folded his arms across his chest. "Let me explain what we just agreed to do. To defeat Kryo Kardia, we are going to—"

"Let me explain it to her, Hal," Rialo said. "I can send her that information through our bond much more quickly than you can speak it."

Hal pursed his lips but nodded, deciding that that was probably the most efficient way to get Anija up to speed.

Turning back to the others, Hal said, "Since we are all in agreement on this plan, I suggest we contact Kryo Kardia immediately and make him this offer."

Surrels blanched. "No way will Kryo Kardia accept any messengers from us. Not without brutally killing them and sending their parts back to us, anyway."

Nege rolled her eyes. "We don't need to go to the Northern Circle to make Father this offer, you fool. I just so happen to have a calling card I can use for long-distance communication that is far more efficient than sending a messenger who will take days, if not weeks, to get there. See?"

Nege pulled out a blank piece of paper from nowhere, flashing it for everyone to see.

Hal nodded. "Thanks, Nege. That will be very helpful. Keershan and I will contact Kryo Kardia using that calling card. In the meantime, we should probably discuss a backup plan in case this doesn't work out."

Surrels sighed in relief. "Thank the gods! I was worried you weren't going to leave us with anything. Yes, let's discuss backup plans in case the bastard known as Kryo Kardia is just as bad as we think he is."

While the rest of the council started discussing contingency plans, Hal let his mind drift. He felt Keershan's familiar warm presence in his mind and heard his Steed's voice say, *Are you all right, Hal?*

I'm fine, Keershan, Hal said mentally. *I'm just thinking about when we should tell the others about what actually happened to us in the challenge.*

Keershan went silent for a moment. *I'm not sure. Perhaps after the duel with Kryo Kardia, assuming he agrees to it.*

I think he will, Hal said. *Nege appears to think that he will consider it, anyway, which is good enough for me.*

Hope so, Keershan said. *Although I am not sure how we will defeat him without Soul Slayer. I doubt Lom will change his mind anytime soon, and I have no idea where to find a rogue Relic Crafter who would be willing to make it for us.*

Hal nodded in response but said nothing. He was thinking back to the second part of the challenge, pondering something that Old Snow had said to them.

Chapter Twenty-One

ONE MONTH AGO.

The winds rushed through Hal's hair as he and Keershan plummeted toward the sea below. The fall was messing with Hal's sense of direction because the sea and the sky kept changing places with each other. It didn't help that both the sea and the sky were blue, which made telling them apart even more confusing.

But Hal was pretty sure they were going to land in the water below and most likely break their backs, if not die upon impact.

Because water, contrary to popular belief, wasn't soft.

But then Keershan extended both of his wings out and soared off to Hal's right. Keershan, however, doubled back quickly, gliding underneath Hal and catching him on his back.

Gasping from the impact, Hal sat up unsteadily on

Keershan as his Steed soared through the endless sky. "Thanks, Keershan. Quick thinking on your part."

Hal was painfully aware of how hoarse his voice sounded from all of the screaming that they'd just done. His throat definitely felt like it, too.

"No problem," Keershan said, flapping his wings at a steady beat to keep them aloft. He glanced down at the open sea below with big eyes. "Dragons *hate* the ocean, so I will do whatever I can to keep us both out of it for as long as possible."

Hal had forgotten about the odd fear of the sea that all dragons had, but he could definitely feel that fear from Keershan flowing through their bond. He did his best not to let it affect him, however, and looked around at their surroundings, trying to get his bearings on exactly where they were.

They hovered hundreds of feet in the air over a sea as smooth as glass. The wind was powerful this far up, making even Hal's short brown hair move about wildly. Fortunately, his bond with Keershan meant that his eyes were protected from the wind. Combined with the heat that Keershan's body naturally generated, Hal was comfortable for the most part, if still slightly woozy from the fall.

But it didn't matter how comfortable Hal was because he did not see any land anywhere. For miles in every direction, it was endless ocean. He didn't even see any boats or rocks poking up out of the water.

"Keershan, do you see any land?" Hal asked, raising his voice to be heard above the howling of the winds. "Because I don't."

Keershan grimaced. "No. I don't see anywhere we

could land at all unless you want to take a dip in the water. And I don't trust that ocean one bit."

Hal could not blame Keershan. Although the ocean was calm and beautiful, Hal noticed that he could not look beneath the surface. The water was just murky enough that Hal could not tell what might be lurking or waiting for them under there.

Suddenly, Hal understood Keershan's fear of the ocean quite well.

The lack of land was problematic. Although Keershan was a strong, young dragon with plenty of energy to spare, Keershan would eventually get tired and need to land soon. Dragons could not fly forever. Even with Hal sharing his energy with Keershan through their bond, Hal estimated that would give them another five, ten minutes of flight time before Keershan needed to land and rest somewhere.

Not to mention eat, Hal thought, feeling his own stomach, which was quite empty at the moment. *Both of us.*

Yet Hal did not see any easy answer to those problems. Unless they could find land soon, they would eventually be forced to land in the ocean.

And something told Hal that the ocean below was the very last place in the world they needed to be. And not just because of the risk of them drowning, either.

"Is this the second part of the challenge, you think?" asked Keershan over the flapping of his own wings and the rushing wind around them. "See how long we can stay in the air before we have to crash?"

Hal bit his lower lip. "The Final Relic might be able to give you more energy. Just let me try to—"

"Won't help," Keershan grunted. "The longer I fly, the

weaker I'll become. The Final Relic is just a bandage. Stupid challenge. Wish we'd never agreed to do it."

Hal rubbed the back of Keershan's neck. "I'm sure we will survive, Keershan. We just need—Hey, what's that?"

Something in the clouds overhead caught Hal's eye, a shadow that did not look like a bird, dragon, or anything else one might normally see in the clouds. He turned his gaze upward, narrowing his eyes to try to get a better look at the object.

Only to realize that it wasn't an object.

It was an island.

Floating in the sky, seemingly of its own accord.

The huge island, probably a mile long and half a mile wide, hung in the air above the ocean, sitting on the clouds themselves. The clouds covered the bottom half of the island, but the surface of the island was quite visible.

The island was covered thickly with a jungle of sorts. In fact, it was covered so thickly in trees and brush that many of the trees were dangling over the edge, like an open-faced sandwich with too many toppings piled too high. Even as Hal watched, a branch from one of the trees broke off and fell into the sea below with a distant *plop*. He did not see any animals within the jungle's trees, although given how tightly packed together they were, perhaps that made sense.

"Are you seeing what I am seeing?" Hal asked Keershan, unable to take his eyes off the floating island.

"If what you are seeing is a flying island, then yes, I am seeing that," Keershan said. "Maybe we are hallucinating together or something."

Hal shook his head. "I don't think so. I think that this must be part of the challenge. Let's go check it out."

Keershan gulped. "Are you sure? What if we land on it

and it falls straight through the clouds because of our weight?"

"If it was going to fall, I'm sure that the island would have fallen a long time ago," Hal replied. "I am sure it is perfectly safe to land on. Besides, the alternative is to keep flying around the sea until you get exhausted, which I am sure that you don't want to do. Right?"

Keershan clicked his teeth together nervously but, with another flap of his wings, changed their direction to the island. "All right, Hal. But the trees look pretty thick. Not sure I'll be able to find a landing place."

As it turned out, however, the thick overgrowth was somewhat illusionary. When Hal and Keershan flew over the island, they saw that the interior was nowhere near as densely thick as the edges were.

A wide-open space stood in the center of the island, near a dark, gaping cave mouth and a sparkling, clear pond. Although the gaping cave was suspicious, the crystal clear pond was inviting enough to make even Keershan relax slightly. They landed on the strip of land—more like a beach, really—between the water and the cavern, more than big enough for both of them.

"See?" Hal said when Keershan landed, gesturing at the island. "The island didn't sink when you landed. We're not as heavy as you seem to think we are."

Keershan looked around the island anxiously. "I suppose you have a point, but this still seems very strange. How come we don't feel any wind up here, even though we are several hundred feet in the air at the least?"

Hal looked at the tall trees on the edges of the island. "The thick undergrowth must be blocking the wind. That's convenient."

"And scary," Keershan said. "What if there are creatures hiding inside those trees that might want to kill us?"

Hal shook his head. "I doubt it, Keershan. As thick as those trees are, they aren't thick enough for anything more dangerous than a bird to hide in. We should take this moment to relax and get our bearings."

Hal jumped off of Keershan's back and landed on the sand, his boots crunching the sand when he landed. Dusting himself off, Hal gestured at the pond before them. "And look at how crystal clear this drinking water is. I don't know about you, but I am pretty parched."

Before Hal could march over to the water to begin drinking, however, he heard a drumbeat from inside the cavern behind them. Pausing in his step, Hal gazed over his shoulder at the cave mouth even as the drumbeat grew louder and louder.

"Drums?" Keershan said, turning around with Hal to face the cavern mouth. He grimaced. "I'm not sure I like this."

Hal nodded. He rested a hand on the hilt of his sword but did not draw it just yet. "I don't care much for it, either. Keep your guard up. We have no idea what is in there."

The drumbeat continued to grow in volume, becoming louder and louder, which made Hal think that the drummer was getting closer to them. Yet even with his night vision activated, Hal's eyes could not pierce the blackness of the cave, meaning that neither he nor Keershan could see what was coming from inside there.

That was, until a figure emerged from within the cave, still banging on his drums, allowing Hal and Keershan to see the figure for the first time.

Hal wasn't quite sure what to make of the drummer.

Humanoid in appearance, the drummer had skin tanned almost black, with a loose grass skirt around his waist. His thin, small arms extended from an almost skeletal chest, his twin drums hanging from his shoulders and stopping in front of his stomach. The drums themselves were covered in odd paintings and symbols and looked quite old.

The drummer's face, however, was the strangest part about him. The drummer seemed to be wearing a wooden mask with two eyes, a mouth, and a nose. At least, Hal *thought* it was a mask, because its expressions kept changing like a real human face.

The drummer stopped drumming when he saw them, however, and came to a stop in front of the cave mouth. Lowering his sticks to his sides, the drummer cocked his head to the side, staring at them with those strange 'eyes,' for want of a better term, from its mask.

Hal and Keershan stared at the drummer, who stared back at them in return. Although the drummer looked frail and nonthreatening, he seemed less afraid of them and more puzzled by their presence on his island than anything.

Why isn't he saying anything? Keershan asked. *This guy's making me nervous.*

I bet you he's a demigod like Erla and her brothers were, Hal replied. *But his silence is strange. Maybe we have to make the first move.*

Hal raised a hand in what he hoped would be taken as a friendly gesture by the strange drummer. "Hello, stranger. I am Halar Norath, a Dragon Rider, and this is my Steed, Keershan. We are here to complete the second part of the challenge."

The drummer cocked his head to the other side before suddenly doing a quick drumbeat on his drums. Unlike the previous beats, this one was quick, almost frantic, like he was saying something quickly.

The drummer then gave Hal and Keershan an expectant look.

Keershan licked his lips and looked at Hal. "You wouldn't happen to play any instruments yourself, would you, Hal?"

Hal sighed. "I don't. He must be messing with us."

"He's not messing with you," said the voice of a young boy from the trees. "He's just speaking the universal language of music."

From out of the trees on the right side of the island came a small boy who didn't look older than five or six. Like the drummer, the boy wore a grass loincloth, although he at least had a normal human face. The boy darted over to stand beside the drummer, who gave his drums a few more beats as if in greeting to the boy.

Hal stared at the boy. "And who are you?"

The little boy stood up straight, although he still only just barely came up to Hal's waist. "My name is Mon. And I will be your guide to the second part of the challenge today."

"Mon?" Keershan repeated. He gasped. "Wait a second. You are *the* trickster god, Mon? From legend?"

Mon shrugged. "I suppose you could say that."

Keershan looked around at the island with more interest now. "Ah, you even have the floating island, although it does not appear to be made out of cream like the legends said—"

"Keershan," Hal said, doing his best not to sound too impatient. "Who is Mon? Is that another ancient legend you have studied?"

Keershan nodded eagerly. "Yes! Before I ran into you in the Desolate Tops, Hal, my research took me to the Solitary Isles just off the coast of Malarsan. I learned from the ruins of an ancient city there that the people of the Solitary Isles had once worshiped a trickster god who had the appearance of a young boy, named Mon, who was said to live on a floating island made of cream."

Hal raised an eyebrow and looked at Mon. "So you are a god."

"Basically," said Mon. He shrugged. "Unlike my fellow deities, however, I no longer actively seek the worship of mortals. I spend most of my days on this island, awaiting challengers such as yourselves to try to make it to godhood."

The drummer chuckled and did another series of fast drumbeats that Hal somehow understood were meant to be sarcastic.

"Don't mind Dorum," said Mon. "He's a bit of a smart-aleck."

Hal folded his arms in front of his chest. "Dorum is his name, eh? How come he doesn't speak?"

"He doesn't speak *your* language," Mon corrected Hal. "As I said earlier, Dorum speaks the language of music because he is the god of music."

"Does he always, er, speak using drums?" asked Keershan.

Dorum shook his head. He tapped his left drum gently before suddenly slapping his right drum.

"He says no," said Mon. "As the god of music, Dorum regularly switches instruments. He's used everything from guitars to harps to trumpets and everything in between, including a few things I didn't even know could be used as instruments. He's always been like this."

"I see," Hal said, although he really didn't, as he didn't understand how one even 'spoke' using music that lacked lyrics. "So, you said this is the second part of the challenge. Exactly what does the second part of the challenge entail, if we may ask?"

Mon jerked a thumb over his shoulder at the open cave mouth. "Easy. This second part of the challenge will require you to sacrifice your mortality inside that cave. Once you can part with your mortality, only then can you truly become gods."

Hal furrowed his brow. "By 'sacrificing our mortality,' do you mean that this is where we will actually become gods?"

Dorum made a series of drumbeats that sounded an awful lot like laughter to Hal.

With a wag of his finger, Mon said, "Your comment amused Dorum. No, this isn't where you ascend. That will be later. This is merely where you show to the rest of the gods—and to the challenge itself—that you are willing to do anything it takes to become a god."

Keershan clawed at the sand. "Sounds easy enough. Just go in there and 'sacrifice' our mortality. Doesn't sound too difficult."

Hal put a hand on Keershan's shoulder, however, to keep him from advancing any further. "Mon, if this is not the part where we will ascend, then what does 'sacrificing our mortality' mean, exactly?"

Mon smiled chillingly. "Why, you will die, of course."

Chapter Twenty-Two

"WE WILL DIE?" KEERSHAN REPEATED IN HORROR. HE took a step back. "Um, I am not sure I am ready to die just yet."

Dorum slapped his drums several times in a slow beat.

Mon nodded. "Dorum says we will all die someday, or at least mortals will. We gods, on the other hand, live forever, assuming we do not get murdered by mortals, demigods, or our siblings, of course."

"I agree with Keershan about his hesitancy," Hal said. "How can we complete the challenge if walking into that cave will kill us?"

Mon shook his head. "Allow me to elaborate. You see, the second part of the challenge is both the easiest and yet most difficult part to overcome. It is where the few who make it past the first part often fail, and why very few mortals have ever successfully ascended to godhood."

Mon began pacing back and forth in front of the cave, arms folded behind his back. "When you step into the cave, the cave will dig deep into your soul. It will forage through every memory, every aspect of your very self, down to the tiniest details. It will look for anything that will disqualify you from moving on and then kill you."

Hal grunted. "Still don't see how anyone is supposed to 'pass' this part."

Mon held up a hand. "But it won't kill you forever. If you are deemed worthy of moving on to the third and final part of the challenge, then the cave will resurrect you, and you will be allowed to walk out of there as if nothing had happened."

Dorum shook his head and rapidly beat his drums.

Mon, coming to a stop, gave Dorum a deadpan look. "Yes, Dorum, I know that 'death' is a big deal to mortals. And yeah, I guess you're also right that the experience will change them one way or another, even if they pass it."

Hal put his hands on his hips. "I don't understand the point of this part of the challenge. What does dying—and coming back to life—teach us about godhood if gods cannot die?"

Mon gave Hal an exasperated look. "It teaches you about the fragility of mortal life, Rider. In essence, it is a symbolic act, showing that you two, the challengers, are willing to give up your mortality in exchange for a shot at divinity. No mortal who clings desperately to their mortality or greatly fears death will ever be good god material, if you know what I mean."

"I don't, actually," Hal said. "The gods in the abode seemed plenty afraid to die to me."

"Only because they knew someone was hunting them down," Mon added. "The reality is that no god should be afraid of death, at least not in the same way that mortals are. There is nothing more mortal, if you think about it, than the fear of death itself."

Dorum slammed his drums once and then folded his arms across his chest.

Mon sighed. "Fine. That, and the fact that you humans have a tendency to get drunk on the tiniest bit of power. But really, I would argue that the fear of death is one of the most mortal fears ever."

Dorum banged his drums, this time with his fists rather than his sticks.

"We'll agree to disagree," said Mon. He turned his attention back to Hal and Keershan. "But for your purposes, this will prove just how serious you two are about becoming gods. Are you willing to face the greatest and final fear that all mortals possess—that is, the fear of death—and give up, through death, the mortal lives you currently live? Or will you cling to your mortal flesh out of fear of the unknown?"

"That sounds easy," Keershan said. "Of course we want to become gods. We wouldn't be in the challenge if we didn't."

"Not so fast, Keershan," Hal said. "We've both been very reluctant about the idea from the start."

"I know," said Mon with a nod. "Your human friend, the one you call Old Snow, has been giving us gods regular updates on your progress. And if you are as reluctant to complete the challenge as you appear to be, then your odds of success, unfortunately, are not as high as you might think they are."

Hal could not disagree with what Mon said, not entirely.

If the cave was able to accurately dig into their souls

and discover their true characters and motives, then Hal thought this might be even harder than the first part of the challenge. The first part, after all, had been a test of character that did not require dying or putting their lives on the line.

But for this second part, it sounded to Hal like they were going to die either way.

And if they did not want to become gods hard enough, then they would stay dead, too.

"Can Keershan and I talk about this first?" Hal said. "We're not on a deadline, right?"

Mon gave Hal a dismissive wave. "Go ahead. Take your time. Although if I were you two, I wouldn't waste too much time talking. After all, you have a world to save, don't you?"

Hal bit his lower lip but did not respond to Mon's comment.

Instead, he and Keershan turned away from the two gods, and Hal said to Keershan, "What do you think?"

Keershan clicked his teeth together, his tail slowly wagging back and forth. "I'm not a fan of the idea of dying, but I also don't see any other way forward for us."

Hal gave Keershan a surprised look. "You mean you think we should go through with it?"

Keershan shrugged. "What else are we supposed to do? It's not like we can go back. We're in too deep now."

"Yes, but doesn't this seem extreme, even going by the standards of the challenge?" Hal said. He gestured at the cave. "If we go in there, we might not come out."

Keershan nodded. "I know that. And trust me, I am as afraid of what might happen in there as you are. At the same time, though, I don't see any other options for us."

Hal pursed his lips. "What if the cave finds us wanting and we just die? Then it will all have been for nothing."

Keershan gave Hal a concerned look. "Are you all right, Hal? I've never seen you this scared before, not even when we fought the Nameless One or Kryo Kardia."

Hal took a deep breath. "I … I guess I am afraid. Because I don't know what is going to happen in there. And I am afraid of dying."

For some reason, Hal did not like to admit that, even to Keershan. He wasn't sure why. The words of Mon flashed in his mind when he said that.

Keershan, however, rubbed his head against Hal's hand. "I understand, Hal. Trust me, I'm afraid to die, too. But at the same time, we have to stop Kryo Kardia, don't we? And the only way to do that is if we complete the challenge and become gods ourselves."

Hal pursed his lips. He felt Keershan's warmth under his hand and flowing through their bond into his body. That helped with some of the anxiety, although it did not dispel his fear just yet. "You're right. We should do this."

"Only if you are ready to do it," Keershan said. He looked Hal in the eyes. "Are you?"

Hal hesitated. He looked at the cave again and shook his head. "No. I'm not."

"Think of something more important to you than your life," Keershan said. "Something that will give you the strength to go forward and do what needs to be done. What are the results if we don't do this?"

Hal bit his lower lip and looked at his feet. "Malarsan will fall. Our friends will be killed. And unlike us, they don't have any chance of being resurrected."

"Exactly," Keershan said. "Now, Hal, I don't want to

pressure you too much, but think about that. About what is at stake here. We already decided we would do whatever was necessary in order to stop Kryo Kardia, didn't we? This is just our chance to prove that we meant that."

Hal took another deep breath. "You're right, Keershan. If this is the only way forward, then we need to walk it. No matter the cost."

Keershan nodded in agreement. "No matter the cost."

With that, Hal and Keershan turned back to the cave, walking side by side up to Mon and Dorum. Mon was sitting on the sand, apparently building a sandcastle, when he noticed Hal and Keershan walk up to them. Dorum was leaning against the cave mouth, tapping out a soft, smooth beat on his drums, while Mon built his sandcastle.

Rising to his feet, Mon said, "So you two are finally ready."

It was a statement, not a question.

"Yes," Hal said. He patted Keershan on the shoulder. "We are ready to begin the second part of the challenge."

Mon folded his arms in front of his chest. "You make it sound like it will take a long time. In truth, the second part of the challenge is the quickest. Once you step in, you won't be inside for very long."

"We know," Hal said. "Now is there anything else we need to know before we begin, or can we just go inside now?"

Mon stepped aside while Dorum walked up to them, still beating his drums softly. "Go ahead. And may luck guide your way."

Hal and Keershan walked past Mon and Dorum, their eyes on the open cave mouth before them. They paid attention to nothing else, until all they could see was the utter blackness of the cavern in front of them.

Stopping at the threshold, Hal and Keershan exchanged a final look.

"Ready?" Hal said.

Keershan smiled. "Yes. Are you?"

Hal took a final deep breath. "Definitely. Let's do this."

With that, Hal and Keershan stepped into the black cave at the same time.

Chapter Twenty-Three

HAL HAD, OBVIOUSLY, NEVER DIED BEFORE. HE'D COME close to dying many times in the past, of course.

But every time Hal had come close to death, he'd managed to avoid it.

Yet death had always been a part of Hal's life, even if he had never experienced it himself. His father dying in the Dragon War, Old Snow's demise, the deaths of so many of his fellow soldiers in the Dragon War ... it seemed like death was always there, as if to remind Hal that he, too, would one day perish.

And that day, Hal knew, was today.

He just didn't know how long it would last.

When Hal stepped over the threshold into the cave itself, he had no idea what to expect. Mon's description of how the cave worked gave him some idea, he supposed, but it was still too vague for his tastes. How did a person die and then come back to life? The only being he knew of who had 'died' and come back to life was the Nameless

One, but even then, the Nameless One had been a god, not a mortal like him. Gods worked by different rules than mortals.

Although perhaps that is what this part of the challenge is supposed to do, Hal thought. *Show us what it is like to be a god.*

And, more importantly, Mon did not describe what death itself would feel like.

I suppose that makes sense, Hal thought as he stepped into the cave. *Mon is a god. I doubt he's ever died, unless he also went through the challenge at some point. I wonder if all of the gods were once mortals who completed the challenge or—*

Hal's thoughts were interrupted, however, as soon as he and Keershan entered the cave. He turned to Keershan, hoping to say something to him, only to realize that he couldn't see Keershan at all. The cave was just too dark, and his night vision could not pierce the shadows.

"Keershan?" Hal said, reaching out a hand to his right, where Keershan had just been. "Keershan, are you there? Keershan?"

Even though Hal said all of these things, he couldn't hear his own voice. The words left his mouth but only silently.

Even worse, Hal could not feel Keershan at all, even though Keershan had been right by his side when they entered the cave, well within reach of his arm. It was like Keershan had simply vanished into thin air, leaving no trace of his Steed.

Hal quickly focused on their bond, but even that proved fruitless. He could no more feel Keershan through their bond than he could feel any other dragon he was not bonded to.

Is Keershan dead already? Hal thought. *Did he fail? Is he not coming back? Is that why I can't—*

Once again, Hal's thoughts were interrupted, this time by a powerful sensation of something much bigger than himself rushing through his body.

In short, it felt like a thousand knives were slashing through every core of his being. And not just his physical body, either. The knives cut into his soul, striking places Hal did not even know existed within himself but which hurt just as much, if not more so, than the parts he did know about.

Hal wanted to scream, but he couldn't.

Images flashed through his mind as the pain overwhelmed him. The first day he met Keershan. Killing the Defacer. Fighting the necrodragon above the city. Entering Dragon Valley. Killing the Nameless One. Seeing the Northern Circle for the first time. Losing to Kryo Kardia. Entering the abode.

And the images kept coming. In fact, the images were an absolute blur now, coming so fast that Hal could not tell what they even were. He wasn't even sure he was viewing his own memories anymore, either.

Then …

It all stopped.

The pain.

The images.

The sounds.

Everything was blissfully, peacefully, wonderfully …

Silent.

And then, not a second later, it all returned in one big flash.

And Hal fell out of the cave onto the beach, screaming

his head off, feeling every nerve in his body on fire. He could not feel anything else. His whole world was never-ending pain. He truly could say that he had never felt anything even close to this before.

But even that, too, faded in time, until Hal simply felt tired. Exhausted.

And all he wanted to do was sleep.

Then Mon's child-like face appeared over him and he said, "Congratulations, mortal! You passed the second part of the challenge!"

Startled, Hal sat up and looked around at his surroundings in alarm, his heart beating faster than Dorum's drums.

Hal was back on the beach between the pond and the cave. From his perspective, it seemed as if no time had passed whatsoever since stepping into the cave and coming out of it. His body even looked exactly the same, too, if slightly sandier due to him having fallen onto the sand.

Hal heard a groan by his side and looked over to see Keershan lying next to him. Aside from looking even more exhausted than Hal, Keershan also appeared normal.

Keershan, Hal said. *Are you okay?*

I am alive, if that's what you are asking, Keershan replied, his voice weaker than usual. *How ... how are you?*

Hal grimaced. *Sandy, but alive.*

Patting his chest, Hal looked up at Mon and said, "That was it?"

Mon nodded, a happy smile on his face. "Sure was! I told you it would be quick, didn't I? The cave doesn't take too long to make a decision once it reads your soul. It's very decisive."

Hal shuddered. "Reading my soul? More like tearing it

apart and putting it back together again. With the sharpest knives in the world."

Mon shrugged. "I've never entered the cave, so I don't know what it's actually like to go in there. Dorum would, though. What do you think, Dorum? Does his description match your experience in that place?"

Hal turned his gaze toward Dorum, who was standing closer to the pond than to the cave. When Mon addressed him, however, Dorum did a series of quick yet soft beats on his drums before pointing at the cave impatiently.

"Oh, that's right," said Mon. "You don't actually die when you go in there, huh? And I guess they did take a little longer than expected to come out."

"A little longer?" Hal said. "What do you mean by that?"

Mon gestured at the cave. "Normally, the challenge only has one challenger at a time, so the cave is only used to dealing with one challenger at any given moment. But since there are two of you, that must have forced the cave to take more time to make sure it fully read your souls."

Keershan gasped for breath and his eyes flickered open. "What exactly *is* that cave, anyway? I've never heard about anything like it in the myths."

"You're asking *me*?" said Mon. "That thing is even older than the gods. Whatever it is, I am just glad that it stays right where it is. Gives me the creeps."

Dorum nodded. He tapped the tops of his drums a couple more times and then turned away from the cave with a shudder.

"Even Dorum thinks it's creepy, although I think he's just putting on a show for us," said Mon. "He spends an awful lot of time in there, despite allegedly finding it creepy."

Dorum actually tossed one of his drumsticks at Mon, striking him in the back of the head. Rubbing the spot where Dorum had hit him, Mon said, "What? If you don't want me saying that, then don't do it."

Dorum glared back at Mon and did a single beat with his remaining drumstick before turning away from Mon, probably still upset about Mon's comment. Hal did not see what was so offensive or upsetting about it, but then again, he barely understood the god of music at all, so he decided not to worry about it too much.

Instead, Hal rose to his feet and dusted off his pants. "Well, I am glad that is over with."

"I am just glad we survived," Keershan said, standing up shakily. "That was the strangest and scariest experience I've ever had in my life."

Mon smirked. "How did dying feel, if you don't mind me asking?"

Hal considered that question. "It felt strange. One moment, I was in absolute pain, the worst pain I'd ever experienced. And then the next was … was …"

"Silence," Keershan said softly. "Total silence."

Hal looked at Keershan in surprise. "How did you know that? I couldn't feel you through our bond."

"Because we experienced the same things," Keershan said. "Remember? We both died. I'd reckon our experiences were similar, if not exactly the same. I literally saw my life flash before my eyes."

Hal nodded. "I did as well. And I think it changed me, changed us, in ways we still haven't fully processed."

Mon chuckled. "Of course! Now that you have died

and come back, your mortality is gone. You aren't fully gods yet, but you are no longer fully mortal, either, at least on a spiritual level."

Hal gave Mon an annoyed look. "What is that supposed to mean?"

Mon wagged a finger at Hal. "You'll find out later. For now, why don't you two go on to the third and final part of the challenge?"

Mon snapped his fingers, and a portal opened up about a dozen yards away from them. The inside of the portal was constantly shifting light and texture, making it impossible to see what was on the other side.

Par for the course with the challenge, Hal thought. *Not telling us anything until we are right in the middle of it.*

"Step through that portal to begin the next part of the challenge," said Mon, gesturing at the portal. "Dorum and I will be cheering you on every step of the way."

Hal narrowed his eyes. "Was that sarcasm?"

Mon shook his head. "Of course not! We genuinely are supporting you. Right, Dorum?"

Dorum, however, still had his back to Mon. His only response was a quick, snide-sounding beat on his drums and a distinct *harrumph.*

"Still upset," said Mon. He looked at Hal and Keershan. "But don't worry about him. See, very few mortals make it this far, and even fewer make it past this part. In fact, the last god who did was…"

Mon trailed off, his green eyes staring into space, like he was reliving a particularly vivid memory.

Hal waved a hand in front of Mon's face. "Hello? Mon? Are you still there?"

Mon snapped out of whatever memory he was reliving

and flashed them a grin. "Of course I am! Anyway, you two should really get going. The third and final part of the challenge is the most difficult, plus you don't want to keep the keeper of the challenge waiting."

"The challenge who?" Hal said.

Mon smiled mysteriously. "You'll see. Bye!"

With that, Mon snapped his fingers, and the ground under Hal and Keershan's feet shifted. The sand formed into a giant hand which then threw them into the portal, Hal and Keershan yelling all the while.

And then they passed through the portal and landed on solid stone flooring face-first.

"Ugh," Hal said, pushing himself up into a sitting position and shaking his head. He looked over his shoulder at the portal behind them, which closed with a soft *pop*. "Not the most graceful entrance to the final part of the challenge, I assume."

"Definitely not," Keershan said, also pushing himself up. He began looking around at their new surroundings. "So where are we?"

Keershan's voice trailed off, making Hal also look around. He understood why.

They stood on a wide stone platform that appeared to float in a dark, endless void. Twinkling lights, like stars, hung in the shadows of the void, while a coldness settled on them that even Keershan's dragonfire could not do away with entirely.

More importantly, however, were the floating stands rising all around them.

Upon which sat every single god and goddess in the world, with Gotcham Nubor himself sitting on a huge throne before them.

Before either Hal or Keershan could react, Gotcham Nubor raised his scepter into the air and said, in a booming, echoing voice, "The challengers have arrived! Let the Duel of Divinity—the third and final part of the challenge —commence!"

Chapter Twenty-Four

"You're sure Kryo Kardia will respond to our attempts to get in contact with him," Hal said to Nege as they stood around the altar in the Forgotten Temple. "And that he will not ignore it."

Nege, standing beside Hal, gave him an offended look. "Of course Father will answer. He always answers calling cards, which is why he gives out so few of them. Otherwise, it would be a waste of perfectly good resources."

"Yes, I've always wondered about that," Fralia said, standing on Nege's other side. "How do calling cards work, exactly? They remind me of our communication necklaces here in Malarsan, but a bit more advanced."

Nege scowled at Fralia. "How am I supposed to know? I just use them. I'm no mage. You'd have to ask an actual Glacian mage that question, but fair warning: They don't answer questions from foreigners about how our magic works."

"Hey, lady," Anija said, standing on the opposite side of

the altar. "Why don't you talk to my friends with a bit more respect? We're all on the same side here, after all."

Nege looked at Anija with an unimpressed expression on her face. "Why don't you make me? Just because we both oppose Father doesn't mean we are friends. It just means we are temporary allies until Father has been defeated. Never mistake my friendliness for anything but political pragmatism on my part."

This is her being friendly *to us?* Keershan asked Hal mentally.

Hal looked over his shoulder. Keershan was sitting on the floor several feet away from them, his tail wrapped around his legs. Rialo and Prika were not here, and neither were Wilme or Surrels, who had all gone to supervise repairs to the damage to Mysteria caused by the wingless dragon's earlier attack.

She's not actively trying to kill us anymore, Hal pointed out. *I suppose, by her standards, that* is *being friendly.*

Keershan shook his head. *You humans are so strange.*

"Anyway, what are we waiting for?" Nege said. She looked at Fralia. "Start the fire. Father will definitely talk to us."

Fralia, looking annoyed at Nege's rudeness, nonetheless raised her hand and cast a simple fireball into the pile of dry wood sitting on the altar before them. A bright, warm fire erupted from the wood, casting orange and yellow hues over the assembled people.

As soon as the flames appeared, Nege threw her calling card into the fire. The calling card turned to ashes as soon as it touched the flames, turning them into blue-white flames that somehow felt cold despite the heat.

"Father!" Nege cried. "It is I, Nege Kardia, your daughter! I demand an audience with you right this very moment."

There was no response aside from the crackling of flames, making Hal wonder if Nege had overestimated Kryo Kardia's response time.

Nege, now tapping her foot impatiently, said, "Father! It is I, Nege Kardia, your daughter! I demand an audience with you right this very—"

"We heard you the first time, Princess," said a familiar snide, high-pitched voice. "No need to repeat yourself. His Iciness has excellent hearing."

Inquirer Dedeket suddenly appeared in the flames. Clad in his colorful robes, Dedeket looked as ridiculous as he always did, only Hal knew that Dedeket's ridiculous appearance hid a very wicked and cunning personality.

"Dedeket?" Nege said in disbelief. "Where is Father? I demand to speak to him right now."

Dedeket winked at Nege. "His Iciness isn't sure he wants to speak with you at the moment. We can see those wretched Malarsans nearby, which means you are probably working with them. He wants me to inquire for him of what you want."

Nege scowled. "To speak to him."

"Why didn't you send a message through Ronix?" asked Dedeket. He looked around. "Where is Ronix, by the way? We haven't heard from him since—"

"I killed him," Nege said coldly. "Prika and I killed him because he tried to kill us."

Dedeket gasped, putting a hand over his mouth, although Hal got the impression that Dedeket was secretly pleased to hear about the demise of his fellow inquirer. "Inquirer Ronix is dead? How very sad. Tragic, even. I will have to inform all of his loved ones, with tears in my eyes, of his unfortunate and unexpected departure from this earthly—"

"Shut it, Dedeket," Nege growled. "Everyone knows you and Ronix hated each other. Your fake tears couldn't deceive even a blind babe in the womb."

Dedeket huffed. "Excuse me for showing basic compassion toward a fellow fallen inquirer. Why, if you were not His Iciness's daughter, I would be absolutely furious with your lack of respect right now."

"You can be absolutely furious later," Nege said. She glared hard at Dedeket. "I wish to speak with Father. Now."

Dedeket adjusted his scarf. "Now that you've spoken so rudely to me, I am not sure I am going to tell your father about your request. Maybe if you were nicer, I would be far more willing to—"

Hal sighed in frustration and stepped up next to Nege. "Forget about Nege. Tell Kryo Kardia that I, Halar Norath, want to speak with him. Now."

Hal used all of his godly authority when he said that. He hated using his godly powers over mortals like that, as it was yet another reminder of the fact that he was no longer mortal. But Hal really did not have time or energy to waste messing with Dedeket, whose silliness was getting on his nerves now.

Dedeket looked at Hal with something like reverence in his eyes. "Huh? Oh, sure. But why am I so eager to obey your request when it is not that much more polite than—"

"Dedeket," Kryo Kardia's voice said from somewhere

Hal could not see. "That is enough. I will speak with them myself."

Dedeket suddenly vanished from view, and Kryo Kardia appeared. Like Dedeket, Kryo Kardia looked about the same as he did the last time Hal had seen him, only this time Kryo Kardia had a hood over his head that hid much of his facial features. No doubt he was trying to hide his scars from the Fracturing spell that the Snow Witches had cast on him.

His purple eyes, however, glowed brilliantly from within his hood, glaring down at Hal and Nege with untold hatred.

"So my favorite daughter has decided to side with my enemies," Kryo Kardia said, his voice full of disgust. "Is this how you repay your father's love?"

"You never loved me," Nege said. "Or any of my siblings, for that matter. You only saw us as pawns to use in your games. Just like your inquirers, your soldiers, and every other living being you have ever interacted with."

Kryo Kardia shook his head. "I always did fear that I may have spoiled you a bit too much, Nege. It appears that I was correct, as you are the single most ungrateful little girl I have ever had the displeasure of raising. Although I am far more disappointed that Ronix failed to kill you. What an incompetent fool."

Somewhere out of view of them, Hal heard Dedeket snicker softly, no doubt amused by Kryo Kardia's put down of his rival inquirer.

Guess they really didn't like each other, Hal thought.

Then Kryo Kardia turned his gaze to Hal. "Hello again, Halar. It has been a while since we last spoke. I see you survived your journey to the Abode of the Gods."

Hal nodded. "That's right. And we didn't just survive. We are stronger than ever. Strong enough to take you down for good."

Kryo Kardia cocked his head to the side. "Such powerful, even godly, words coming from such a tiny man and his even tinier dragon. Drunk with power already and it hasn't even been two months."

Hal pointed accusingly at Kryo Kardia. "The only one drunk with power here is you, Kryo Kardia. Or should I say, Kralot?"

Kryo Kardia tensed. "I see that those wretched women told you a lot about me. Too much."

"They told me enough," Hal said. "In any case, it doesn't matter what the Snow Witches told me. I'm here to make you an offer you can't refuse."

Kryo Kardia folded his arms across his chest. "Would that happen to be the unconditional surrender of the Malarsan Army to my forces? If so, that would save me a great deal of time, effort, and resources that would be otherwise wasted conquering your tiny kingdom."

Hal shook his head. "No. I want to challenge you to a trial by combat. You and your dragon, Frozas, against me and my Steed, Keershan, in a single duel that will determine the outcome of the war."

Kryo Kardia tapped his chin. "How interesting. It has been ages since the last time an enemy from a country I invaded challenged me to a trial by combat. I had honestly thought that practice was long dead."

"You mean this isn't the first time you've been challenged to duel?" Hal said.

Kryo Kardia shook his head. "Not in the least. In the early days of the Glaci Empire, when I was first invading and conquering rival nations, I regularly received these challenges all the time. After the Glaci Empire grew to a certain size, however, the challenges stopped coming in, but I do miss them. It was always amusing to crush the hopes and dreams of a weak people, in the form of their chosen Champion, right in front of their eyes."

Hal bit his lower lip. "Does that mean you are going to accept my offer, then?"

"I may," Kryo Kardia said, "but before I do so, I note that you have not named a time or place for the duel to begin. Your challenge isn't complete until you are able to show me those details."

Nege sighed. "I knew something would go wrong. You can't trust Malarsans to do anything—"

"No problem, Kryo Kardia," Hal said. "I challenge you to a trial by combat at the border of Malarsan and Hosar in two weeks at the close of the day."

Kryo Kardia gave Hal an impressed look. "So you did think this through, after all. I see you've done your research into the old ways."

Nege looked suitably embarrassed, but Hal did not mock her. He kept his gaze firmly on Kryo Kardia. "Now, do you accept the time, location, and date of the duel, or do you not?"

Much to Hal's surprise, Kryo Kardia nodded. "I accept your offer, Halar Norath. But before I fully commit, exactly what is at stake for both of us during this duel?"

Hal pointed at himself. "If Keershan and I lose, then we will surrender the kingdom of Malarsan to you. The kingdom of Malarsan will peacefully join the Glaci Empire and there will be no need for your forces to invade, destroy, kill, or pillage anyone or anything within the borders of the kingdom."

Kryo Kardia stroked his chin thoughtfully. "That is a rather tempting offer, but what if I lose? What then?"

Hal took a deep breath. "If you lose, the Glaci Empire is forbidden from invading or annexing the kingdom of Malarsan in any way, shape, or form. Citizens from the empire may continue to visit Malarsan and trade will still be allowed between us, but you will respect our sovereignty and independence forever."

Hal knew it was a gamble to lay out their demands in such stark terms. He frankly expected Kryo Kardia to reject it, but at the same time, Hal did not regret making that demand. He knew that Kryo Kardia would likely not even consider it a possibility that he might lose to them and therefore did not have to worry about being unable to invade the country at a later point.

Plus, he doesn't yet realize that we are going to kill him, Hal thought.

Kryo Kardia appeared to be considering Hal's offer. "Such stringent demands, yet I can respect a man who knows what he wants and isn't afraid to ask for it. Very well. I accept your offer, but I would like to modify the terms slightly. Specifically, what will happen if Frozas and I defeat you two in battle."

Hal cocked his head to the side. "What would you like to change?"

Kryo Kardia smiled wickedly. "If I defeat you two and you are still alive, then you two will become my slaves and the entirety of the Malarsan Dragon Rider Order will fall under my control, along with all of the relics and everything else that your order has."

Hal furrowed his brows. "Wouldn't conquering Malarsan already give you those things?"

"Would it?" Kryo Kardia said. "Your Dragon Riders have no reason to stay in Malarsan should I defeat you. There is nothing to stop them from packing up and leaving the kingdom for safety elsewhere. I merely wish to ensure that this does not happen."

I don't like that, Hal, Keershan said. *This sounds like Kryo Kardia is just trying to cover all his bases.*

Only if he wins, Hal reminded Keershan. *And we aren't going to let him win, remember? I think this is fine. We will be okay. It will never happen. Trust me.*

Keershan did not respond. Hal did, however, sensed that Keershan was not exactly convinced about that, but Hal knew they didn't need to worry.

So Hal said, "Fine. I accept your modifications to the challenge. Do you accept my challenge?"

"I do now," Kryo Kardia said. "Thus, in two weeks' time, I will see you and your Steed for the duel that will determine the final outcome of this war. I expect nothing less than your best."

"Trust me, Kryo Kardia, you will definitely get our best," Hal said. "More than our best, actually."

"I am looking forward to it," Kryo Kardia said.

With that, Kryo Kardia vanished from view, and the blue flames turned back to their normal orangeish-red. They burned warmer now, too, although Hal still felt quite cold for some reason.

"Hal," Anija said from the other side of the altar. "Why did you agree to give Kryo Kardia control over the Dragon Riders if he wins?"

Hal gazed at Anija. "Do you really think Kryo Kardia

will beat us? It doesn't matter what we promised him. We could have promised to make him a god and the end result would still be the same. Either way, he will fall."

"I wouldn't be so sure about that myself," Nege said. "As much as I hate Father, I know first-hand how powerful he is. He is not a foe to be underestimated, especially considering how you have already lost to him twice."

Hal gripped the hilt of his blade tightly. "This time will be different. We are stronger now. And we will have a powerful new weapon, too. Right, Keershan?"

Keershan raised his eyes, a puzzled look on his face. "But we don't even know where to find someone who could build the Soul Slayer for us."

"Soul Slayer?" Fralia questioned. "What's that?"

"A weapon that will put an end to Kryo Kardia once and for all," Hal replied. "We need to find a Relic Crafter to build it. And no, not Lom. We already asked him and he said he could not do it for us."

"Is that why you asked for the two weeks to prepare?" asked Anija. "So you can find this Relic Crafter who will be willing to build it for you?"

Hal nodded. "Yes. We're going to need all the time we can to prepare for that."

"We also want to make sure that the Malarsan Army has time to prepare, too," Keershan said, "because we suspect that Kryo Kardia may not be so eager to respect our agreement as he appeared."

"I doubt Father will break a trial by combat agreement," Nege said with a shake of her head. "He loves the old ways too much. Plus, it's a sacred vow that one does not break on a whim. It would make him look weak to go back on his word, even if we are the only people who know about it."

"Weak to who?" Anija questioned. "That's what I'd like to know."

"To us, his enemies," Nege said. "And the last thing Father wants anyone to see him as is weak."

Hal shrugged. "I also don't care about your father's insecurities. We need to find the rogue Relic Crafter that Lom told us about. Keershan and I will likely need to leave the kingdom to find him, as I doubt there are any other Relic Crafters in Malarsan other than Lom."

"What about that identification sphere that Lom gave us?" Keershan said. "Could that be used to track down the rogue Relic Crafter?"

Hal pulled the metallic sphere out of his shirt pocket and rolled it in his hands. "I'm not sure. Lom made it sound like it's only good for identifying oneself to a Relic Crafter. He did not say anything about the sphere being able to actually locate them."

Even as Hal said that, however, a yellow light on the sphere suddenly blinked on. Then a map of Malarsan blinked into existence above it, causing Hal to almost drop it in surprise.

"What the heck is that?" Anija said as she walked around the altar toward them.

Hal blinked. "I-I am not sure. It looks like a map of—"

"Malarsan," Lom's voice said from behind them. "Although I am surprised to see that it still works."

Hal looked over his shoulder to see Lom, his tools hanging from the hooks in his belt, walking up to them. The Relic Crafter wore a serious expression on his face, which contrasted sharply with his usual cowardly one.

"Why does your identification sphere have a map of Malarsan inside it?" Keershan said.

Lom came to a stop and stared at the map. "All identification spheres have a map of the world in them. Regardless of which country you are in, the sphere will update its location to show you a map of the country you are currently residing in."

Hal stared at the sphere in amazement. "How does it know what country it is in? And how does it find a map that accurately reflects its current geographic location?"

Lom gestured at the ceiling. "The spheres receive such information from certain artificial stars in the sky far above. It's too complicated to explain to non-Crafters like yourselves, but that's more or less how it works."

Hal thought Lom was right. The idea of artificial stars somehow sending information to the sphere was too much even for his godly mind to wrap around. He was half-tempted to hop on Keershan's back and fly up into the sky to see such stars close up but decided against it, as they had no time for such frivolous activity.

"What is the purpose of the map inside the sphere?" asked Fralia, eyeing the map with interest. "Is it supposed to help you figure out where you are?"

Lom nodded. "Yes. It also helps the Relic Crafter in question if they need to travel around said country or if, like myself, they end up in another country."

Hal looked at the map again. "Seems useful, but I am not sure how this will help us find the rogue Crafter you told us about."

Lom gestured at the map. "The sphere can also show you the locations of other Relic Crafters, if they are nearby and their identification spheres are active."

Keershan frowned. "But weren't you telling us that you Relic Crafters don't know where each other are?"

"We normally don't," Lom said, "but in case of emergency, we do have our spheres. I haven't used mine in a long time, however, so I can't say if I know if anyone is close by or not."

Hal glanced at the sphere in his hand. "How do we locate other Relic Crafters using this sphere?"

As soon as Hal said that, the sphere flashed blue and started whirring and vibrating in his hand.

"That's how," Lom said sardonically. "It's voice-activated, so if you say the right thing, the sphere will 'hear' it and immediately start looking for whatever you ask it to. I doubt, however, that you will find anything especially useful, seeing as Malarsan's Relic Crafter has been dead for a long time. It will probably only show me and—"

Lom stopped speaking abruptly when first one red dot, then two, flashed on the map. The first red dot was toward the northern end of Malarsan, right on top of Mysteria. Hal guessed, even without Lom's explanation, that that was supposed to be Lom.

The second red dot, however, was located in the center of the kingdom.

"The capital," Hal said in disbelief. "There is another Relic Crafter in the capital."

Lom gulped. "Uh-oh."

Hal gave Lom a puzzled look. "What do you mean by that?"

Lom rubbed the back of his neck. "I mean that if there is another Relic Crafter *here*, then that doesn't bode well for us. Especially if they are the rogue one I think they are, although truthfully, I don't actually know any rogue Relic Crafters personally."

Hal looked at the map again, narrowing his eyes. "Then we will go to the capital, find this Relic Crafter, and ask him to make the Soul Slayer for us. We don't have much time, so let's get to it."

Chapter Twenty-Five

SURRELS WAS STILL SURE THAT HAL AND KEERSHAN WERE not being entirely upfront with him and the others about what changes they had undergone during their time in the Abode of the Gods.

After all, there was no way they could have flown all the way to the capital in less than a day. Even knowing that dragons could fly quickly, Surrels also knew that dragons had their limits and needed to rest. Especially Keershan, who, as a smaller-than-normal dragon, probably needed to rest more than usual.

Yet here they were three days later, walking the busy streets of the capital, Hal looking no worse the wear for having made the flight. Surrels supposed it helped that they had spent a couple of days recuperating in Castle Lamor, which helped, but Surrels suspected that that had been more for his benefit than Hal's.

And the fact that Hal was younger than him did not seem to account for the difference in recovery time, either.

"Any more information from your magic talking ball?"

Surrels asked Hal in a low voice as they walked through the streets of the capital.

Hal shook his head underneath his hood. "No. And why is everyone staring at me when I'm wearing a hood? This was supposed to keep me from being recognized."

Surrels pursed his lips and looked around at the crowds around them. While most people kept walking, many of the citizens cast not-so-subtle glances in Hal's direction. And Surrels knew they were looking at Hal specifically because their eyes completely skipped Surrels, almost like he didn't exist.

"I don't know," Surrels said. "I think it would be difficult for the most famous hero in all of Malarsan to walk the crowded, busy streets of the capital and not be noticed."

Hal frowned. "Well, then I'll just become more obscure."

Surrels blinked and suddenly Hal looked less familiar even to him. The shadows in his hood seemed to obscure his features more and what little was visible no longer reminded Surrels much of Hal. Indeed, if Surrels hadn't been walking by his side, he would have thought Hal had been replaced by a total stranger who bore only the vaguest resemblances to Hal.

Whatever Hal did seemed to work, too, because the people who had been staring at him abruptly looked away or went back to whatever they had been doing before they saw him.

"How did you do that?" Surrels asked incredulously as they walked.

Hal gave Surrels a puzzled look. "How did I do what?"

Surrels gestured at the crowds around them. "Made people look away from you. Was that magic or something?"

Hal shrugged. "I have no idea what you are talking about, Surrels. All I did was hike my hood up a little bit more. You must have a very active imagination."

Surrels narrowed his eyes. He knew what he saw, and he wasn't sure why Hal was lying about it.

Must be some of that divine power that the gods gave him, Surrels thought. *But it didn't work on me for some reason. He must be able to control what others see or something.*

"Why not ask your talking ball where this rogue Relic Crafter is?" asked Surrels as they turned a corner.

Hal sighed. "I've tried, but every time I ask it a question that specific, the sphere goes silent. But Lom said it would vibrate once I got close enough and would vibrate more the closer we get to wherever this rogue Relic Crafter is hiding."

"Is it vibrating now?" Surrels said.

Hal came to a stop, forcing Surrels to stop as well, and looked at the pocket in his pants where he presumably kept the sphere. "No, not right now. We need to keep walking. It was vibrating harder earlier. I think we are still on the right track."

Surrels bit his lower lip but did not argue with Hal, even though they'd been walking the streets of the capital for almost half an hour now with no luck. Sure, the capital was the biggest city in Malarsan and had plenty of hiding places for anyone who did not want to be easily found, but Surrels still thought they should have found the rogue Relic Crafter by now.

But Surrels decided that Hal seemed to know more about this mystery Crafter than he did, so he kept his mouth closed as they continued to search the streets for any sign of this Crafter.

As they walked, Surrels reflected on what had happened after Kryo Kardia accepted Hal's challenge a few days ago.

Hal had called another meeting of the council, mostly to inform them that Kryo Kardia had indeed accepted his challenge for a duel in two weeks' time. Surrels had been genuinely surprised when Hal announced that, as he had not thought that Kryo Kardia would ever agree to such a thing. Evidently, Kryo Kardia was far more prideful than he thought.

The next order of business, then, had been to find a 'rogue' Relic Crafter who was apparently somewhere in the capital and ask said Relic Crafter to make a powerful weapon for Hal and Keershan that would supposedly allow them to kill Kryo Kardia once and for all. Surrels thought that 'Soul Slayer' was a rather ominous title for a weapon, but he also wanted to see Kryo Kardia finished for good as much as anyone, so again, he did not object.

To prepare for the upcoming duel, Hal, Keershan, Fralia, and Surrels had returned to the capital to seek out the rogue Crafter while Anija, Rialo, and Wilme had stayed in Mysteria to prepare the site of the duel at the border with Hosar.

Surrels and Fralia had accompanied Hal and Keershan for two reasons.

One, Surrels and Fralia both lived in the capital. As Surrels was the general of the Malarsan Army and Fralia was the archmage of the Mage Academy, they both needed to be physically present in the city for their respective jobs. Indeed, Surrels and Fralia had only been in Mysteria to discuss the war with Anija and the other members of the council.

The second reason, of course, was to help Hal and

Keershan find the Relic Crafter. Granted, Surrels had been saddled with that duty. Due to the secretive nature of this mission, the four of them had decided that only Hal and Surrels should be actively searching the city for the rogue Crafter. This was because Keershan, although smaller than most dragons, was still too big to walk through the capital without clogging traffic or drawing attention to themselves. It was easier for two human beings to blend in with the crowds than it was for a dragon, in other words.

As for why the mission needed to be secret, that was dead simple: Surrels knew that the Glaci Empire had spies in Malarsan. He did not know who these spies were, exactly, or where they were, but his own military spies had reported that the Glaci Empire had sent spies into Malarsan in preparation for the war. Hal did not want Kryo Kardia to know about Soul Slayer, so Surrels and Hal had to keep this mission under wraps until the duel.

In fact, that was why Hal had asked Surrels to join him. Surrels's past experience as a Black Soldier meant that he was used to covert missions and had a lot of experience successfully pulling them off. He still couldn't quite remember everything he had done as a Black Soldier, but many of his memories had returned over the last month, so he knew what to do.

It was, however, depressing. Surrels was starting to think that he'd never leave his past as a Black Soldier behind. Between being tricked by Tenka into killing Old Snow and now sneaking around looking for this rogue Relic Crafter, Surrels wondered if he would ever get a chance to slow down and spend time with his children and their families.

I am getting too old for this crap, Surrels thought. *Hal might not be bored of it yet, but I sure am.*

Unfortunately, the war with the Glaci Empire meant that Surrels couldn't put aside his duties just yet. Even if all he wanted to do was retire and live in the countryside outside of the capital with his family, he couldn't do that until at least the war with the Glaci Empire was dealt with.

Which might be in as little as a week and a half at this point, Surrels thought.

At least Surrels *was* able to walk the streets of the capital without fear of being arrested. When Regent Akei took power and learned the truth about Tenka's role in Old Snow's unfortunate death, Akei had sent messengers to the entire kingdom declaring Surrels innocent of his crimes and restoring him to his old position as the general of the Malarsan Army. Thus, Surrels was no longer a criminal in the eyes of the law.

That did not make Surrels feel any better about his future, however. He found himself wondering how Kendo, his son, and Lila, his daughter, were doing. Lila was due to give birth to his first grandson very soon, but Surrels knew he would not be there to see it happen.

And Hal hasn't even bothered to ask me about it, Surrels thought, scowling softly as he and Hal turned another corner. *Perhaps he doesn't care.*

Without warning, Hal came to a stop in front of an alleyway and said, "The sphere. It's vibrating."

Surrels also stopped as Hal pulled the sphere out of his pocket. The sphere was, indeed, vibrating softly in Hal's hand, making little to no noise.

"Does that mean we are close?" asked Surrels.

Hal nodded, looking around the street in which they stood. "We should be. Unfortunately, the sphere doesn't exactly say where we should go. But it seems to be vibrating in front of this alleyway."

Surrels peered down the alley. It looked like most of the alleyways in the capital: Full of garbage tossed there by the residents living in the surrounding buildings and by people walking past the alley. It smelled like it, too. Surrels spotted a single rat sitting atop a pile of trash before it dove out of sight, presumably due to seeing them.

Wrinkling his nose, Surrels said, "Are you absolutely sure this is the right place, Hal?"

Hal turned toward the alley and the sphere vibrated even harder. "The sphere seems to be."

Hal walked into the alley, and Surrels reluctantly followed. Although he did not see any human beings in the alley, Surrels just didn't like walking into the trash. The stench of rotten food reminded him far too much of the sewers beneath the city.

Hal, however, seemed patently unbothered by the stench. He just held his sphere out, pointing it this way and that, perhaps trying to hone in on whatever the sphere was pointing him toward. The sphere, to its credit, kept vibrating harder and harder the deeper into the alley they went.

"We're getting closer," Hal said excitedly as they walked. "I bet we'll find the Relic Crafter soon."

Stepping over an overturned trash can, Surrels said, in a dry voice, "I hope so. This trash reeks."

Hal suddenly came to a stop in the middle of the alley and turned toward a particularly large pile of garbage. Holding the sphere toward the pile of garbage, Hal said, "I think this is it."

Stopping beside Hal, Surrels looked at the garbage

skeptically. "Hal, you *do* realize that this is garbage, right? Unless the Relic Crafter we are looking for is made out of literal garbage, I am not sure this is the spot."

Hal shook his head again. "Not the garbage. But what's *behind* the garbage."

Hal held up a hand, and a blast of divine light shot out and smashed through the garbage pile, instantly vaporizing it.

And revealing a hidden wooden hatch at the base of the building, like an entrance to a wine cellar.

"A hidden hatch?" Surrels said uncertainly. He looked at Hal. "Do you think that is where the Relic Crafter is?"

Hal nodded. "Must be. Come on. Let's go find our rogue."

Chapter Twenty-Six

THE WOODEN HATCH OPENED WITH A VERY LOUD screeching sound that made Surrels wince as Hal opened it. "Guess this Relic Crafter guy must not be very good about keeping the hinges of his front door oiled."

Hal, stepping back from the open hatch, cocked his head to the side. "I think it's possible that this hatch hasn't been opened in a while. Just look at the steps."

The open hatch revealed a stone staircase that disappeared into the darkness. There were no light sources from what Surrels could see, but Hal drew his sword and illuminated it, allowing them to see further into the cellar. Giving Surrels one final look, Hal said, "What are we waiting for? Let's go."

Hal went down the steps into the cellar, and Surrels followed. He made sure to close the door on their way in, however, not because he wanted to be trapped down here, but because he didn't want anyone following them. Surrels did not think that any Glacian spies had been following them, but just to be sure, he wanted to keep the door closed. That way, if someone did try to follow in after them, they would hear the hinges creak and they would not be taken by surprise.

As soon as Surrels closed the hatch, the staircase fell into pitch-black darkness. Or would have, if not for Hal's shining sword, which gave them more than enough light by which to see.

This allowed Surrels to see that the staircase went down deeper than expected. It also turned a corner up ahead, making it impossible to tell what might be awaiting them below. The air was musty and stale and the stairs themselves were dusty and cracked, which did nothing to soothe Surrels's nerves.

Yet Hal showed no fear or discomfort as he walked down the stairs. Surrels followed closely behind him, hand on the hilt of his sword. He did not want to be taken by surprise in case their rogue Relic Crafter friend did not want any guests.

"So this Relic Crafter," Surrels said as they walked down the stairs. "What do we know about him?"

"Not much," Hal said with a shake of his head, his voice echoing slightly in the enclosed space. "Even Lom was surprised to learn that there was another Relic Crafter in Malarsan. He is probably rogue, which means he violated the Relic Crafter oath, but other than that, I know as much about him as you do."

"So how do we even know he will be able to craft this Soul Slayer sword you keep talking about?" Surrels asked. "What if he can't?"

"All Relic Crafters can make the Soul Slayer," Hal said confidently. "At least, that is what Lom told me. And seeing as Lom has no reason to lie to me, I see no reason not to believe him."

"I see," Surrels said. He pursed his lips. "If this Relic Crafter really is a rogue, like you said, then how do we know he will want to work with or help us?"

"We don't," Hal said. "But I can be pretty persuasive when I need to be. I will make him an offer he can't refuse."

Surrels shook his head. "Whatever you offer him, please make it quick. This place gives me the creeps."

"It will be fine," Hal said. "We will—whoa!"

Hal's foot stepped off the last step, and he nearly fell. But Surrels caught him at the last moment and pulled him back.

Looking at Hal in alarm, Surrels said, "What was that? Did you trip over something?"

Hal, panting slightly, looked down at the stairs under their feet. "No. There's a missing step here."

Hal was right. The next step was missing. In fact, now that Surrels was looking, many of the steps ahead of them were missing, leaving large gaps between the remaining stairs.

"That's odd," Surrels said. "Where did all of the steps go? Stolen, perhaps?"

Hal scratched the back of his head. "Who would steal steps? That doesn't make a lot of sense. They probably got broken off from age or overuse or something like that."

Surrels licked his lips and gazed at the steps again. "Then we will just have to watch our steps so we don't trip and fall again."

Hal smiled. "Actually, I've got a better idea. Hang on."

Hal grabbed Surrels's shirt collar and suddenly launched forward. The two flew through the air, heading down the stairs at a shocking speed, causing Surrels to cry out until they reached a landing at the bottom of the steps.

As soon as they landed, Hal let go of Surrels, who immediately staggered to the side and leaned against the nearest wall, panting and sweating.

"What was that?" Surrels said, looking at Hal in disbelief.

Hal, patting dirt off his pants, flashed Surrels a playful grin. "Short flight. It's a new ability I got from the gods. It lets me fly for short distances at a pitch. Figured it would be faster and safer than walking down those terrible steps."

Surrels shook his head. "My stomach disagrees."

Hal cocked his head to the side. "You mean you can handle flying through the air at high speed on the back of a dragon, but a short hop down the stairs makes you sick?"

Surrels scowled at Hal, rubbing his stomach. "Because you didn't warn me what you were going to do. And I'm not as young as I used to be."

Hal shrugged. "Fair enough. Next time, I'll warn you. Anyway, let's go see what's behind *this* door."

Hal pointed at another door in front of them, this one made of metal and stone. It did not appear to be locked as far as Surrels could tell, although something about it still made him feel uneasy just looking at it.

"I bet the Relic Crafter we're looking for is behind that door," Hal said. He held up his glowing sword. "I'll go in first."

Hal grabbed the door handle and pushed the door open. It opened with even louder creaking sounds than the wooden hatch, but Hal did not hesitate to step inside. Not wanting to be left alone in the darkness, Surrels followed him inside as quickly as he could.

And was surprised by what he saw.

The illumination from Hal's glowing sword revealed a large underground chamber that Surrels had certainly never seen before, much less knew existed. Shelves after shelves filled the chamber, each shelf covered in boxes and crates full of objects that Surrels could not quite make out. Even so, Hal's sword was not quite bright enough to show the whole room, which spoke to how big it actually was.

"What is this place?" Surrels said, looking around the chamber in awe.

"Must be the Relic Crafter's workshop," Hal said. "Reminds me of Lom's old workshop back in the Northern Circle, only much bigger."

"Well, I still don't see another Relic Crafter anywhere," Surrels said. "Are you sure that this is the place?"

Hal pulled the sphere out of his pocket again and held it up. "It's not vibrating anymore, but Lom told me that it would stop vibrating once we found the Crafter we are tracking."

Surrels huffed. "Maybe it's broken, because—"

Surrels was interrupted by a roaring fire nearby. A massive furnace suddenly roared into existence to their left, casting a bright orange hue over them both. The furnace illuminated the room even more, huge columns of fire erupting inside it.

"What the—?" Surrels said with a start, looking at the furnace in shock. "A furnace—? Where did that come from?"

Hal quickly took up a battle position, his eyes darting around. "Most Relic Crafter workshops have furnaces, so not surprising. If this one is already active, however, then that means that our rogue is definitely here. We just need to find him."

Hal then looked toward the room as a whole and shouted, "Crafter! Show yourself!"

There was no response other than the crackling and roaring of the flames nearby, making Surrels feel uneasy. He reached for his own sword but never got a chance to draw it because he heard a soft *click* nearby.

Then, without warning, all of the boxes and crates on the shelves before them shuddered. They vibrated hard, shaking harder and harder, until spider-like legs erupted from beneath them, breaking through their cardboard and wooden exteriors. Their legs lifted up the boxes, which then jumped down from whatever shelf they were on to land on the floor. The *thunk, thunk, thunk* of hundreds of boxes and packages hitting the floor at once made Surrels cringe, even with the roaring flames behind them.

In less than a minute, hundreds of boxes and crates of various sizes—each one supported by four spidery mechanical legs—surrounded Surrels and Hal on all sides. Surrels immediately drew his sword as he and Hal went back to back, keeping a careful eye on the odd creatures, which had yet to start attacking them.

"What in the gods' names are these things supposed to be?" Surrels said. "Monsters?"

One of the boxes—about the size of a watermelon—suddenly leaped toward Surrels, who batted it out of the air with his sword.

Or tried to. The box actually wrapped its spider-like legs around the blade of his sword and clung to it tightly, throwing Surrels off balance. He nearly fell to the floor himself before Hal caught the back of his shirt and jerked him back.

Unfortunately, the sudden jerking, combined with the extra weight of the box spider clinging to his blade, made Surrels drop his sword. As soon as his sword hit the ground, a dozen other similar box spiders surged forward and dragged his weapon away, the clicking of their feet mixing with the screeching sound of Surrels's sword as it was dragged across the stone floor.

"My sword!" Surrels cried out in alarm, reaching toward the box spiders.

Hal, however, pulled him back again, saying, "Don't! I don't know what these things are, but they are dangerous."

"Dangerous is putting it very lightly, young man," said a deep, slightly muffled voice from between a nearby set of shelves. "Like their creator, they love to take things apart and put them back together again. Especially living beings."

"Are you the rogue Relic Crafter?" Hal called out, his voice strong and confident despite how outnumbered they were.

The deep voice chuckled. "Rogue? You must know some of my brothers and sisters if you insist on using *that* outdated terminology to me. I consider myself a progressive, unrestricted by our silly old traditions that have no place in the post-Fall world."

Surrels bit his lower lip. Although he knew Hal would protect him, he could not help but feel very vulnerable without his sword. All he had left now was his backup knife, which he doubted would be enough to protect them should the box spiders attack again. "Mr. Rogue Relic Crafter, we need your help."

"Need my help?" said the rogue Relic Crafter. "Is that why you sneaked into my workshop, armed with weapons, and bypassed all of my security measures? You seem more like assassins to me. And I hate assassins."

The flames from the furnace burned hotter than ever, making Surrels's forehead break out into a cold sweat. Hal, oddly, seemed entirely unaffected by the heat. He simply lowered his glowing sword to his side. "We did not come here to kill you. We are not assassins. Like Surrels said, we came here because we need your help."

The Relic Crafter laughed. "You must have mistaken me for someone who cares about your silly little problems. Let me guess, you want a weapon or tool of some sort to help you resolve some dumb human problem, yes?"

"Basically," Hal said, "although our problem is neither silly nor dumb. It is of utmost importance. And it will affect you, too, if you don't help us solve it, er—?"

"You wish to know my name?" said the Relic Crafter. "Very well. I might as well show myself. It will be the last thing either of you are likely to see."

The Relic Crafter stepped out from the shadows, allowing Surrels to see him for the first time.

This Relic Crafter bore only a vague resemblance to Lom. Whereas Lom was thin, this Relic Crafter was bulky, each one of his four arms bulging with muscles. He wore thick iron armor that was scarred and pitted from use, stained with soot. Each arm ended in a large steel mallet, gripped tightly by his four arms.

His face was covered by a metal mask that left his mouth and eyes visible but hid the rest of it. Even so, Surrels noticed scars trailing from the corners of his mouth up into his mask, implying that the rogue's face was probably not pretty to look at.

"I am Vexo," said the rogue Relic Crafter. "And I am the only Relic Crafter in the world willing to make weapons for anyone who can afford my prices."

Chapter Twenty-Seven

"Vexo, eh?" Surrels said. "Odd name."

"It's an ancient Relic Crafter name that means 'hammer,'" said Vexo. He gripped his hammers tighter. "Each Relic Crafter is named after our preferred crafting tool. I prefer hammers, hence why I am named that."

That made Surrels wonder what Lom's name meant in the Relic Crafter language. He didn't know Lom well enough to guess at what his preferred crafting tool was, although he recalled seeing Lom use hammers a lot in his work, too.

Then Vexo's eyes darted to Hal. "A Dragon Rider. Haven't seen one of those in a while. I guess the rumors of the rebirth of the Dragon Riders are true."

Hal cocked his head to the side. "How did you know I was a Dragon Rider just by looking at me?"

Vexo gestured with one of his hammers at Hal's head. "You are clearly wearing the Final Relic, which I assume you used to kill the Nameless One again. Correct?"

Hal raised an eyebrow. "You seem to know a lot about the outside world."

"Of course," said Vexo with a snort. "Unlike my brethren, I travel the world. I've been as far north as the Abode of the Gods and as far south as the Dark Pit. My journeys have taken me to the Sky Kingdom, to the depths of the ocean, and even into the jungles of Tipjok. My current base of operations is this city, although you got lucky because I was just about to leave."

"Leave?" Surrels said. "Why?"

Vexo gave Surrels a deadpan look. "I am not interested in getting caught up in your hopeless war against the Glaci Empire. I know enough about your kingdom's pitiful army to know that the Glaci Empire will crush it as easily as a young child crushes an ant under his shoe and with as much enjoyment."

Surrels scowled. "I am the general of the Malarsan Army, Vexo. Might want to watch what you say."

"Then that explains why the Malarsan Army is so weak," said Vexo. "Now, when that woman was in charge, Queen Marial, I believe her name was, she was a true leader. She invested heavily in the Malarsan Army, creating new weapons and finding new ways to use old weapons. War magic as a discipline wouldn't even exist without her. She was a smart woman, let me tell you."

"And she also was in cahoots with the Nameless One," Hal pointed out. "You know, the evil god who wanted to destroy the world?"

Vexo shrugged. "No one's perfect. But wouldn't it be nice to have had those demons on your side now? They could have been useful allies against the Glaci Empire. Funny how hindsight makes everything clearer, doesn't it?"

"You are definitely a strange Relic Crafter," Surrels said. "Not like Lom at all."

"Lom told you where to find me?" Vexo said. "I haven't seen that coward in ages. I am surprised he referred you to me, although that does explain how a couple of humans like you found me."

"Lom told us you could help us with our problems," Hal said. "That you could build a weapon for us."

"I undoubtedly could," said Vexo, "but whether I will is another question entirely. Unlike my fellow Crafters, I don't build anything for free. My only limit is what I charge for my work."

"Why?" Surrels said. "I thought you Relic Crafters built things because you loved building things. And I also thought that your people had stopped building weapons because of how the relics were used."

Vexo laughed. It was a long, loud, sarcastic sound that echoed throughout the workshop. The sound sent shivers down Surrels's spine, although Hal did not seem terribly disturbed by it.

"The Relic Crafter oath is from a bygone era when something like that might have made sense," Vexo said, his laughter dying down to a mere chuckle. "We signed it because we foolishly believed that limiting our creativity and output would, in some ways, make the world a more peaceful place. How wrong we were. Wars continued to rage in our absence, even if our weapons were no longer at their center."

"So you lost faith in your own ideals, then," Hal said.

Vexo sneered at them. "That would imply I ever believed in them in the first place. I never considered the oath permanent, even if many of my peers did. It was my liberal interpretation of the oath that got me in trouble with my fellow Crafters and is why I must keep on the move constantly. Frankly, I am surprised you found me."

Surrels noticed Vexo reach up and touch one of the scars on his face when he said that. Surrels wondered if the scars had come from whatever his fellow Relic Crafters had done to him when he had broken the oath.

Hal tapped the floor with his foot. "What do you do now? Sell your services to the highest bidder?"

"More or less," said Vexo. "In my defense, I don't advertise my services. I merely build up a reputation in the black market over time and allow potential clients to reach out to me first. I've made a lot of money that way, enough to live comfortably for the rest of my life."

"But you still keep building things," Surrels said. "Even though you are obviously well enough off."

Vexo's right eye twitched. "You were not wrong when you said that my people love to build things, although it is more like a compulsion. We *must* be working on or creating something at all times, even if we are not being paid to do so. We get very strange if we go too long without building anything. It's an annoying compulsion much of the time, but I've found ways to channel it productively, as you can tell."

Vexo's comment about them getting very strange when they go too long without making things caused Surrels to think about Lom. The Relic Crafter had seemed like an anxious wreck when he first arrived in Malarsan, but over the last couple of months, Lom had calmed down quite a bit. Surrels understood that Lom had been a prisoner of the Snow Witches for a long time prior to arriving in

Malarsan, which meant he had probably not been allowed to make anything during that time.

Fascinating, the things you learn about from talking to other people, Surrels thought.

"We want you to build us a weapon," Hal said. "One powerful enough to defeat Kryo Kardia."

Vexo tilted his head to one side. "And what sort of weapon would that be? A cannon big enough to blow him into pieces? I could easily construct such a thing, but it would not be very practical to—"

"No," Hal said with a shake of his head. He met Vexo's gaze. "We want the legendary Soul Slayer. And we think you can make it."

Vexo stared in silence at Surrels and Hal for a long time, making Surrels feel rather nervous. It didn't help that Vexo's expression was difficult to read, having become as blank as a piece of paper.

Finally, Vexo laughed. "You want *me* to build *you* the infamous Soul Slayer, the only weapon that we Relic Crafters have ever made that even we think is pure evil? My, you must be either very shortsighted, very greedy, or both."

"I know exactly what I am asking for, Vexo," Hal said. "The Soul Slayer is necessary if we are going to stop Kryo Kardia once and for all. It is the only way to ensure that he will not come back."

Vexo put his hammers in the loops of his belt and folded his upper two arms in front of his chest while his lower two arms fixed themselves on his hips. "And why should I care? I am already planning to be out of here by the time the Glaci Empire invades. I have no dog in this fight."

"Kryo Kardia isn't going to stop with Malarsan, and you know it," Surrels said. "That man is going to take over the entire world if he can manage it. Soon, there won't be anywhere safe for you to hide. Or anywhere safe for anyone to hide, for that matter."

Vexo shrugged. "No empire lasts forever. In my time, I've seen empires rise and fall, kingdoms flourish and despair. But I might be willing to make the Soul Slayer for you for the right price."

Hal raised an eyebrow. "So you have no moral qualms with reconstructing an evil weapon?"

"Because good and evil are such subjective terms, obviously," said Vexo. "And besides, I've always wanted to try my hand at rebuilding such a powerful weapon. In my opinion, the Soul Slayer was a masterpiece of Relic Crafter design, surpassing even the Final Relic in sheer power, beauty, and usage."

"Yet you haven't," Hal said. "Perhaps you are more hesitant about crafting it than you appear."

Vexo pursed his lips, which was the first time so far that Surrels had seen any hesitation or worry in Vexo's appearance. "It would be the most complicated weapon I've ever built, the culmination of my life's work. I do not fear it. I fear that I will not make it as good as I can."

"I'm sure you will be able to," Hal said. "So name your price. How much do you want us to pay in exchange for the Soul Slayer? And can you make it in a week and a half?"

Vexo tapped his chin thoughtfully. "It's not that simple, Rider. Not only are you asking me to build a legendary weapon that has not existed in eons, but you are asking me to build it faster than I have built anything else before, which will inevitably impact my travel plans and potentially put my life at risk should the Glaci Empire decide to invade Malarsan before I finish the weapon."

"They won't," Hal said. "I can promise you that."

"Even so, it's a big ask," said Vexo. His eyes darted to the helmet on Hal's head. "I doubt there is enough money in the kingdom's treasury to pay for Soul Slayer. Instead, I will ask for the Final Relic."

Hal immediately put a hand on his helmet while Surrels said, "The Final Relic? You can't be serious."

"But I am," said Vexo. "The relics were some of our finest creations. And the Final Relic was the finest of them all, even if it is lacking in the sheer power that the Soul Slayer had. One of the reasons I came to Malarsan in the first place, after all, is because I heard rumors of the Final Relic being here. It would be fun to study and take apart so I can replicate its design to sell to others down the line."

Hal scowled. "The Final Relic is not a weapon for you to sell. It is a tool I have used to defend Malarsan from evils such as the Nameless One."

"Be that as it may, it's still the only object I would even consider taking as payment for constructing the Soul Slayer, especially on such short notice," said Vexo. "But if you refuse my generous offer, then I am afraid I will have to ask you to leave my workshop and never, ever return."

Hal stepped forward. "We can't do that. We need the Soul Slayer. And we need it as soon as possible."

Vexo rolled his eyes. "If you can't pay me for it, then I can't make it for you. But if you really insist on rudely staying on my personal property, then I guess I will have to get rid of you myself."

A mechanical hand suddenly lowered from the ceiling and grabbed Hal around the waist. Before either Hal or

Surrels could react, the mechanical hand lifted Hal up and threw him directly into the open furnace. Hal yelled as he disappeared inside the burning flames, his screams quickly being overwhelmed by the roaring of the burning furnace.

"Hal!" Surrels said in alarm. "No!"

"Unfortunately, the Final Relic does not provide constant protection against fire, so your friend is probably dead," said Vexo. "Don't worry. You will soon join him in the next life."

The *click, click* of spider legs reminded Surrels of the box spiders. The mechanical constructs had resumed moving in on Surrels, who drew his backup knife from his belt and waved it threateningly at the box spiders. "Don't any of you get any closer or I'll—"

"Or you will what, human?" said Vexo. "Open them with your knife? My box spiders are not strong individually, but should be more than capable of overwhelming you."

Surrels bit his lower lip. He knew that Vexo was right. Surrels would not be able to fight off hundreds of box spiders on his own, even if he had the proper weapons to do so. Maybe if Hal was still alive, Surrels would have stood a chance.

As it was, however, Surrels knew that his time had come.

That was, until the furnace made odd groaning noises, causing Surrels to look over his shoulder. The box spiders had come to a stop as well while even Vexo gazed up at the furnace in confusion.

"What is that noise?" Surrels said. He glanced at Vexo. "Something wrong with your furnace?"

Vexo narrowed his eyes. "Impossible. I just recently finished repairs on it. It should not be—"

Boom.

A shining light smashed through the front of the furnace, sending chunks of burning metal flying everywhere. As the light flew, beams of light shot out of it, striking the box spiders surrounding Surrels and either destroying them outright or making them explode. Surrels himself was crouching on the ground, hands over his head, although none of the light beams came even close to hitting him.

Vexo stared in astonishment as his box spiders got zapped one by one. "What the—? What is going on—?"

The shining light flashed down toward Vexo, landing right in front of him. A moment later, the light faded, revealing a very much still alive Hal, the tip of his sword pointed at Vexo's throat.

Hal looked pretty good for someone who had just been thrown into a furnace. His armor and clothing were completely untouched while his body radiated pure unadulterated power and energy unlike anything Surrels had felt before.

And Hal, to put it lightly, did not look very pleased.

"I asked nicely before," Hal said, his voice hard. "Now, I am done asking nicely. Kneel."

Vexo suddenly fell to his knees before Hal, who lowered his sword to his side. Hal gazed down at Vexo with contempt while Vexo stared up at Hal with his mouth open in shock.

Surrels couldn't believe what he was seeing. Not only had Hal somehow escaped the furnace unscathed—which Surrels doubted even a Dragon Rider could do—he had also somehow forced Vexo to kneel with one word. Just what had happened to Hal to change him so much?

The answer to Surrels's unspoken question came from an unlikely source: Vexo, who, staring up at Hal, said, "Ahhh, I see. You drank the elixir, didn't you?"

Hal tensed. "I drank no such thing."

Vexo chuckled. "No, you clearly did. It explains much about you that puzzled me, particularly how you survived being thrown into a burning furnace that should have vaporized you under any other circumstance. You really are no ordinary human, and not just because you are a Dragon Rider wearing the Final Relic, either."

"Hal, what does Vexo mean?" Surrels asked, rising to his feet now that it was safe to do so, the smell of burning wood and metal from the destroyed box spiders filling his nostrils. "What is elixir?"

Vexo's eyes darted back up to Hal. "You mean you haven't even told your friend yet? Well, it's not my place to do so. But it does explain many things."

Hal had his back to Surrels, so Surrels could not see what Hal's expression looked like. He could guess, however, that Hal was not happy, based on his body language.

"I want you to build Soul Slayer for me," Hal said. "And do it without pay."

"Without pay?" Vexo repeated. "Isn't that slavery?"

Hal leaned toward Vexo and said, in a cold voice, "Your payment is your life."

Vexo paused. "I suppose that is a good form of payment. Very well. I will build the Soul Slayer for you, free of charge."

Hal stood up. "Thank you. I expect it to be ready in a week and a half."

Vexo nodded. "I can have it done in a week. Don't underestimate me."

Hal nodded in return and turned away from Vexo. Walking away from Vexo, Hal said, "Come on, Surrels. We've done what we need to do here. Let's go back to the others and report back on the success of our mission."

Surrels followed Hal without hesitation, although he did look back over his shoulder at Vexo. The rogue Crafter had risen back to his feet and was sweeping up the remains of his destroyed box spiders. He did not look particularly happy.

But Surrels was not worried too much about Vexo's happiness.

He was mostly worried because Hal, in his view, had been acting almost exactly like Kryo Kardia back there, using his power to force others to do his bidding against their will.

I just hope that there's still some of the old Hal I know in there somewhere, Surrels thought, turning his attention back to Hal's back. *Otherwise, I am not at all sure that killing Kryo Kardia will solve all of our problems.*

Chapter Twenty-Eight

"IS IT ME OR DOES HAL SEEM TO HAVE BEEN ACTING strange lately?"

Surrels kneeled in the dirt in his garden. Ten days had passed, but they had been hard days. He wiped the sweat from his brow and looked over at Anija. The female Dragon Rider stood just outside the short wooden fence he had set up around his small garden, her arms folded in front of her chest, a frown on her youthful features.

"What do you mean?" Surrels said, wiping his dirty palms on his pants. "Are you referring to the eternal glow that seems to follow him and Keershan everywhere they go? Because I am almost certain at this point that they are deliberately doing it to make themselves look cooler."

Anija shook her head. "The glow doesn't bother me. It's how Hal and Keershan act. They act like they're better than us."

Surrels pursed his lips and glanced at the glowing soft flower at his knees. "They do seem a bit snippier than usual, but they are under a lot of stress. After all, they're going to decide the fate of the entire country today, assuming Kryo Kardia shows."

Anija raised an eyebrow. "You make it sound like you don't think he will."

Surrels shrugged as he rose to his feet, picking up his pail and digging tool as he did so. "All I'm saying is that Kryo Kardia really has no reason to agree to this. The Glaci Empire could easily crush Malarsan in a day, if that. I still expect him to not show up or maybe give his men orders to initiate the invasion if he should lose."

Anija, recalling how smug Kryo Kardia had looked when he had agreed to the trial by combat, shook her head again. "I wouldn't be so sure about that. Kryo Kardia is a lot of things, but a liar, I think he is not."

Surrels cocked his head to the side as he walked over to a flower bush on the other side of the paddock. Kneeling in front of the glowing white flowers, Surrels took his watering can out of his pail and began pouring water on the flowers' roots. "I don't know what makes you think Kryo Kardia is above lying. His whole shtick is being deceptive and under-handed. Even if he does show up, expect him to do something to try to throw Hal and Keershan off their game."

Anija huffed. "Probably, but that's different from refusing to show up. Either way, Hal and Keershan will be in for the fight of their lives. Let's get back to talking about them."

Surrels looked up from his gardening at her, annoyance on his face. "Why? If you have a problem with their atti-tudes, why not go and tell them yourself?"

Anija hesitated. "I think you know why."

Surrels sighed. "Okay, I do. They are definitely not as easygoing as they used to be. If you'd seen how Hal treated that Vexo guy in the capital. Well, let's just say he reminded me a bit too much of Kryo Kardia at that point."

Anija nodded. "See? That's what I am worried about. I am worried that Hal and Keershan might have gotten too much power for them to deal with. It's going to their heads."

"Are you worried that they might abuse their power?" Surrels said. "Which is an understandable worry, seeing as power has a tendency to corrupt, although I don't think they've crossed that line yet."

"They are treading dangerously close to it, though," Anija said. "Plus, I still think they are hiding something from us about their time in the abode and how they got their power."

Surrels nodded. "Agreed. Anytime I or anyone else has asked them for details, they've been pretty vague. Hal even told me that mortals are apparently not allowed to tell other mortals about what they saw in the abode, as apparently the gods don't like that."

Anija snorted. "I'm sure the gods care about that, and it has nothing to do with Hal and Keershan deciding to keep secrets from us."

Surrels put the water pail down and bent down closer, clearly examining the white flowers for any defects. "Agreed, but unfortunately, there's not much we can do about it, I'm afraid. We'll just have to wait for Hal and Keershan to be ready to tell us in their own time."

Anija narrowed her eyes. "I suppose you have a point. Anyway, choosing to garden on the day of the trial itself seems like an odd decision to me."

Surrels glanced up at Anija before returning his attention to his flowers. "It's not for fun. I told Hal and Keershan I wanted to give them a Life Flower before they entered the ring with Kryo Kardia. That way, they will be able to heal themselves and hopefully survive, even if they lose."

Anija rolled her eyes but said nothing to that, mostly because Surrels's plan wasn't entirely bad.

The Life Flower was a legendary, almost mythical, flower that could heal all injuries, cure all illnesses, and supposedly even bring the dead back to life. Anija had yet to see any hard proof of that last one, but both she and Surrels had benefited from the healing properties of the Life Flower before, so she knew it was the real deal.

Normally, the Life Flower was a once-in-a-lifetime event. But somehow, Surrels had managed to grow a small but productive garden inside a cave well outside the boundaries of Mysteria, a cave illuminated by magical artificial light. Due to how rare and difficult to find Life Flowers were, Surrels had chosen this spot so that, even if Mysteria was destroyed, the Life Flower would continue to bloom.

Or so Surrels had told Anija. Personally, Anija believed Surrels chose this place because it gave him privacy from the rest of the world.

Probably why he isn't super eager to talk to me, Anija thought. *I'm invading his space, although honestly, I need someone to talk to other than Rialo about this, and Surrels is the only other person I feel would understand my concerns.*

"I see," Anija said. "I guess that makes sense, although I feel like Kryo Kardia isn't going to give Hal or Keershan time to use the Life Flower."

"I'm sure they will find time to use it," Surrels said. He frowned deeply. "The trouble is that I need to figure out which one is ready to be picked. Life Flowers can only be used for healing at specific points in their development. Pick them too early and they do nothing. Pick them too late and their healing properties are significantly weaker. You have to pick them when they are just right."

"And do any of them look 'just right' to you?" asked Anija.

Surrels hesitated before suddenly reaching down and cutting a flower from its stem. Holding up the glowing white flower, Surrels said, "This one definitely does. You can tell their readiness by how brightly they shine. The brighter they shine, the more ready they are for being used."

Anija raised an eyebrow. "Huh. How did you figure that out?"

Surrels stood up, carefully depositing the plucked Life Flower into a small leather bag hanging from his side. "Trial and error, mostly. Life Flowers aren't the most intuitive plants to grow, to put it lightly."

Anija shook her head again. "Honestly, I am amazed you could figure out how to grow them at all. That gardening skill of yours is something else."

Surrels's smile faded slightly and his gaze became somewhat distant. "It was my wife, Tonya. She was a great gardener. Taught me everything she knew so we could garden together. She'd even joke that I was better than her, although in my opinion, Tonya was much better than I ever would be. She'd probably grow twice as many Life Flowers as I have in half the time."

Anija scratched her chin. "Your wife sounds like a hell of a woman. I'd have loved to have met her."

Surrels sighed. "Yes, she certainly was. Now I need to take this Life Flower to Hal and Keershan, so why don't we go back to town? We should have time before Kryo Kardia shows up."

Anija nodded once more. She turned to leave the cave, only to hear Rialo's voice in her head say, *Anija! Are you there?*

Pausing in her step, Anija replied, *Yes, Rialo, I am here. What's up?*

Kryo Kardia's personal war balloon, the Frozen Heart, *has been spotted by the border guards,* Rialo said. *That means that Kryo Kardia will be here any second.*

Anija felt anxiety rise within her when Rialo said that. She took a deep breath, however, and said, *Surrels and I will be at the border as quickly as possible. See you later.*

Okay, Rialo said. *But you don't have to come if you don't want—*

No, I want *to be there,* Anija said firmly. *I definitely do not want to miss this, not for anything.*

All right, Rialo said. *The Clawfoot Clan and I will be there as well. See you soon.*

"What's the matter?" Surrels said as Rialo's voice faded from Anija's mind. "You look like you just saw a ghost."

Anija looked over her shoulder at Surrels, giving him a strong look. "Kryo Kardia is here."

Surrels's eyes widened in surprise for a moment before a calm and collected expression replaced his surprise. "Then I guess we need to get going, eh?"

Anija did not reply. She simply walked out of the cave with Surrels right behind her, doing her best not to let her fear and anxiety overwhelm her.

And it had nothing whatsoever to do with whether Hal

and Keershan would win or lose or even what the ultimate fate of the kingdom would be.

It was personal.

Far, far more personal.

Because Anija was about to come face to face with the man who might very well be her real father.

Chapter Twenty-Nine

NORMALLY, THE BORDER BETWEEN MALARSAN AND HOSAR was unremarkable. Thickly wooded, a single dirt road ran from the base of the Desolate Tops through the forest, eventually connecting to Hosar's major highway. The forest, mostly on the Malarsan side of the border, had suffered a lot of damage since the start of the war, but it was still respectably thick with towering oaks, crystal clear streams, and an abundance of wild animals that the Dragon Riders' Steeds liked to hunt every now and then for food and fun.

But today, as Anija and Surrels walked down the main road from Mysteria to the base of the Desolate Tops, the border was positively brimming with people and activity on both sides. On the Malarsan side, at least a dozen Dragon Riders and their Steeds stood on the small cliffs overlooking the forest, keeping their eyes on the skies above and the ground below for any trouble. war mages and soldiers from the Army walked among the citizens, clearly trying to keep some semblance of order in a part of the country that was normally empty but today was full of people.

Hundreds of Malarsans loitered around the border, with more than a few stalls and traveling merchants having set up shop to hawk food, drinks, and anything else they could sell the people who had come from all over the kingdom to watch the duel. The smell of fried lamb filled the air, and Anija noticed even a handful of hatchlings standing in line to buy their food. Anija had never seen this many people at the border before, and not all of them were from Mysteria, Giant's Foot, or the surrounding areas, either.

When Hal and Keershan had announced to the town of Mysteria that Kryo Kardia himself would be showing up to duel, that news had spread like wildfire throughout the entire kingdom. Anija even spotted a few fishermen from the southern coast sitting on some rocks nearby, eating their fried lamb or drinking booze and laughing and joking with each other.

But the Malarsan side of the border was nothing compared to the Hosarian side. Hundreds, if not thousands, of people had gathered over there, and most of them did not appear to be Hosarians. From what Anija could tell, it looked like people from all over the Glaci Empire's many provinces had traveled to watch the duel.

Clearly, both the Malarsans and the Glacians were excited about the duel.

"Wow," Anija said as she and Surrels walked past a juggler who was entertaining a group of young children by juggling glowing glass spheres. "I knew we'd been getting some travelers in Mysteria over the last few days, but I didn't realize we'd gotten *this* many people."

Surrels scowled. "I don't like it. People are treating this duel like it's some form of entertainment when it's actually what will determine the future of the whole country."

"And that's what makes it so exciting, Father," said a familiar young voice nearby. "What is more dramatic, more pulse-pounding, more intense than a duel between two of the most powerful men in the world for such high stakes?"

Anija whipped her head to the side to see a young man with a dragon tattoo covering half his face walk up to them, a half-eaten stick of what appeared to be chicken in his right hand and a big grin on his face.

Surrels's jaw dropped. "Kendo? I didn't know you were going to be here. When did you arrive?"

Kendo smirked at Surrels and jerked a thumb over his shoulder. "Yesterday. As for why, that's easy. I am here to watch the duel of the century, naturally. And maybe make a little bit of money while I am at it."

Anija followed Kendo's thumb to a small booth set up where a line of hungry-looking people stood, purchasing the same chicken sticks that Kendo held, along with dragon-shaped jewelry. A man and a woman, who Anija did not recognize, stood behind the booth, serving the customers. Based on how long the line was, Anija guessed that Surrels's son was doing quite well for himself.

"Are you selling food and trinkets to the spectators?" Surrels said. His eyes narrowed. "And how did you get both Lila and Spai in on this? Where is Cha?"

"Cha?" Anija repeated. "Who is that?"

"My nephew," said Kendo casually, "who is currently taking a nap in the tent behind our stall over there. One-year-old children seem to sleep a lot."

Anija nodded and looked at Surrels. "I forgot that you are a grandfather now. That seems kind of weird."

Surrels gave Anija an annoyed look. "What? Do I need to grow a big white beard or something to look like a proper grandfather now?"

"Don't get yourself so riled up, Father," said Kendo. He gestured at the man and woman standing behind the stall servicing the spectators, who Anija assumed were Lila and her husband Spai. "I promised my sister and her husband half of the profits from our little business venture. We've already almost sold out of chicken sticks, so I'm going to have to go make some more so our hungry customers don't go over to the competition. I expect sales to skyrocket once Kryo Kardia himself is actually here."

"We heard he already was," Anija said. She scanned the skies, which were empty. "But I don't see his ship."

"It's still a good ways out, although I expect him to be here any minute," said Kendo. He grinned. "Just think of all of the chicken sticks and dragon jewelry we'll sell. I might be able to retire young."

Surrels smirked. "Good idea. You can then become your older sister's nanny for Cha in exchange for housing, since you obviously don't have a home of your own. I'm sure Lila and Spai will appreciate the help around the house."

Kendo cleared his throat. "I-I mean, if this business takes off, I will obviously have to devote more time to it, maybe open a permanent location in the capital

or something. You know, become gainfully employed and contribute to the kingdom's economy and all that."

Anija frowned. "Is that why you are doing this? Because you aren't with the Dead Dragons anymore?"

Kendo nodded. "Yes. Ever since Father got me out of

prison, I've decided to turn over a new leaf. No longer will I engage in illegal or ethically questionable businesses. I will be a good, law-abiding citizen who makes his profits honestly. And look, I am even employing my own family."

Surrels pursed his lips, but Anija did not see what he was so upset about. Although Anija did not know Kendo nearly as well as Surrels did, she understood that Kendo had been involved in organized criminal activity from a young age. Running an honest business operation seemed like an improvement to Anija, although she noted that he still liked those expensive cigars, if his smoke-scented breath meant anything.

"Well, I am glad that you are not getting into trouble, at least," Surrels said. "And I hope you have a plan for getting Lila, Spai, and Cha out of here in case the duel doesn't go in our favor."

Kendo draped an arm around Surrels's shoulders. "Of course! We will definitely make a quick escape if needed, although personally, I have great faith in our champions. I've heard rumors that they now wield god-like power far superior to anything that Kryo Kardia wields. Is that true?"

Anija glanced around the area but did not see either Hal or Keershan. "Yes. They are almost gods themselves at this point."

Kendo whistled. "Amazing. Although right now, my main concern is figuring out how to sell my wares to the Hosarians over there."

Anija gazed across the border at the huge crowd of Glacians, who were buying things from their own merchants. "You mean you can't just go over there and set up another stall?"

Kendo shook his head. "Unfortunately, no. The Glaci Empire forbids individual foreign merchants such as myself from setting up shop within their borders. I was just talking to a friendly Glacian merchant who came over to see how my stall was doing, actually. He told me that if I wanted to sell my stuff there legally that I'd need to pay fifty percent of my revenue in tariffs to the empire due to being a non-citizen from another country."

Anija looked at Kendo in surprise. "Fifty percent? That's outrageous."

"And the reason why only the bigger foreign merchants have been able to make headway there," said Kendo. He chuckled. "Not since the war started, though. The vast majority of non-Glacian merchants who did business in the empire, especially from Malarsan, got kicked out when Kryo Kardia declared war. But I foresee a time in the not-too-distant future when Glacians and Malarsans will once again be trading with each other peacefully and profitably."

"You do?" Surrels said.

Kendo nodded and waved his half-eaten chicken stick toward the border. "Sure! If Hal wins, then Malarsan will remain an independent country and we will be in a position to negotiate better trade deals with the Glaci Empire. If Kryo Kardia wins, however, Malarsan will be absorbed into the Glaci Empire and then we, as new Glacian citizens, will be able to trade freely with the rest of the empire free of those expensive tariffs. From a business perspective, this duel is a win-win situation for us."

Anija frowned deeply. *So that is why he's so upbeat. No matter who wins, his business opportunities will be more or less the same.*

You humans have a funny way of finding ways to capitalize on dangerous situations, Rialo said in her head suddenly. *We dragons aren't quite that talented.*

Anija looked up in the sky in time to see Rialo and half a dozen other Clawfoot Clan members—the elders who served under Rialo—soar in. They landed on some of the higher peaks, mostly because the ground was too crowded for them to safely land. Anija waved at Rialo, who waved a wing back at her in response.

Only the greedy humans like Kendo, Anija said. *Some of us actually understand what is at stake here. And profits are the least of our concerns.*

Very true, Rialo said. *We will keep an eye out for Kryo Kardia up here. Have you seen or heard from Hal or Keershan yet?*

No, Anija said, feeling a little anxious. *Have you?*

I have not, Rialo said. *Last I heard, they were in the Forgotten Temple, but I did not stop by on my way up here to check on them.*

I'm sure they are just waiting for Kryo Kardia to, you know, actually appear, Anija said. She glanced at the skies again. *Because he still isn't actually here.*

And you are sure you are okay with that? Rialo asked.

Anija bit her lower lip, trying to ignore Surrels and Kendo, who were now apparently discussing private family matters that did not involve her.

Ever since Anija had learned that Kryo Kardia was possibly her real father, Anija had been dreading this day. She did not think that she and Kryo Kardia would interact much, seeing as Hal was Kryo Kardia's main target, but she was worried about how she might react when he finally got here, nonetheless.

On one hand, Anija had always wanted to know, on some level, what her past was and who her parents were. She'd simply ignored those questions for the longest time because she did not think that she would ever find out, aside from what Shadow Mask and some of the older Dark Tigers had told her when she was growing up in the guild.

On the other hand, knowing that Kryo Kardia might be her actual father made her feel physically ill, especially after finding out about his role in the deaths of her parents. She could not imagine living with Kryo Kardia or wanting to get to know him better, like she assumed she would have if she had known her parents.

In fact, Anija wasn't quite sure what that made her. She didn't look like any of the Glacians, lacking their signature blue skin. She'd always assumed she was a Malarsan like Hal and the others, but now she had to deal with her possible heritage: That of Glacian royalty, daughter of one of the evilest men alive. It was even worse than finding out that Shadow Mask was her real dad.

Yet Anija did not feel torn about her allegiance. She wasn't planning to betray Malarsan or her friends. Whatever her connection to Kryo Kardia might be, Anija's real loyalty lay with the kingdom and her friends. She did not care one bit for Kryo Kardia.

That was when Surrels suddenly elbowed her and said, "Look who else has chosen to join us."

Snapped out of her thoughts, Anija looked to see a smartly dressed young boy beside a tall, bearded man in flowing red robes walking among the crowd that had assembled to watch the duel. Half a dozen well-armed soldiers clad in golden armor escorted the man and the boy. The boy was looking around at everything with big eyes while the older man's eyes kept darting around, no doubt watching out for any potential dangers.

Anija blinked. "Is that Prince Stebo and Regent Akei? I didn't know they'd be here."

"Guess I forgot to tell you about that," Surrels said. "Stebo told me he wanted to see the duel. And as it is traditional for the rulers of each country represented in a duel to view it in person, both he and Akei had to show up. Glad that Stebo looks like he's having fun, at least."

Kendo eyed Stebo and Akei and their bodyguards with obvious interest. "The regent *and* the future rightful king of Malarsan are here? I wonder if they remember how I helped save Stebo's life and would like to repay me for that honor."

Surrels put a hand on Kendo's shoulder. "Don't. The elite guardsmen aren't going to let anyone near Stebo, and for good reason. Stebo is still a target for people upset with the current state of the country. Best not to give the guardsmen reason to bash your skull in."

"Yes, but what if Stebo, like most young boys, is hungry and wants a delicious chicken stick to sate his hunger?" said Kendo with a wink. "I could point them to my stall. Especially after they hear how cheap my chicken sticks are. Stebo could buy one for every one of his elite guardsmen and the regent as well. No way he can say no to that."

Anija resisted the urge to roll her eyes at Kendo's pragmatism, but then she heard Rialo say mentally, *He's finally here.*

Looking up into the sky, Anija had no trouble spotting it: The *Frozen Heart*, the flagship of the Glacian Air Navy, hovered through the sky just beyond the Malarsan and Hosarian border. People on both sides of the border stopped whatever they were doing to stare at the incoming war balloon or point and whisper to each other. It was certainly an impressive sight, although Anija did not know where Kryo Kardia planned to land the war balloon, as there were too many trees, especially on the Hosarian side, to land such a large vehicle.

More impressively, the Glacian Dragon Riders flew around the war balloon, acting like an escort. Anija's eyes were drawn to the huge mountain of a man riding on the crimson dragon at the forefront of the war balloon, who she remembered was Prince Compe Kardia, Kryo Kardia's eldest. Compe looked quite regal, especially in his golden armor that reflected the sun overhead brightly.

Although apparently, they were not going to land the *Frozen Heart* at all. What appeared to be a huge anchor dropped from the underside of the *Frozen Heart* and crashed somewhere among the trees on the Hosarian side of the border, sending birds flying up from the trees in shock, squawking and chirping as they did so.

As for the Glacian Dragon Riders, half of them landed on top of the *Frozen Heart* while the other half landed in a wide-open area near the border itself, which Anija realized had likely been set aside for their use. Compe was among the ones who landed, jumping off his Steed as soon as they touched down and marching over to the border.

"Citizens of the kingdom of Malarsan and fellow citizens of the Glaci Empire," Compe said, his voice booming loud enough to be heard by everyone, likely enhanced by the mask he wore over his face. "I am Prince Compe Kardia, firstborn of Emperor Kryo Kardia, and current Captain of the Glacian Dragon Rider Corps. His Majesty, my father, Emperor Kryo Kardia himself, shall be here shortly to begin his duel with your champion."

The Glacians cheered when Compe said that, but a

stern look from the Prince made the Glacians calm down immediately. Evidently, they had jumped the gun.

Turning his gaze back to the Malarsans, Compe said, "But first, where are *your* champions? That is, Captain Halar Norath and his Steed, the dragon known as Keershan?"

Anija bit her lower lip and looked around. She had noticed Hal and Keershan's absence but hadn't worried about it until now.

They didn't run away, did they? Anija said to Rialo.

Rialo shook her head. *No. My little brother, Keershan, is too brave and proud to run away from a fight.*

Then where are they? Anija asked.

As if in answer to her mental question, a brilliant light suddenly shone from the peaks of the nearby Desolate Tops. Shining brighter than the sun, the white light rose from the peaks before suddenly shooting down to the border, causing all of the people on both sides of the border nearest the line to scramble to get out of the way.

Everyone, that was, except for Compe, who watched with folded arms across his chest as the light drew closer and closer.

The light landed on the ground with a soft rumbling noise before dying down, revealing Hal and Keershan standing on the Malarsan side of the border. They stood opposite Compe, who gazed up at them with impassive eyes that reminded Anija of how Kryo Kardia looked whenever he was looking at someone he did not care for.

As for Hal and Keershan, they looked as impressive as always. Their glowing gold-and-white armor gave them a fairly regal look themselves, if not divine. Keershan was even wearing extra armor himself now.

But it was the new sword at Hal's side that really caught Anija's interest. In contrast to the gold-and-white colors of her two friends, the black sheath of the sword stood out darkly. It even filled Anija with a growing sense of dread, despite knowing that it was in the hands of her friends.

The Soul Slayer, Rialo said. *I didn't know that they actually had it.*

Apparently they do, Anija thought. *Hope it's as useful as they seem to think it will be.*

The Malarsans cheered for Hal and Keershan when they appeared, wildly chanting their names over and over again. Yet Hal and Keershan did not seem to be listening to the cheers from the people, as their eyes were fixed on Prince Compe, who stood before them.

"Hello, Prince Compe Kardia," Hal said, his voice also loud enough for everyone to hear clearly. "Keershan and I are here. We are ready to duel with your father."

Compe nodded. "Then let it be—"

"Wait!"

Inquirer Dedeket suddenly burst from the Glacian crowd, coming to a stop right beside Compe. Putting his hands on his knees, Dedeket panted hard. "Oh, I am not as young as I used to be."

"Dedeket?" Compe said, a hint of annoyance in his voice as he turned toward the inquirer. "Why are you interrupting us?"

Straightening himself—although still significantly shorter than either Compe or Hal—Dedeket said, "With all due respect, Your Majesty, we must do things the correct way or otherwise not do them at all! I came up with a brilliant introductory speech for your father that I simply must deliver. It is of utmost importance."

Compe sighed heavily. "Fine. Say what you are going to say. And no. More. Got it?"

Dedeket nodded. "Of course! I understand you perfectly. Now let me find that speech."

Dedeket stepped forward and, after digging through the seemingly endless folds of his robes, pulled out a folded piece of parchment. Unfolding it, Dedeket cleared his throat and said, in a much louder voice than before, "I hereby introduce His Iciness the Glaci Emperor Kryo Kardia himself, God-Emperor of the Glaci Empire and Defender of the Seven Realms, and king of the Glacian Dragon Riders!"

Without warning, a massive white dragon flew out from the *Frozen Heart*. Flapping its wings hard, the white dragon soared toward the border, and upon its back sat Kryo Kardia himself.

Frozas, Rialo thought with a scowl. *Haven't seen her since the Fang Clang left the kingdom.*

Anija grimaced. *She looks as bad as Kryo Kardia now. Wonder if she's suffering from the same curse that he is.*

Anija was not wrong. Although white from a distance, it became obvious, the closer they drew to the border, that Frozas herself did not look as good as she used to. Her scales were now closer to gray than white, and even her eye color looked more sickly green than anything.

Frozas soon landed on the Hosarian side of the border, next to Compe and Dedeket. Compe stood his ground, but the winds created by Frozas's landing knocked over Dedeket, who fell onto the ground and appeared to get tangled up in his own robes.

But no one paid any attention to Dedeket. All eyes were

now on Kryo Kardia himself, who sat, wearing his frozen crown, upon Frozas's back.

"Thank you for the introduction, Dedeket," Kryo Kardia said. He gazed at Hal and Keershan. "It is the only one I will need to crush these two for good."

Chapter Thirty

ANIJA GULPED. SHE HAD FORGOTTEN HOW TERRIFYING KRYO Kardia actually was in person. Despite standing a good distance away from Kryo Kardia, she could feel the cold air radiating off him and Frozas. It was cold enough to force both the Malarsans and Glacians closest to the border to back away, shivering as they pulled their coats more tightly around their bodies.

Hal and Keershan, on the other hand, did not appear at all intimidated by Kryo Kardia's cold air. They simply stood their ground, meeting Kryo Kardia's and Frozas's dismissive looks without flinching. Anija admired that they were seemingly unafraid of Kryo Kardia at all, which was not how she or anyone else watching them felt at the moment.

"I wouldn't be so sure that you will crush us, Kryo Kardia," Hal said. "We're not the same weak mortals we were when we first fought you two months ago."

Kryo Kardia smirked. "Yes, you are much shinier. I fail to see, however, how that will help you to defeat me."

Keershan growled. "We're not just going to defeat you. We are going to kill you and prove to your own subjects that you aren't the god you like to make yourself out to be."

Anija raised an eyebrow. *Damn. Keershan can be pretty fierce when he wants to be.*

I know, Rialo said with more than a hint of pride in her voice. *I am pleased to see that he is finally embracing his dragon heritage. I cannot wait to see him gouge out Frozas's eyes.*

Anija also forgot sometimes just how bloodthirsty dragons could be. While the stereotype of a mindless, rampaging beast hellbent on destruction largely did not apply to most dragons, Anija knew from experience that said stereotype definitely had at least a hint of truth to it.

She also found herself worried about Hal and Keershan. Their bravery in the face of Kryo Kardia and Frozas was admirable, but at the same time, their viciousness was out of character for both of them. She glanced at Surrels and noticed he seemed as anxious as she did.

Kendo, on the other hand, was already rubbing his hands together. "Good! They are both here. That means the duel is going to start any minute now. I need to get the fryers going. We will sell out."

With that, Kendo ran off back to the stall that he and his sister ran.

But Anija thought Kendo severely underestimated how many people would be willing to buy more stuff from him or the other merchants now that all four champions were here. On either side of the border, Malarsans and Glacians lined up at safe distances from Hal and Kryo Kardia, sitting on the ground, rocks, or stumps and fallen trees to watch the fight. Most people were too absorbed with the fight itself to care about buying more things from the merchants.

Even a few merchants had closed up shop in order to watch the duel.

That was not surprising. As Kendo himself had stated, this was the duel of the century, the fate of a kingdom and an empire on the line.

And the souls of our friends, Anija thought, watching Hal and Keershan closely, *which may be more important than the kingdom or the empire.*

Hal rolled his shoulders. "We're ready to begin the duel when you are, Kryo Kardia."

"Of course," Kryo Kardia said. "But before the duel begins, we must first go over the rules properly. Dedeket, please."

Dedeket, having now untangled himself from his own robes, walked up beside Frozas. He was shivering but obviously trying to hide it, although he couldn't hide the frost forming on his robes.

"Y-Yes, sir," said Dedeket. He looked up at Hal and Keershan. "P-Perhaps you are unfamiliar with the rules of the trial, but—"

"We know how this works already," Hal said shortly, never taking his eyes off of Kryo Kardia and Frozas. "We are ready to move on."

"But the spectators do not," Dedeket said. "For this duel to be more fair and enjoyable for the spectators, it behooves us to educate them on how this will work."

Hal sighed. "Fine. Read the rules to them. But make it quick."

Dedeket nodded. He turned toward the Malarsans and Glacians and said, "Spectators of the duel! You are about to witness the first trial by combat in over half a millennia. The champions from the kingdom of Malarsan are Halar

Norath and his Steed, Keershan. The champions from the Glaci Empire are, of course, His Majesty Emperor Kryo Kardia and his Steed, Frozas, chief of the Fang Clan."

Anija cocked her head to the side. She did not see the value in repeating information everyone already knew, although Dedeket seemed to be getting to the point quickly. He probably did not want to freeze to death.

Clearing his throat loudly, Dedeket continued. "At stake is nothing less than the fate of the kingdom of Malarsan itself. Should the Malarsan champions win, the kingdom shall remain independent of the Glaci Empire, and the Glaci Empire will sign a treaty ensuring that we will never, ever invade the kingdom or attempt to annex it in any way, shape, or form for as long as either state exists. If, however, the Glacian champions win, then the kingdom of Malarsan will formally join the Glaci Empire as another province, along with all of its Dragon Riders and Steeds."

Anija glanced at Stebo and Regent Akei when Dedeket said that. The future king and his uncle stood nearby, Stebo chewing on a chicken stick while Akei watched the duel with a grim expression.

"How did you get Stebo and Akei to agree to the duel?" Anija said, looking at Surrels.

Surrels shrugged. "I bluntly told them that we stood no chance of victory against the empire whatsoever in a traditional military engagement and that our best bet was—and still is—to let Hal and Keershan have a swing at Kryo Kardia. Stebo trusts me more than pretty much anyone and Akei is a rather reasonable man, so they agreed that this was the best way to tackle this particular problem."

Anija nodded, although she could not help but privately wonder what would happen to Stebo and Akei if Hal and

Keershan lost. Would they still be allowed to rule Malarsan, just as governors instead of kings, or would they lose their royal titles as well?

I'm much more concerned about them losing their lives, Rialo said. *Something tells me that Kryo Kardia would not appreciate potential challengers to his power or leave leaders in charge of his provinces who might be able to sway the people away from him.*

Anija could not disagree with that.

"As for the rules, they are quite simple," said Dedeket. "A trial by combat is always to the death. Once it begins, none of the champions participating can back out, surrender, or run away. Spectators are allowed and even encouraged, but no one outside of the duel is allowed to interfere. Should a spectator or ally of one of the champions attempt to help or intervene, the trial shall be nullified and normal warfare shall resume between the nations involved in the trial."

That did not surprise Anija. Yesterday, Hal and Keershan had called a meeting with both the council and the Dragon Rider Order as a whole to warn them not to even attempt to intervene in the duel. Even if Hal and Keershan were getting beaten to death by Kryo Kardia and Frozas, Hal had said, no one was to do anything. Hal and Keershan did not want to risk losing the duel on a simple technicality.

Which Anija understood. Losing because you accidentally violated the rules was worse than losing because the other guy was stronger, faster, or just better than you in some way.

But Anija also had to admit that it would be difficult for either her or Rialo not to want to step in should Hal and Keershan get hurt. Anija believed that they would survive, but she knew that there was a big difference between what one thinks one would do and what one would actually do in the real situation.

"The champions themselves may use whatever tactics, strategies, tools, weapons, magic, or anything else they may want to use during the duel," Dedeket said. "In fact, there are no rules against fighting 'dirty' or using so-called 'underhanded tactics' to get an edge over your opponent. Anything goes unless the champions agreed to certain limitations beforehand."

"We did not," Kryo Kardia said simply. "We will use everything we have at our disposal to ensure our victory."

Dedeket nodded. "Then I believe that covers the rules. As the official keeper of the trial, I will be the one to announce the victor when it becomes apparent."

Hal held up a hand. "Hold on. The rules of the trial require two keepers, one from each nation, to ensure fairness and accountability. We still haven't picked ours yet."

Dedeket sighed. "Fine. Who have you chosen to be your keeper?"

Hal jerked a thumb over his shoulder. "Surrels."

Surrels, looking slightly surprised by Hal pointing him out, nonetheless adjusted his shirt and walked over to where Hal and Keershan faced Kryo Kardia and Frozas. As he passed Hal, Surrels handed Hal something, although it was too small for Anija to see what it was. She could guess, though, remembering what Surrels had said earlier about giving Hal one of his Life Flowers.

He definitely won't put up with any funny business from Dedeket, Anija thought as Surrels turned from Hal and Keershan and walked until he was just outside the circle that the champions stood inside, coming to a stop there.

Dedeket walked over to Surrels's side, although he did

not greet him. Instead, he simply turned back toward the champions and said, "All right! Does everyone understand the rules of the trial now?"

Hal, Keershan, Kryo Kardia, and Frozas all nodded. Hal rested his hand on the black sword at his side while Kryo Kardia raised his spear, ice energy floating around it. Keershan clawed at the ground and snarled while Frozas clacked her teeth together and flapped her wings, sending dust and dirt flying into the air.

"Then let the trial by combat begin!" Dedeket and Surrels said at the same time.

Chapter Thirty-One

WITH A FLAP OF HER MIGHTY WINGS, FROZAS FLEW straight up into the air. Keershan, however, was quick to follow, his own wings beating hard and sending them soaring up after Kryo Kardia and Frozas.

"Where are you going?" Hal called out after Kryo Kardia and Frozas, raising his voice to be heard above the roaring winds and the flapping of dragon wings all around him. "Is the great Kryo Kardia running away already?"

Hal, of course, knew that Kryo Kardia wasn't running. He had simply taken to the air, likely believing that he would have an advantage in the sky, thanks to Frozas's mobility.

Just like in our last fight back in the Northern Circle, Keershan said. *Only this time, we are fighting on* our *turf.*

Hal agreed. *And we have a secret weapon he definitely won't see coming.*

Hal touched the leather grip of the Soul Slayer as that thought passed through his head. He had only received the Soul Slayer from Vexo two days ago, which was faster than he had expected to get it. It had given Hal time to test the Soul Slayer, which was both lighter and sharper than any other sword he'd ever owned or used.

Indeed, the Soul Slayer felt like it had been made just for Hal, which it had. Vexo told him that he had designed the hilt to be comfortable in Hal's grasp.

The only part that Hal had not yet tested was its supposed ability to eat the souls of its victims. Hal had considered going out into the woods and killing random animals to see if it would work, but that had seemed too cruel to him, plus he wasn't sure if animals actually had souls like humans or dragons anyway. Nor had Hal even thought about testing it on other people because that would be even worse.

But Vexo had assured Hal that the Soul Slayer would indeed eat the souls of its victims. Hal would have asked Vexo how he knew that without using it himself, but given Vexo's moral flexibility, Hal did not want to think too much about what kind of testing Vexo had done on the sword prior to giving it to Hal for his use.

Yet Hal could certainly feel the power of the Soul Slayer whenever he touched or used it. It was a dark power that reminded him of the demons, especially the Nameless One. He half-wondered if Vexo had infused demonic energy into the Soul Slayer, but he had not asked about that, either.

All Hal cared about now was using it to kill Kryo Kardia.

Nothing else really mattered.

Frozas suddenly came to a stop in the air, beating her wings hard to keep her and Kryo Kardia afloat. Hal and

Keershan came to a stop several feet opposite them, staring them down with hard eyes as Keershan hovered.

"I take it you didn't want any prying eyes," Hal said. He glanced at the ground far below, where even the dragons looked like ants. "Although our fellow Dragon Riders will be able to see us no matter what."

Kryo Kardia smirked. "Yes, but they will not be able to hear us. Besides, the spectators don't need to see us fight. Whoever's corpse hits the ground first will tell them who won and who lost."

Hal gripped the handle of the Soul Slayer tightly. "Why did you actually agree to this duel? It seems very risky. What if you lose? Wouldn't that be embarrassing for you?"

Kryo Kardia shook his head. "Spoken like a true peasant. If you had built a worldwide empire like mine, you wouldn't even be asking this question."

Frozas began to fly in a circular pattern, forcing Keershan to start flying in the opposite direction. This resulted in the two dragons circling each other slowly in the air, like a couple of sharks sizing each other up before going in for the kill.

"Enlighten me, then," Hal said, "because I fail to see how you benefit from this."

Kryo Kardia grinned. "Do you know how I got my reputation as a powerful emperor who takes what he wants and has no equal? I got it by winning these very same duels. More importantly, I made these duels into spectator events in themselves."

Hal raised an eyebrow. "What do you mean?"

Kryo Kardia gestured toward the ground below. "Traditionally, duels such as this are to be attended only by the champions, the keepers, and their respective armies. Very rarely would non-military civilians show up. But when I first began expanding the empire's borders, I would send out invitations across the empire and to the enemy nation's people to watch what would surely be an entertaining and exciting battle."

"And it worked?" Hal said.

Kryo Kardia nodded. "Quite. By decisively crushing the opposing champion, not only would I save us precious time and resources that would have been wasted on a traditional war effort, but I also established myself in the eyes of both the Glacians and the people of the opposing nation as a powerful leader who is not to be crossed. It helps that these events are often quite profitable for our imperial businesses, of course."

Hal nodded. "I see. It's about establishing your reputation."

"Or re-establishing it," Kryo Kardia said. He glanced at the ground below. "I still saw hope in the eyes of some of your fellow Malarsans. And among my own people, I saw hints of doubt, hesitation, worry about the outcome of this duel. How could I not, then, agree to take your challenge and prove to both of our peoples that I am who I say I am and how foolish it is to continue to resist me?"

Hal licked his lips. He had definitely seen a lot more hope among his fellow Malarsans than he had expected. Likewise, the Glacians, although obviously excited to see their emperor defeat Hal, had seemed less enthusiastic than he otherwise thought they would have been. Their cheers for Kryo Kardia had certainly sounded less enthusiastic than the Malarsans' cheers for him had, anyway.

Not that popular opinion mattered much to Hal, however. He knew they were going to win no matter what.

"Just wait until we crush you in front of your subjects," Hal said. "Then they'll know you aren't nearly as tough or powerful as you like to make yourself out to be."

Kryo Kardia chuckled. "It amuses me still how much confidence you have in yourselves. Whatever power the gods may have given you won't help you even slightly against the power that I wield."

Keershan snorted. "Whatever dark magic you have is nothing in comparison to the divine energy now flowing through us. You will see that soon enough."

Hal gripped Soul Slayer tighter than ever. "Enough talk. Let's let our weapons do all the talking for us."

Kryo Kardia leveled his spear. "For once, I actually agree with you. Let us see who is the true champion and who will live and who will die."

Kryo Kardia suddenly unleashed a blast of ice at them, forcing Keershan to bank to the side. Hal, gripping Keershan's saddle with one hand tightly to avoid falling off, drew the Soul Slayer from its sheath and pointed its black blade at Frozas.

A beam of light energy exploded from the tip of the Soul Slayer, although it looked different to Hal. Rather than being a pure beam of light, shadowy lines intertwined with the beam, giving it an almost drill-like appearance.

Must be the Soul Slayer's magic, Hal thought.

But Hal did not dwell on it. He just watched as the beam lanced toward Frozas, who was not nearly fast enough to dodge it.

But Kryo Kardia thrust his hands forward and a wall made of ice appeared between the light-dark beam and him and Frozas. The light-dark blast exploded the wall of ice, vaporizing it and creating a steam cloud that was quickly dissipated by the strong winds in the sky around them.

Yet when the steam disappeared, neither Kryo Kardia nor Frozas were anywhere to be seen.

"Damn it," Hal said, whipping his head this way and that as they flew. "Where did they go?"

"They must be hiding in the clouds," Keershan said. He grinned. "Why not make them show themselves?"

Hal smiled back. He raised the Soul Slayer over his head toward the sun and, drawing upon the godly power within, unleashed a blast of heat and light that exploded in every direction at once.

The explosion ripped through the surrounding clouds, instantly vaporizing them and revealing a startled-looking Kryo Kardia and Frozas hovering in the air not too far away.

Not giving them time to react, Keershan fired a stream of golden dragonfire at them. Frozas valiantly tried to fly out of the way but she still got hit in the chest by the drag-onfire, causing her to cry out in pain and fall. Kryo Kardia yelled as he and Frozas plunged to the ground below.

However, Frozas wrapped her wings around them and, in a move that even Hal considered impressive, dove out of the fall. Her wings sprang from her sides and she and Kryo Kardia flew back up, this time rushing toward Hal and Keershan with shocking speed.

Hal, however, was ready for this. Keershan darted toward Frozas, dragonfire building in his throat. Hal could see Frozas's throat also glowing with building drag-onfire while the tip of Kryo Kardia's spear glowed brightly with ice energy. They kept flying toward each other, neither side slowing down, until Hal saw the dragonfire from his sword reflecting off the whites of Kryo Kardia's eyes.

"Up!" Hal cried out.

Keershan immediately banked up and just in time, because Frozas unleashed her blue dragonfire at the same time. Kryo Kardia, however, thrust his spear up, firing a huge ice beam at the two of them as they flew over Kryo Kardia and Frozas.

Hal, at the same time, fired his own dragonfire infused with divine light. The two beams met in the middle and exploded, the blast sending both dragons hurtling in different directions. Hal himself actually fell off of Keershan before Keershan caught him safely.

Thanks, Keershan, Hal said mentally as Keershan beat his wings.

Thank me later, Keershan said. *This duel isn't over yet.*

That was true. Frozas had already recovered from the blast and was now hovering away from them again. Kryo Kardia looked unharmed but even he was panting slightly, although given his undead nature, Hal wasn't quite sure how that worked.

Regardless, Hal lowered his sword. "Do you yield? If not, we can do this all day."

Kryo Kardia snarled. "Foolish peasant. There is no such thing as surrender in a trial by combat. This will only end when one of us is dead."

Hal smirked. "Come on, Kralot. You know you can't win. Might as well let Keershan and I do our thing."

Hal meant that. He could tell that Kryo Kardia, despite whatever dark magic he used to expand his lifespan artificially, was starting to tire out. Even if Kryo Kardia hadn't been getting tired, Frozas almost certainly was. Even taking into account Kryo Kardia and Frozas's bond, there was still a limit that the Steed had, and she was likely rapidly approaching it.

Hal and Keershan, on the other hand, were gods who could not tire. At least, they could not tire as easily or quickly as mortals. Hal was still unsure if it was impossible for them to get truly tired or not, but either way, he foresaw no way for them to lose this.

Kryo Kardia, however, sat up straighter and glared at Hal and Keershan. His eyes landed on the Soul Slayer. "That sword. How interesting. It resembles the legendary Soul Slayer of myth."

Hal smirked again and waved the Soul Slayer at Kryo Kardia. "That's because it is. And because it is, I am pretty sure you are going to die today."

Kryo Kardia narrowed his eyes. "That's assuming I even give you the chance to use it on me."

"As long as this duel continues, it's only a matter of time before I do," Hal said. He pointed the Soul Slayer at Kryo Kardia. "Now, why don't we put an end to this waste of time you call a duel? It's time to——"

Hal was interrupted by his hand, the same one that held the Soul Slayer, freezing over. The sudden drop in temperature made Hal cry out in surprise and let go of the Soul Slayer, which fell toward the ground below.

"Hal!" Keershan said in alarm. "The Soul Slayer!"

Clutching his freezing hand, Hal said, "Get it, Keershan! Before——"

A huge shadow fell over them, and Hal looked up in time to see Kryo Kardia and Frozas flying upon them. But Kryo Kardia, rising to his feet, jumped off of Frozas's back and tackled Hal off Keershan's back.

The two Dragon Riders suddenly plunged to the ground below, grappling with each other as the world spun all around them. Kryo Kardia's grip on Hal's shoulders was as strong as iron, making it difficult even for Hal to break it.

Then they landed on a hard, wooden flat surface that separated them. Hal rolled to one side while Kryo Kardia rolled to the other. Even so, Hal rose to his feet, as did Kryo Kardia, although Hal took a brief moment to see where they had fallen.

They stood on top of the *Frozen Heart*, which had a wooden landing pad that ran the length of its top. Based on the claw marks on its surface, Hal guessed that this was where Frozas and other dragons regularly took off from and landed upon whenever they rode on the *Frozen Heart*.

"There," Kryo Kardia said, wiping black blood from the corner of his mouth. "Much better ground on which to fight."

Hal gazed at Kryo Kardia, noting how dented his armor was from the fall. "Was this your plan? To separate Keershan and me?"

Kryo Kardia nodded. "Of course. Everyone knows that Dragon Riders are weaker when they are physically separated from their Steeds. I trust that Frozas will keep your dragon busy."

The sound of roaring and growling in the sky overhead made Hal glance up to see Frozas and Keershan darting in and out of the clouds. They snapped and snarled at each other, shooting fireballs or avoiding fireballs from the other through impressive aerial maneuvers.

But Hal had no time to focus on them. He looked at Kryo Kardia and raised his fists. "Very well. If it's an even fight you want, then let it be. Although we are not equals."

Kryo Kardia smiled mysteriously. "We most certainly are not."

With that, Kryo Kardia held up his hand over his head.

And caught the falling Soul Slayer.

Hal's eyes widened as Kryo Kardia examined the Soul Slayer in his hands. "You. How?"

Kryo Kardia glanced at Hal. "How did I calculate the exact speed and trajectory of a falling sword I have never personally handled before to ensure I would catch it? It isn't magic. It's simply math, although at a higher and faster degree than your mere mortal mind can comprehend."

Hal stepped forward, his hands glowing with divine light. "I am no mortal, Kryo Kardia. I am a god. And I am going to smite you."

Hal thrust his hands forward and unleashed a blast of pure divine light at Kryo Kardia.

At the same time, Kryo Kardia snapped his fingers and the floor under their feet glowed red.

Hal had just enough time to register the glowing red light before he suddenly felt much weaker. The divine light blast dissipated into nothingness, and Hal himself felt like he could barely stand.

"Huh?" Hal said, looking down at his hands. "What happened? Why do I feel so weak?"

"Because, in the end, that is all you are," said Kryo Kardia's harsh voice. "A weak, pathetic mortal only playing at being a god."

Hal looked up in time to see Kryo Kardia's boot coming at his chest. Kryo Kardia's kick sent Hal flying backward, and he crashed into the wooden landing pad, every bone in his body screaming from the pain of the blow.

And before Hal could recover, he suddenly found himself staring down the black tip of the Soul Slayer.

At the other end of the Soul Slayer was a triumphant-looking Kryo Kardia, who gazed down at Hal with clear smugness on his features.

"Where did your godly powers go, Halar?" Kryo Kardia said. "Is it possible you might have stumbled into a trap?"

Hal gasped. "The ship. Somehow, you stole my godly powers. How?"

Kryo Kardia cocked his head to the side. "I've stolen nothing from you, Halar. I only activated the anti-divine energy field spell that I put on my ship prior to showing up here. I am glad to see that it worked."

"But how did you know that Keershan and I have godly powers?" asked Hal. "We tried to keep it a secret."

Kryo Kardia laughed. "As if I am too dumb or slow-witted to put two and two together. Once Compe informed me of your return from the abode—and once I learned about Vilona's demise—I realized that you and Keershan were not just empowered mortals, but outright gods. You have no idea how many hours it took me to find this spell in the oldest, darkest books I own, not to mention the amount of time and moulash it took to make it work without alerting you or your dragon to its existence."

Hal breathed hard. "So as long as I am here, I can't use any of my godly powers."

"Correct," Kryo Kardia said. "For all intents and purposes, you are a mortal once again." He raised the Soul Slayer above his head. "And I can't wait to see what this weapon, designed for killing me, will do to you."

Hal gulped, but there was nothing he could do. He was

still reeling from the shock of losing his divine powers, even if only for a moment. He could only stare in horror as Kryo Kardia raised the Soul Slayer higher and higher above his head, knowing that it would come down any minute and kill him.

This was not going how Hal had envisioned it going at all.

Old Snow was right, Hal thought as his life flashed before his eyes. *I shouldn't have been so eager to challenge Kryo Kardia to a fight.*

Chapter Thirty-Two

ONE MONTH AGO.

Hal was almost overwhelmed by the godly aura that filled the stadium in which he and Keershan now stood. Everywhere he looked, he saw gods and goddesses seated, cheering and screaming, although Hal realized that they were not cheering for him and Keershan.

Rather, they were cheering for their deaths.

As for Gotcham Nubor, he lowered his scepter to his lap and gazed down on Hal and Keershan with what might have been respect in his eyes. "Welcome to the Duel of Divinity, the third and final part of the challenge, Halar Norath and Keershan Clawfoot. I am impressed that you made it this far."

"I am, too, but for different reasons," Old Snow said, his voice coming from Hal's left.

Looking to his left, Hal saw Old Snow standing a few feet away from them. He stood a little straighter than he had before, looking almost like he'd aged down a few years. His eyes shone with fatherly pride.

"Wait, what is going on here?" Keershan said, looking around the stadium in bewilderment. "What is the Duel of Divinity?"

"It is the third and final part of the challenge," Old Snow said. "If you complete this challenge, then you will both be eligible to become gods."

Hal narrowed his eyes and glanced at the stands rising up all around them. "And why are all of the other gods here?"

"This is how the final part is traditionally done," Old Snow said. "The idea is to let the gods welcome you to the fold if you win or cheer your demise if you lose."

Keershan's wings slumped. "So we're basically entertainment for the gods."

"That's more or less what humans are to the gods, yes," Old Snow said. "But it's much more than that. The power of a god is not something that the gods wish to give away lightly. It is something they want to be sure they are giving away to the right person, or people in your case. Godly power in the wrong hands would be very dangerous."

Hal folded his arms in front of his chest. He was still trying to process their recent death and resurrection, and now Old Snow was telling them that they were going to have to duel someone in front of all of the other gods. That was rather stressful to think about.

Even so, the entire challenge had been stressful from beginning to end, so Hal decided that they could handle a little bit more stress. He sensed it would all be over soon.

"How does this Duel of Divinity work?" Hal said. "Who, exactly, are we going to duel?"

"I can answer that," said Gotcham Nubor, his voice bellowing from his throne above them. "In the Duel of Divinity, you will duel the previous winning challenger of the challenge. That is, the individual who came before you and successfully completed the challenge."

"Who would that be?" Hal said, although he had a sinking feeling he knew.

Gotcham Nubor held out his hand. "Come, challenger. Reveal yourself to your opponent."

A portal of dark energy suddenly appeared on the floor on the other side of the stadium, energy crackling from within. Two claws suddenly emerged from within the portal, grabbing both sides of the opening and pulling out the person to whom they belonged.

Hal felt his breath catch in his throat when he saw who their opponent was. "No. It can't be."

"This is a joke, right?" Keershan said, also unable to take his eyes off the figure standing before them. "Because if so, we are not laughing and this isn't funny in the slightest."

Old Snow, his arms folded behind his back, shook his head. "I am afraid not. You must indeed duel him if you wish to complete the challenge."

Hal's hands balled into tight fists, his knuckles turning white from the stress he put on them. "But we've already fought him once before. Why do we need to fight him again?"

As for who they were talking about, it was the dark figure who stood on the other end of the stadium. Tall and imposing, the demonic figure was someone who neither Hal nor Keershan had ever thought they might see again.

The Nameless One, the god of darkness and demons,

stood in the stadium, horns curling from his forehead, a wicked grin on his face. Large, bat-like wings extended from his back, his clawed hands balled into tight fists. His tail, covered in crystalline red spikes, swung back and forth behind him while his crimson eyes gazed upon them.

But Hal had to admit, he looked different. The Nameless One's form was shimmery and slightly transparent, almost like he wasn't actually real.

Not that that seemed to matter to the gods, however. The appearance of the Nameless One caused the other gods to sneer and stare with dread at him. Even Gotcham Nubor, who had summoned the Nameless One, seemed ill at ease, shifting slightly in his throne, clutching his scepter more tightly than before.

"What is this?" Hal said to Gotcham Nubor, gesturing at the Nameless One. "Why—no, *how* did you bring back the Nameless One? Keershan and I killed him already."

Gotcham Nubor shook his head. "That's because this isn't the original Nameless One, who is indeed dead and gone forever. This is a shadow of the original Nameless One, crafted from the memories and shades left behind by him when he perished at your hands. He has all the powers and strength of the original but none of the intelligence, so don't bother talking to him."

Hal pursed his lips. "I still don't like this. It seems too risky to bring back the Nameless One, even as a shade."

"He is little more than a puppet who is entirely under my control," said Gotcham Nubor. "He cannot cause any trouble, even if he had the consciousness necessary to desire such a thing. Observe."

Gotcham Nubor snapped his fingers and the Nameless One suddenly knelt before rising again. "As you can tell, this thing is the Nameless One in name only. His original spirit is long gone. Using information from the challenge and the gods' collective memories of him, I created a shade of the Nameless One who is every bit as powerful as the original but utterly lacking in free will."

Despite Gotcham Nubor's assurances that the Nameless One was merely a puppet and nothing more, Hal was not sure that the other gods were quite as convinced. They seemed to view the Nameless One shade with far more hostility than a mere puppet deserved. No doubt they were all remembering what the Nameless One had done before his original death.

Hal looked up at Gotcham Nubor again. "You said that we'd be fighting someone who completed the challenge before us. Were you referring to the Nameless One?"

Gotcham Nubor nodded. "Yes. Well over five thousand years ago, the Nameless One, then a mortal, entered the challenge and completed it. He became like one of us, which, in retrospect, was a terrible mistake on our part."

Hal's hands balled into fists. "You mean you guys could have stopped the Nameless One but didn't? Why?"

"Because, despite being gods, we do not know *everything* there is to know, Halar," said Gotcham Nubor. "Including the future. We can know only the past and the present. It is not our fault that the Nameless One went mad with power and had to be killed."

Hal pursed his lips. More and more, he found himself wondering why anyone put faith in these so-called 'gods' if they were no more powerful or able to prevent tragedy than the average mortal. They certainly did not seem like the all-powerful, wise beings that he'd learned about growing up.

"Well, this should be easy," Keershan said. He glanced

at Hal's helmet. "We killed the Nameless One before. We can easily do it again."

Gotcham Nubor shook his head. "It won't be quite that easy this time, even with the Final Relic. For you see, the Nameless One you killed was recently resurrected and therefore weaker than he was before his first death. This Nameless One, however, is based on the power he wielded at the height of his reign of terror, before his first death."

Ah. Now Hal understood why the other gods looked and acted so nervous and hostile. The Nameless One, back in his day, had been a powerful, evil god who had been cast out of the abode by his fellow deities for his evil actions. Although Hal did not know the exact details of the Nameless One's fall, he guessed they hadn't been pretty, based on how scared the rest of the gods seemed to be of him.

And indeed, Hal thought that this puppet version of the Nameless One did look bigger, stronger, and more intimidating than the one they had killed in the mortal realm. He still doubted this puppet would be that much more difficult than the original, but decided not to take it too easy this time.

"And furthermore, you will be under certain limitations during this duel," said Gotcham Nubor. "For example, you won't be able to use the power of the Final Relic to fight the puppet."

Hal and Keershan started, with Hal saying, "What? But the Final Relic is the only weapon that can kill the Nameless One. How are we supposed to win without it?"

"That is for you to figure out," said Gotcham Nubor coldly. "Furthermore, if you lose, you and Keershan will not only be thrown out of the abode, but you will die."

"Why?" Keershan said. "What does killing us accomplish?"

"You know far too many secrets about the challenge," said Gotcham Nubor. "We cannot risk you telling other mortals about it, which would ruin the integrity of the challenge and make it far too easy for future challengers to ascend to godhood. So you had better win if you want to survive."

Hal bit his lower lip. He understood the gods' logic well enough, but that did not make it any less nerve-wracking to think about.

"But before the duel actually begins, we will give you two five minutes to plan how you will handle this duel," Gotcham Nubor said. "Old Snow may advise you two as to the best strategy to take in regard to this duel. Once those five minutes are finished, however, the duel will begin."

A five-minute timer suddenly appeared in the air above Gotcham Nubor's head and began rapidly ticking down.

Hal, turning his attention away from Gotcham Nubor, said to Old Snow, "How are we going to beat the Nameless One without the Final Relic?"

Old Snow stroked his chin. "I am surprised you are asking me that question. I thought the solution was obvious, which worries me a bit that you two apparently haven't figured it out yet."

Keershan tapped the sandy floor of the stadium thoughtfully. "I guess we could always use dragonfire, which is generally pretty effective against demons, but—"

"Dragonfire is not the answer, either, at least not the total answer," Old Snow said. He gestured at Hal and Keershan. "The two of you already have everything you need to defeat the Nameless One again. You have the same power that the original Dragon Riders drew upon when they defeated him the first time before the Fall."

Hal raised an eyebrow. "And that is—?"

"Your bond," Old Snow said simply. "The bond between a Rider and Steed is absolute, one of the strongest of its kind in the whole world, because it makes both the Rider and the Steed stronger than either one is alone. Why do you think the Nameless One and his demons were so terrified of Dragon Riders that they spent five thousand years trying to erase every hint of their existence of them from history? And why else do you think that Kryo Kardia has been so eager to add Dragon Riders to his military despite the Glacian Army already being the most powerful military without it?"

Hal scratched the back of his head. "But even before the Fall, the original Dragon Riders used the Final Relic to kill the Nameless One."

"Only in conjunction with the power that their bonds gave them," Old Snow said. He sighed. "You still have yet to realize the full power of the bond between Rider and Steed. I would be disappointed, but this knowledge has been lost for many years. So it is no surprise that even you two don't know about it, as I only learned of it myself after I died."

Hal pursed his lips. Thanks to the actions of the Nameless One and his demons, the original history of the Dragon Riders was lost to history. Although Hal, Anija, Keershan, Rialo, and the other Riders and Steeds had made good progress in recovering a lot of the missing information, there was still a lot they didn't know about.

"Can't you just tell us what we need to learn?" Keershan said. He glanced at the timer. "We've got less than two minutes left."

Old Snow shook his head. "Unfortunately, just as I told you, I am not allowed to give you any crucial information that might help you complete the challenge. The hints I've given you are my limit. All I can say is that you must deepen your bond even further and truly become *one*."

Old Snow put a lot of emphasis on the word 'one' for some reason, but Hal had no time to ponder it before a loud bell rang throughout the stadium as the timer reached zero.

"The timer is up!" Gotcham Nubor called out. "It is time for the Duel of Divinity to begin. challengers, get ready."

Hal looked at Old Snow one last time. "Thanks, Old Snow. Without your help, we wouldn't have made it this far."

Old Snow dipped his head toward them, a strangely sad expression on his face. "I know. Just be careful. Not all is as it seems."

More riddles, Hal thought, turning away from Old Snow and hopping onto Keershan's back, who walked over to the edge of the circle in the stadium. *I wish Old Snow would just speak plainly sometimes.*

You heard him, Keershan replied. *He's not allowed to give us any cheats. We have to figure out how to defeat the Nameless One on our own.*

Hal sighed as Keershan came to a stop. *I still can't figure out what he means by us becoming 'one.' I feel like our bond is strong enough already. What more could there be to it?*

Keershan growled softly at the Nameless One. *We might*

have known if not for the actions of the Nameless One's followers. At least burning him will be fun, *if nothing else.*

Agreed, Hal said. He paused. *Something just occurred to me, Keershan.*

Keershan flicked his ears toward Hal. *What?*

If the Nameless One was the last person who completed the challenge before us, that doesn't make sense, Hal said. *After all, the Nameless One is already dead. And we know that the gods try to find replacement gods as soon as possible.*

Meaning you think that someone already went through the challenge before us and took on the duties of the Nameless One? Keershan said. *Good point. But if so, who—*

Another bell rang loudly, interrupting Keershan, as Gotcham Nubor shouted, "Let the Duel of Divinity begin!"

Deciding to worry about that later, Hal drew his sword and said, "Let's get him, Keershan!"

Keershan nodded. With a flap of his wings, they went flying toward the Nameless One, who raised his claws, which glowed with shadow energy.

But they were faster.

His sword blazing with dragonfire, Hal swung his blade at the Nameless One's neck. His sword cut straight through the Nameless One's neck, severing his head from his body and sending it flying across the stadium. The Nameless One's body collapsed onto the sand as his head hit the ground and rolled for several feet before coming to a stop at one of the walls.

Skidding to a stop on the sand, Keershan looked over his shoulder at the dead Nameless One, his eyes wide with confusion. "Was that it? Did we win?"

Lowering his sword, Hal rubbed the back of his neck. "I guess so. The Nameless One looks pretty dead to me."

Keershan smiled. "That was even easier than expected! Guess we get to become gods now—"

Tendrils of pure shadow erupted from the ground around them. The tendrils wrapped around Hal's arms and legs, lifting him off of Keershan's back and suspending him in the air. Even thicker tendrils wrapped around Keershan's legs, pinning him to the ground, despite his best efforts to pull away from them.

"What the—?" Hal said, glancing back at the Nameless One's corpse. "How—? I thought the Nameless One was dead. How is he still using his powers?"

"He isn't," said Old Snow's voice. "But I am."

Old Snow stepped out of the shadows from the overhang at the entrance to the stadium. He looked normal.

Except for his eyes, which now glowed the same shade of red as the Nameless One's eyes had.

Chapter Thirty-Three

"OLD SNOW?" HAL SAID IN HORROR, STARING AT OLD Snow. "Why are your eyes red? Why can you control shadows?"

Old Snow sighed. "I warned you, didn't I? Nothing is at it seems here."

The tendrils holding Hal suddenly twisted and threw him to the side. Hal went flying through the air before crashing into the opposite wall and sliding down it. He tried to rise to his feet, but more tendrils rose from behind him and wrapped around his body, holding him against the wall.

"Hal!" Keershan roared. "No!"

Keershan redoubled his efforts to escape, but the tendrils were not quite done with him. They lifted him into the air and slammed him down onto the sand once, twice, three times. Through their bond, Hal felt Keershan's pain almost as keenly as he felt his own.

Despite that, Keershan didn't give up. His throat glowed with building dragonfire before a particularly thick shadow tendril wrapped around his mouth and slammed it shut. Wisps of smoke rose from the corners of Keershan's mouth as his dragonfire died down, deep-throated growls emitting from his throat as Keershan struggled to free himself.

"I hate having to do this," Old Snow said as he walked forward, gazing from Hal to Keershan and back again. Shadow energy swirled around the tip of his cane. "But I have no choice. The challenge demands it."

"I don't understand," Hal said through gritted teeth. "Are you the new god of demons?"

Old Snow came to a stop in a spot that was directly in the middle of Hal and Keershan. His eyes darted from side to side as he looked at both of them. "Yes. Chosen by the gods, I went through the challenge before you two and successfully completed it."

"B-But you're a ghost," Hal said. "I thought only living mortals can do the challenge."

Old Snow raised an eyebrow. "I do not recall saying that. That was obviously an assumption on your part. The truth is, any mortal, living or dead, can, with permission from the gods, take on the challenge. It is easier for mortals but still very possible for the dead."

Hal felt the coldness of the tendrils around his body sapping his strength, but he ignored it for now to focus on Old Snow. "Why didn't you tell us?"

"It's like I told you," Old Snow said. "The keeper of the challenge is not allowed to tell the challengers what is coming up. I tried to give you hints, but it is a difficult line to toe."

"How come we didn't see you in the abode along with the other gods?" Hal said. "You were there, weren't you?"

Old Snow smiled sadly. "Not quite. I was already in the

challenge when Shirataka was dead, preparing it for your arrival. I knew you would make it here eventually, so I wanted to make sure it was ready for you and Keershan when you arrived."

Hal bit his lower lip. "But why? Why become the new Demon God? You remember how evil the Nameless One was. Why are you walking in his footsteps?"

Old Snow's eyes darkened. "Because what *I* want isn't important. For the balance of the universe, it is necessary for all divine positions to be filled. Gotcham Nubor, as powerful as he is, is in no way, shape, or form able to take on the responsibilities of all of his fellow gods. It had already been over a year since the Nameless One's demise and they still hadn't found a replacement."

"What about when he first died?" Hal asked. "Why didn't they replace him then?"

"Because his first death was not a true death," Old Snow said. "Although he lacked a physical body and was locked away, the Nameless One technically was still alive and capable of fulfilling most of his duties. It has only been recently that there has been a need for a true replacement, hence why I was offered the job as soon as I died."

Hal gulped. "So this entire time, you knew we'd have to fight you if we want to win."

Old Snow nodded again. "Yes. Bearing that knowledge has been difficult, to say the least. But now, no more secrets. No more riddles. Just a simple duel between you two and me."

Hal nodded. "So you aren't going to go easy on us, huh?"

Old Snow shook his head and raised his staff, its tip glowing darkly with shadow energy. "No. As both the keeper and the final challenge itself, I am obligated to see this duel through to the end. Either way, by the end of this match, nothing will be the same."

Hal nodded again. He figured as much.

At the same time, however, Hal did not want to fight Old Snow. Even knowing that he couldn't actually kill Old Snow, the thought of bringing physical harm to his friend was almost enough to make Hal want to surrender.

But then Hal thought about Keershan, struggling to free himself from Old Snow's shadows. He thought about Fralia, Surrels, Anija, Rialo, Wilme, and the entire Dragon Rider Order and the kingdom of Malarsan. He thought about Kryo Kardia and the Glaci Empire who were posed to invade, conquer, and destroy his nation.

And finally, Hal found the strength he needed to see the challenge through to the end.

Meeting Old Snow's eyes, Hal said, "That is fine, old friend. I know you are just doing your duty. And I promise to give you my best."

Old Snow spread his arms. "Then come at me, Hal, Keershan. Show me and the other gods that you aren't just mortals, that you aren't just Dragon Riders, but are worthy of becoming gods yourselves. And, more importantly, that you can fight and live as one."

There was that word again. 'One.' Hal still did not understand Old Snow's hints, but he felt like he was starting to wrap his mind around it.

Drawing on his bond with Keershan, Hal grabbed the tendrils holding him against the wall and channeled drag-onfire through his hands. Dragonfire erupted from his palms, the hot flames instantly vaporizing the tendrils that had been holding him down, the fire burning away at the coldness that had sunk into his limbs.

With a roar, Hal rushed toward Old Snow, who raised his scepter, no doubt to block Hal's blows.

But Hal wasn't aiming for Old Snow.

When he got close enough, Hal jumped over Old Snow's head. Old Snow, seemingly unprepared for his action, swung his staff at where Hal had once been. The new Demon God seemed to realize his mistake, however, whirled around to face Hal, clutching his scepter tightly.

Yet Hal did not take advantage of the opening. When his feet touched the ground behind Old Snow, Hal darted toward Keershan, who was still pinned down by the shadow tendrils wrapped around him. The tendrils had wrapped around Keershan so tightly that his scales now looked even blacker than Rialo's.

But Hal rested one hand on Keershan's ice-cold body and channeled dragonfire through his palm. Dragonfire covered Keershan's body in an instant, vaporizing the shadows and freeing Keershan, who immediately rose to his feet.

"Thanks, Hal," Keershan said, flapping his wings to get the creaks out of them. He looked at Old Snow and frowned. "I wish we didn't have to do this."

Hal nodded. "Yes, but it's for the best. If we don't do this, then no one will be able to stop Kryo Kardia."

Keershan sighed. "You are right. Hop on."

Hal immediately jumped onto Keershan's back, taking his usual spot on the saddle. Once he was settled in, Hal pointed his sword at Old Snow. "We're ready for Round Two. And this time, we *will* win."

Old Snow actually smiled. "I look forward to you earning your victory very soon."

The ground underneath Keershan's feet rumbled and Old Snow's shadow suddenly expanded from underneath his feet until it covered every inch of the stadium floor. The temperature in the stadium easily plunged fifty degrees in a moment, forcing Hal and Keershan to draw even more upon Keershan's internal heat to keep them from freezing.

Massive shadowy tendrils ending in spikes rose from the ground around them, each tendril about twenty feet in height. The tendrils formed a partial dome over Hal, Keershan, and Old Snow, their sharpened tips pointed directly at them.

"In the mortal realm, you killed the Nameless One before he could show you the true power that the Demon God wields," Old Snow said, his own voice starting to sound deeper and darker. His eyes glowed red. "Allow me to show you the power that the original Dragon Riders struggled to deal with on their own. And we will see if you can handle it any better than they did."

Chapter Thirty-Four

"OUCH," SAID DEDEKET, HIS ARMS FOLDED BEHIND HIS back. He smirked at Surrels. "Looks like this trial is about to come to an end very soon. Have you dug out a grave big enough for both of your champions yet?"

Surrels, who had been watching the battle in the skies as anxiously as anyone, tore his gaze away from the duel just long enough to glare at Dedeket. "Have you?"

Dedeket snorted. "Please. Everyone knows that His Iciness will not—*cannot*—lose. He has already separated Halar and Keershan from each other. See?"

Dedeket gestured at the *Frozen Heart* hovering in the air above the trees on the Hosarian side of the border. From this angle, it was impossible to see how Hal and Kryo Kardia's fight was going, but Surrels did not feel particularly good about it. He thought he caught a glimpse of Kryo Kardia's frozen crown above the edge of the war balloon but he wasn't sure.

He could, however, see Keershan and Frozas in the sky. The two dragons darted in and out of the clouds with amazing grace and agility, shooting fireballs at each other or moving in close to feint and strike with their claws and tails. This was the first time Surrels had seen two dragons tangle in the air, and it made him all the more grateful that he was a human and not a dragon.

Surrels and Dedeket, as the keepers of the trial, had been watching the duel more closely than anyone else. Thus far, Surrels had not seen anything that would disqualify Kryo Kardia and Frozas from winning, which bothered him slightly.

Hal and Keershan can win without any tricks, Surrels told himself. *Just need to have faith in them. They've escaped worse situations before.*

The fight did not seem to be ending anytime soon, however, so Surrels let his gaze wander for a moment to see what everyone else was doing.

Everyone on both sides of the border was watching the sky duel with rapid interest. Even Kendo had seemingly closed up shop so that he, Lila, and Spai could sit on the ground and watch the fight. He spotted Anija sitting on Rialo's back on the cliffs overhead, apparently having climbed up there to join her Steed. Fralia and Wilme sat beside each other on the grass not far away from Surrels and Dedeket, both looking rather anxious but especially Fralia, who had her hands over her mouth.

The Glacians looked about as tense and interested as the Malarsans. Prince Compe was sitting on the back of his dragon again, his arms folded in front of his chest, seemingly the only one who did not look worried about his father's fight against Hal and Keershan.

He's probably just hiding his worries, Surrels thought dismissively. *I bet Kryo Kardia teaches his children not to show emotion, even if they are afraid themselves.*

"Has Father been killed yet?" said a familiar female voice behind Surrels.

Surrels started and looked over his shoulder to see Nege and Prika walking up to him. Nege was in her battle armor, spear at her side, while Prika had his wings folded behind his back. Both were giving Surrels an expectant look, especially Nege. Her gaze practically demanded that Surrels answer her question and that it better be a good answer, too.

"It's not over yet," Surrels said, turning to face them, "if that's what you are asking."

Dedeket, however, whirled around on the spot and glared at Nege. "So there you are, you traitor. How dare you show your traitorous face here in person. Why, if I had my way—"

"Silence, Inquirer," Nege said without missing a beat. "I never cared for your opinions before Father betrayed me and I am even less inclined to care about them now."

Dedeket's hands balled into tight fists, shaking hard, but Surrels thought Dedeket seemed too angry to respond.

"What brought you out here, Nege?" Surrels said. "I thought you and Prika wanted to stay in Mysteria in case Hal and Keershan lost so you could make a quick escape."

Nege stopped several feet from them, along with Prika. "We realized that if your champions lose, there will be nowhere safe for us to flee to. The Glaci Empire has a long reach."

"And we know that no one can hide from Kryo Kardia for very long," Prika said. He shuddered. "Or Frozas, for that matter. She isn't very tolerant of traitors to the clan, I can assure you. That's why she and Kryo Kardia get along so well together."

Surrels nodded. He had not given much thought to Kryo Kardia's Steed, Frozas, who was chief of the Fang Clan. Originally the second largest dragon clan in Malarsan, the Fangs had left the kingdom after the Dragon War, citing Marial's enslavement of the dragons at the end of the war as the primary reason why they relocated to the Northern Circle.

But Surrels wondered if Kryo Kardia had offered Frozas something else in addition to safety from humans by moving to the Glaci Empire. Perhaps he'd offered to punish the Malarsans in exchange for the loyalty of the Fang Clan, which Surrels could certainly understand the appeal of from Frozas's perspective.

Unfortunately, Surrels knew little about dragon politics as it was, so he could not say for sure. He just hoped that Keershan would be able to handle Frozas even without Hal's help.

That was when Surrels felt a cold presence behind him. He looked over his shoulder to see Prince Compe staring directly at them, having finally torn his gaze away from the duel in the sky.

Or rather, Prince Compe was glaring directly at Nege and Prika, along with the other Glacian Dragon Riders. They all seemed to be trying to kill Nege and Prika from a distance with their eyes alone, although Surrels was pretty sure that Dragon Riders did not have the ability to shoot death beams from their eyes.

Nege, for her part, merely glared right back at them. "And I see that all of my equally traitorous siblings have shown up, too. Of course they did. They want to be 'good' children and support our father, even though he deserves none of that support."

"You have always been a mouthy girl, Nege," said Dedeket, "but even I didn't anticipate you betraying His Iciness. Just you wait. When His Iciness kills the Malarsan champions, then swift justice will be executed on you and your Steed."

Nege raised her spear. "I am this close to just impaling you for your big mouth."

Dedeket abruptly raised his hands. "Wait! T-The rules of the trial dictate that no harm can come to the keepers of the trial. It is absolutely forbidden. In fact, if you even so much as lay one finger on my fine robes, that will count as a loss for your champions."

Surrels furrowed his brows. "Are you sure that's in the rules? I mean, it makes sense, but—"

"It is," said Dedeket hastily. He put a hand over his heart. "And I know the rules by heart because I spent the last two weeks memorizing them for this moment. I intend to forget them as soon as His Iciness crushes your champions, however, because they really aren't necessary to know in everyday circumstances."

Nege lowered her spear. "Fair enough. But as soon as Hal and Keershan win, watch your back."

A shadow fell over Surrels as a deep male voice behind him said, "*If* Halar and Keershan win."

Surrels looked over his shoulder again to see Prince Compe standing behind him. He had not even heard the large prince approach, which caused him to take a step back from Prince Compe.

But Prince Compe didn't even acknowledge Surrels's existence. His blue eyes focused on Nege as if she was the only other being worthy of his attention in the general area.

"Big brother," Nege said. "What brings you over here, other than to tell me how much I hurt you by betraying our family?"

Prince Compe blinked. "I'm not hurt. I just wanted to warn you that the outcome of the duel matters, perhaps, less than you'd think."

"What do you mean?" Surrels said. "If Hal and Keershan win, then Malarsan will be safe. It's about the only thing that matters."

Prince Compe finally looked at Surrels, though it was with a hard gaze that made even Surrels hesitate. It reminded him far too much of the deceased Prince Tenka Hojara, who had also had a tendency to treat anyone who was not a royal with contempt and bitterness.

"Silence, commoner," said Prince Compe. "This conversation is not for you."

Surrels scowled. "Given how I am the general of the Malarsan Army *and* a keeper of the trial, I'd say your little conversation *does* involve me."

Prince Compe turned fully to face Surrels. "I am the crown prince of the Glaci Empire and a Dragon Rider, second only to my father. Perhaps you'd like to rethink your lack of respect."

Surrels met Prince Compe's gaze, not hesitating, despite feeling more scared than he let on. "Boohoo. I've killed demons before. I can handle bratty princes like you just fine."

Prince Compe snorted. "Believe what you want. It will change nothing. Only the battle in the sky will—"

Boom.

The *Frozen Heart* was now on fire. Shuddering, the ship tilted from side to side, slowly but surely lowering to the trees below.

"The *Frozen Heart* is crashing!" said Dedeket in alarm. "If it falls into the forest——"

Prince Compe grunted. "On it."

Prince Compe rushed back to his Steed and his fellow Riders. Once Prince Compe climbed onto his Steed's back, the Glacian Riders took off into the air toward the falling war balloon, no doubt trying to make sure it did not crash on all of the spectators.

And it wasn't just the Glacian Riders, either. The Malarsan Riders, led by Anija and Rialo, also shot into the air toward the crashing airship, their mighty wings flapping loudly in the wind.

"What happened?" Surrels said in alarm.

Dedeket shook his head. "I have no idea. But if I had to hazard a guess, I would say that His Majesty Kryo Kardia obviously defeated your champion." He smirked at Surrels. "I would recommend praying to whatever inferior gods you Malarsans worship because you are going to need their help now that——"

A loud roar filled the air, a roar like that of a dragon's. Yet it was far louder, deeper, and stronger than any dragon roar that Surrels had ever heard in his life, making him wonder where it was coming from.

That question was answered quickly, however, when Surrels saw Keershan breaking off from Frozas toward the falling *Frozen Heart*. Surrels thought Keershan might be trying to help control the descent of the ship only to see two figures falling off of the *Frozen Heart*.

Even from a distance, Surrels had no trouble identifying

the figures as Hal and Kryo Kardia. And Hal, oddly, was glowing a bright golden light, as was Keershan, the two shining like stars as Keershan drew closer and closer to him.

Finally, Keershan darted underneath Hal, catching him on his back before he could plunge into the forest below. As soon as Hal made contact with Keershan, however, the two were instantly obscured by a sphere of bright light that completely enveloped both of their forms.

At the same time, Frozas, flapping her wings rapidly, caught Kryo Kardia before he could land on the ground below. Frozas then banked away from the sphere of light that held Hal and Keershan, clearly trying to put some distance between them and the sphere. Frozas then came to a stop a good distance from the sphere, her wings flapping as a shaken-looking Kryo Kardia sat up on her back.

Both of their eyes were fixed on the sphere of light that had once been Hal and Keershan. In fact, the eyes of pretty much everyone were on the sphere, aside from the Dragon Riders trying to keep the *Frozen Heart* from crashing into the spectators. Surrels himself couldn't tear his eyes away from the sphere.

"What is this?" said Dedeket. He gave Surrels an accusing look. "What are your champions doing? A Malarsan trick?"

Surrels looked at Dedeket in confusion. "How am I supposed to know what they're doing? I've never seen them do this before. It looks like—"

The sphere of light suddenly contracted before exploding, briefly blinding Surrels and everyone else in the vicinity. Surrels even covered his eyes, hearing Dedeket gasp in shock and pain from the unexpected blast.

Once the light faded—which seemed to take an eternity

—Surrels finally lowered his hands and looked up at Hal and Keershan.

Or rather, at where Hal and Keershan had once been.

Because a new figure hovered in the air where Hal and Keershan had once existed, clutching a golden sword and shield in his hand. Supported by huge yellow dragon wings, the figure faced a bewildered Kryo Kardia and Frozas with clear determination in his body.

Dedeket blinked rapidly. "What the hell is *that?*"

Surrels smirked at Dedeket. "Better get digging, Dedeket. Because I think your champions are going to need it."

Chapter Thirty-Five

THE SOUL SLAYER CAME DOWN ON HAL WITH FRIGHTENING speed, driven by Kryo Kardia's intense strength. Hal, however, rolled out of the way at the last possible second, causing the Soul Slayer to slam into the wooden platform hard enough to make a thick, ugly crack.

Rising to his feet, Hal blasted Kryo Kardia with another fireball, but Kryo Kardia deflected it with an armored fist easily. Yanking the Soul Slayer out of the platform, Kryo Kardia turned toward Hal, a wicked grin emerging from the crumbling skin of his face.

"There's nowhere to run, Halar," Kryo Kardia said, his voice full of glee and triumph. He raised the Soul Slayer. "I can feel how much this sword hungers for the souls of the innocent. How ironic is it that this weapon you thought would kill me will actually be what kills you and your Steed in the end?"

Hal narrowed his eyes. He didn't want to admit it, but Kryo Kardia had a point. Hal could not get close to Kryo Kardia so long as he wielded the Soul Slayer. Hal knew that even a simple cut from the Soul Slayer would cause him unimaginable spiritual pain.

But without my divine powers, I can't fight him evenly, Hal thought, scowling. *Kryo Kardia has the edge on me up here.*

That was the main problem. Even without the Soul Slayer, Hal should have been able to overpower Kryo Kardia through sheer divine power alone. Yet Kryo Kardia had already figured that out and even come up with a way to counter Hal's divine magic.

I need to get off the war balloon, Hal thought, backing away slowly from Kryo Kardia. *That's the only way I can even the playing field between us.*

Of course, Hal was well aware that Kryo Kardia would not allow him to leave. Even if Hal jumped, he'd just plunge to the ground below. Granted, his new godly nature would protect him from the brunt of the fall, but Hal did not want to test exactly how injured falling from great heights was for gods versus humans. He suspected that falling from great heights was not fun, no matter how powerful and godly one was.

Even more, Hal realized that they would need to pull out one last trump card to beat Kryo Kardia. He knew he couldn't get the Soul Slayer back from Kryo Kardia, but fortunately, the Soul Slayer was not the only secret weapon that Hal and Keershan had brought along. It was simply the easiest.

Thinking quickly, Hal contacted Keershan via their bond, saying, *Keershan! I've got a plan.*

Good, Keershan said, who sounded distracted, *but you'll have to fill me in on it later. Frozas is very distracting.*

All you need to know is that you will have to catch me, and then we will have to merge, Hal said.

As Hal expected, that last word caught Keershan's attention. *Merge? Are you sure? The last time we tried to do that—*

We have no choice, Hal said. *Kryo Kardia has the Soul Slayer. It's our only shot.*

Okay, Keershan said finally. *Just give me the signal and I'll try to disengage from Frozas.*

Hal smiled to himself. *Don't worry. You will definitely know the signal when you see it. Everyone will, actually.*

Not sure I like your tone, Keershan said. *In my experience, that's the tone you use whenever you're about to do something incredibly dangerous, stupid, or both. Good thing I am used to going along with your dangerous, stupid plans that somehow always work out in the end.*

Hal nodded, but before he could respond, he saw the Soul Slayer coming at his face.

Muting his bond, Hal jumped backward, narrowly avoiding the tip of the Soul Slayer, which passed by his face. Staggering backward, Hal moved quickly even as Kryo Kardia advanced on him, the emperor's longer legs allowing him to take greater strides than Hal could.

"What are you running from, Halar?" Kryo Kardia said in between swings of the Soul Slayer. "I thought you were going to kill me. I suppose even the power of the gods isn't almighty, now is it?"

Hal did not reply to that. He was too busy dodging Kryo Kardia's slashes to say much of anything. He was just looking for the right opportunity to strike, but he needed to find an opening.

Or force one, Hal thought. *Because even though I don't have access to my divine magic at the moment, I do have access to another powerful weapon.*

Leaping back from Kryo Kardia, Hal activated the Final Relic. He felt power flow through his body as his armor turned to gold and his skin glowed white. The power swept away the pain and exhaustion that had nearly overwhelmed him, filling his limbs with newfound strength and agility.

Just in time for the Soul Slayer to come flying at him.

But Hal charged, going faster than Kryo Kardia expected. He got into Kryo Kardia's guard and slammed his fist into the emperor's stomach, making Kryo Kardia gasp in pain. Yet Kryo Kardia reacted quickly, slashing at Hal.

Hal, however, rolled to the side, avoiding the Soul Slayer as the weapon tore through the wooden landing zone they stood upon. Rolling to his feet, Hal shot several spheres of light at Kryo Kardia, but Kryo Kardia deflected them all with the Soul Slayer as easily as rocks.

"So you are using the power of the Final Relic again," Kryo Kardia said, raising the Soul Slayer before him. "As I recall, however, it wasn't of much use to you during our last fight."

Hal narrowed his eyes. "That's because I am not going to use it to fight you."

Kryo Kardia raised an eyebrow. "You aren't? Then what, exactly, *are* you going to do?"

Hal cracked his neck. "The Final Relic, despite being infused with godly power, isn't affected by your anti-divine magic spell. I am guessing this is because the divine energy it has is indirect, which is why I am still able to use it."

Kryo Kardia nodded. "Yes, but as I said, it won't do you any good. The Soul Slayer will still slay your soul."

Hal took a deep breath. "Only if you live long enough to get to do that."

With that, Hal launched straight up into the air, causing

Kryo Kardia to look up at him in surprise. As Hal rose, he drew upon the power of the Final Relic and his bond with Keershan, creating a huge fireball over his head that rapidly grew in size. The heat and flame licked at the back of Hal's neck but he barely felt it thanks to the protective energy of the Final Relic.

In seconds, the fireball was about the size of Keershan, blazing white-hot in Hal's hands. Kryo Kardia even had to partially cover his eyes due to the bright light emanating from the fireball, narrowing his eyes as he continued to watch Hal.

"Take this!" Hal yelled.

With that, Hal threw the huge fireball down toward Kryo Kardia. Kryo Kardia, apparently not too stunned, turned and ran, clearly trying to get to safety.

But if Hal had done it right—and he was pretty sure he did—then soon, there would be nowhere safe for Kryo Kardia to run to.

The fireball smashed into the top of the *Frozen Heart*, but it did not stop there. It smashed through the landing zone, tearing through the war balloon. The sound of burning wood and metal and hissing air as the helium from the war balloon shot out of the damaged flagship filled the air as the *Frozen Heart* itself careened from side to side before suddenly falling down toward the trees below.

The blast from the explosion sent Kryo Kardia flying. The god-emperor flew over the side of the *Frozen Heart* as his ship descended toward the Hosarian forest below, yelling at the top of his lungs.

Hal would have found that amusing save for the fact that he, too, had nothing supporting him now.

And so Hal plunged toward the forest below himself, yelling as the wind rushed past him.

Keershan! Hal called out mentally as he fell. *Any second now would be great!*

Coming! Keershan said.

Hal heard the flapping of wings and looked over to see Keershan—bloodied and wounded from his battle with Frozas—soaring toward Hal. Behind Keershan, Hal also spotted Frozas shooting toward the falling Kryo Kardia, no doubt trying to catch him before he fell.

Hal, however, ignored Kryo Kardia and Frozas in order to focus on Keershan. His eyes connected with Keershan's and he could feel their bond opening and expanding.

But it was more than that. In the brief time between their eyes connecting and Keershan catching him, Hal felt his bond with Keershan practically explode. He opened everything to Keershan, absolutely everything, holding nothing back, doing exactly what Old Snow had taught him and Keershan to do back during the challenge. He felt Keershan doing the exact same thing, their open bonds combining and merging into something newer and greater than either of them had ever thought possible.

And so, when Hal finally made physical contact with Keershan, a blinding sphere of white light erupted all around them. It was so bright that even Hal could not see. Neither could Keershan, for that matter.

Describing what happened in the next few moments was impossible using human words. It was, at once, both a physical and a spiritual union unlike anything that either of them had experienced in their lives. Whatever was Hal's became Keershan's and whatever Keershan's, Hal's.

In seconds, the process came to an end. Hal felt his own

consciousness fading, but he could also sense Keershan's consciousness fading.

No, fading wasn't the right word. They were merging into one, becoming better, stronger together than apart.

And finally, after what felt like an eternity of waiting, the process ended.

And then Hal and Keershan opened their eyes at the exact same time.

They floated in the air above the Malarsan and Hosarian border in exactly the same position that they had been in when Keershan caught Hal.

Only now, Hal did not feel like he was sitting atop Keershan. Nor did Keershan feel like he was having to carry extra weight on his back like he always did whenever Hal rode upon him.

No, they both felt weightless and as one. Hal did not feel like a Rider, and Keershan did not feel like a Steed.

It worked, Keershan said in their conjoined mind. *I can't believe it.*

Why not? Hal asked. *It worked last time, didn't it?*

I suppose, Keershan said. *I'm just kind of excited because this is the most amazing development in human-dragon relations ever. We're actual Dracoknights now.*

Hal nodded, but he immediately turned his attention to the world beyond their body. He knew that the duel was still ongoing and that they did not have time to marvel over their new body, even though he had to admit, it was pretty cool.

It appeared that Frozas had indeed successfully caught Kryo Kardia before he crashed into the ground below. Kryo Kardia sat atop Frozas's back, one hand clutching her reins, the other still firmly holding the Soul Slayer.

But Kryo Kardia and Frozas wore identical expressions of shock and incredulity at the sight of Hal and Keershan's combined form. Hal could feel the eyes of the spectators below and somehow sensed that they were every bit as shocked as Kryo Kardia and Frozas. That included their friends and allies, who they definitely had not told about their secret beforehand.

"Impossible," Kryo Kardia said, his voice hoarser and more ragged than before. "What sort of magic is this?"

Hal and Keershan grinned and raised their hand. "The magic of our bond."

A beam of golden flame shot toward Kryo Kardia and Frozas, instantly covering them both in flame.

And causing both of them to scream.

Hearing the screams of Kryo Kardia and Frozas as they burned to death caused Hal to remember how their duel with Old Snow had gone at the end of the challenge what felt like a lifetime ago now.

Chapter Thirty-Six

ONE MONTH AGO.

Old Snow's shadow tendrils shot toward Hal and Keershan with the swiftness of striking snakes. In fact, Hal even thought they looked a bit like snakes, their bodies moving and swaying with the agility and grace of those reptiles.

But Hal, channeling dragonfire through his sword, spun around, slashing at the tendrils as they struck. Keershan, too, alternated between breathing dragonfire at the tendrils or slashing at them with his claws or occasionally biting them with his teeth. They made good progress in the fight that way, batting the tendrils aside or burning them to a crisp.

Unfortunately for them, however, the tendrils just kept coming. For every one they managed to destroy, another two or three would take their place. Even drawing upon his bond with Keershan to give him extra strength and agility, it took all of Hal's skill just to make sure a stray tendril did not get through and strike him.

A particular shadow tendril launched forward, slashing at Hal's wrists. Hal easily disintegrated it with his sword only for a burning, yet oddly cold sensation to ripple across his back. Gasping, Hal looked over his shoulder to see that a tendril he hadn't noticed had slashed his back, leaving a bloody wound where it had struck.

The tendril reared back and tried to strike again, but Hal spun around and cut it into pieces with several well-placed swings from his own sword. The tendril disintegrated into wispy darkness, although Hal got only the barest of reprieves before at least a dozen tendrils appeared out of nowhere and went straight for him.

But Keershan leaped out of nowhere and, opening his mouth, unleashed an overwhelming stream of dragonfire that completely obliterated the shadow tendrils. In fact, Keershan kept going, spewing red-hot dragonfire in a continuous stream, spinning in a circle, burning away every shadow tendril that tried to get too close.

Ducking to avoid getting caught in Keershan's dragonfire, Hal said, *Thanks for the save, Keershan!*

No problem, Hal, Keershan said as he kept pouring dragonfire onto the shadows around them. *But don't celebrate just yet. Old Snow is still a threat and I am running low on dragonfire.*

Hal nodded and glanced toward Old Snow. The keeper of the challenge and their old best friend had not moved an inch from his position on the other side of the stadium. Hal knew this fight would not end until they defeated Old Snow, but right now Old Snow had them pinned down with his tendrils.

Although Hal now saw that Keershan had created an

opening for him to exploit. By continuously breathing drag-onfire, Keershan made it almost impossible for the shadow tendrils to get too close to them.

That's the idea, Hal, Keershan said mentally. *Go and attack Old Snow before I run out of dragonfire!*

Without responding, Hal took off toward Old Snow, drawing upon his bond with Keershan to run faster than he normally could. He never took his eyes off the old man, gripping the worn leather hilt of his sword as tightly as possible.

But then a wall made of literal shadow rose up in Hal's way. Hal, however, jumped into the air and barely made it over the wall, landing on the ground on the other side with a roll. Rolling to his feet, Hal swung his sword at Old Snow, aiming for his face.

Hal's sword, however, just collided with Old Snow's staff. Old Snow did not even budge under the impact, nor did he turn his gaze toward the sword. Old Snow kept his demonic red eyes on Hal's face the entire time, blocking Hal's sword with ease.

"You aren't doing it right," Old Snow said. "If you want to defeat me, you have to *think.*"

Old Snow shoved Hal backward, causing Hal to stag-ger. Hal did, however, manage to jump backward in time to avoid another swing from Old Snow's staff.

"Think?" Hal said as he landed. "Think about what? How to defeat you?"

Old Snow twirled his staff in his hands. "No. That's not what I am talking about. You have to think about what I told you earlier, about how to truly realize the power of the Dragon Riders, if you wish to win the challenge."

Hal narrowed his eyes. "But I thought you weren't supposed to tell us how to defeat you."

"I did not," Old Snow said with a shake of his head. "But I gave you enough hints that you should be able to figure it out on your own. Or, at least, I thought I did. Perhaps I put too much faith in your reasoning abilities."

Hal raised his sword and took a step toward Old Snow, only for his foot to get caught in something. Catching himself at the last second, Hal looked down at his feet and saw that they were covered in shadowy goop that made it impossible for him to move anywhere.

"And pay attention to your surroundings!" Old Snow said.

Wham.

Hal wasn't sure what happened, but he was now lying on the sandy, shadowy floor of the stadium, his head spinning. He heard the laughter of the gods rising all around him, which told him that something amusing must have just happened.

Unfortunately, having a headache made it difficult for Hal to laugh, even if he had known what everyone was laughing about.

Old Snow suddenly appeared above Hal, clutching his staff, his red eyes gleaming from within his white hair and beard. He looked more disappointed than anything.

"Have you learned nothing about what it means to be a Dragon Rider?" Old Snow said. "Or even how to fight?"

Hal blinked and felt blood leaking from his nose. He opened his mouth to respond, only to hear a roar of surprise from behind him. Craning his neck, Hal immediately spotted the source of the roar.

Keershan was being held down by the shadow

tendrils. Although he spat sparks from his mouth, they were too weak to do much against the tendrils, which had Keershan pinned to the ground. Keershan was obviously trying to free himself but just as obviously was having no luck in relying on his physical strength alone. He guessed that Keershan was just about out of dragonfire at this point.

"Keershan!" Hal said, reaching out a hand toward him.

The butt of Old Snow's staff crashed down on Hal's outstretched hand. Hal cried out as his hand broke and he tried to yank it back but just couldn't because of the pressure that Old Snow was putting on his hand. He looked up to see Old Snow still glaring at him.

"Neither Keershan nor you would be in this situation if you had just worked together, you know," Old Snow said. He dug his staff deeper into Hal's broken hand, making Hal groan. "I really do want you two to win this challenge, but I can't let you win that easily. The other gods would not allow it."

Hal took a deep, shuddering breath and said in a tight voice, "We *are* working together. That's what Dragon Riders do."

Old Snow shook his head. "No, you are not. Just because you two share a bond does not mean you are fully taking advantage of it. To defeat me, you will need to go one step further in your bond with Keershan and achieve a power that neither of you have alone."

Hal blinked. "What does that—"

Old Snow slammed his staff into Hal's hand again, causing Hal to yell in pain. "I can't tell you. Figure it out yourself."

Hal took another deep, shuddering breath but didn't

bother opening his mouth to talk. He suspected he would just scream in pain if he tried talking verbally again.

Mentally reaching out to Keershan, Hal said, *What do you think Old Snow means about taking our bond one step further? Ring any bells?*

No, Keershan said in frustration. *I am not sure what he expects us to do. We already fight together as a good team. We have the strongest bond of any Rider and Steed pair that I know of. We're about as close as a Rider and Steed can be without actually becoming one person.*

Hal's eyes widened. *Becoming one person. You don't think that's what he means, do you?*

Keershan rumbled uncertainly. *Perhaps? I don't know. That seems impossible. How could we become one person? Do we even want to become one person? What would happen to us as individuals if we tried that?*

No idea, Hal said. *But it's the only thing that makes sense. I remember how Rialo was able to use her bond with Anija to take over her body briefly back in the Northern Circle. If Riders and Steeds can take over each other's bodies, it's not that far-fetched to think that we can combine into one being using the same method.*

By opening our bonds fully into each other, you think? Keershan asked. *Rialo told me that is how she took over Anija's body from a distance, although she could only maintain that level of connection for a brief period.*

It's our only shot at completing the challenge, however low our odds might be, Hal said. *Ready to give it a try?*

In the physical world, Hal saw Keershan lick his lips uncertainly. *Okay, but you'll have to free me first.*

Don't worry, Hal said. *I've already got a plan for that.*

Returning his attention to the physical world, Hal looked up at Old Snow. From his perspective, it had taken several minutes to converse with Keershan about their plan for defeating Old Snow.

But Hal knew from experience that mental conversations were infinitely faster than conversations in the real world. He guessed that, from Old Snow's perspective, it had probably been less than ten seconds, if that.

Meaning Old Snow didn't quite know what was going to happen next.

Gritting his teeth, Hal said, "Thanks for the hint, old man. I now know exactly what we need to do."

With that, Hal grabbed Old Snow's staff with his other hand and channeled dragonfire through it. Old Snow's staff went up in flame, causing Old Snow to grunt and let go of his staff, which dropped onto the sand by Hal's side.

But Hal ignored that. He jumped to his feet and, ignoring his broken hand, rushed toward Keershan. He crossed the gap between him and Keershan in less than a second and, raising his sword, slashed at all of the tendrils holding down Keershan. The tendrils turned to wisps under each blow from his burning sword until Keershan was free again.

Rising to his feet, Keershan met Hal's gaze. "Ready?"

Hal nodded. "Yes."

With that, Hal, keeping his gaze level with Keershan's, opened his bond as fully as he could. At the same time, he felt Keershan's bond open wide as well.

Hal, truthfully, had no idea what he was doing. Neither did Keershan, for that matter. The two of them were going off what amounted to little more than a wild hunch and hoping it worked out.

But even as Hal opened his bond, he sensed a strong urge to open it even further. He didn't know where this urge

came from. It almost seemed to be coming from the Final
Relic, like his very relic was telling him to keep going no
matter how scary or weird it might seem.

So Hal finally threw his full self into it. He channeled
all of his hopes, fears, memories, desires, interests, beliefs,
ideals, and everything else that made him who he was
directly through his bond. He channeled it into Keershan's
bond.

At the same time, Hal felt all of Keershan enter him,
too. He suddenly found it difficult to tell when he ended
and Keershan began. Every blink of his eyes changed his
perspective. Sometimes he was in his body staring at Keershan, other times he was in Keershan's body looking at *him*,
and then sometimes he felt like he was staring at both his
and Keershan's bodies at once.

The entire process would have probably scared him
under normal circumstances, but right now, it felt like the
most natural thing in the world. He dove deeper into Keershan as Keershan did the same to him.

In seconds—in the half-blink of an eye—the process
ended.

And Hal breathed.

And Keershan breathed.

"What?" Hal said aloud, although his voice sounded
deeper to him for some reason. "What happened—? Did it
work?"

"Not sure," Keershan said, whose voice came out of
Hal's mouth, "but I think it did."

Hal raised one of his hands.

And froze.

Because his hands now ended in thick dragon claws.

Yet when Hal looked down at his body, he did not see

Keershan's body. He saw a humanoid body with two arms and legs ending in sharp dragon claws. He felt a spiked tail behind him, waving back and forth. He even felt wings attached to his back, currently folded, but he suspected that he could open them at a moment's notice.

Even better, the pain and exhaustion from before had completely gone away. Both of Hal's hands no longer hurt, and both worked as perfectly as ever. Hal himself felt stronger and taller and faster than he ever had at any point in his life.

"Amazing," Hal said, looking down at his—at *their*—new body. "What is this—?"

"You finally figured it out," Old Snow said. "I was wondering when you would."

Hal and Keershan raised their head to look at Old Snow, who was still standing not far from them.

Only this time, Old Snow wore an expression of pride on his face.

He was apparently the only one who did, however. The rest of the gods were staring in stunned silence at Hal and Keershan, their expressions ranging from shocked to confused and even to anger. But they were mostly shocked. Even Gotcham Nubor appeared to be at a loss for words, which was saying something, as the king of the gods always seemed to have something to say.

"We became one, somehow," Hal said, balling his claws into fists. "But we still don't understand *how*."

Old Snow smiled. "You have unlocked the final secret of the Dragon Riders, the ability that made them such a force to be reckoned with that even a dark god like my predecessor feared them: Unity."

Keershan blinked. "Unity? What do you mean?"

Old Snow spread his arms. "As you are well aware, a Dragon Rider pair is formed when a human and a dragon form a bond. Often, this bond requires a relic to create, establish, and maintain, although bonding can happen naturally. Yet when the initial bond is created, it is often weak. bonds between a Rider and Steed take years to fully mature and deepen and strengthen, but there is an endpoint to that growth, and not just death, either."

"Unity," Hal said in realization. "Becoming one."

Old Snow nodded. "Exactly. When a Dragon Rider pair achieves Unity, that is the process of becoming one single individual. Now, you don't stay in that form all the time, of course. But once achieved, you can use it on command, although it takes many years to master."

"So this is what all Dragon Rider pairs are working toward," Keershan said. "All these years, I've read about the previous 'unity' between humans and dragons that existed before the Fall. I did not think it would be quite so literal, though."

"There is, of course, a metaphorical aspect to it as well," Old Snow said, "but for Dragon Rider pairs like you two, it is quite literal."

Hal flexed his muscles. He had always wondered what being a dragon felt like. *This is amazing, Keershan. I didn't know, even when we were separate, that you felt* this *strong.*

Thanks, Keershan said, *although I find the concept of standing on two legs pretty weird. How do you stay upright all the time? It feels weird.*

Snapping out of his thoughts, Hal said to Old Snow, "Thanks for all of the hints. I am sure you are going to regret it, given how we will now use our power to defeat you."

Old Snow smirked. "There is a difference between *knowing* something and knowing how to do something, Hal. And what did I just tell you about paying attention to your surroundings?"

Something hard and heavy slammed into Hal's side, sending him flying. Hal and Keershan slammed into one of the walls on the opposite side of the arena, prompting another wave of laughter from the watching gods.

But Hal, ignoring the derisive laughter of the gods, rose unsteadily to his feet and raised his head to see what had attacked them.

A massive demon now stood in the center of the arena. Vaguely bearlike in appearance, the demon was missing a head. Instead, it had hundreds, perhaps even thousands, of tentacles flailing wildly in place of where its head would have been if it had been a normal creature. It stank of death, too.

Despite lacking any visible eyes, the demon turned its 'head' toward them, the slapping sounds of its tentacles making Hal's scales crawl.

"What the hell is that?" Hal said in horror, taking a step back.

Old Snow shrugged. "One of my demons. And a rather powerful one at that, although I am sure that the first Dracoknight in ages should be able to handle it without issue."

Hal bit his lower lip. "I—"

Hal did not get to finish his sentence before the demon surged forward. Its tentacles extended out from its neck and wrapped around his and Keershan's arms and legs. A sickening coldness flooded Hal and Keershan's shared body, making them shiver even despite the shared warmth from the dragonfire inside them.

Old Snow's eyes glinted in the light from the torches along the walls as the demon drew Hal and Keershan deeper into its mouth. "I am proud of you two for finally figuring out what I have been trying to teach you. But just because you know how to merge does not mean you know how to use your new power. Or that you will survive long enough to learn how to use it."

Chapter Thirty-Seven

ANIJA WASN'T QUITE SURE WHAT HAPPENED.

Nor was Rialo, for that matter. The Dragon Rider pair hovered in the air, Rialo's wings beating against the air, staring in confusion and disbelief at the dragon humanoid figure who had once been Hal and Keershan floating not far from them.

Anija normally wasn't one to stare, but since the other Dragon Riders had already taken care of the crashing *Frozen Heart*, Anija had taken the time to watch this unexpected turn of events. She was vaguely aware that the other Dragon Riders had already guided the *Frozen Heart* away from the battlefield, thus protecting the innocent civilians on both sides, but that was all she knew about that situation.

She could only watch as the new figure's golden dragonfire—which reminded her of the Final Relic's dragonfire, only somehow more 'holy,' for want of a better term—bathed Kryo Kardia and Frozas. The screams of pain emanating from Kryo Kardia and Frozas were both some of the best and most horrible sounds that Anija ever heard. Best because they implied that those two were dying horrible deaths. Most horrible because she did not think their deaths were entirely natural.

Rialo, too, stared. Through their bond, Anija sensed that Rialo was even more confused than she was.

And that scared Anija, because Rialo always seemed to understand things better than she did.

What happened to Hal and Keershan? Anija asked, hoping to get a good answer from Rialo.

I have no idea, Rialo said. *I've never seen anything like that figure before. He's not a dragon, but neither is he a human. I have no idea what he is.*

That was even more troublesome.

Even so, Anija said, *But hey, at least he's defeating Kryo Kardia and Frozas. Whatever Hal and Keershan did, it must have worked.*

Rialo rumbled underneath her uncertainly. *Maybe. We'll just have to wait and see.*

As soon as Rialo said that, the humanoid dragon cut off his stream of golden dragonfire and lowered his sword and shield to his side.

Surprisingly, Kryo Kardia and Frozas had not been burned to ash, like Anija had thought they would be. But they were virtually unrecognizable. Frozas's snow-white scales had been scorched pitch-black and were horribly melted. Kryo Kardia wasn't much better, with his blue chipped skin now as black as Frozas's scales. One of his eyes had even been melted shut.

They hovered in the air for the barest of split seconds before abruptly plunging to the ground below. Kryo Kardia and Frozas crashed into a series of tents on the Malarsan side of the border that had been the merchant stalls set up to serve the spectators. Fortunately, all of the merchants had closed shop as soon as the trial started, which meant there had been no one inside any of the tents when Kryo Kardia and Frozas crashed.

Silence reigned across the border for what felt like an eternity as all eyes turned toward the dragon humanoid hovering in the sky overhead. Even Anija did not quite know what to think or feel.

That is, until the humanoid dragon figure raised his sword into the sky and said, in a voice that sounded like a combination of Hal and Keershan's voices, "The trial by combat is over! Kryo Kardia and his Steed, Frozas, have been defeated by us. We, Halkeer, are the winners of the trial. Therefore, the Glaci Empire must end all military incursions and activities in and around the kingdom of Malarsan effective *immediately*."

When Halkeer—which Anija thought was a strange name, although certainly less of a mouthful than saying their two names separately—said that, they did not merely sound like victors announcing their triumph in a challenge.

They spoke with the absolute authority of the gods themselves, as if by speaking alone, they could write reality as they saw fit.

Not that Anija would even consider disagreeing with them, however. From her position in the sky, Anija thought that Kryo Kardia and Frozas looked quite dead. Even if they weren't, Anija knew they were in no shape to keep fighting.

Cheers went up from the Malarsan side as every single person who had arrived to spectate the event went wild. Fireballs fired by fire mages flew up into the sky and exploded like magical fireworks to celebrate this victory. The cheers were so loud that Anija could hear them even from up in the sky, loud enough to make her cringe slightly and even cover her ears.

Although Anija did not cover her ears too much. She, too, was cheering for Halkeer, as was Rialo, who roared her approval.

As for the Glacians on the Hosarian side of the border, they looked more stunned than anything. No doubt they were trying to comprehend how their emperor, who had styled himself as a god, had been defeated by some random Dragon Rider from Malarsan. The Glacian Dragon Riders, who hovered well away from Anija and Rialo, stared in disbelief at their fallen emperor as well.

Except Prince Compe. Out of all of the Glacians, he looked less confused or stunned and more angry. His hands balled into tight fists as he gripped the reins of his Steed, his dark eyes peering out from the eyeholes of his mask at Halkeer.

Guess he's just upset that Daddy didn't win, Anija thought, not even bothering to hide her own smirk this time. *That's what happens when you cross Malarsans.*

But then the good mood was immediately ended when a familiar annoying, high-pitched voice called out, "Wait!"

The voice, probably magically magnified, was loud enough to drown out all of the cheering from the Malarsans. Anija herself followed the sound of the voice and saw that it came from Inquirer Dedeket, who stood on the ground below where the Malarsan and Hosarian borders met. His arms crossed in front of his chest, Dedeket glared up at Halkeer with pure anger in his eyes.

"What do you want, Dedeket?" Halkeer said, more

than a hint of contempt in his voice. "Your king is dead. We won the trial."

Dedeket shook his head. "Not quite. Prince Compe!"

Prince Compe and his Steed rushed down to Dedeket, who climbed on the dragon's back, before they took off into the air again. Anija watched with annoyance as Dedeket, riding behind Prince Compe on the dragon's back, soared toward Halkeer.

What is that idiot doing? Anija said. *Is he trying to overturn the results of the duel?*

Rialo growled. *If so, that will finally give me the excuse to burn that little sycophant I have been waiting for all year.*

Halkeer glared at Dedeket and Prince Compe as they approached him. "What do you mean, 'not quite'? Kryo Kardia and Frozas are dead. We killed them ourselves."

Prince Compe's dragon came to a stop several dozen feet away, flapping his wings rapidly, as Dedeket peered around Prince Compe's large frame to look at Halkeer. "First, you have not actually proved that His Iciness or his Steed are dead. So you can't just go around saying that. And second, this was a duel between His Iciness, his Steed, and Halar Norath and Keershan of Malarsan, which definitely did not involve you."

Halkeer narrowed his eyes. "What are you talking about? We *are* Halar Norath and Keershan."

Dedeket cocked his head to the side. "Are you? You don't look—or sound—much like either. Even if your composite parts are Halar Norath and Keershan Clawfoot, it's obvious that your strange ability to merge has created an entirely new being who has no right to participate in this trial. That alone should disqualify you from being crowned winner of this duel."

Anija's jaw fell. *Is this idiot really rules-lawyering to Halkeer? Right after seeing what he did to his boss?*

No one ever said Dedeket was wise, Rialo said with a snort.

"And what gives you the right to make that judgment, worm?" Halkeer demanded. "You're just a mortal. And a rather weak, annoying one at that."

Dedeket sat up straight in his seat behind Prince Compe. "Because I am one of the keepers of the trial, mortal or not. Did you forget that I had already memorized all of the rules of the trial? And you just broke the most fundamental rule of trial by combat: Allowing a new person to intervene in a formal trial with agreed-upon participants."

Halkeer opened and closed his mouth incredulously. "I... what? Are you even listening to yourself speak?"

Dedeket flashed Halkeer a wicked grin. "Of course. I love the sound of my own voice almost as much as I love the sound of His Iciness crushing the bones of his enemies underneath the heels of his boots. And since you broke the rules, that means that the entire trial and all related agreements are void."

Halkeer's eyes widened. "Wait, if the trial is void, then that means—"

"War is still on," said Prince Compe, interrupting Halkeer without hesitation.

Anija's eyes also widened. *Crap. Did we just win the battle, only to lose the war?*

Without waiting for Halkeer's response, Prince Compe and Dedeket turned to the Glacians on the Hosarian side of the border and Dedeket said, "Proud citizens of the Glaci Empire! As keeper of the trial, I have determined that the Malarsans have violated the rules of the trial, thereby disqualifying Halar Norath and Keershan Clawfoot from winning the duel! Through their own foul treachery, the Malarsans have shown themselves to be dishonest and untrustworthy fellows and fully worthy of unleashing the full wrath of the Glaci Empire upon their kingdom!"

The Glacians below began yelling and sneering at the Malarsans. Although their screams and shouts rapidly mixed together into an incoherent mess of noise, Anija got the general gist of their rude words and shouts.

Damn it, Anija thought. *This is possibly the worst possible way this could have ended. Because even if Kryo Kardia and Frozas are dead, the Glaci Empire is still far stronger and bigger than we are.*

I know, Rialo said grimly. *It looks like we will have no choice but to fight.*

Anija heard the flapping of wings all around her and looked to see that the Malarsan Dragon Riders had joined her, with looks of worry and concern on their faces. As for the Glacian Riders, they had flown over to Prince Compe and Dedeket, silently joining them as they formed a loose circle around Halkeer.

Halkeer, oddly enough, did not look afraid or even worried about the Glacian Riders. He simply cast a gaze around them as if they were barely worth his notice.

Wish I had that level of confidence, Anija said.

Confidence doesn't mean much when one is outnumbered a dozen to one, Rialo said. *We need to help Hal and Keershan before they get overwhelmed by the Glacians.*

Anija nodded. She raised her sword, ready to order the Malarsan Riders to fly to Halkeer's aid, but as it turned out, she did not need to do that.

A deep rumbling sound came from within the pile of smashed tents where Kryo Kardia and Frozas had fallen.

The sound was loud enough to draw everyone's attention to the sight, including Halkeer and the Glacian Riders.

The rumbling sound just grew with intensity, however, gradually rising higher and higher. A cold wind suddenly blew through just then, cold enough to make Anija shiver despite her protective armor and heat from Rialo.

What is going on down there? Anija thought, staring in horror. *I thought Kryo Kardia and Frozas were dead.*

Dedeket did say that we had not confirmed that they were dead, Rialo said, her voice tense. *Be ready for anything, Anija. We have no idea what will happen next.*

Rialo was more right than even she knew.

Because in the next instant, everything changed.

Thick, twisting tendrils of ice suddenly erupted from the pile of destroyed tents, forcing the few Malarsans who had still been nearby to scatter. Yet even as the tendrils emerged, they changed forms, forming huge hands at the ends of them.

And they were all going toward Halkeer and the Glacian Riders.

"Hal!" Anija screamed. "Keershan! Watch out!"

But Anija should have saved her screams not for Halkeer, but for the Glacian Riders.

Because the ice hands caught each Rider and Steed pair with surprising speed, catching even the Glaci Riders off-guard. The only pair who avoided capture were Prince Compe and his Steed, who quickly flew out of the way of the hand that tried to grab them.

Yet the ice hands did not seem to care because they immediately pulled all of the struggling Glacian Riders toward the site of Kryo Kardia and Frozas's demise.

Hovering above the pile of burning and destroyed tents, the ice hands paused.

But they did not release the Glacian Riders. Instead, sickening green energy pulses went down from the captured Riders and their Steeds into whatever was hidden underneath the destroyed tents. Each pulse seemed to make the Glacian Riders weaker and weaker because they gradually stopped resisting the ice hands.

In seconds, all of the Glacian Riders had stopped trying to fight back at all. They hung limply in the ice hands, their bodies as unmoving as rocks.

They're dead, Rialo said in a tight voice. *He killed them.*

Anija didn't have to ask who 'he' was because she already knew.

Even if she hadn't, however, the identity of the man in question became obvious in the next instant when the ice hands suddenly shattered, dropping the corpses of the Glacian Riders onto the ground.

The shattered ice, however, did not merely dissipate. A cloud of ice shards shot up into the air until it was level with Halkeer. It then rapidly took shape before the eyes of everyone in the vicinity, and in seconds, a new being hovered in the air where Kryo Kardia and Frozas had once been.

The new being appeared to be a fusion of Kryo Kardia and Frozas. Humanoid in appearance, the figure wore snow-white scales and armor, with bluish-white wings extending for several feet from either side of his huge body. Massive muscular arms ended in thick claws that clutched a long spear that ended in the head of a dragon, a sphere of glowing blue dragonfire swirling within it.

But it was the face that most got Anija's attention. The

figure's face was that of a bone-white skeleton, icy blue eyes glaring out from the empty eyeholes at Halkeer.

"What is that?" said one of the Dragon Riders flying near Anija, a rookie whose name Anija could not immediately recall off the top of her head.

Prince Compe and Dedeket, hovering a good distance away from the new figure, also gave him wary looks.

"Kryo Kardia?" said Prince Compe, hesitation in his voice. "Is that you?"

The new figure glanced casually in Prince Compe's direction. "Yes. Although I must say, I am very disappointed by your lack of familial loyalty, unlike your siblings, who gave their lives so I may have mine back."

Kryo Kardia pointed a single finger at Prince Compe, and a concentrated stream of ice fire shot at him.

That was the best word Anija could use to describe the substance that Kryo Kardia fired at Prince Compe. It looked like fire and ice unnaturally melded into one, leaving a trail of steam behind it, although it moved too fast for Anija to get a good look at it.

And it definitely moved too fast for Prince Compe to dodge. The beam lanced through his chest, right where his heart would be, and Prince Compe immediately slumped forward on his Steed. His Steed must have felt the pain, too, because he cried out in pain and descended toward the ground, a shrieking Dedeket on his back as they fell.

Anija, not wanting the dragon to crash into the people below, indicated for Rialo to go after him. Rialo shot toward the seemingly dead Prince Compe and his Steed. Anija paid little attention to the fight going on overhead, her focus primarily on Prince Compe and his Steed.

Although Anija was not the only one who went to save

them. Half of the other Malarsan Riders joined her and, reaching Prince Compe at roughly the same time, they caught his falling Steed and directed him toward an open space on the Hosarian side. It was difficult for Anija to tell if Prince Compe was dead or not, but she decided he was in good hands now and looked back up at Kryo Kardia and Halkeer.

Not much had changed. The two still hovered in the air facing each other, staring each other down, as if daring to make the other make the first move.

But then Halkeer cried out and launched toward Kryo Kardia, who did the same. The two charged toward each other, screaming at the tops of their lungs, before colliding in the middle.

And positively exploding.

Chapter Thirty-Eight

WHEN HALKEER AND KRYO KARDIA CRASHED INTO EACH other, Surrels had not expected a massive explosion to follow.

A huge blast of light erupted from the two, completely obscuring them from view and forcing Surrels to cover his eyes to avoid getting blinded. The light, however, lasted only for a few seconds before fading, allowing Surrels to lower his hands and see things better.

Halkeer and Kryo Kardia were rapidly trading blows with each other. It was almost impossible for Surrels to keep up with them. In fact, it *was* impossible for him to follow their attacks. They moved with truly divine speed, and Surrels had no idea who was winning and who was losing. They seemed evenly matched to him and he didn't like that one bit.

"Damn it," said Kendo, standing beside Surrels. He was looking at the pile of tents that had been the merchant row, a frown on his face. "Why didn't Hal and Keershan kill Kryo Kardia and Frozas over someone else's tent? At least I am pretty sure we made a profit before the duel began, so I suppose I can't complain."

Surrels tore his gaze away from the duel in the sky to look at Kendo in disbelief. "We just saw Kryo Kardia absorb the life force of his own children to power himself up and you are more worried about your business losses?"

Kendo shrugged. "It's not like my worrying about Hal and Keershan—or whoever that new person is—is going to change the outcome of the duel. Although it does make me want them to win all the more, if only to teach Kryo Kardia a lesson."

Surrels shook his head. He supposed this was better than Kendo being in organized crime, although he wasn't sure how much of an improvement this actually was. Perhaps Kendo was simply less likely to end up back in jail this way than if he'd gone back to the Dead Dragons or some other criminal group.

"Surrels!" Fralia said. "Surrels! We need to talk."

Surrels turned his head in Fralia's direction and saw Wilme running alongside the young woman. The two women reached Surrels and Kendo quickly, coming to a stop, Fralia putting her hands on her knees as her dark hair hung on either side of her head.

"What's the matter, Fralia?" Surrels said, frowning. "Did you see something?"

Fralia shook her head and pointed across the border. "No. I just sense some *very* dark magic emanating from that forest. As in, necromancy."

Surrels's eyes widened. "Wait a minute, didn't Hal and Anija say that Kryo Kardia is a necromancer? You don't think—"

"That he's going to unleash his undead minions on us?" Wilme finished for him. "Yes, that's exactly what we think."

Surrels gulped. "But that would violate the rules of the trial, wouldn't it?"

"You heard Dedeket, Father," said Kendo, gesturing at the sky. "Hal and Keershan technically already violated the rules of the duel and therefore nullified whatever agreement they'd made with Kryo Kardia. That means that this is effectively no longer an actual trial by combat, meaning there is nothing to stop the Glacians from invading Malarsan right this very instant if they want."

Surrels opened his mouth to try to argue against that, but he didn't get to before greenish-black lights erupted from the woods on the Hosarian side of the border. The Glacians who had been watching the duel in the sky immediately turned their gazes to the woods around them, worried looks on their faces.

And Surrels didn't blame them because in the next instant, a veritable horde of undead creatures burst out from within the woods. The undead creatures—largely humanoid in appearance, although it was hard to tell for sure from a distance—immediately began attacking the Glacians themselves. They killed several Glacians before the nearest Glacian soldiers realized what a threat they were and started attacking them, although Surrels did not think they would be able to defeat the seemingly never-ending horde as the zombies flooded out from the trees.

"Why are they attacking their own allies?" said Kendo in shock, watching as the zombies tore through Glacians. "Aren't they Kryo Kardia's subjects, too?"

Fralia pursed her lips. "What better way to expand your

undead forces than killing innocent people and adding their bodies to your army?"

Fralia was right. Surrels saw a particularly unfortunate Glacian soldier get dogpiled by at least a dozen zombies, who immediately went to attack the next unfortunate soldier. When the zombies left, the first soldier rose up as one of them and assaulted one of his former living mates, the two stuck in a life-or-death struggle as the living soldier tried to fight off the zombie.

"Damn it," Surrels said, putting his hands on his head. "Not good."

"Understatement of the year, Father," said Kendo, taking a step back. "Now if you will excuse me, I think it's time for me and my sister and her husband to make our leave."

Surrels whipped his head toward Kendo in surprise. "Make your leave? To where?"

Kendo gestured at the zombies. "Anywhere but here. Frankly, given this recent turn of events, we might just skip the kingdom entirely. Perhaps there is a land beyond the southern seas that Kryo Kardia won't be able to reach."

"The war isn't lost yet," Surrels said. He balled his hands into fists. "But you may have a point about you and Lila needing to flee. The battlefield is no place for civilians."

"We're going to fight?" Fralia questioned Surrels.

Surrels nodded as he drew his sword. "Yes. We have no choice. If those zombies cross the border, then it will spell doom not just for Mysteria, but for Malarsan as a whole. We need to stop them here, even if that means working with the Glacians themselves."

"Do they even want our help?" asked Wilme doubtfully.

"I suspect they'll take whatever help they can get," Surrels said. "Fralia, gather the mages. I'll lead the soldiers to battle."

"What about the Dragon Riders?" Fralia said. "Couldn't they help—"

The sound of clashing swords overhead made Surrels and everyone else look up again.

Halkeer was no longer alone against Kryo Kardia. It appeared that most of the Malarsan Riders had joined him, flying in a tight circle around the dueling gods and attacking wherever Kryo Kardia left an opening. A few did, however, break off to deal with the zombie infestation, although given how intermingled the zombies were with the Glacians, that made it difficult for the Riders to attack from the sky.

"The Riders are busy dealing with Kryo Kardia," Surrels said. "Plus, they can't risk breathing fire on the zombies without harming innocent people. We are on our own for the moment, for better or worse."

Wilme pursed her lips. "I will go back to Mysteria and get help."

Kendo raised a hand. "We'll go with her and make sure she gets there."

Surrels gave Kendo a surprised look. "Didn't realize you wanted to help."

Kendo shrugged. "I'm not a soldier, mage, or Dragon Rider, but that doesn't mean I can't still help protect my kingdom from those monsters."

A surge of fatherly pride rose up inside Surrels when Kendo said that, but he did not give himself time to focus on it.

Instead, Surrels turned around and, raising his sword

into the air, yelled, "Soldiers of the Malarsan Army! To arms!"

With that, Surrels rushed toward the border and was rapidly joined by the hundred or so soldiers that had been present for security forces. The drawing of swords and the clanking of armor intermingled with the heavy footfalls and battle cries of the Malarsan soldiers, the soldiers falling into a familiar arrow-shaped battle formation that they had practiced time and again over the last year.

So when they struck the zombie horde, they hit them with the force of the hundred soldiers they were. Surrels instantly beheaded a zombie that had been terrorizing a young woman and her child before stabbing another zombie in the chest and kicking it down, where one of his fellow soldiers stomped its head to paste under his boot.

Up close, the zombies looked—and smelled—even worse. They really did appear to be the reanimated bodies of dead Glacians, although their blue skin had turned gray and brittle over the years. They stank of flesh and dirt, which, intermingled with the blood shed by the innocents, made it unpleasant for Surrels to breathe, although he barely focused on that.

A deep, masculine yell, followed by the whooshing of fire and the sound of burning flesh, caught Surrels's attention just as he beheaded another zombie. Briefly pausing, Surrels looked over in the direction that the yell had come from.

It was Prince Compe. The wounded Glacian Rider, clutching his chest, had dismounted from his injured Steed to fight off the zombies trying to attack them. Dedeket lay flat on the back of Prince Compe's Steed, shaking hard and looking like he was scared out of his mind. The three of them were backed against a large tree, which meant that the zombies couldn't surround them, but they were trapped nonetheless.

Prince Compe, despite his injuries, was putting up a good fight. Well over a dozen dead zombies lay at his feet, with more joining their fallen brethren every time he swung his sword or unleashed a fireball. Interestingly, Prince Compe alternated between channeling dragonfire through his sword or through his fists, allowing him to alternate his strikes.

But it was clear that the zombie horde—which just seemed to grow bigger and bigger— would overwhelm Prince Compe eventually.

So Surrels, gripping his sword, called several other Malarsan soldiers over and rushed over to help Prince Compe. Surrels led the charge, slashing and hacking at the backs of the zombies that were too focused on Prince Compe to notice or pay attention to him.

As a result, Surrels cut a clean path through the zombies to Prince Compe in record time. But by the time he got to Prince Compe, one zombie—a fat man wearing some kind of ancient black armor—had broken through. Prince Compe tried to slash it but the fat zombie merely blocked his attack with its arm guard, knocking his sword out of his hand. The zombie slammed its fist into Prince Compe's chest, right where his wound was, and sent Prince Compe staggering to the ground.

The zombie raised its fists, likely to finish off Prince Compe, but Surrels was faster. With a single, well-aimed swing of his sword, Surrels sent the fat zombie's head flying in a random direction, where it struck another zombie that had been getting a little too close for comfort and knocked it down, where it was immediately beheaded by one of Surrels's soldiers.

Panting and sweating, Surrels looked down at Prince Compe and asked, "Are you all right?"

Prince Compe did not look all right to Surrels. His chest armor was covered in blood and not all of it was zombie blood, either. The bits of skin visible beneath his mask were as pale as snow, and he was breathing very hard.

At the same time, however, Prince Compe did not cry or show weakness. He simply glared up at Surrels with hateful eyes and said, "So this is how I die."

Surrels blinked. "What?"

Prince Compe cocked his head to the side. "Are you not going to kill me? I am weaker and more wounded than I ever have been before. This is the most vulnerable I've been in my life. And since the rules of the trial no longer apply, anyone can do anything to anyone else."

Surrels's eyes flicked up to Prince Compe's Steed, a black-and-gray dragon with greenish-blue eyes that eyed him warily. "I'm no expert on Dragon Riders, but I thought your bond with your Steed would heal you."

Prince Compe shook his head. "It's not that simple. My bond with Woppa is not as strong as it could be. Plus, Kryo Kardia's attack cast a degradation spell on me. Nothing other than life magic can heal me now." He looked at Surrels again. "So do it. Kill me. Get it over with. I know you want to. It's what I would do if our roles were reversed."

Surrels bit his lower lip. Killing Prince Compe was tempting to his Black Soldier instincts. Prince Compe, after all, appeared to be second only to Kryo Kardia himself in the Glaci Empire's hierarchy. Taking out Prince Compe would undoubtedly make the Glaci Empire weaker and Malarsan stronger or at least safer. Especially if Halkeer successfully killed Kryo Kardia again.

That was what a Black Soldier, trained in espionage and assassination, would do.

But then Surrels thought about Tonya and his family.

And thrust his hand into his pocket and pulled out the Life Flower in it and held it out to Prince Compe. "Take this."

Prince Compe stared at the Life Flower suspiciously. "Is that some kind of poison? That seems like a very round-about way of—"

"No, you royal brat," Surrels growled. "This is the legendary Life Flower. Apply it to your wounds and it will heal you."

Prince Compe actually gasped. "The Life Flower? You must be lying. The Life Flower is only a legend."

Surrels shook his head. "This is from my garden, not from legend. Now take it. Unless you *want* to die, of course."

Prince Compe appeared extremely suspicious of Surrels now. Nonetheless, he took the glowing Life Flower from Surrels's palm and brought it over to his chest. As the Life Flower left Surrels's hand, Surrels felt a miraculous warmth flow through his body and he recalled another legend of the Life Flower, that it only bloomed to save the life of someone who had not yet completed their destiny.

That warm feeling ... was that the Life Flower telling me well done? Surrels thought, watching as Prince Compe applied the Life Flower to his chest wound. *But it's not sentient, is it?*

Surrels did not know the answer to that question. He just watched as the Life Flower flashed against Prince

Compe's chest before dying down, the light fading from its petals as it turned back into an ordinary white flower.

Prince Compe's chest wound was cleaned and closed up. Additionally, Prince Compe himself looked like he'd just received an adrenaline boost. His eyes were wider and bigger, his breathing had returned to a normal steady rhythm, and he appeared stronger and happier overall.

"It worked," said Prince Compe in disbelief, staring at the dead flower in his hand now. "The Life Flower actually worked."

"You're welcome," Surrels said, hoping he wasn't going to regret saving the life of a man who was currently his enemy. He held out a hand toward Prince Compe. "Need a hand?"

Prince Compe stared at Surrels's hand with hesitation for a moment before clasping it tightly and rising to his feet. Surrels was surprised at how heavy Prince Compe was, but he did not show any weakness as he helped the prince to his feet.

Letting go of Surrels's hand, Prince Compe stared at Surrels uncomprehendingly. "Why did you save my life? You could have killed me."

Surrels met Prince Compe's gaze. "Because I am not your father. I don't kill my children for my own selfish reasons."

Prince Compe nodded, although Surrels could tell that Prince Compe didn't quite understand that. Surrels was not surprised. He guessed Prince Compe was not a father himself yet, so he obviously didn't understand what being a good father meant.

"Prince Compe!" said Dedeket's shrill voice behind

him. "What in the world are you doing fraternizing with the enemy?"

Prince Compe turned around and Surrels looked around him to see Dedeket—his nice robes now much messier than usual—stomping up to them. The inquirer came to a stop right in front of Prince Compe, who, Surrels noted, was at least two heads taller than Dedeket and twice as wide.

"He saved my life, Dedeket," said Prince Compe. "I am not sure that makes him the enemy anymore."

Dedeket blew a raspberry. "He saved your life, did he? Do you not understand that this man is the general of the Malarsan Army and a sworn enemy of His Iciness Kryo Kardia and the Glaci Empire as a whole? By accepting his help, you have unintentionally betrayed the empire itself!"

"But his men are fighting the zombies and protecting our fellow citizens," said Prince Compe, gesturing toward the battle raging behind Surrels. "He has nothing to gain from helping us."

Dedeket walked up to Surrels and poked him in the chest with a single finger. "I bet you do! You're probably hoping to turn us against His Iciness. Well, your Malarsan tricks won't work on me. I am a worldly and wise inquirer who is familiar with the many intricacies of court politics and international relations. In any political situation, there are always layers, like in an iceberg, layers upon endless layers of intrigue all for the exact purpose of helping politicians and generals get ahead in the great game. No, sir, you definitely do not fool Inquirer Dedeket, Grand Inquirer of the proud and honorable Glaci—"

Bang.

Dedeket lay on the ground at Surrels's feet, a rather

large bump developing on his head where Prince Compe's armored fist had struck him.

Surrels grimaced at Prince Compe. "You didn't have to hit him *that* hard."

Prince Compe lowered his fist. "Dedeket has always annoyed me. It's not my fault he gave me an excuse to quiet him for once."

Surrels tried not to smile at that. "Anyway, glad we are on the same side, at least for now. Will you help us kill the zombies?"

Prince Compe nodded. "Of course. I will assemble whatever men have not yet fallen to Kryo Kardia's Undead Legion and order them to help your soldiers."

Prince Compe's Steed coughed behind him. "It won't work. They'll just keep coming. And unlike living beings, the dead don't get tired."

Prince Compe pursed his lips. "Woppa is right. The Undead Legion is fragile but also self-sustaining and unable to be worn down through conventional means."

Surrels glanced at the sky where Halkeer, the Dragon Riders, and Kryo Kardia were stuck in a huge air battle that was still very much impossible to follow. "Kryo Kardia is the source of their power, right? So if Halkeer kills Kryo Kardia, then the Undead Legion will die with him."

Woppa clacked his teeth together. "Not that simple. There's likely a necromancer in the woods who is animating the zombies, probably one of Kryo Kardia's Disciples."

Surrels furrowed his brow. "Disciples?"

Prince Compe cast a glance toward the woods. "Yes. Kryo Kardia, in addition to us as his sons, has followers who he teaches the forgotten arts of the kingdom of Many to. They aren't nearly as powerful as Kryo Kardia, but they are proficient necromancers."

Surrels grimaced again. "So someone will need to head into the woods to kill whoever is animating the zombies?"

"That is the only way to ensure their defeat, yes," said Prince Compe with a swift nod. "Can you do it?"

Surrels sighed. "Looks like I'll have to, although actually finding the necromancer will be difficult. Those woods are very dark."

Prince Compe snapped his fingers. A Glacian mage suddenly appeared out of nowhere, though based on her ripped robes, she had clearly been in the middle of fighting the zombies.

"Yes, Your Majesty?" said the Glacian mage with a bow. "What do you require?"

Prince Compe pointed at Surrels. "Escort the Malarsan general into the woods to find the necromancer who has brought these zombies to life."

The Glacian mage stared at Prince Compe in alarm. "Escort the Malarsan general? But isn't he—"

Prince Compe gave the mage a very Kryo Kardia-like death glare. "This is an order, not a request."

The mage gulped and bowed again. "Yes, sir, Your Majesty, sir."

Surrels bit his lower lip but said nothing as he and the Glacian mage ran into the woods together. He just hoped that they would be able to find the necromancer in time to kill him and that Prince Compe would uphold his end of the deal and work with his soldiers to keep the zombies in check.

But I suspect he will, Surrels thought as he ducked to

avoid a low-hanging tree branch. *The real question is, will Halkeer be able to defeat Kryo Kardia?*

Surrels did not have the answer to that question.

So he prayed to the gods silently, asking them to give Hal and Keershan the strength they needed to win.

Because they needed it.

Chapter Thirty-Nine

Not to distract you or anything, Hal, but did you just hear Surrels? Keershan asked.

Hal, who was currently in control of Halkeer, dodged a slash from Kryo Kardia. He backed away at the last second, allowing Anija, Rialo, Ragnol, and Dinne to bathe Kryo Kardia in dragonfire. That attack forced Kryo Kardia to protect himself with some kind of black ice barrier that did not melt despite the heat of the flames.

Surrels? Hal repeated. *No way. He's all the way down there and we're all the way up here. No way we could hear him above all the fighting and screaming below.*

But I'm sure I heard his voice, Keershan protested. *It sounded like he was praying to the gods to help us.*

Hal paused briefly. He recalled Gotcham Nubor telling them after the challenge that they would be able to hear any prayers from mortals that mentioned their names, even if they were not being prayed to directly. That had been the one godly power they had not experienced yet. *Maybe you're hearing his prayers to the gods and because we are technically gods, that means we can hear him, too.*

Makes sense, Keershan said. *But I guess we'll worry about that later. Kryo Kardia is still a threat.*

That was the understatement of the century.

Despite the presence of the other Dragon Riders to back them up, Kryo Kardia still proved a formidable opponent. He had already taken out almost all of the other half-dozen Riders who had joined Halkeer. That was why the only two Dragon Rider pairs left were Anija and Rialo and Ragnol and Dinne.

Then Ragnol and Dinne charged toward Kryo Kardia, Ragnol screaming at the top of his lungs as he swung his battle ax at Kryo Kardia while Dinne swiped at him with his claws from below in a clear double-attack formation that Hal recalled teaching them what seemed like a lifetime ago now.

Only for Kryo Kardia to dodge both attacks easily and slam his fist into Ragnol. The blow sent Ragnol falling off Dinne to the ground below, forcing Dinne to break off his own attack to rescue Ragnol. Given how limp Ragnol appeared, Hal guessed that Ragnol was out of the fight for now.

Which left just him, Keershan, Anija, and Rialo against Kryo Kardia.

Hal hovered dozens of feet away from Kryo Kardia while Rialo flapped over to join them. Hal could sense Rialo was tiring out, as was Anija, although the two did their best to put on a strong face as they hovered side-by-side with Halkeer above the woods far below them.

"Is this the best that the famous Dragon Riders of Malarsan have to offer?" Kryo Kardia said, his voice sounding like a deeper and hoarser version of his normal voice. "Will I have to kill every single Dragon Rider in your pathetic little kingdom before you finally yield?"

Hal scowled but did not respond to that. Instead, he said, "How did you do that?"

Kryo Kardia cocked his head to the side. "Survive your initial attack? Isn't it obvious? I took the life force of my Steed and my children and their Steeds and added it to my own. Otherwise, I would have almost certainly died then."

"You mean you didn't achieve Unity with Frozas like we did?" Hal said in surprise.

Kryo Kardia smirked. "Of course not. To achieve Unity requires many years of developing a bond between Rider and Steed, and in my old age, I've grown quite impatient with anything that takes a long time to master. My bond with Frozas was never that close, even though we did work quite well together when she was alive."

Hal raised an eyebrow. "So this is basically just a perverted version of Unity. You forced Frozas to become one with you and killed her, didn't you?"

Kryo Kardia flexed his muscles. "More like I consumed her soul in order to graft it onto my own. It's a process I have repeated many times over the thousand or so years I have lived, although with different people whose knowledge, skills, or talents I wanted for my own. I then used my dark magic to add parts of her body onto my own. And now, I am more powerful than I ever have been before, powerful enough to match the strength of a god."

Beside Halkeer, Anija seemed to do a double-take. "Powerful enough to match a god? How would you know that? I don't see any gods around here."

Kryo Kardia smirked again. "Look right beside you. There is a god right next to you."

Anija and Rialo turned their gazes to Halkeer, and Anija's jaw dropped. "Wait. *You* two are gods now? Since when?"

Hal cringed. "Er, since the challenge of the gods. It was our reward for completing it."

Hal was annoyed that he had to reveal this to Anija and Rialo now of all times. But Kryo Kardia had somehow figured it out, so Hal saw no point in hiding it from them anymore. They had much bigger problems to worry about.

"How come you didn't tell us?" Rialo demanded. "It would have explained so much."

"We didn't want to worry everyone," Keershan said. "Because by becoming gods, that means we will have to leave the mortal realm eventually. We won't be allowed to stay with you guys in Mysteria anymore."

Anija still seemed to be processing this revelation based on her shocked expression. "A lot of weird things about you two make *so* much sense now. Like how you were able to destroy all those war balloons a while back on your own and stare down the Glacian Riders like they were nothing."

"We will discuss this later," Hal said. He turned his attention back to Kryo Kardia. "The real question is, how did you figure that out?"

Kryo Kardia cocked his head to the side. "Aside from the obvious divine power you radiate like the sun, I also once participated in the challenge of the gods."

Keershan gasped. "You mean you participated in the challenge of the gods? No one told us that."

Kryo Kardia nodded. "It was ages ago, long before either of you were born. Unfortunately, despite completing the challenge, the gods did not like me. So they refused to give me my rightful reward and sent me back to the mortal realm, expressly forbidding me from coming back to the Abode of the Gods for any reason."

"So that's how you knew Vilona," Hal said in realization. "You must have met her then."

"That I did," Kryo Kardia said. "The abode is also where I learned of the existence of the dark magic that I now currently possess. I was in line to become the next god of darkness, but once I was kicked out, I was forced to find *other* means to equal the power of the gods."

Hal furrowed his brow. "And I take it you are planning to return to the abode at some point to get your revenge."

"Of course," Kryo Kardia said. "Why else do you think I have been so interested in getting your relic? I need all the power I can get if I am to challenge the gods themselves and invade the abode. The Dragon Riders are the only mortals in this realm who have come even close to challenging the power of the gods, hence why I have done my best to build up a Dragon Rider force of my own."

"That's insane," Anija said. "You aren't a god."

Kryo Kardia chuckled. "Correct. I will become *greater* than a god. I will wield enough power to make the gods themselves kneel before me. Every knee under the heavens shall soon submit to the might of Kryo Kardia, the God Emperor of the whole world!"

Hal raised his golden sword. "Not unless we stop you. We can still kill you, you know. You aren't a god yet."

"Can you?" Kryo Kardia said. "Without the Soul Slayer, killing me, even with your divine power, will be considerably more difficult. It may even be impossible."

Hal suddenly remembered Vexo's words to him when

he gave him the Soul Slayer. Actually, it had been less Vexo's words and more Vexo's general smug attitude, as if he knew something that Hal did not.

He knew we wouldn't be able to use the Soul Slayer to stop Kryo Kardia, Keershan said, clearly thinking the same thing as Hal. *And he took our money anyway.*

Hal scowled. *I know. But there's a reason he's considered a rogue Relic Crafter, after all.*

Shaking his head, Hal pointed his sword at Kryo Kardia, golden fire swirling around the tip. "We'll see about that. As I said, you still aren't a god yet."

Kryo Kardia spun his spear before him. "Then what are you waiting for, Halkeer? Come at me, if you really think you can stand against my might."

Hal bit his lower lip. He glanced at Anija and Rialo and said, "You two, go help the others below. We'll handle Kryo Kardia."

"And leave you to fight this madman by yourself?" Anija demanded. "I don't think so. We might not be able to merge like you and Keershan, but that doesn't mean we are cowards who will run away from a fight."

"It's not about bravery," Hal snapped. "It's about your safety. You two don't stand a chance against him. Now *go.*"

Hal used his divine authority when he said that last word. He hated using it to essentially override Anija and Rialo's free wills, but he knew how stubborn the two of them could be, both individually and collectively. He needed them both gone.

Fortunately, it seemed to work. Anija and Rialo both wore hesitant expressions on their faces before nodding and flying down to the ground below. Hal half-expected Kryo Kardia to attack them, but the emperor of the Glaci

Empire paid them no attention. His icy blue eyes were fixed on Hal and Hal alone, white-blue dragonfire curling around his spear.

"Thank you for getting rid of the interlopers," Kryo Kardia said. He raised his spear. "Their absence will make this battle far sweeter. I have never killed a god before. It will be interesting."

Hal scowled. "Unlike you, we *have* killed gods before. Trust me, it's not easy."

With that, Hal and Keershan launched toward Kryo Kardia, their voices crying out as one from Halkeer's mouth. Golden dragonfire erupted along the blade of Hal's sword, glowing almost as brightly as the sun.

But Kryo Kardia dove to the side, easily avoiding their sword, and slashed at them with his spear. Hal, however, raised his shield just in time to block the spear, though the impact still forced him to roll through the air to get out of Kryo Kardia's reach.

We can't beat him through sheer physical power alone, Keershan said. *Might I suggest we access some of that godly energy we've been saving more directly?*

Hal smirked. *I like your thinking. Let's see exactly what the god of light can actually do.*

Kryo Kardia, obviously, was not privy to their mental conversation. He simply shot toward them again, flapping his wings hard, spear leveled at Halkeer's chest.

But Hal raised his hand toward the sun, and a bright, blinding light erupted from his palm. The light grew in brightness more and more until it had obscured nearly everything. The light slammed into Kryo Kardia, who cried out in surprise as the light blinded him.

But it didn't blind Hal. Due to being the gods of light,

Hal and Keershan could not be blinded by light unlike mortals or other beings. They could see as well in blinding light as in normal light, and right now, that gave them the biggest possible advantage over Kryo Kardia, who could not.

That was how Hal could see Kryo Kardia floating in the air, one hand over his eyes, clearly trying to prevent himself from permanently losing his eyesight. That meant his guard was down entirely, which Hal fully intended to take advantage of.

Gripping his sword tightly, Hal shot toward Kryo Kardia again. His wings beat against the winds as he drew closer and closer to Kryo Kardia, his eyes on the emperor's neck, which he would strike in order to behead him.

Without making a sound, Hal swung his sword at Kryo Kardia's neck.

But Kryo Kardia tore his hand from his eyes and caught the blade of Hal's sword with his bare hand. Between the sharpness of the blade and the dragonfire rushing along it, Kryo Kardia's left hand made disgusting squelching and burning sounds.

Yet Kryo Kardia showed no fear or concern. He just stared at Hal with sightless eyes that made Hal's stomach churn.

"What—?" Hal said in disbelief, staring at Kryo Kardia. "How can you still see—?"

Kryo Kardia chuckled. "I am undead. My eyes, technically speaking, do not work, and haven't for some time. But I don't *need* eyes to kill you."

Kryo Kardia suddenly slammed his spear into Hal's gut. Hal cried out in pain as Kryo Kardia's spear went through his stomach and out the other side. While not the worst pain Hal had felt in his life, it was certainly far worse than he'd expected to feel in his godly state. Even Keershan felt it, his screams filling Hal's mind as Kryo Kardia dug his spear into his stomach.

"That's right," Kryo Kardia hissed. "Scream. Beg for mercy. Mercy you will never get."

Kryo Kardia yanked his spear out of Hal's stomach and brought the butt of his spear down on the back of his head. The blow sent Hal hurtling toward the ground below, his head spinning, his golden blood freely trailing behind him as he fell toward the trees.

As Hal and Keershan fell to the forest below, Hal's mind returned, one last time, to the final minutes of the last part of the challenge, and how they managed to get out of that situation.

Chapter Forty

THE BREATH OF THE TENTACLE-HEADED DEMON MADE HAL and Keershan feel sick to their stomachs. If feeling sick to your stomach was bad when you were just one person, it was far worse when you were two people sharing the same body. The stench reminded Hal of death and mold, making it difficult for him to think clearly.

Why is this demon so strong? Keershan asked mentally. *We should be able to escape from it easily!*

No idea, Hal said. *We're not gods, so we aren't that much stronger than it. We just need to focus.*

That, of course, was easier said than done. Between the cold, slimy tentacles sapping their limbs of energy and the god-awful stench of the demon's breath, focusing on anything was a challenge in itself. Even with the new-found clarity from having merged, they were not immune to pain or what pain could do to you when applied in just the right places in just the right way.

Hell, Hal and Keershan couldn't even focus on what the

gods might be doing. Hal guessed, however, that very few of them were disappointed with how this match was going.

They're probably happy that we mere 'mortals' are being put in our place, Hal thought, anger rising in him. *They probably think we deserve this.*

I wish we could teach them a lesson, Keershan said. *Or at least show them why we 'mere' mortals aren't so mere.*

Hal felt Keershan's anger join his own and become something far stronger and hotter than anything they could feel on their own. The anger rose inside their new combined form, sending dragonfire through their limbs, driving away the relentless cold of the demon's tentacles and giving them some of their old strength back.

The demon, apparently sensing this change, tried to pull them in even faster than ever. But Hal and Keershan, their minds cleared by their anger, resisted with all their might. The demon's tentacles started to smoke where they touched Hal and Keershan's skin as they grew hotter and hotter, yet the demon still did not let go or yield.

Keershan, Hal said. *Why don't we give this monster exactly what it wants?*

Keershan rumbled approvingly. *Sure. Let's burn it.*

Hal nodded. He returned his focus to the external world and, drawing upon the dragonfire within him, unleashed it in one huge blast.

And this time, Hal did not unleash it from his hands, like normal. Nor did it even come from his mouth alone.

No, Hal and Keershan unleashed the dragonfire from their whole body. Fire exploded from their whole form in every direction, white-hot, hot enough to melt even dragon scales.

And the demon, who had brought them within mere inches of its 'mouth,' took the brunt of the blast.

The demon didn't even get to scream before the dragonfire explosion completely devoured it. For a second, all Hal and Keershan could hear, see, feel, taste, and smell was fire and the burning of demon flesh.

But then the dragonfire died out, and Hal and Keershan found themselves standing in a huge pile of ash that had once been the demon. Their body was still on fire, however, acting more like fiery armor than anything.

They faced down a startled-looking Old Snow, his jaw hanging open.

That was his mistake.

Without hesitation, Hal and Keershan launched toward Old Snow, sword swinging, screaming at the top of their lungs.

Old Snow raised his staff to block the sword.

And his staff snapped clean in two when Hal and Keershan's dragonfire sword slammed into it.

Old Snow instinctively closed his eyes, but at the last possible second, Hal and Keershan stopped the sword within an inch of Old Snow's face. It was just close enough to singe the hairs on Old Snow's white beard but not close enough to actually hurt him.

"Do you yield, god of demons?" asked Hal and Keershan, their voices coming from their combined mouth at the same time.

Old Snow slowly opened his blood-red eyes and blinked at the sight of the dragonfire blade burning mere inches from his face.

Then Old Snow nodded ever-so-slightly. "I yield, Halkeer. I yield."

As soon as Old Snow said those words, Hal and Keershan felt a shift in the room's atmosphere. Lowering their sword to their side, Hal and Keershan looked around the stadium.

The gods had gone utterly silent again. The expressions on their faces ranged from impressed to fearful to annoyance, although all of their faces were tinged with shock. No doubt they had not expected to see Hal and Keershan win the challenge or even just defeat Old Snow.

The sound of two hands clapping broke the tense silence, drawing Hal and Keershan's attention to Gotcham Nubor's throne.

The king of the gods was clapping for them. He was even smiling now, oddly enough.

"Good show, Halar Norath and Keershan Clawfoot!" Gotcham Nubor said, his voice ringing across the arena. "And congratulations on passing the challenge! You have done what very few mortals have ever accomplished. For that alone, you will be forever ingrained in the memories of the gods for as long as the universe breathes."

Slowly, the rest of the gods joined in with the clapping and cheering, until soon nearly every single god and goddess in the room was congratulating them. Even Demo, who was little more than a purple sphere, appeared to be spinning and rotating faster than usual in excitement. The god of the dragons was clapping with the other gods, using his forelegs to pull that little feat off.

And, of course, no one was clapping harder than Old Snow. The smile on his face told Hal and Keershan all they needed to know about how proud the old man was of them.

I can't believe it, Keershan said. *We won. We did it. We completed the challenge.*

I can't believe it, either, Hal said. *I wonder what the next steps are—*

A burning pain erupted inside their chest, making both Hal and Keershan cry out. A bright flash of light blinded them both and suddenly Hal found himself lying on the sandy floor of the arena, staring at an equally bewildered Keershan, who was staring at his claws like he'd never seen them before.

"Huh?" Keershan said, his eyes wide as he turned his claws over. "I'm four-legged again? I mean, I can't complain, but—"

"Your Unity form must have worn off," Old Snow said with a nod. "Frankly, I am surprised it lasted as long as it did."

Hal looked up at Old Snow in confusion. "What do you mean? I thought we had achieved Unity, the ultimate goal of all Dragon Riders. Why did we separate?"

Old Snow leaned on his staff, which was now back in one piece for some reason. "Much like when you first bonded, achieving Unity takes a lot of practice to do and even more practice to maintain. Uniting your bodies and minds requires a ton of energy. It is frankly a miracle that you two achieved Unity as soon as you did, much less that you maintained it for that long. For that alone, I predict that you two will make excellent Dragon Riders, although I supposed that is rather obvious."

Hal flexed his hands. It felt weird having normal human fingers again rather than claws. He wasn't sure he liked it.

"Will we be able to merge again?" asked Keershan as he rose to his four feet, shaking the sand off his scales.

"Sure," Old Snow said. "But not for a few days, at least. It will take time for your bodies to recover from and adjust to the changes caused by merging. With time, you will be able to maintain Unity for longer and longer periods of time, but for the moment, they will only last a little while before your bodies return to their original separate conditions."

Hal felt the breastplate of his chest armor. It only bore a vague similarity to the scales that dragons had and felt nowhere near as strong as the scales that he had had during his merge with Keershan. He almost didn't like his human form anymore, although he had to admit that the lack of a tail and wings did feel a lot better.

Gotcham Nubor suddenly flew from his throne toward them. Landing on the sandy floor of the arena a few feet away, Gotcham Nubor spread his arms. "Again, I must congratulate you two for completing the challenge. I honestly had low expectations for both of you, but you have proved yourselves worthy of apotheosis."

"Apothe-what?" Hal said as he rose to his feet, dusting sand off his pants.

"Ascension to godhood," Old Snow explained. "That's just the fancy word for it."

"The *proper* word for it, you mean," said Gotcham Nubor. "It is important to know the proper names of things, for names, like knowledge, have power linked to them. To know a thing's name is to, in some way, control the thing in question."

"Right," Hal said. "So what now? Are we just instantly promoted to godhood on the spot or is there another three-part challenge we need to undertake before we can ascend?"

Gotcham Nubor shook his head. "No, the actual ascension process is quite quick. Raniel!"

The flapping of wings overhead made Hal and Keershan look up in time to see a familiar winged angel flying toward them. It was Raniel, the Captain of the Guard in the abode. He looked much the same as he had back in the abode, although Hal noticed a couple of bottles of some kind of golden liquid tied to his waist.

"Raniel?" Keershan said in surprise, staring at the angel as he landed. "What are you doing here? I thought only challengers and the gods themselves were allowed into the challenge."

Raniel gave Keershan an annoyed look. "His Majesty King Gotcham Nubor allowed me to enter. So congratulations, I suppose, for winning."

Hal could tell that it pained Raniel to congratulate them on anything. No doubt it would take Raniel some time to adjust to the idea that a couple of mortals were now higher in the divine hierarchy than he was, even if those mortals had to become gods in order to be so.

Gotcham Nubor held out a hand toward Raniel. "The elixirs, please."

Raniel quickly untied the bottles from his belt and handed them to Gotcham Nubor without saying another word.

Gotcham Nubor then held the bottles out to Hal and Keershan. "Drink these and you will become gods."

Hal narrowed his eyes. "What are 'these' exactly?"

"Divine elixirs," Old Snow said. "By drinking these elixirs, your essence will change. You will go from being mortals to gods."

"Once you drink them, the entire process should take

approximately five minutes," said Gotcham Nubor, "less if you are particularly compatible with godhood."

"What does that mean?" Keershan said.

"That refers to any divine essence you may already have in you," Old Snow explained. "If you were demigods, for example, the ascension process would take less time than if you were mortals."

Hal took both of the elixirs, which felt smooth and warm in his hands, like freshly-brewed coffee. "Neither of us is part-god, so I assume it will take time for us to ascend."

"Perhaps," Old Snow said vaguely. "But either way, in no more than five minutes, you two will be gods forever."

Hal licked his lips. He undid the stoppers on both bottles and brought up one to his lips and held the other one to Keershan's mouth. Meeting Keershan's gaze, Hal said, "On the count of three, we will both drink at once. Okay?"

Keershan nodded. "Got it."

Hal took a deep breath. "One. Two. Three!"

As soon as that last word left Hal's mouth, he dumped the entire elixir into his mouth. At the same time, he tipped Keershan's elixir into his open mouth, feeling the liquid drain from the bottle quickly.

The elixir tasted *wonderful*. It vividly reminded Hal of the warm goat's milk that his mother would feed him when he was ill as a young child. It brought feelings of comfort and safety inside him, helping him to relax as the buttery drink went into his mouth and down into his body.

All those feelings of comfort and safety, however, vanished in a second.

They were replaced by white-hot fire.

And not dragonfire, either.

It was simply fire that burned within, destroying everything in its path.

And there was nothing Hal—or Keershan—could do about it.

Chapter Forty-One

SURRELS DECIDED THAT ZOMBIE HUNTING WAS NOT FOR HIM.

That might have been an odd thought to have under any other circumstance, but given the hordes of undead creatures threatening to overwhelm both Malarsan and Hosar, Surrels thought this was the perfect time to consider his preferences in that area.

Fortunately, the undead were not exactly observant. Although Surrels and his escort, the Glacian mage who identified herself simply as Pilas, had to make their way past the zombies to find the necromancer, the zombies barely paid them any attention. Perhaps the scent of fresh living flesh beyond the woods was too much for them to ignore, or maybe they thought that two measly humans would not be enough to fill their stomachs by themselves.

Of course, it helped that Pilas was using some kind of hiding spell to prevent them from being spotted. Pilas tried to explain how the spell worked to Surrels, but she used a lot of big magical words that flew over Surrels's head completely.

All Surrels understood was that the zombies could not see them, and even if the zombies did somehow see them through the concealing spell, they would just think they were a couple of trees or a bush or something and continue to ignore them.

As Surrels noted earlier, zombies weren't exactly the smartest.

And because the zombies made no effort to hide their tracks, it was easy for Surrels and Pilas to follow the rough path they had made through the woods back to its source. Even so, they had to move slowly because Pilas' mage robes kept getting caught on branches and bushes. It eventually got to the point where Pilas tied her robes more tightly around her body to prevent them from catching on to things.

"How much longer until we find the necromancer?" Surrels said, keeping his voice to a whisper to avoid alerting the zombies to their existence.

"Not far now," Pilas said, also keeping her voice low as she ducked underneath a low overhanging branch. She pointed ahead. "He's just beyond those trees. At least, I think he is, based on the dark magic I sense."

Surrels pursed his lips but put his hand on the hilt of his sheathed sword as they approached the coming tree line. Reaching the trees, Surrels and Pilas peered through the gap at a sight that Surrels would never forget.

A large graveyard sat in the middle of the forest. A large abandoned graveyard, based on how overgrown the weeds were among the rotting headstones and how rusted the metal fence surrounding it was.

But it had clearly seen a lot of action recently. Most of the graves were ripped open, piles of dirt and wood everywhere. Even as Surrels watched, more and more zombies burst out from graves, toppling tombstones and sending dirt flying everywhere as they marched in a line out through the graveyard's open gates.

Most of the undead, however, came from the huge stone tomb set in the center of the graveyard, from which a steady stream of zombies emerged. A dark figure in a hood and cloak stood near the entrance, his hands glowing a sickly green color as he chanted words in a language that reminded Surrels of the sound of breaking bone.

"What is a graveyard doing all the way out here?" Surrels said, raising an eyebrow. "I've been to Hosar several times and have never even heard of such a place."

Pilas pursed her lips. "This is the graveyard of the former royal family of Hosar, who His Majesty had put to death after the empire conquered the country. The Hosarian royal family ruled Hosar for generations, so this is where their dead were traditionally buried. As well, this graveyard is where most of the Hosarian soldiers who perished in the border skirmishes with Malarsan over the centuries were buried, as it was considered too much trouble to bring their bodies back to be buried in their hometowns. Hence why there are so many zombies."

Surrels gave Pilas a surprised look. "You sure know a lot about Hosar."

Pilas furrowed her brow. "That's because my family is from Hosar, so I grew up hearing all of the stories from my grandparents. This graveyard became abandoned after Kryo Kardia conquered it. That is probably why he agreed to have the duel at the border."

Surrels nodded. "Definitely. It gives him a near-endless supply of zombies to work with. Makes a lot more sense than hauling a bunch of corpses from the Northern Circle down here."

Pilas nodded in agreement. She pointed at the hooded figure. "That man must be the necromancer who Kryo Kardia sent out here to act as backup. I've only seen one other necromancer before this one, but they're very distinctive."

"Gotcha," Surrels said. "Since you seem more familiar with necromancy than I am, what do you think would be the best way to approach this guy?"

Pilas stroked her chin. "I have not fought a necromancer before, but if they are anything like normal mages, then they are usually physically weak. If we can sneak up on him and get him from behind, we might be able to kill him before he even realizes we're here."

Surrels blinked. "So we need to assassinate him, in other words."

Pilas nodded again. "More or less. Why? Do you have experience in that area?"

Surrels gripped the hilt of his sword more tightly. "Far too much. With your concealing spells, I could probably sneak up on him without him or his minions being the wiser."

Pilas pursed her lips. "A risky plan, but I suppose it's also our best. I will stay here and act as backup in case you fail to kill the necromancer."

Pilas waved a hand over Surrels and he suddenly felt a cold, watery sensation wash over him even though he was perfectly dry. Looking at his body, Surrels did not see anything out of the ordinary.

"I put a camouflage spell on you," Pilas explained. "To

anyone but you and me, you will look like you are part of the general environment."

"You don't think the necromancer will sense the moulash on me or something?" Surrels said.

Pilas shook her head. "He shouldn't, as he is clearly too busy summoning the undead to pay attention to anything else. I caution against making sound, however, because people can still hear you."

Surrels gave her one last nod before making his way through the tree line. He moved quickly but quietly, heading to the other side of the graveyard. His Black Soldier instincts, honed from years of experience, kicked in, and he suddenly found it easier to move quieter than a ghost.

When Surrels circled the graveyard, he darted out into the open, doubled over. He found a gap in the metal fence that he slipped through easily and made his way toward the necromancer, whose back was now to him. Up close, the necromancer seemed bulkier than he expected, although Surrels figured he was just wearing a bulky cloak.

More importantly, the necromancer appeared totally focused on the zombies streaming from the mausoleum. And thanks to the slapping and grunting noises made by the zombies, Surrels doubted the necromancer could hear anything, especially something as quiet as Surrels's footsteps.

Closer, Surrels thought, slowly unsheathing his sword. *Closer. Closer.*

When Surrels got within two feet of the necromancer, he paused. He needed to wait for the right moment to strike. However defenseless the necromancer might have appeared, Surrels knew that he only had one real shot at taking this guy out. If he missed or his attack only injured but did not actually kill the necromancer, then Surrels would almost certainly end up as one of his zombies.

So Surrels mentally counted down the seconds until it was time to strike.

Three.

A zombie wearing a crown shambled out of the mausoleum, nearly stumbling over its own oddly-shaped feet before joining its fellow zombies.

Two.

Two zombies—these ones appearing to be twin women wearing the same white grave clothes—emerged from the mausoleum with surprising quietness, only the clacking of their jaws indicating that they were on the move.

One!

Surrels rose to his full height and raised his sword over his head.

Then Pilas' scream abruptly pierced the air before ending just as abruptly.

Before Surrels registered what happened, the necromancer spun around and kicked Surrels in the gut. The blow knocked Surrels to the ground, causing him to drop his sword. He tried to rise to his feet, only for a couple of burly zombies in rusty armor to appear on either side of him and grab his arms. Surrels struggled to break free of their grasp but their grips were stronger than steel.

"Well, well, well," said the necromancer, standing up straight as he dusted off his cloak. "What have we here? A Malarsan assassin? How cute."

Surrels gazed up at the necromancer, who he could now see was nowhere near as thin or reedy as he had first assumed. In fact, the necromancer was buffer than Surrels, his muscles straining against his shirt. He looked like he could easily bench Surrels and then some.

More creepily, however, were his eyes, which glowed the same unnatural green color as his hands.

"How did you know?" Surrels said. "I was camouflaged by—"

"By that silly little girl hiding in the bushes?" the necromancer interrupted Surrels. "You don't think I have zombies hiding in the woods around me for exactly this sort of Malarsan trickery? Her corpse will make an excellent addition to my collection."

Surrels gulped. He felt bad about poor Pilas, but he felt even worse for himself. He had failed to stop the necromancer, which meant that the Malarsans and Hosarians would inevitably be overrun.

The necromancer picked up Surrels's sword and turned it over in his hands. "Cheap iron, which is to be expected from such a poor kingdom as yours. Still, I think it should be more than sufficient for killing you and adding you to my collection."

Surrels grimaced as the necromancer raised his sword over his head. He knew that struggling was pointless.

But then, a sudden coldness descended on the entire graveyard, making Surrels and the necromancer shiver. The zombies, naturally, did not react, probably because they could not feel anything.

"Coldness?" said the necromancer, looking around in alarm. "It can't be His Majesty, can it—?"

A loud wailing sound suddenly erupted from the woods around the graveyard, causing both Surrels and the necromancer to look around in confusion. The necromancer, especially, whipped his head this way and that, his green eyes trying to spot the source of the wailing.

"Where is that sound coming from?" said the necromancer. He glared at Surrels. "Is this another one of your Malarsan tricks?"

Surrels gulped again. "I-I have no idea where this noise is coming from, either."

The necromancer narrowed his eyes. "Liar. And a terrible one, at that."

The necromancer raised his hand again only for a rolling wave of ice-cold mist and fog to rush out of the trees around them. Accompanied by the wailing sound, the mist quickly covered the whole graveyard, limiting Surrels's line of sight to less than two feet in front of him.

That allowed him to see the necromancer well. The necromancer was now completely ignoring him, turning on the spot, a concerned frown crossing his face.

"Who is there?" the necromancer called, his voice echoing in the mist. "Show yourselves! Or else I will have my zombies tear this whole forest apart until they find you!"

No response. The wailing had also gone silent, although in this case, it was less comforting and more ominous.

The necromancer took a deep breath. "Playing the silent game, are you? Very well. It's your funeral."

The necromancer raised a hand, perhaps to summon his zombie horde, and that was when *it* appeared.

From out of the mist emerged a creature straight out of Surrels's worst nightmares. Tall and skeletal, the creature wore thick furs and a coat torn at the edges. Eyes white as snow shone from within its black eyeholes as it reached out with long, skeletal fingers toward the necromancer.

The necromancer gasped. "What in Kryo Kardia's name is that—"

The creature grasped the necromancer's shoulders and pulled him toward its mouth. The necromancer screamed in sheer terror and struggled against its grip, but his efforts didn't even make the creature budge.

The creature then 'kissed' the necromancer. That was the best word Surrels could use to describe its action. It brought its mouth against the necromancer's, instantly silencing his screams. He continued to struggle against it, however, but his struggling became weaker and weaker until soon he stopped entirely. His body went limp in its hands, but the creature kept sucking as if trying to get every last drop of whatever it had sucked out of him.

Then the creature broke off its 'kiss' and dropped the dead necromancer onto the ground. As soon as the necromancer's lifeless body landed, the zombies holding Surrels suddenly let go of his arms and collapsed. Surrels, not one to look a gift horse in the mouth, snatched his sword off the ground and waved it at the creature.

"I-I have no idea what sort of monster you are, but you don't scare me," Surrels said. "Try to kiss me and you'll find out I am a harder target."

A shrill elderly female voice laughed from within the mist. "How cute that you think you could resist Guardian. Ah, to be young again."

The creature, evidently named Guardian, suddenly shrank back into the mist. It grew smaller and smaller until it ended up inside a ceramic jar that an elderly woman held, which she quickly put the lid on.

But it was not just one elderly woman, but three. They stood side by side in the mist and, aside from the identical hats and robes, they looked completely different. One was short and stout with a frog-like face, while the second was tall and thin with an extremely long nose.

Only the woman in the middle, who was neither too tall nor too short, looked like a normal middle-aged woman to Surrels, although her ice-blue eyes and snow-white hair made him doubt that.

Surrels gulped. "Who are you and why did you save me?"

The tall woman gave Surrels an offended look. "Didn't Hal and Keershan tell you about us? Is this the thanks we get after all we've done for you ungrateful Malarsans?"

Surrels blinked. "Wait. Three sisters. Witch hats. You're the Snow Witches of the Wastes!"

The short woman grunted. "Took you long enough. I see you are more brawn than brains."

The tall one smirked. "Oh, I *like* brawny guys. You wouldn't happen to be single, would you, General Surrels?"

"Sisters, please show some respect to one of Hal and Keershan's friends," said the middle woman. She looked at Surrels. "Although it seems like Hal has told you about us, allow me to make proper introductions. I am Boca, the oldest sister, and these are my younger sisters, Kiko and Ericha, respectively."

Surrels lowered his sword, staring at the Snow Witches uncertainly. "Well, this is certainly a surprise. Hal told us about you, but he didn't quite capture your, er—"

"Radiant beauty?" Ericha offered.

"Incredible intellect and charm?" Kiko added.

Surrels bit his lower lip. "Your *great* magical ability. You three are clearly very talented magical users."

Ericha pouted. "Yes, I suppose we are that. But don't you think we're beautiful? Or at least *I* am?"

"Flirt later, sister," said Boca. She gazed at the dead necromancer with utter contempt. "I cannot believe Kralot shared our knowledge of necromancy with others."

"I can," Kiko said. "He's disrespected us in every other way. Why wouldn't he do it this way?"

"You mean you ladies taught him how to summon the dead?" Surrels said. "That doesn't seem wise."

Boca gave Surrels an aloof look. "It doesn't matter at this point. We followed the *Frozen Heart* here to watch the duel. We suspected that Kralot would not play fair, which is why we located the necromancer, as we intended to take him out to aid the Malarsans."

Surrels glanced at the dead necromancer and lifeless corpses strewn around his feet. "You certainly succeeded in that. Always nice to have backup."

"So where are Kralot and Hal and Keershan?" asked Ericha, glancing around the graveyard. "We just got here, so——"

Something hot and burning suddenly broke through the trees. It shot directly over their heads and slammed into the Hosarian royal family mausoleum, smashing straight into it. Surrels and the Snow Witches ducked, covering their heads with their hands, but as it turned out, they didn't need to do that.

"What was that?" said Kiko, lowering her hands from her head and gazing at the mausoleum in confusion. "A meteor?"

Surrels, suddenly feeling like he knew where he'd seen that fire before, rushed over to the smashed mausoleum entrance. Coming to a stop in front of the wreckage, Surrels felt his heart tighten at the sight.

Hal and Keershan—no longer Halkeer—lay among the rubble of the mausoleum. Though they appeared to still be alive, they were barely moving, their armor cracked and missing in several places. Golden blood leaked out of Hal's crown while Keershan had blood dripping out of the corner of his mouth. Hal had a gap in his stomach armor like he had been stabbed, although to Surrels, it looked like the wound had healed already.

Surrels took a deep breath and looked over his shoulder at the Snow Witches. "This is no meteor. It's Hal and Keershan. They're—"

"About to be very dead very soon," Kryo Kardia's chilling voice said from within the mist.

Kryo Kardia, in his full humanoid dragon form, appeared in the mist like a ghost himself. He landed on the main path to the mausoleum, crushing the fallen zombies under his clawed feet, and rose to his full height, a wicked grin on his face as he spun his spear in his hands.

And Surrels suddenly realized just how screwed they were.

Chapter Forty-Two

HOVERING ON RIALO'S BACK ABOVE THE BATTLEFIELD THAT had once been the Malarsan and Hosarian border, Anija saw Halkeer vanish into the forest, followed shortly by Kryo Kardia, who was clearly chasing the two of them.

She only noticed because the zombies—which had been fighting so vigorously against the combined forces of the Malarsans and Glacians—had abruptly fallen to pieces a second or two ago. It had been very strange. One second the zombies were ravenously tearing at any living flesh they could get; the next, they lay flat on the ground like the corpses they were. That left everyone feeling very confused, aside from Anija, who had an inkling of what might have happened.

Surrels must have taken out the necromancer that Prince Compe told him about, Rialo said mentally, her voice sounding quite pleased. *Remember? Prince Compe told us.*

That had been another unexpected turn of events. Prince Compe and the remaining Glacian soldiers and mages had sided with the Malarsans against Kryo Kardia's

Undead Legion. Evidently, Surrels had saved Prince Compe's life from said demons, and Prince Compe saw this as a way to repay Surrels for that act of kindness.

Wiping the sweat from her forehead, Anija said to Rialo, "Yeah. But Hal and Keershan clearly need our help."

Looking over her shoulder, Anija shouted, "Ragnol! You're in charge now. We're going to help Hal and Keershan."

Ragnol, who sat on Dinne as they hovered over the Malarsan side of the border, nodded in understanding. Clutching his chest where Kryo Kardia had punched him, Ragnol immediately began barking orders to the Malarsans and Glacians alike, who immediately started to follow his orders. Mostly, they appeared to be doing cleanup of the fallen zombies as well as tending to the wounds of those who had been harmed by the Undead Legion.

Before Rialo could take off, however, Fralia shouted below, "Anija! Rialo! Wait!"

Looking down at Fralia standing on the ground, Anija shouted back, "What?"

"I want to come with you to help Hal and Keershan!" Fralia said, gesturing at the woods.

Anija raised an eyebrow. "Are you sure that would be a smart idea? Kryo Kardia is—"

"I don't care," Fralia replied. She met Anija's gaze sternly. "Hal and Keershan are my friends, too, you know."

Anija pursed her lips but found she could not argue with Fralia. Although the archmage always seemed too timid to Anija, she had to admit that Fralia could be quite persuasive when she wanted to be.

So Anija had Rialo swoop down and allow Fralia to

jump on her back. Just as Fralia wrapped her arms around Anija's waist for support, Rialo took off, flying above the tops of the trees, scanning the woods below for any sign of Hal and Keershan or Kryo Kardia.

"See them yet?" Fralia yelled over the whipping winds around them.

Anija suddenly pointed straight ahead at a plume of smoke rising not far from them. "There! They must be over there!"

Rialo picked up speed without Anija even telling her to. In seconds, they reached the site of the plume, causing Rialo to slow down just enough to keep them hovering in the air.

It appeared that Hal and Keershan—now separated into two individuals again—lay in the ruins of what appeared to be an ancient mausoleum, injured and barely moving. Kryo Kardia stood before the entrance to the mausoleum, spear in hand, which glowed with power. He faced Surrels and the three Snow Witches, of all people, who Anija certainly had not expected to see here.

Worryingly, the Snow Witches, who Kryo Kardia normally feared, now looked afraid of *him*.

"Move aside, women," Kryo Kardia said. He raised a clawed hand and clicked his claws together. "Unless you wish to die with your friend, that is."

"Is that any way to talk to your mothers, Kralot?" Ericha asked. "Show some respect."

Kryo Kardia sneered. "You women aren't my mothers. You are nothing more than annoying thorns in my side who I will be more than happy to remove."

"You won't win, Kralot," said Boca softly. "The Fracturing will take you."

"Not if I become a god, it won't," Kryo Kardia said. He pointed his spear at them, and ice-blue energy mixed with a sickening green color began building at its tip. "But I have no time to argue. If you wish to die here, then I will be more than happy to accommodate that request."

The Snow Witches threw up some kind of magical barrier that resembled a hexagon beehive, but Anija intuitively sensed that it wouldn't withstand whatever attack Kryo Kardia was going to shoot at them.

Rialo, Anija said mentally, *let's kick his ass.*

Rialo growled and rushed toward Kryo Kardia. Opening her mouth, she unleashed a powerful blast of dragonfire at his back.

But Kryo Kardia whirled around and unleashed his energy blast at *them.* The energy blast shot through the air, carving a path through Rialo's dragonfire, before colliding with Rialo's face.

Rialo roared with pain and went spiraling to the ground below. Anija, grabbing Fralia, jumped off of Rialo's back. At the same time, Fralia raised her hands, which glowed green.

A powerful gust of wind caught Anija, Fralia, and Rialo. The wind allowed Anija and Fralia to land safely in the graveyard, while Rialo crashed into the trees just beyond the fencing. Anija felt Rialo's pain through their bond but could also tell that Rialo was still alive, which made her supremely grateful. She could not, however, see where Rialo had crashed in the trees.

Staggering upright, Anija glared at Kryo Kardia. "You bastard. You will *definitely* pay for that."

Kryo Kardia smirked. "Is that any way for a daughter to talk to her father?"

"Daughter—?" Fralia looked at Anija in confusion. "Anija, what's he talking about?"

"Nothing," Anija said, drawing her daggers from her side. "He's lying. Don't listen to him."

Kryo Kardia cocked his head to the side. "Why do you deny the truth in front of your friends? Are you trying to avoid reality? That's not very healthy, you know."

Anija bit her lower lip but looked at Fralia. "Yes, Kryo Kardia is my father. At least, we think so. He got my mother, who was a member of his harem, pregnant somehow, and she and my stepfather fled to Malarsan where the Dark Tigers killed them. I only just found out."

Fralia's jaw dropped. "Wow. That is quite the revelation."

"Indeed," Kryo Kardia said. He held a hand out to Anija. "Anija, I am going to give you one—and only one— chance. Join me and I will make you not merely a princess, but a goddess, just as I will become a god. We will rule the Glaci Empire together as father and daughter, just as we should have the entire time."

"But I thought you wanted to kill me," Anija said slowly.

Kryo Kardia shook his head. "No. Not after losing my other children. Even Compe has deserted me for the Malarsans. You are the only one I have left."

Anija scowled. "Your offer doesn't tempt me in the least, 'dad.' I know how you treat your children. You'll only use me as long as I am useful to you and then discard me as soon as I am no longer necessary. I would spit in your face if you were close enough."

A slightly disappointed look flickered in Kryo Kardia's eyes. "Very well. It appears that I will have to kill *all* of my ungrateful, disobedient children. I suppose I will simply have to start again, perhaps with the grandchild of General Surrels."

Surrels, who stood behind the Snow Witches, pushed past them just then, glaring harder at Kryo Kardia than Anija had ever seen Surrels glare at anyone before. "Keep your corpse-like hands away from my grandson."

"Agreed," said a high-pitched female voice overhead. "You don't need *his* grandson when you have a perfectly loyal daughter to rule with you."

Nege and Prika suddenly flew down from the trees overhead. As soon as Prika landed in the graveyard, Nege hopped off his back and walked over to Kryo Kardia. Anija noticed that she had a sword sheathed at her side instead of her usual spear.

Guess she lost her spear or something, Anija thought.

Kryo Kardia whirled toward Nege, glaring at her. "Loyal? If that is a joke, Nege, I am not laughing. You were the first of my children to betray me. I ought to kill you this very instant."

Nege stopped several feet from Kryo Kardia and knelt in front of him. "With all due respect, Father, I thought you of all people would have realized my defection to the Malarsans was a lie."

"A lie?" Kryo Kardia repeated skeptically. "In what way?"

Nege gazed up at Kryo Kardia, a smirk on her face. "To trick the Malarsans into letting their guard down and spilling their secrets to me, I pretended to be offended at you sending Ronix to kill me. In truth, I always planned to betray them. I simply never told you because it was of utmost importance that the Malarsans trusted me and did not suspect I might have ulterior motives for 'helping' them. Especially Hal and Keershan over there."

Anija pointed accusingly at Nege. "I knew it! I knew from the start that we couldn't trust your spoiled little ass. Of course you were playing us the whole time. Lying bitch."

Nege flashed another smirk at Anija. "That's no way to talk to your long-lost sister, Anija, although truthfully, we aren't really related by blood, so I suppose it doesn't matter."

Kryo Kardia stroked his chin. "Yes, that makes far more sense than you betraying me. You always were my favorite child, Nege. You always displayed far more loyalty to me than any of your siblings. How could I have so foolishly believed you would ever even consider betraying me? You fooled even me with your deceptions."

Nege rose to her feet and smiled a smile that Anija wanted to wipe off her smug face personally. "I apologize for causing you so much harm and inconvenience, but it was necessary to make sure that my plan worked."

"It worked wonderfully," Kryo Kardia said. He held out a hand to her. "Now join me, Nege, and we will kill every last person in this graveyard. For your loyalty, I will give you anything you want, up to half of my empire, if that is what your heart desires."

Nege started walking closer to Kryo Kardia, arms folded behind her back, a thoughtful expression on her face. "*Anything* my heart desires? Well, I really just want one, simple thing, Father."

"What is it?" Kryo Kardia said. "Name it and I will ensure you get it as soon as we return to the Northern Circle."

Nege stopped less than a foot from Kryo Kardia and looked up into his eyes. "No need to wait until we go home to give me what I want. You can give it to me right here, right now, in this very moment."

Kryo Kardia frowned. "And what would that be? My crown?"

A wicked grin crossed Nege's face. "Your life."

In one smooth motion, Nege drew a black sword from her sheath—the Soul Slayer—and stabbed it directly into Kryo Kardia's chest.

Kryo Kardia gasped. He looked down at the sword in his chest, disbelief and horror on his features. "No ... it cannot be."

Nege grinned even more. "It is. The legendary Soul Slayer."

With that, Nege twisted the blade farther, and Kryo Kardia cried out as the sword drained his soul. Kryo Kardia was completely still, seeming frozen by the Soul Slayer. His blue skin gradually faded to a dim gray and his breathing became harsh.

But then Kryo Kardia punched Nege in the face. The blow sent Nege staggering backward onto the ground, a dazed expression on her face as blood leaked from her nose.

Stepping backward, Kryo Kardia grasped the hilt of the Soul Slayer with both hands and growled, "No. I will not perish like this."

"You're right, Kryo Kardia," Hal said, his and Keershan's voices mixed together. "You will perish like *this* instead."

Halkeer suddenly launched out of the mausoleum, sword blazing with dragonfire. Kryo Kardia whirled around, his eyes wide with shock.

Just in time for Halkeer to bring his sword directly down on Kryo Kardia's forehead.

In the next instant, Halkeer met Kryo Kardia's eyes and uttered one word:

"Burn."

Kryo Kardia's entire body erupted into flame. Kryo Kardia himself cried out in utter torment as the dragonfire tore through his whole body, burning away his skin and melting his armor. It would have been a difficult sight for Anija to watch if not for the fact that it was Kryo Kardia who was dying.

Seconds later, the dragonfire disappeared, leaving nothing more than a blackened skeleton that had once been Kryo Kardia. Halkeer yanked his sword out of the skeleton's forehead and landed on the ground in front of it.

Then the blackened skeleton—Soul Slayer still embedded in its chest—collapsed into a pile of ash.

Chapter Forty-Three

HAL BLINKED. ONE MOMENT, HE AND KEERSHAN HAD BEEN one again, having merged just long enough to be able to finish off Kryo Kardia.

In the next, however, he and Keershan were separate beings once more. The transition was less jarring than it had been the first time, but this separation left Hal feeling strangely weak. He leaned on his sword for support, his legs shaky, while Keershan looked like he was barely making it as it was.

Keershan took a deep, shuddering breath. "Did we do it?"

Hal nodded, looking at the pile of ash that had once been Kryo Kardia, atop which sat the Soul Slayer. "We did. This time, we definitely did."

"Hal!" Fralia said all of a sudden. "Keershan!"

Hal looked up to see Anija and Fralia running over to them. Fralia was practically crying while Anija was smiling. He heard footsteps behind him and looked over his shoulder to see Surrels and the Snow Witches also approaching them, all of them looking happy as well.

Except, oddly enough, Boca, who wore her usual serious expression.

Why isn't Boca happy that Kryo Kardia is dead? Hal thought in annoyance. *Did she forget how evil he was?*

But she raised him as her own, Keershan pointed out. *Even if they had a falling out at some point, I bet Boca still thought of Kryo Kardia as her son.*

Hal pursed his lips. Now that Keershan pointed that out, he noticed that the other Snow Witches did not look quite as happy as he thought at first. They appeared to be putting on happy faces for everyone else's sake.

Not that Hal had time to ponder that further, however, before Fralia reached him. "Hal! I am so glad that you and Keershan not only killed Kryo Kardia, but are safe and sound!"

Hal, already weakened from spending too much time merged with Keershan, took a deep breath. "Thanks, Fralia, but breathing is becoming difficult."

Fralia let go of Hal and stepped backward, a sheepish expression on her face. "Sorry, Hal. I'm just so relieved this is finally, *finally* over."

Anija nodded. Her arms folded in front of her chest, she looked at Kryo Kardia's remains dismissively. "Yes. And he got the only fate someone like him deserved. Frankly, I think he deserved worse, but this is fine, too. Hopefully he'll get tortured in the afterlife."

"Not likely," Nege said, who had also approached the group. She gestured at the Soul Slayer. "The Soul Slayer allegedly destroys a person's soul, meaning—if I understand this correctly—that Father did not ultimately go on to any afterlife. He simply ceased to exist."

There was no mourning or grief in Nege's voice when she said that. She sounded somehow even more gleeful than Anija, which made Hal grateful that she had chosen to side with them.

"How did you find the Soul Slayer, anyway?" Anija said. "I thought you had run away as soon as the duel started."

Nege shook her head. "When I saw Hal drop the Soul Slayer after destroying the *Frozen Heart*, I knew such a weapon couldn't go missing forever. I had hoped to use it myself, and I am pleased to say that I did."

"So what are we going to *do* with the Soul Slayer?" asked Surrels uncertainly, staring at the weapon. "Isn't it supposed to be pure evil or something like that?"

Boca stepped forward. "My sisters and I will take it and destroy it. We will ensure that it does not end up in the wrong hands."

Anija gave Boca a skeptical look. "And how do we know that *you* aren't the wrong hands?"

"Let's just say that we have experience dealing with evil artifacts and leave it at that," said Ericha.

"I trust them with it," Hal said. He shuddered. "It was always a gamble to use, anyway. Best to get rid of it so that no one else in the world decides to use it."

Anija made a humphing sound but clearly did not argue with them about it.

"Glad that is out of the way," Surrels said, putting his hands on his hips. "But what do we do now?"

"End this war," said Prince Compe's voice from the forest.

From the woods around them emerged Prince Compe and his Steed, Woppa. But they did not come alone. The hundreds of Glacians and Malarsans who had come to witness the duel—and later participate in the battle against the Undead Legion—followed him. With his large size and mask, Hal thought that Prince Compe looked a lot like his father.

"Seriously?" Anija said, turning to face Prince Compe as he and Woppa walked through the broken gateway into the graveyard. "After we literally saved your life, you *still* want to go to war with us?"

Prince Compe came to a stop before them, his eyes impassive, though they did glance briefly at the ashes of Kryo Kardia. "As Kryo Kardia's eldest son and heir, I am in line to take the throne, which I will do as soon as I return to the Northern Circle. That means I, and I alone, can decide when to end this war."

Hal bit his lower lip. Like Anija, he, too, was frustrated that Prince Compe seemed interested in continuing the war. Granted, as a literal god, Hal could smite him on the spot, but he decided to wait and see what Prince Compe did next before acting.

Prince Compe then met Hal's eyes. "And I say that this war, unjustly started by my father, is *over*."

Prince Compe raised his voice when he said that, no doubt to make sure that everyone in the forest heard his pronouncement.

The reaction was mostly stunned silence from both the Malarsans and the Glacians. Even Stebo and Regent Akei appeared startled by Prince Compe's decision, exchanging puzzled looks with each other.

"You're not joking, are you?" Hal said.

Prince Compe shook his head. "This is no joke. Ever since Kryo Kardia started this war, I have always felt uneasy about it. I served him willingly, however, because, like so many other Glacians, I believed that he had our best interests at heart. But after today, it is obvious that my adoptive father never cared for anyone but himself."

Prince Compe looked at Nege. "That means you may return to the Northern Circle with me if you wish, sister, you and your dragon."

Nege sighed in relief. "Finally! You have no idea, brother, how difficult it has been these past two weeks having to live like a peasant. I cannot wait to return to my room in the citadel and live like the princess I truly am."

Hal resisted the urge to roll his eyes, but Anija did not.

Surrels raised a hand. "That's nice and all, but what about future relations between Malarsan and the Glaci Empire? What are you going to do?"

Prince Compe nodded. "Firstly, I will end all military activity in and near Malarsan. Secondly, I will work closely with Regent Akei—and, hopefully in the future, Prince Stebo—to build an equal partnership with the kingdom of Malarsan in which we will respect your right to independence and no longer seek to unduly influence your country. We will, of course, discuss these in more detail over the coming weeks, months, and years, but I am hopeful that we will create a fruitful partnership for both of us."

Hal nodded. "Sounds good to me. In the meantime, however, why don't we all go back to Mysteria and have a feast? I am sure that Wilme and the cooks in town will be able to throw something together to celebrate this great victory."

Prince Compe bowed. "I would be honored to attend a

feast with you, as would all of the Glacians who traveled this far to watch this duel."

"*I* wouldn't be!"

Startled, Hal looked around, trying to spot who had said that, when his eyes fell on Dedeket. The Grand Inquirer was in chains near the front of the group, chains held by Ragnol, who glared at Dedeket like he was an annoying dog.

"Silence, Inquirer," said Prince Compe, turning to face Dedeket. "As the heir to the Glacian Throne, I have the authority to end this war and alter our relations with Malarsan or any other country we interact with."

Dedeket spat on the ground. "You are no legitimate heir! You are a traitor to the Glaci Empire. His Iciness would not have wanted a traitor like you to sit on the throne. When we get back to the Northern Circle—"

Ragnol suddenly wrapped a thick cloth around Dedeket's mouth, instantly muffling the mouthy Inquirer. Dedeket, however, continued to ramble, and based on his tone, he was obviously referring to Prince Compe with a lot of less-than-kind words.

With that, the group as a whole turned and made their way out of the forest back to the border. Hal and Keershan, however, left the graveyard last, taking up the rear of the large group.

The mood in the group, overall, was one of happiness and relief. It seemed like both the Malarsans and Glacians were glad that the war was over and that there was hope for a peaceful future between them. Already, Hal saw Surrels, Stebo, and Akei speaking with Prince Compe and Nege about what these peaceful relations between their respective countries might entail.

I'm glad everyone is so happy, Keershan said. *I just wish we would be able to stick around to join them.*

Hal nodded again. They both knew that they would have to leave the mortal realm soon, which would require them to say goodbye to everyone they had known and loved in their mortal lives.

That caused Hal's mind to drift back to the last part of their recent trip to the abode, right when they were about to return to the mortal realm.

Chapter Forty-Four

TWO AND A HALF WEEKS AGO...

"This is utterly ridiculous and unfitting for new gods," said Raniel for what felt like the millionth time. "There is no need to go back to the mortal realm."

Hal, standing on the Endless Cliffs, looked over his shoulder at Raniel. "We're not leaving forever."

"Just long enough to take out Kryo Kardia," Keershan added with a growl, clawing at the ground.

"But you are *gods* now," Raniel argued. He gestured at them. "Gods do not care about what happens in the mortal realm unless it is truly dire. You are debasing yourselves for what, mortal sentimentality? Do you even realize how much you are embarrassing not just yourselves, but all of the gods with this silly decision of yours?"

Although Hal was still trying to figure out exactly what kind of powers a god like him had, he was sorely tempted to smite Raniel for his incessant babbling.

Fortunately, it was Gotcham Nubor, who had accompanied them beyond the Gates of the Gods and now stood near Raniel, who said, "Silence, Raniel. As gods, they rank far higher than you in the hierarchy of the universe. You must show them the respect that they deserve, regardless of how you may personally feel about them."

Raniel shut his mouth and looked at his feet, clearly quite ashamed.

A nice perk of being a god is that Raniel can no longer openly disrespect us, Keershan pointed out. *I could get used to that.*

Hal chuckled, but then Gotcham Nubor said, "Still, despite Raniel's disrespect, I share my concerns with him. Leaving the abode so soon after becoming gods yourselves may not be the wisest decision."

Hal looked at his body. Aside from the glowing white light and their golden armor, neither he nor Keershan looked substantially different than they did before drinking the divine elixirs.

But Hal certainly *felt* different. He felt stronger, more powerful, far beyond even what the Final Relic made him feel like. He now understood why the gods often seemed so aloof and arrogant.

If one felt like *this*, then it was difficult, if not impossible, to *not* be arrogant.

Hal looked back up at Gotcham Nubor. "Thank you for your concerns, but even if we are gods, we still have a lot of friends and loved ones out there who need our help. Just a few loose ends to tie up before we come back here for good."

"Where is Old Snow, by the way?" Keershan said, looking around in confusion. "I thought he was going to see us off."

"Lord Rikas is busy with his duties as the current Demon God," said Raniel stiffly. "He told me to say goodbye for you in his place, which is why I am here in the first place and not doing my actual job of protecting the abode."

Hal frowned. He knew he would see Old Snow again eventually, but he'd hoped that Old Snow would see them off anyway.

Keershan smiled at Hal. "Don't worry, Hal. I am sure we will see Old Snow again when we return after tying up those loose ends you mentioned."

Gotcham Nubor frowned. "That is exactly what I am worried about. I fear that your attachment to your mortal friends will lead you to act foolishly. As gods, we can only be impartial once we cut off all ties to the mortal world that we may have once had."

"If you think that, then why are you letting us go down there at all?" Keershan asked, gesturing with his head at the edge of the cliffs. "Why not force us to stay here? As the king of the gods, surely that is within your power to do."

Gotcham Nubor glanced over the cliffs, a harsh look on his face. "Because Kryo Kardia must pay for his murder of Shirataka. If Kryo Kardia had not had Shirataka killed, I wouldn't allow either of you to leave the abode."

"Special circumstances require special decisions, then," Hal said.

Gotcham Nubor nodded. "More or less."

Hal licked his lips. "Don't worry, Your Majesty. Keershan and I will deal with Kryo Kardia and be back here before you know it."

Gotcham Nubor met Hal's gaze. "Will you truly be able to let go of your mortal friends when the time comes?"

Hal hesitated for a split second before nodding again. "Yes."

"Very well," said Gotcham Nubor. He gestured toward the cliffs. "Then you may leave. But as soon as you finish your work in the mortal realm, we will call you back here. And you will never be able to live in the mortal realm ever again."

Hal bit his lower lip and looked at Keershan, who looked back at him.

Then the two looked back to Gotcham Nubor and said, "We understand."

Gotcham Nubor lowered his hand. "Then go. And may the universe itself be with you."

Hal and Keershan nodded, and Hal jumped onto Keershan's back. Getting into a comfortable position, Hal looked down at Keershan and said, "Ready?"

"Ready," Keershan said.

With that, Keershan jumped over the side of the cliffs. His wings snapping open, Keershan soared toward the base of the cliffs, away from the Gates of the Gods. Neither Hal nor Keershan looked back.

They kept their eyes firmly focused on the direction of their next and final destination.

The kingdom of Malarsan.

Their home.

Chapter Forty-Five

"Hal?" Fralia said. "Hal, are you there? Hello?"

Snapping out of his thoughts, Hal gazed at Fralia, who stood opposite him and Keershan in the lobby of the Forgotten Temple. "Hmm? What?"

"You looked like you'd fallen asleep there," Anija said. "Which, I mean, I understand because these meetings can get pretty boring, but the meeting hasn't even started yet and you're already asleep."

Hal shook his head and rubbed the back of his neck. "Sorry. I was just remembering things."

"We both were," Keershan said with a nod, rubbing his head against Hal's leg. "We've been through a lot together, haven't we?"

"I think we've *all* been through a lot," Surrels said, standing off to Hal's left. He sighed and looked around the Forgotten Temple. "This really brings me back to when we first met. I tried to kill you, but then you guys captured me and used me to get into the capital. I really thought you guys were going to kill me at some point." He sighed. "But hey, at least I got my family and my life back. If I'd known that back then, maybe I wouldn't have been so mean to all of you."

Anija, standing off to Hal's right, snorted. "I remember being super pissed off about having to work with you guys and waste time that could have been spent on stealing valuable things. And if I'm being honest, I'm still not entirely sold on the idea of being the new captain of the Dragon Riders or hanging out with you questionable individuals."

Hal chuckled. "I think you will do just fine, Anija, you and Rialo. I trust you two to lead the Dragon Rider Order and School more than anyone else."

Rialo, sitting before the massive mural of the final battle between the Dragon Riders and the Nameless One, flashed her teeth at Hal. "Of course we will. Although I must say, I will miss you, little brother, even if I find it hard to believe that you are actually a god now."

Keershan chuckled. "I can't believe it, either. But it's true."

Rialo shook her head. "This is too much like the stories mother used to tell us. A disgraced dragon runt brings peace between the humans and dragons and then ascends to godhood along with his human friend."

"Make sure to add that he was a very studious dragon in your retellings," Keershan said with a wink. "That way, you can encourage the hatchlings to value their minds as well as their claws."

Rialo huffed. "I still don't see book learning in the Clawfoot Clan's future, but I suppose I can ensure that your efforts to restore and preserve our history will not be forgotten."

"Are you sure that you guys *have* to leave?" asked Lom, who stood next to Fralia, a worried expression on his face. "I know that you two are gods now and all, but I think I speak for all of us when I say we will miss you."

Hal pursed his lips. Based on the suddenly somber expressions of his other friends, Hal knew that Lom really was speaking for everyone.

That was the difficult part. It was the night after the celebratory feast held after the defeat of Kryo Kardia. That morning, a group of war balloons had shown up at the Malarsan and Hosarian border to transport Prince Compe, Woppa, Princess Nege, Prika, and all of the other Glacians who had shown up to watch the duel back to the Northern Circle. Prince Compe had profusely thanked Hal and the others for their generosity and hospitality and vowed to begin work on renewing relations between Malarsan and the Glaci Empire as soon as he got back to the Northern Circle.

That included expanding the Dragon Rider Order to the Glaci Empire. Although Prince Compe and Princess Nege were the only two Glacian Riders who had survived, they still had a ton of stolen relics left over from Kryo Kardia's efforts to make his own Dragon Rider Order. Most of the relics would be returned, Prince Compe promised, to Mysteria, and any potential Glacian Riders, along with their Steeds, would be sent first to Mysteria to bond and train.

The way Hal saw it, the Dragon Rider Order needed to expand. He had a vision of a worldwide Order of Dragon Riders from across all nations. He hoped that the order would become a protector not just of one country or Empire, but the whole world, to keep it safe from threats like the Nameless One and Kryo Kardia alike. Hal just wished that he and Keershan would be able to lead it themselves.

But I am sure that Anija and Rialo will do a fine job, Hal thought, glancing at them. *They have the same vision as us.*

After the Glacians left, Hal had called the council—aside from Wilme, who was busy overseeing the efforts to clean up the wreckage at the border—together to tell them the truth about, well, everything. How he and Keershan became gods, the restrictions Gotcham Nubor had put on them, and everything else.

Including why they needed to leave not just Malarsan, but the whole mortal realm, forever.

And now, tonight was the night when Hal and Keershan would be leaving. They had decided to make sure that their closest friends were there when they left so they could say one final goodbye. Hal and Keershan had already said goodbye to Hal's mother, who had traveled to Mysteria to watch the duel like everyone else.

"We don't like this any more than you guys do, but yes, we have to leave," Keershan said with a sigh. "Gotcham Nubor was extremely clear about that."

"So you can't even visit us?" Surrels said, furrowing his brow. "Or even write us?"

Hal shook his head. "As gods, we are supposed to cut off all ties to the mortal realm to maintain our objectivity. That means we cannot visit or even write to you unless we need to."

Anija smirked. "So next time a power-hungry tyrant decides to threaten the world, you guys will show up for that, right?"

Hal smiled. "Maybe. But either way, we have to go."

Those words tasted bitter in his mouth. This might very well be the last time he ever saw his friends. He and Keershan would undoubtedly outlive them, as well as everyone else in Malarsan that they knew.

But Hal did not say that. He could see that his friends already knew that.

"Then I guess this is goodbye," Surrels said.

Hal nodded again. "Yes. But more than that, it's a thank you. I want to thank each and every one of you for helping Keershan and me. Without you guys, I am pretty sure we'd have both died a *long* time ago."

"That's right," Keershan said. "And if fate should ever decide to make our paths cross again, well, perhaps we will see you guys again, after all."

Everyone else nodded. No one said anything, because truthfully, there was not much to say.

That was when a familiar elderly voice said, "Beautiful goodbyes. Reminds me of how much I miss all of you."

Old Snow walked out of the shadows between two pillars, looking much the same as he had before his death. He certainly didn't look as demonic as he had back in the challenge.

"What the——?" Surrels said, his eyes widening. "Old Snow? What are you doing here?"

Old Snow smiled at everyone. "Gotcham Nubor sent me to guide Hal and Keershan back to the abode. He wanted to make sure that you two did not linger in the mortal realm, which means we must be leaving right away."

"Right," Hal said. "We were planning to leave soon anyway. Might as well go now. Bye, everyone."

Everyone waved goodbye as Hal, Keershan, and Old Snow walked toward the exit to the Forgotten Temple. Hal waved goodbye as they walked while Keershan wagged a wing as a dragon way of waving. Even Old Snow gave them a quick wave, though quickly stopped once they left the temple.

Lowering his hand to his side, Hal sighed. "I wish we did not have to go. I am going to miss everyone."

"Same," Keershan said. "But you heard Gotcham Nubor. We're gods now. So we might as well act like it."

Old Snow smiled and glanced at the Forgotten Temple. "We may be gods now, but that does not mean we will be gone forever."

Hal gave Old Snow a puzzled look. "Why wouldn't we be? Aren't we supposed to live in the abode?"

"Only because you do not have a temple here in the mortal realm in which to visit," Old Snow said. He patted the stone doors of the Forgotten Temple. "I think this place would make a fine temple for the new gods of light, personally. An idea I might have mentioned to Lom on our way out without either of you two noticing."

Hal could not help but smile. "That would be wonderful, Old Snow. Just wonderful."

Old Snow nodded. "Indeed. But for now, we must go. Do you mind if I catch a ride with you two?"

Keershan shook his head. "Not at all, Old Snow. Not at all."

With that, Hal and Old Snow climbed onto Keershan's back. As soon as they were seated comfortably on Keershan's saddle, Keershan flapped his wings once, twice, thrice, and then they were soaring in the air north, back to the abode of the Gods.

Back to their new home.